Black Knight Squadron

Book 1

Foundations

By John Chapman

To Kris

Those too lazy to plow in the right season will have no food at the harvest. Proverbs 20:4

"The only moral judgements in war are made by the victors, and victorious armies are led by those who have mastered the latest, most efficient tools of their trade."
William Manchester; The Last Lion Vol.2: Biography of Winston Churchill

Black Knight Squadron General Order No. 1:

Do not expect someone else to do for you what you can do for yourself.

To learn more about the Black Knight Squadron saga, and to see more content, including pictures, lessons learned, maps and updates, find us on Facebook by searching @blackknightsquadronbooks

Table of Contents

Chapter 1

Consolidated Brick Corp
Alliance, Ohio

      Chris Mason was frustrated. His job as the manager of the Brickyard was usually fulfilling; he enjoyed the challenge of keeping a century old brick plant in operation and profitable, and the people he worked with were salt of the earth. While only 29 years old, Chris was mature beyond his years, and his ability to fix almost anything combined with his natural leadership abilities and willingness to work hard had led to his appointment as the plant's manager the year before. He started working at the plant in high school, and had quickly risen in responsibility. He'd never had another job and didn't particularly want one.

      His frustration this morning stemmed from the actions of one of his employees, Carl, a man twice his age, who seemed to lurch through life in an endless cycle of putting in a half ass workday, getting drunk in the evening, then waking up late to start the cycle all over again. About 20 minutes ago Carl brought in a load of sand. While dumping the load in the aggregate shed, a brand-new structure Chris had worked hard to design and build, Carl had managed to put the top 7 feet of the dump bed through the roof of the building. When Chris asked Carl what the hell happened Carl told him "I was dumping the load and when I tilted the bed, it felt sluggish, so I goosed the hydraulics. I guess the sluggishness was the bed hitting the ceiling joist". Chris was struck dumb for a moment. When he found his voice he asked Carl, "Why did you have the bed up inside the shed at all?" Carl just shrugged his shoulders and said, "I thought it would be faster to unload."

      Chris didn't trust himself to speak, but finally managed "Go sit in the office while I take some pictures and call corporate." Chris took some pictures and thought about how he was going to word his report so corporate HR couldn't stop him from firing Carl this time. After he took some pictures and wrote down the truck number, Chris walked out the open front of the shed and pulled out his smartphone to call corporate, when he noticed something was wrong.

It took him a couple of seconds to realize it was quiet. The usual rumble of a working brickyard was absent. "What the hell happened now?" Chris said out loud, "did we lose power?" It was early December, there was some snow on the ground and it was cold, but the sky was clear. Chris shrugged it off and told himself to focus on one problem at a time, and looked down at his phone. He pushed the home button and nothing happened. His phone wasn't even displaying the date and time like usual. As Chris was trying to figure out what was wrong with his phone, he heard a godawful screech of metal tearing, and looked up in time to see a dump truck smashing through the corner of the shed from the direction of the road, then plow over Carl, who was standing next to the building smoking a cigarette. The truck, loaded with 25 tons of gravel, barely slowed down.

The driver, getting no response from the brakes, turned the wheel hard right, turning the entire 80,000-pound monster over onto its left side, spilling a sea of gravel onto the ramp and finally stopping the truck on its side about 150 feet from the corner of the shed. Chris managed to sprint into the shed and avoid the carnage, but one of the yard's frontend loaders wasn't so lucky. When the noise stopped, Chris stopped running and turned to look back. He was having a hard time processing what he was seeing but began to walk back toward to wreckage, shaking his head to try to clear his mind. As he walked Chris realized he had his phone in his hand, and tried to wake it up again. Nothing. "What the hell is going on?" he shouted, more out of frustration than seeking answers.

Chris ran to the frontend loader, climbing up the dune of gravel trying to see inside the cab. When he got where he could see, Chris could see the operator had been thrown from the open cab, and he couldn't see him. He realized the guy must be buried in the gravel. Chris heard voices and people climbing up the gravel, and yelled "Somebody got buried, get some shovels. Someone run to the office and call 911!" A couple of minutes later someone yelled, "I found him!" off to Chris' right. Chris got up and stumble-ran through the gravel to where everyone else was converging. When he got there, he saw several people clawing frantically at the gravel around a heavily tattooed hand and arm, but they were having trouble because no matter how much gravel they scooped away more would pour back down into the hole. He recognized the arm immediately, because of the sleeve tattoos, as belonging to Willy, one of the equipment operators who worked at the shed.

A couple of minutes of rough labor had Willy's limp body being lifted down off the gravel pile and laid on the ground. Chris kneeled down next to him and could see immediately Willy was dead. His head was lying at the wrong angle, and he wasn't breathing. Chris was having a hard time keeping his emotions under control; Willy was a good man and one of the "old hands" who had worked at the brickyard longer than Chris had been alive. Chris stood up, and suddenly remembered seeing Carl getting hit by the truck. He ran around the gravel pile to the corner of the shed but pulled up short when he saw Carl, or what was left of him. Carl was in several pieces, torn apart by the force of the truck combined with the sharp metal of the shed corner that had been torn off the building during the collision.

It was more than Chris could take; he dropped to his knees and vomited. Chris thought he was tough, and in a lot of ways he was. But Chris had only touched death in the clinical world of a funeral home. Seeing the bodies of two people he called friends in the immediate aftermath of a chaotic death shook Chris deeply. He began to lock up as his mind focused on the grisly scene in front of him, when Carol, one of the office workers, ran up to him crying. As Chris stood up and tried to compose himself, Carol ran into his arms and started cry-talking in a long stream of consciousness "I tried to call 911 but the power is out and none of the phones work and my cell phone is dead" Carol took a ragged breath "and I went into the bookkeepers' office to see if Margret's phone worked and she is slumped over her desk. What is going on?"

The rest of the yard guys and a few of the office employees had gathered around Chris. He looked up and asked if anyone else's cell phone worked. Everyone fished their phone out of their pockets and Chris heard lots of mumbling. No one's phone would wake up or show any indications of life at all. "Shit!" Chris mumbled. He raised his voice "Everyone, go try to start your cars." Most looked confused, but as he broke away from Carol to run to his car, another of his guys, Ed, let out a curse of realization and began sprinting to the employee parking lot. He beat Chris there by seconds.

Chris hit the unlock button on his key fob as he ran, and almost fell down when he reached the door and snatched the handle, expecting it to open, but it remained locked. He fumbled for the key, got it in the lock, and was able to manually unlock the door. He jumped in the seat, turned the ignition, and nothing happened. No door dings, no lights on the dash, nothing. "Please start," he said out loud, "This cannot be happening". Still nothing. His Subaru was dead.

Ed had a little better luck. His 1971 Chevy truck started as usual. Ed did notice none of his gauges worked, but given his suspicions about what just happened, he didn't care. Ed left his truck running and jogged to Chris' Subaru, where he found Chris getting out. "Anything?" Ed asked. "Nope. It's dead." Chris replied. Ed let out a long breath and said, "You thinking what I'm thinking?" Chris looked at him for a minute and said, "EMP". Ed nodded his head and said, "We need to check the area and make sure, then we need to get to the range." Chris nodded and opened the back hatch on his car while Ed went back to his truck. Nothing more needed to be said; they had trained together and been friends long enough to know what needed to be done.

Chris took off his jacket and opened an old Blue Force Gear DAP pack on top of the stuff in his trunk. He pulled out a Blue Force Gear chest rig with some AR mags and a medical kit already in it, and put it on. He put his Carhart work jacket back on over the rig and zipped it up. Next, he pulled his EDC pistol, a Glock 19 with a Trijicon RMR milled into the slide, and did a press check. Then he checked the RMR, but it was dead. He cursed to himself and unloaded and field stripped the pistol quickly. He unzipped his jacket and found the right allen wrench and spare 2032 battery in his vest, then changed the optic's battery. When he tried to turn the optic back on, it was still dead. "Crap, the EMP must have gotten it." he said to himself. The backup iron sights would have to do, he thought. He realized he wasn't carrying a spare magazine for the Glock, and rooted around until he found one in his bag. It was loaded with the ball ammo he used on the range instead of the Federal HST hollow points he liked for "social occasions", but it would have to do.

Realizing he didn't have a spare pistol mag pouch with him, he put the mag in his pocket and grabbed his rifle, a BCM Recce 16. He loaded the carbine with a 28-round mag and cycled the bolt. Out of habit, he checked the Aimpoint T1 he used as an optic and his Surefire Scout light and B.E.Meyers MAWL laser, then realized all three were working. He didn't understand why his rifle optic would work while his pistol optic was fried, but quickly decided to stop looking a gift horse in the mouth. Whatever it was, he was thankful to not be facing the Apocalypse with an iron-sighted carbine. It also gave him hope that his brand new TNVC Sentinel night vision goggles had survived. He worked so hard to save the money for them.

Chris started sorting through the gear and ammo he had in his trunk, when Ed backed out of his parking space and pulled over to the Subaru. Ed Jumped out and Chris could see he had already put on his plate carrier and all his mag pouches were full. Ed said, "I wish I had spent the money on a Team Wendy Helmet now. Just grab all of your crap and put it in the bed bro, you can sort it out later". Chris realized Ed was right, and started grabbing bags and throwing them in the truck bed. Once the three bags and his tent were loaded, Chris cross-loaded the cases of 5.56mm and 9mm ammo he kept in his trunk for training. He was at the range every day and never knew what kind of training he would be able to jump into, so he always kept a lot of ammo in his car.

When he was done, Chris closed his hatchback and driver door. He stopped for a second and closed his eyes to gather himself. He thought about Amanda, his new wife, and thanked God she was at the police department, where she worked as a dispatcher. She would be safe there for a couple of hours while they figured out what was going on. Chris opened his eyes and let out a breath, feeling better about the situation, and jogged to Ed's truck. As he tried to jump into the passenger seat of the truck, his rifle swung on the two point sling, wedged against the seat, and used his momentum to punch him squarely in the testicles. Chris saw stars and let out a "oof", then collapsed against the door. *So much for having my crap together* flashed through his mind. Ed was looking right at him when it happened, and burst out laughing. "Good thing there isn't much to hurt there," Ed said. Chris felt like vomiting again, the pain was so intense. But the embarrassment overwhelmed his pain receptors and Chris gingerly found his seat and closed the door. Ed was still laughing at him as they drove back to the aggregate shed.

When they got to the shed, none of the employees were there. Ed noticed a man sitting on the high side of the overturned dump truck, and assumed he was the driver who careened out of control. He nodded his head at the guy to make sure Chris saw him, then stopped the truck and turned to Chris and said, "Hey, you alright little buddy?" Chris flipped him off and said, "I'm fine, and you're a dick." Ed thought of a witty comeback but decided instead to say, "Common, we still got work to do." while smiling at Chris. Chris flipped him off again, but got out of the truck and began carefully walking over to the dump truck.

"What happened?" Chris yelled up at the driver. The driver didn't look down at Chris, but shook his head and said, "I don't know man. I was turning into the lot when the engine died and I had no power. I hit the brakes but they didn't work either." The driver then looked down at Chris and continued talking, "I tried to get the load all the way in to the ramp, but I was going too fast and misjudged the turn. I remember hitting the building but everything went black after that." Chris told the driver, "OK. I have to go find my employees and figure out what's going on." The driver said, "Is the fire department and an ambulance on the way? I'm hurting pretty bad, man." Chris replied, "No, none of the phones work. I think we may be on our own." The driver started asking questions but Chris was already headed to the office to try to find his people.

As Chris passed the truck, Ed said, "Hey bro, I'm going to walk up to the road and see if any traffic is moving." Chris, deep in thought, didn't look up, he just said, "Ok, I'll be in the office." When Chris got to the office, he found three of his employees, Carol, Jeff and Bonnie, sitting in the main office area. Carol was curled up in a ball on a chair, crying softly. Jeff, the sales manager, and Bonnie, a sales clerk, were standing in front of the TV trying to get it to turn on using the remote. Jeff looked over his shoulder when he heard Chris and said, "Trying to get the TV on to get some news…" Jeff stopped talking when he saw Chris' rifle on the sling. "Why the hell do you have a gun Chris?" Jeff thundered. "The power goes out and you're going all Rambo?" Chris stopped, looked at Jeff and said, "Shut up Jeff. You're an idiot." Jeff puffed up with indignation and started to speak, but Chris cut him off, "Jeff. Shut.

11

The. Hell. Up" biting the words out. Chris had always disliked Jeff, and he didn't have the time or patience to deal with his douchebaggery right then.

Chris said, obviously speaking to all three of them, "Listen up. I am pretty sure we have been hit with an electromagnetic pulse, from either the sun or a nuke. You guys need to get home and take care of your families." "That's a bunch of horse crap Chris, the power is just out" Jeff said, in his best condescending voice. "I'm not here to convince you Jeff," Chris said slowly, trying to calm himself down. "I'm just taking the information we have and drawing a conclusion. If you want to stay here, be my guest." Bonnie told Chris "My car won't start, can you give me a ride home?" Chris told her Ed's truck was the only one that would run, and they would drop her off on their way out of town. Bonnie said, "I'll go grab my stuff and meet you at the truck." Chris told her to wait for him. He didn't trust Bonnie, and he didn't know if Ed had left the truck running. He wouldn't put it past Bonnie to just steal the truck. She was generally a pretty selfish person.

Chris asked Bonnie, "Can you see if you can get Carol ready to go home?" Bonnie said she would try. Jeff interrupted, "I can take care of Carol." Bonnie just looked at Jeff and said, "I'm sure you'd like that Jeff, but I'll take care of her." Jeff started to say something, and Bonnie got in his face, "What? You have something to say? You want me to tell them about how you tried to 'take care of' me," Bonnie used her finger quotes "that night I got drunk at the Mexican restaurant?" Jeff looked pissed but he just turned around and sat down at a desk.

Shaking his head, Chris went into the bookkeeping office and checked on Margret. As Carol feared, Margret was indeed dead, at least as far as Chris could tell. Chris remembered hearing something about her having a pacemaker, and supposed the EMP, or whatever it was, had stopped her heart. That was a damn shame; Margret was not only a great lady, but she grew up in the 30's and knew how to can and garden. She would have been a real asset if this was indeed "the big one". Chris ripped the curtains down off the window behind Margret's desk and covered her up, then said a prayer over her.

The next hour or so was a frenzied mess. Ed returned to tell Chris that there were a bunch of cars dead on the road on their street,

Mahoning Avenue, as well as on State Street, the major connecting road through town; and that there were a lot of people just milling around. He said he didn't see any cars moving at all. Chris and Ed then checked all the heavy equipment on the property to see if anything still ran. They found a frontend loader, a backhoe and a bobcat that started right up. All three had been stored in a metal equipment shed with the doors closed. Ed said, "Whatever it was, it seems to be stopped by metal buildings." Chris thought for a minute and said, "Yeah, the optic on the pistol I was carrying outside when it happened was fried, but the one on the carbine that was inside my car is fine." They both thought about it for a minute, then Ed said, "Well, whatever it is we need to get moving. We shouldn't leave those bodies out; the animals will get to them."

So before they left, Chris used the Bobcat to move Margret, Carl and Willy's bodies to the ramp and collapse the gravel pile onto them, burying them in a tomb of about 10 feet of rock. They both felt terrible about it, but it was the best they could do under the circumstances. When he got off the Bobcat, Chris walked to the mound and said, "Lord, please watch and protect the souls of these good people. Please give us strength and wisdom as we deal with whatever this disaster becomes."

After the burial, Chris met Ed and Bonnie at Ed's Truck. Chris asked where Carol was, and Bonnie said, "She and Jeff disappeared when I went to get my stuff from the car and bring it here. I hope she's OK." Chris was upset that Jeff may be taking advantage of Carol, a young single mother, in the times ahead, but couldn't think of anything to do about it right this minute. Chris then asked if anyone had seen the injured dump truck driver, but no one had. They looked for the guy for a few minutes, but couldn't find him. Chris called them back together at Ed's truck and said, "I'm not wasting any more time on that guy. He's a grown man and will just have to deal with it." Bonnie and Ed both nodded and loaded up in Ed's truck without another word.

As they pulled out of the property and turned north onto Mahoning Avenue for the first leg of their trip, to drop Bonnie off at home about 4 blocks away, Ed looked past Bonnie, who was sitting between them, and with a straight face told Chris, "Look on the bright side; God fired Carl for you." Chris just sighed and shook his head.

Chapter 2

City Police Range
Alliance, OH

Mark Wallace showed up for work early. It wasn't that he was late very often, but getting up at 5AM to be at the range by 7AM for a class got harder the older he got. He usually rolled in 15 minutes or so before class, making him the butt of many an hour of jokes by the range manager, Kyle Wilson. In addition to being the range manager at the police training facility where Mark taught almost every day, Kyle was Mark's boss on the SWAT team, and was one of Mark's closest friends. Kyle knew all of the buttons to push to get Mark wound up, and usually pushed them with ruthless efficiency. It was a source of much entertainment, but Mark didn't mind; if you were a delicate flower or were easily butt-hurt, being a SWAT officer and tactical trainer probably wasn't your calling in life.

Mark was a semi-retired police officer, who moved to Ohio several years previously after a law enforcement career in California and several years of traveling around the world teaching SWAT teams. He and his partner, David Wells, owned and operated a firearms and tactics training company that catered to police SWAT teams and some armed citizens who took their training seriously.

With the current unrest in the country leading to increased threats against the police, and a greater awareness by citizens of the need to train to a higher level, they were very busy. Mark kept his experience fresh by serving as a volunteer police officer in Alliance, where he was one of three Team Leaders on the City's part-time SWAT Team. He and David also did a lot of free classes for officers from all over the state. He liked helping the good guys be better fighters, and felt a responsibility to teach whatever he could to as many cops and responsibly armed citizens as possible.

Mark had been traveling to Alliance to teach courses for many years, and when the opportunity came up for him to move to

Ohio and teach there full time he jumped at it. The range facility at Alliance was world class, and was the result of many years of work by Kyle, the Chief of Police, City government, and large amounts of support from the firearms industry and the local community. It had everything needed to do advanced training, but its real advantage was the range was not restricted to law enforcement training; civilian students could take most of the courses offered there as well.

This was unusual, as most law enforcement agencies didn't want the hassles or perceived liability of allowing citizens to train with them. Hundreds of responsibly armed citizens took advantage of this policy every year, training right alongside professional lawmen and gunfighters. The down side of the range, if there was one, was it was located inside the perimeter of the City's water treatment plant, but nothing is perfect. The good news was after a while you got used to the smell of fresh poop.

Most important to Mark, however, was that he rarely had to travel anymore. His wife, Kasey, was happy to have him home most nights, and he had gotten tired of watching his family life slip away while he was on the road. Mark knew that moving to Ohio had played a large part in saving his marriage; and he was very aware and thankful for the part Kyle and the City had played in making the move possible.

Mark's business partner, David, lived in Indiana, where he worked his "day job" as a heart surgeon. David would drive up to Alliance to teach classes frequently. He hadn't always been a cake eating heart doctor; David started his adult life in the US Army, where he was a Special Forces 18D (SF Medic... kind of a demi-doctor with mad combat skills) and sniper for 8 years, before letting the GI bill carry him away to medical school. While they made an unusual pair, based on life and professional experience, David and Mark meshed very well; and they had been all over the world teaching cops and military units together. They had settled on Alliance as a home base for their business after deciding their families deserved better than them being on the road all the time.

Alliance was a perfect home base for a law enforcement and civilian firearms training business because of the facility Kyle and the city had built. Situated on a little more than 5 acres, the "range" was actually a very compact but fully functional training facility. When you entered the gate the first building on the left was the bathroom. These weren't just any bathrooms but a stand-alone building sporting some of the nicest "facilities" on any range Mark had ever seen. And he had seen a lot of ranges. Next to the bathrooms was the range's vault, a large purpose-built government certified storage building for weapons, ammo and other dangerous materials. The vault was a key component in attracting government training business, because visiting teams could secure their equipment there and not have to keep it in the hotel in town when not training.

The next building on the left was the range office. A small stand alone 20'X20' building, it had been the only structure on the range when Kyle had taken over. Built in 1961, the range office had served as the range classroom until the erection of the next building on the left, the classroom. A very large metal structure built in 2016, made possible by a donation from Blue Force Gear the classroom had two rooms; one large and the other small. The classroom had 5 large rollup garage doors that allowed for maximum flexibility in how the classroom was used.

Behind the classroom was the range's crown jewel: an 8000-square foot ballistic shoothouse with a catwalk. This part of the range was the most commonly used feature of the facility; hosting civilian, law enforcement and military training almost 250 days a year. Beyond the classroom was the range's parking area for military vehicles. Opposite the classroom, on the right side of the range from the gate, were the facility's breaching ranges. An entire row of breaching obstacles allowed the SWAT team and range staff to teach all of the skills necessary for mechanical, ballistic and explosive breaching.

Next to the breaching range was a 50-yard pistol and carbine range, capable of accommodating up to 20 shooters at a time on either paper or steel targets. The back corner of the 50-yard range also boasted an aircraft cabin simulator, used to train air marshals from around the word. Beyond both the military parking area and the 50-yard range was a beautifully manicured 300-yard range, equipped with a full complement of steel targets.

All of the range's facilities, along with many off-range training areas for realistic urban and rural training, and the support of the City's government, combined to create an almost perfect environment for modern tactical training. The decision to base their training business at Alliance had been a no-brainer for Mark and David.

*

It was easier being early today because the class Mark was teaching wasn't scheduled to begin until noon, so he was able to get up at a more reasonable hour and still be at the range 2 hours early to set up the shoothouse for the day. Mark was happy that David was in town to teach the Advanced Close Quarters Battle (CQB) course with him, and today was day one of the class. It was the last class of the year and the entire range team was ready for a break after a long, busy, 10-month training season.

Being pretty pleased with himself because he beat Kyle to the range for once, he unlocked the office, made coffee and poured a cup. Then Mark lit a cigarette and leaned against the front bumper of his Yukon, intent on meeting Kyle when he pulled up so he could rub it in that he beat him to work. It was a beautiful winter day, with a clear blue sky contrasting the 28-degree temperature. Life Was Good. Mark thanked God for his Arcteryx cold weather gear, and enjoyed his coffee. After about 10 minutes, the shine started to wear off of his grand plan to get over on Kyle, so he opened the back hatch on his SUV, unlocked the Truck Vault, and started getting his personal gear ready for the long day of teaching tactics.

As Mark was pulling his plate carrier out of the vault, Kyle pulled up and backed into his usual spot. Kyle got out of his decrepit Chevy Trailblazer and pretended for a moment not to see Mark, then as he walked to the passenger side of his SUV he looked up, appearing startled, and said, "Oh, you scared me. The last thing I expected was for you to beat me to work. Ever." Kyle then laughed uproariously and said, "Got you good!" Mark just grinned and shook his head. Kyle had been a cop for over 25 years, and before that served in as an Infantryman in the Ranger Regiment. This combination of life experiences gave Kyle an interesting sense of humor. It was hard not to love Kyle, even when he was being a 4th grader trapped in a 47-year-old man's body. Kyle continued to laugh to himself while he got his gear out of his Trailblazer and walked into the range office. Mark grabbed his helmet bag and 3rd line assault pack, picked up his plate carrier, and lugged his gear into the office. After setting his gear down he refilled his coffee and sat down in the camp chair that served as his office seat.

Mark asked Kyle, "So, are you ready for this training season to be over or what?" "Oh, hell yes," Kyle replied, "It's going to be a busy day with both your CQB class and our own SWAT training today, but I'm looking forward to the end of the week. Friday night I'll be on the road to my dad's place in West Virginia to kill as many deer as DNR will let me shoot." Mark chuckled and asked him, "Do you want to merge SWAT training with day one of the CQB course? We only have 8 students in the CQB course, and could handle all 18 of our SWAT guys." Kyle thought about it for a few seconds and said, "That would help me out if you don't mind doing it that way. It would let me get a bunch of admin stuff done today so I can get out of here early on Friday." "No worries," Mark said, "The team will be here at 11, and I'll brief the other team leaders and get everyone ready to train once the regular students get here. I will use my team as assistant instructors. With that many students, we will need the extra eyes in the shoothouse." Kyle said, "Thanks Bro," and then turned to his computer to start working.

Mark left the office and ran into David, who had just arrived, and after a quick bro-hug, briefed him on the addition of 18 more dudes to the class for the day. David took it in stride, and just said, "Awesome, we will have a great day. I brought the family with me, so we will have to go grab Kasey and get some dinner after class." David spent so much time in Alliance he had purchased a home, and his wife and kids frequently came with him to town.

Mark and David spent the next 45 minutes or so picking up the shoothouse and getting the furniture, target stands and targets ready for the first few runs. By then the Team's SWAT officers had all arrived and were ready to train, so Mark put them through the quick qualification they shot twice a month to test their basic skills. By the time they were done, all of the open enrollment Advanced CQB students had shown up. David was ready to begin the course in-briefing for the CQB class when Mark and the rest of the team walked into the classroom. "Find a seat, brothers, and we will get to work," David said. The SWAT guys took off their gear, and everyone took a seat. Another training day at the range was underway.

"How is it even possible I'm sweating right now?" Lee, one of the CQB students, asked a couple of hours later. Lee was ditching his gear in the classroom after the first full speed team scenario in the shoothouse, getting ready to do the after action for the run. After he racked his rifle and got his helmet and vest off, he continued, "I swear I never moved faster than a walk, but I'm smoked." "Dan would be happy to towel you off." said Ronnie, one of the SWAT guys. Everyone laughed, and when it quieted a little Dan piped up with, "No really, I'll towel you off bro." Everyone laughed even harder. "Dan retains his title as 'gay chicken' champion for the day," Mark said in a loud voice. "Now, find your seats.

Mark sat down inside the classroom and lead off the after-action review while David stood just outside the door and checked his phone for text messages from his "day job". About halfway through the first team's comments the lights in the classroom went out and they heard the heater stop running. At the same time, David mumbled, "What the hell just happened." while he tried hitting the home button on his phone to get it to wake up. "I just charged this thing an hour ago," David said. Mark heard David's comment so he stood up and pulled out his phone to give it to David to do whatever he needed to do. Mark's phone woke up fine, but David noticed immediately it had no cell signal and would not connect to the range's Wi-Fi. David stuck his head in the door and said, "Everyone, do me a favor and check your phones,"

All 26 guys in the classroom checked their phones, and they all powered up, but no one could get a cell signal or Wi-Fi. As Mark was about to speak, Kyle came in the classroom and said, "Are any of you guys having problems with your phones? The power went out, my phone won't turn on, and my laptop died." Everyone just looked at each other for a couple of seconds, then David looked directly at Mark and said, "We should all try to start our cars before we freak out." Mark's mind immediately flashed to his wife Kasey, but he forced down the worry. Kasey was an accomplished police officer, assaulter and sniper in her own right; and she had a cool head in emergencies. If this was bad, she could hold her own until they linked up.

Within 3 minutes, when none of their cars would start, there was little question in any of their minds about what happened. Their only real confusion was why the phones of the guys who were in the classroom at the time of the event still powered up. Lee, an electrical and computer engineer by trade, pointed at the classroom building and said, "Metal building disrupted the pulse. We should all check our optics, lasers and lights on our carbines; they were in the classroom too. We should also check anything inside our vehicles that wasn't wired into the car, like hand held radios, night vision, tablet computers, stuff like that." Mark said, "If that is the case, we might be able to salvage a lot of useful equipment."

Kyle got a look on his face, turned around, and ran to the stand-alone vault next to the office. Mark chased after him and helped Kyle open the door. Kyle went directly to the radio rack inside the vault and turned one on. It worked. "You know, having comms that still work is going to be a Godsend during whatever this is bro," Kyle said. Mark nodded his head and said, "That, and if the vault hadn't been grounded correctly, those 700 blasting caps might have made for quite a show." Kyle shivered involuntarily. Mark said, "We need to do an inventory of every single piece of equipment, ammo and explosives we have on site; I have a feeling things are about to get sporting." Kyle couldn't disagree. He just nodded and started counting spools of det cord.

Chapter 3

Summit County Courthouse
Akron, OH

The Common Pleas courtroom stunk particularly bad today. Usually the small room filled with low cost lawyers, cops in court with 3 hours of sleep after working the 3rd watch, and the never-ending parade of hygiene challenged defendants offended the senses, but today's bouquet was foul enough to gag a third world garbage truck driver. Kasey Wallace, a part time police officer in Tallmadge, an Akron suburb, was waiting her turn to testify in a minor heroin possession case stemming from a traffic stop, and the defendant's lawyer was late. This delay forced Kasey to endure the smell she had learned to associate with the slow-motion collapse of society.

To pass the time, Kasey watched a defendant who was sitting in front of her in the gallery, a 20-something girl with the twitch and teeth of a meth abuser, surfing Snapchat on her smart phone in direct contradiction of the rules as laid out by the Bailiff prior to the court being called into session. As Kasey was contemplating giving the Bailiff the 'head nod / fingerpoint' to alert him to the transgression, the lights went out in the courtroom. Winter power outages weren't unusual in Akron, but Kasey noticed the look of confusion on the girl's face and saw that her phone's screen had gone black. She watched as the girl tried to wake up the phone without success.

The Judge spoke over the murmuring in the court, saying, "Everyone keep your seats please, I'm sure the power will come back on in a moment." Sunlight streamed through the courtroom windows, and Kasey decided to just relax; there was nothing she could do about the delays, and getting impatient wouldn't help anything. After several minutes, another Deputy Sheriff came into the courtroom, approached the Bailiff, and whispered in his ear while holding and gesturing at his cell phone. The Bailiff then asked the court clerk, "Becky, do you know why the UPS power strips didn't keep the computers on?" "No." Becky looked frazzled, and stammered, "I don't understand. They have always kept the computers working before. They must be bad."

The Bailiff approached the judge, and after speaking to her he called the courtroom to rise and the judge adjourned for the day. All of the docketed cases were continued, and everyone filed out of the court. As soon as Kasey broke the threshold of the courtroom into the hallway she snatched her phone out of her purse and hit the power button. Nothing happened.

Kasey had been a cop for a while, had attended all the usual DHS briefings and in-service trainings about EMPs. While she was married to one of the foremost SWAT trainers in the country, with access to people, equipment and information most cops didn't even know existed, she was no slouch herself; Kasey was a qualified SWAT officer, and the only State certified female Police Sniper in Ohio. Kasey had a decisive mind, and before she even exited the stairwell she had decided that she was going to treat this situation like an EMP or solar flare, until proven otherwise.

When she burst out the door of the courthouse into the sunlight, her fears were solidified. High Street in front of the courthouse was a mess of stalled vehicles with people milling around in the road. Kasey knew time was now of the essence, and sprinted across High Street to the parking garage and down to the lowest basement level where she always parked. As she ran she prayed the parking level was low enough underground to save her SUV from the effects of the pulse.

When she hit the bottom of the parking garage stairs and could see her 2018 Chevy Equinox she started hitting the unlock button on her key fob. Nothing happened; no lights, no sound, nothing. Now she was concerned, because even if the vehicle survived the pulse, her key fob had been exposed to the pulse, and her SUV was "keyless". If the fob was dead she wouldn't be able to get in the car or get it started. When Kasey got to the small SUV, she remembered the valet key option they had paid extra for when she bought the vehicle a couple of months ago. She ripped the plastic cover off the right side of the driver's door handle, exposing the valet key slot. Then she fumbled with the key fob and removed the valet key, then used it to unlock the door; breathing a sigh of relief that at least she could get to her rifle and armor even if the car wouldn't start.

When Kasey sat in the driver's seat, she immediately noticed a couple of lights on the dash were working, and breathed even easier. She pushed the start button, and was surprised the Equinox started right up. The passive chip in the valet key must have been enough to tell the vehicle's computer she wasn't a thief and it was ok to start. Kasey quickly opened the back hatch and got her SWAT carbine, a BCM short barreled rifle, out of its bag, loaded it, and got back in the driver's seat and closed the door. She wedged the rifle between her right leg and the center console. Kasey didn't think things would get too violent yet, but she would be a 105-pound attractive female driving one of the few working vehicles through a city that wasn't known for its domestic tranquility in the best of times. While she was already armed with her Glock 43 off duty pistol, she viewed that as a backup and wanted a serious fighting gun close at hand for this drive.

Kasey thought about her and Mark's two children who lived 2000 miles away in Idaho, and felt herself starting to panic a little. The kids were adults now and living on their own, but Kasey had a mother's instinct, and the kids were only in their early 20's. She decided to close her eyes for a second and calm down. Panic was her enemy; clear thinking and decisive action would get her back to her husband, and eventually get her children to safety. She took a moment and prayed, "Heavenly Father, please guide me and give me strength to get home, and do what is necessary to fulfill your will for my life. Please protect my husband and the kids. In Your Son's Name, Amen." Now that her mind was right, she opened her eyes and drove out of the lot.

Kasey was able to drive up to the ground level and find an exit gate that wasn't blocked by a stalled vehicle, but the ticket machine wouldn't work to lift the little orange stick that passed for a gate. As she sat and thought about whether or not to "ram" the gate, she noticed a man standing in High Street next to a stalled car pointing at her and yelling. Kasey couldn't hear him, but from the angry look on his face she could tell he was working up the gumption to come take her SUV. That realization made her decision for her; she hit the gas, rammed the gate, and sped away. She turned right onto High Street, weaving around the stalled cars, and immediately busted a left then another left to get onto Broadway. Kasey continued to bob and weave around the stalled vehicles and walkers in the road, trying not to hit anyone, but not endangering herself or her now precious vehicle. As she came to the intersection at East Market Street, traffic thinned out, and she was able to speed up. After she passed Market Street, Kasey realized she should have gone that way in order to avoid the freeway on the way home. She quickly made a U-turn and drove the wrong way on Broadway until she got back to Market, then made a left.

About 4 blocks down she saw a stalled Akron PD car in the road with an officer standing behind it unloading equipment from the trunk. When the officer heard Kasey's SUV approaching, he stood up, turned around, and looked at her. Kasey immediately recognized the officer as James Roberts, known by everyone as JR. Kasey felt a wave of relief flash over her. The Wallace and Roberts families went to the same church, and Kasey and Sarah, JR's wife, were in many of the same women's groups in the church. JR was on the Akron SWAT team and he and Mark trained together all the time. Kasey and JR had also been classmates in the State Basic Sniper School, and talked frequently about police sniper related topics.

Kasey screeched to a stop, causing JR to run behind his car and come to the low ready with his pistol. Kasey stepped out slowly and yelled, "JR, it's me, Kasey." Only then did JR recognize Kasey's personalized license plates, LNGSHOT. JR stepped out and jogged up to Kasey. They shared a quick hug, and JR asked, "Are you OK? Why does your Equinox run?" Kasey replied, "I'm OK. It was parked in the courthouse parking structure basement. The pulse didn't get to it."

JR asked Kasey, "So, you think it was an EMP too?" Kasey said, "Yeah. I can't think of anything else that would do this, can you?" JR said, "No. I am surprised no transformers blew up though." Kasey nodded, "Yeah I didn't think of that, but it is strange." Kasey shook it off and told JR to cross load his gear into her SUV. He turned to do so while Kasey reached into the driver's seat, grabbed her carbine, and pulled security. When he was loaded JR said, "Ready." Kasey replied, "Lets go." When they were moving, JR said, "Can you take me home? Sarah is off work today. It's on the way to your house, if you want to stay off the freeway." Kasey said, "Of course. Are you and Sarah coming to Alliance with me?" "Is that where you're going?" JR asked. Kasey said, "Yes. I'm stopping by our condo first to take what ammo, guns and food I can with me, but I'm only stopping there long enough to load up. If I take too long Mark will think I'm stuck somewhere and leave a trail of bodies all the way to Akron trying to find me. He knows I was in court today." JR agreed with that, and thought about going to Alliance while keeping his eyes facing out pulling security. Kasey let him think.

JR was torn. He knew his oath as an Akron Police officer dictated he return to the station, report for duty, and die fighting the dirtbags who were even now probably heading out to smash windows to steal TVs and sneakers. Without transportation and communications, the 500 officer Akron Police Department was doomed to lose the battle against several thousand hood rats, probably within the first 48 hours. His duty as a man drew him to protect his wife; to get her to a place of safety and then evaluate the situation from there. Of all of the places within traveling distance of his home, he knew Alliance offered the best chance of safety for his wife. The range facility there had the equipment and numbers of highly trained people that would give them the capability to survive. He also trusted Mark and Kyle to organize a quick response to this event, whatever it actually was. He would talk to Sarah before he said anything out loud, but his mind was made up. They would go to Alliance with Kasey.

As they rounded the corner turning onto North Adams Street, intending to cut behind the Akron City hospital, Kasey was startled to see a white guy in a red flannel shirt standing in the middle of the road about 75 yards in front of them, pointing what looked like a shotgun at the SUV with one hand while gesturing them to stop with the other. She blurted out, "Contact front." And let off the accelerator. JR said, "My rifle is in my bag. Can I borrow yours?" Kasey levered the carbine up and over the center console, handed it to JR, then started accelerating right at the man. The narrow road and high curbs meant she had nowhere else to go. The guy in the road put his left hand on the shotgun and fired a shot at them. Kasey ducked instinctually but nothing hit them. JR yelled, "Stop with my side towards him." Kasey got the SUV stopped about 40 yards from the man with the gun, with JR's door about 45 degrees offset from the guy who by now had racked another round and was firing again. The shot missed Kasey and JR again, not surprising either of them given the fact he was shooting a shotgun and they were over 40

25

yards away. Kasey thought *Thank God he isn't shooting slugs.* JR rolled down the window, crouched in the seat until he could stabilize the carbine on the sill, centered the Aimpoint's dot on the man's chest, and pressed off 4 shots. It felt to JR like a drill in a vehicle tactics class. Neither JR nor Kasey could see where the shots hit but the man fell down on his back like a puppet with the strings cut.

Kasey and JR sat in silence for a moment until Kasey broke the tension by saying, "Well, 25 minutes into the apocalypse and you're already on the scoreboard JR." JR was quiet for a minute, finally breaking his silence with, "It's going to be a short apocalypse if everyone is as dumb as that guy. Let's get moving." As they drove past the man's body, giving it as a wide berth as possible, JR said, "Stop real quick. I should grab that shotgun." Kasey stopped and JR jumped out, ran over to the guy, and dead checked him by poking him in the eye with the muzzle of Kasey's rifle. When the man didn't move JR grabbed the shotgun off the ground and jogged back to the SUV. After he was in and they were moving again Kasey said, "Please tell me there is still ammo in that thing. I'd hate to think we killed a guy who was out of ammo." JR checked the magazine of the Remington 870, and found one round in it. He then opened the action and a round popped out. "Yep, two rounds in it." JR said. Kasey just breathed a sigh of relief and kept driving.

JR rolled down his window, and asked Kasey to roll down the others. It was cold as hell, but he didn't want to eat glass if one of the windows was hit. JR reloaded the shotgun with the OO Buck rounds that came out of it, figuring to use up those two rounds first, saving their limited 5.56mm rifle ammo. As he engaged the safety on the shotgun, JR noticed an "Akron Hospital Property" tag with an inventory number on the side of the receiver. *Dammit,* he thought. JR prayed he hadn't just killed an Akron Hospital Police officer in plainclothes who was trying to commandeer a vehicle. If so, the guy was an idiot. Shooting at them first from that far away when armed with a shotgun was just a dumb move. Still, it would suck if he had just killed a brother cop. JR pushed the thought out of his mind; he had to focus on getting to Sarah, then protecting her and Kasey until they could get to Alliance.

The remaining 12 minutes of the trip to JR's house near Goodyear Heights Park was uneventful. When they pulled up in the driveway JR jumped out and went in the front door. Kasey shut the

SUV off, hoping to not draw the attention of JR's neighbors to the running vehicle. In a couple of minutes the garage door came up, Kasey started the Equinox again, then turned around and backed into the garage. JR lowered the door by hand and Kasey came with him into the house. Once inside, she saw Sarah sitting on the couch staring at the wall. Kasey walked over to her and sat down. "Are you OK sis?" Kasey asked her. "I'm trying," Sarah said, "it's a lot to take in. I thought it was just a power outage, but my phone wouldn't work; and when I decided to go to Grace (the church they all attended) to kill some time, my car wouldn't start." Kasey asked if JR had told her what they thought was happening, and Sarah said, "Yeah, he just did. It's all so unbelievable. I'm not sure what to think. Can't the government fix it? I mean it's just some electronics, right?"

"Unfortunately, I don't think so sis." Kasey replied. "Whatever this is has probably affected the entire country. The power grid is down and the vast majority of cars are dead, probably permanently. The problem is too big. It will take years to restore basic services like power, water and sewer. I think we are on our own for a long time honey." Sarah sighed and nodded, then said, "We aren't on our own; the Lord is with us." For the first time since things fell apart Kasey felt thankful. Kasey had trouble forming close friendships with women; she found most of them to be shallow, soft and dependent on others. Sarah was such an emotionally strong woman, with such a deep trust in God that Kasey felt overwhelmingly lucky to have her as a friend.

JR came back into the living room lugging a big duffle bag. He set it down and sat on the arm of the couch next to Sarah. He closed his eyes for a second, gathering his thoughts, and told Sarah, "Honey, I think we need to go to Alliance until this blows over." He had a whole list of reasons and arguments prepared, expecting her to object. Instead she just said, "I agree." He stared at her for a moment, and she said, "Baby I trust you; and if you and Kasey are right, this could change the world for the rest of our lives. What do we need to pack?" JR had always loved and admired his wife, but never as much as that moment. She was a woman to ride the river with.

"I love you Sarah," JR said, then continued, "OK, we have very limited space in Kasey's Equinox and she still has to load a bunch of stuff at her house, so I already packed as many of our outdoor clothes and shoes in this duffle as I could fit. I need you to pack underwear and all your heavy socks in a backpack then fill the rest of it with whatever toiletries will fit. Then grab our little document safe and put as many of our hard copy pictures in it as you can, along with whatever flash drives we have in the house. I need to sort guns and ammo and load whatever bottled water we have in the house into the SUV. After that, we will grab whatever canned goods and boxed dry food we have and take all of that. I'd really like to be back on the road in 20 minutes if we can." "I'll do the food," Kasey said. They all got to work.

It took 35 minutes until they were ready to pull out. JR ended up leaving most of his guns in the safe and locking it up; there just wasn't room in the SUV. He did take all 4000 rounds of 5.56 and 1000 rounds of 9mm ammo he had, along with 500 rounds of .22LR he found. In addition to his work guns already in the Equinox, he only took his work precision rifle, a Tikka T3x Tac A1, and his Ruger 10/22 rifle. Everything else would have to keep for now. They found 2 cases of water and about 1 medium cardboard box worth of food and packed that in the SUV next to their clothes and small safe.

JR put Sarah in the back seat behind Kasey, who was driving. He uncased his work carbine, a Hodge Defense 14.5 inch carbine. When he function checked the gun, the Aimpoint was toast from the pulse, but his Magpul iron sights would do the job until he could figure something out. He armed Sarah with the 10/22, and told her to only shoot outside the SUV. Before her car door closed, Sarah said, "I forgot our bibles." and ran inside to grab them. She returned quickly with the 2 bibles in hand and got back in the SUV.

When they were ready Kasey started the Equinox and JR opened the garage door. Kasey pulled out, JR closed the garage and jumped in the passenger seat, and they were off. JR was thankful none of their neighbors came out to gawk at the working vehicle, and perhaps try to take it. JR was a former Marine with combat deployments and had a couple of shootings as a police officer, but would be perfectly happy going the rest of his life without killing anyone else. Today's events so far made him suspect it was not to be.

The drive to Kasey and Mark's place in Cuyahoga Falls was fast. Kasey was able to stay on residential streets until the last half mile, and they only encountered one problem. When taking a shortcut through the Chapel Hill Mall Parking lot a Cuyahoga Falls Police officer on foot tried to wave them down. Neither Kasey nor JR recognized the guy and they just went around him. As they passed him he started yelling and put his hand on his pistol. JR brought his carbine up into view and pointed it at the officer, who saw the gun and JR's police uniform and turned around and walked the other direction.

Kasey backed into her driveway a few minutes later, and gave JR the key to the front door. He did the "in the front door / open the garage routine" and Kasey backed in. JR closed the garage and they huddled there. Kasey said, "JR, load as much of that 5.56 ammo as will fit in the cargo area and put cases of 9mm on the back-seat floorboard. I'll open the safe. Please grab all of the rifles and put them on top of the 9mm ammo. There are only about eight rifles, the rest are already in Alliance. Put the three cases of Hornady 168 Amax ammo for our sniper systems on the back-passenger side seat and stack whatever .22LR you can find on top of that. I'm going to grab our clothes and shoes." Sarah said, "I'll grab food and whatever water you have and wedge it in where I can." "Thanks sis," Kasey said. "There are several buckets of Wise LTS food in the pantry. Please grab that too." Sarah said, "You got it."

They went to work. First, Kasey grabbed her drag bag containing her Sako M10 sniper rifle, her shooting tripod and sniper assault pack, and threw them in the Equinox. She didn't want to forget them. Next, Kasey went into their master bedroom closet and stopped cold; she would miss her heels. She never got to wear them enough, but she did have a thing for them. That train of thought led her to a sad place, angry at the world for disrupting her and Mark's life. This condo was the smallest place they had ever lived together, but it held so many great memories. Like any couple, in their years of marriage Kasey and Mark had good times and bad; but they had never been happier together than since they moved to Ohio. This condo represented that to Kasey for some reason and she was going to miss it. She allowed herself wallow in it for a minute then realized she had to stay focused on the mission or she would let everyone down. Kasey squared her shoulders and got to work.

Mark had invested heavily in Arcteryx and Crye uniforms and cold weather gear for them both. They spent a lot of time on the range or on SWAT callouts in the cold and he always said, "This sucks enough without fighting your own gear. Buy it right, buy it once." She grabbed every piece of uniform and cold weather gear she could find. It was a substantial amount but she realized it might be a really long time, if ever, before they could get more. Kasey also suspected their operational tempo and new lifestyle would be hard on uniforms. She packed all of it. Next, Kasey packed both of their Bibles out their nightstands and set their home defense BCM rifle on top of one of the bags.

When she was finished, Kasey had two large Eagle deployment bags stuffed to the gills with boots, uniforms, coats, Bibles, family photos, underwear and toiletries. After she lugged them out to the garage and made them JR's problem to load, Kasey went to the shelves in the garage and grabbed her and Mark's Mystery Ranch bug out ruck sacks, and all of the loose pouches and plate carriers she could find, and put them in the "stuff wherever it will fit" pile next to the SUV. Next, Kasey grabbed two large totes full of AR15 magazines. They were very heavy, and she asked JR to strap them to the roof. Again, she suspected they would need them, and they wouldn't be making anymore for a while.

When they were done the Equinox looked like something out of a circus. Every cubic inch was stuffed with something, with barely enough room for the three of them to squeeze in. JR and Kasey talked about the route they would take to get to the range in Alliance. There was no way to get there without getting on I-76 but they planned a way to minimize that, sticking to back roads as much as possible. Within 30 minutes of arriving JR locked the safe and opened the garage door. After Kasey had pulled out and the door was closed, the three of them said a prayer and hit the road. After going less than a mile Sarah said, "I have to pee."

Chapter 4

Liberty Avenue, Ward 2
Alliance, OH

Dylan Nowak hadn't been in a gunfight, but he'd thought about it some. It wasn't that Dylan wanted to shoot someone; in fact it was quite the contrary. He just knew the odds of being able to avoid a gunfight during his career while working as a cop in post-industrial Ohio were pretty small; especially for a cop like him who actively sought out dope dealers and violent criminals. Dylan knew that if he sat on his ass and never aggressively investigated anything he would probably be alright, but he just wasn't built like that. What it really came down to was Dylan had 5 children at home, and was determined that he would stack whatever bodies were necessary in order to get back to his kids.

Dylan knew he was lucky to be a Patrolman for the Alliance Police Department, because he could go to pretty much any training he wanted to, for free, at the Department's range. The range hosted most of the big name firearms and tactics instructors throughout the year and Dylan took as many carbine, pistol and patrol tactics classes as his shift commander would allow. At least once a month he was at the range for several days working on his gunfighting skills.

During his 5 years as a policeman, his drive to pursue criminals had landed Dylan in more than his share of hot water. His name appeared constantly in the local newspaper, usually as the subject of some indignant community organizer's tirade against the inherent brutality of the cisgendered male dominated police state. People cursed Dylan's name in the bars, heroin shooting galleries, and flophouses of Stark County; usually by people who were on probation, parole, or supervised release because of his police work. Even some cops disliked Dylan, sometimes because he made them look like the lazy active duty pensioners they were.

That's not to say Dylan was perfect. Sometimes, especially when he was a new guy, his enthusiasm to separate criminals from society overran his understanding of the procedures designed by his Department to ensure the details of the law were indeed followed. He had been unsuccessfully sued a few times, but the Chief of Police always backed his guys when they were in the right. Because of all this Dylan's relationship with the community, especially the more economically challenged parts of it like Ward 2, was strained (to put it nicely).

However, despite the pain he caused in the collective asses of the Chief of Police, Mayor, and City Counsel, Dylan had something they all knew the City desperately needed. He was a natural gatherer of intelligence. Despite his reputation in the community, hood rats, street dealers, and addicts talked to Dylan. Usually more than they should. He had the gift of gab which, when combined with his instinctual understanding of how human networks functioned and a good memory for names, made him particularly dangerous to those seeking to break the law and get away with it.

For example Dylan had recently been developing information on a new criminal organization in the area known by his snitches only as the "Bookie Organization". While he wasn't sure yet how the gang had gotten its name or who was controlling it, he was sure the Bookie Organization was a very real group of criminals who worked together to distribute dope. Massive amounts of prescription opiates, heroin, fentanyl and carfentanil were being distributed throughout Stark County, including in Alliance, by the Canton based Bookie Organization. In fact, the latest micro-spike in opioid overdoses, over and above the already historically high rate, seemed to coincide with the first rumblings Dylan heard about the Bookie Organization using carfentanil, a synthetic opiate designed for use in elephants, as a cutting agent for their heroin.

Dylan hadn't been able to develop much specific information about the Bookies yet, but no one else in the county on the law enforcement side even seemed to know they existed. The Bookie Organization appeared to Dylan like a big dirty iceberg floating through the sea of cultural decay and learned dependency most of Stark County had devolved into. Not much was visible above the surface, but he knew it had be big and dangerous beneath the waves.

This lack of information had led to Dylan's current situation: sitting in his marked patrol car in the middle of Ward 2, watching a known "hub" drug house on Liberty Ave near South Street in

Alliance, looking for someone he didn't recognize. A pill user named Brenda who he arrested yesterday told him her boyfriend got his pill deliveries from Canton every day at this house. He figured if anyone he didn't recognize came out of the house it would make for a good investigative stop. Maybe he could identify someone tied directly to the Bookies. It could be a thread to pull on if nothing else. Dylan sipped his coffee and texted with his wife while he waited.

While all of Alliance had suffered decline in the now 20 year-long slow-motion collapse of the area's industrial economy, Ward 2 had become the physical manifestation of the city's economic and societal decay. All manner of illegal vices and other symptoms of a broken culture radiated like a starburst from Ward 2's four square miles of once vibrant single family homes on tree lined streets. Of the city's four electoral wards, Ward 2 was the most densely populated, economically depressed, and violent. While containing about 30% of the city's population, Ward 2 accounted for over 70% of police services.

About 30 minutes after Dylan parked to watch the house, a red Nissan Sentra pulled up and a black guy got out, then walked up to the door. As he climbed the porch steps Dylan saw him use his right hand to grab a bulge on his right hip and hitch up his sagging pants. *Bingo!*, he thought. Dylan just observed a reason to Terry Search the guy. He watched the subject go inside and come back out 3 minutes later, then get in his car and leave. Dylan got behind the Nissan and initiated the traffic stop. Ten minutes later Dylan had one Raymond Hilton, a 25 year old man with an address in Canton, Ohio, in custody for being a felon in possession of a handgun and possession with intent to distribute of 13 grams of individually packaged 1-gram bags of Heroin and 39 prescription pills. The $7800 in small bills Dylan found in Hilton's pocket would help support the distribution charge. Hilton was handcuffed in the back of the patrol car while Dylan sat in his driver's seat and worked on the tow report for the Nissan on his in-car computer. Dylan had Hilton by the short hairs and they both knew it. They also both knew Hilton would eventually answer Dylan's questions about the Bookies in an effort to avoid a long stay in prison.

As Dylan was about to Mirandize Hilton and start the delicate dance of interrogation, his patrol car died and his computer blacked out. Dylan was stunned for a second. He'd just finished the tow report but hadn't saved it yet. That was a lot of work. Dylan sighed and turned the ignition key but nothing happened. No click of the starter, no lights on the dash, nothing. *What the hell,* he thought. He noticed the in-car radio was dead as well, which was never supposed to happen; it was wired directly into the battery. He figured the alternator was dead and had drained the battery, so he keyed up the mic on his portable radio and called dispatch. Nothing. Dylan grabbed his cell phone out of the center console and speed dialed dispatch. The call wouldn't connect. He looked and saw the little circle with a slash where his signal strength should be, meaning he had no cell signal at all. He couldn't figure out what was going on so he got out of the car and looked around.

Doors were opening all up and down Liberty Avenue, and people were walking out onto their porches. The lady who lived in the house where Dylan was parked asked him, "What up Nowak (for some reason everyone referred to him by his last name, even the public)? Why da power out? Its cold up in dis house without no heatin'!" "Your power is out Malinda?" asked Dylan. "Hell yeah it out." Malinda said, "I callin the power people to complain. I paid my bill an errything." Malinda tried using her Obama phone to call, but she couldn't get it to work. Dylan left her to it and walked to the rear of his car.

Dylan wondered what the hell could cause everything to shut down like this. The power going out, his car dying and electronics not working all at the same time were obviously connected. Dylan remembered his training on EMPs but he thought those were caused by nuclear weapons going off, and he hadn't seen or heard anything unusual on the horizon or in the sky. Besides, his cell phone wasn't dead, it just couldn't connect to a tower. He was stumped. He sat back down in his cruiser for several minutes and just thought. The neighborhood that was normally teeming with noise and movement was eerily quiet. No rap music brought tidings of easy money and baby mamas as it bellowed from open windows; no 20 year old electric furnaces could be heard wheezing away attempting to keep sedentary bodies warm who should instead be at work in the middle of a weekday. No $600 cars with rusted through mufflers could be heard lurching through the hood. The only noise Dylan could hear was the periodic raised voice of some upset soul complaining that the racist Trump must have shut off their Obama phone or how the white man was trying to freeze them all to death.

Dylan slowly came to a decision. Whatever this event was he didn't think it would be fixed quickly. He had to get off this street before people started to realize this was a serious situation, and began testing him. If they realized he couldn't call for help things could get ugly. He was about 15 blocks from the station and decided he would walk Hilton to the station and figure it out from there. He stood up and looked around.

Dylan walked to the back of his patrol car and opened the trunk. He took off the exterior armor carrier he wore on patrol. It was only a soft armor carrier, and he wanted level 4 plates and his rifle mags for this walk. He didn't know exactly why he felt that way but Dylan always followed his gut. Besides, the minute he walked out of sight of his patrol car a clock would start ticking until someone worked up the balls to break into it and set it on fire. He threw his Velocity Systems plate carrier over his patrol uniform, checked to make sure all three mags in the pouches were loaded, and grabbed his rifle. He charged his rifle, closed the trunk and gathered up the gun, dope and money he had taken off Hilton, shoving it in a cargo pocket in his uniform pants. Dylan then got Hilton out of the back seat. Hilton, seeing Dylan's rifle and different armor asked, "What the hell dude?" Dylan said, "First, I'm not your dude. My car is dead. We're walking to the station." "That don't make no sense. Have another car come get me." Hilton demanded. "I ain't bein' walked to jail like no dog on a leash. It's cold up in here!" Dylan replied, "Shut up. You have the right to remain silent. Do that."

Dylan had to manually lock all the doors after figuring out the electronic lock button didn't work, forcing him to play the convict shuffle with Hilton as he tried to control him and walk around the car. That accomplished he had to do that same thing to Hilton's Nissan. Finally, Dylan was ready to move. He took a firm hold on the handcuffs holding Hilton's hands behind his back and started walking. Dylan planned on going north on Liberty until they reached Milner St, then skipping west to the alley that paralleled Liberty and turning north again. He reasoned this would allow them to move with the least amount of exposure.

35

They hadn't even reached the corner of Milner when the first round snapped overhead. "Shit," Hilton exclaimed as he ducked and almost fell over. "Let me go. They ain't gonna let you walk outta here. This place gonna explode." Dylan lifted Hilton's arms up by the cuffs and said, "Run." He kept a strong grip on Hilton's cuffs and pushed him forward. They reached Milner Street and turned the corner. Dylan slowed them to a walk and looked around. Behind him on Liberty Avenue he saw three young males watching them intently. He didn't see any weapons, and shoved Hilton back into a jog and turned the corner into the alley going north. As they were rounding the corner Dylan looked back at the young men and saw one of them take off running north on Liberty Ave while the other two moved to follow him.

Dylan knew he was in serious trouble now. It didn't matter if the kid who ran north on Liberty was going to get in front of him in an effort to trap him, or if he ran to get more people to do the same thing. Either way Dylan was sure he was being enveloped. After years of technology, organization and the law allowing him to be the hunter in this urban jungle, he now had no ability to communicate or travel quickly. Dylan was now the hunted. As Dylan's mind focused on the primal fear he now felt, Hilton decided to act. Hilton stopped abruptly causing Dylan to collide with his back. As Dylan recoiled off the criminal's back, Hilton mule kicked him squarely in the abdomen just above his wedding tackle. Dylan went down like a bag of cement dropped from a roof.

The unexpected attack caught Dylan completely by surprise, mainly because in his mind he had started to view Hilton as an ally. After all they were both running from people shooting at them. Such was not the case. Hilton was a savage; raised by his culture from birth to be a predator and exploiter of the weak. His only motivation was personal gain and individual power. He knew that these Alliance hood rats weren't shooting at him, they were shooting at this cop. If he could get away from the cop he would find help and shelter among them.

Hilton turned around and began kicking Dylan as he lay on the ground, intending to soften him up so he could run. Instead his boot must have connected with Dylan's head because the cop went limp. Hilton jumped on Dylan and managed to get the keys off his duty belt. It took a couple of moments but Hilton was able to unlock one of the handcuffs binding his wrists then bring his hands around front and get the other hand free. Hilton tossed the cuffs aside and dug into the officer's cargo pocket looking for his dope and money. Grabbing a handful of both, along with his favorite "Glock fo-ty" the cop had taken from him, he quickly stuffed it all in his pocket. He took the clip (as he thought of it) for his Glock out of the officer's pocket and loaded it up and stuffed it in his pants.

Hilton stood up and began to walk away but realized he could use that rifle the cop was wearing. It wasn't an AK but he had seen people shoot ARs on YouTube, and figured he wanted one. He bent back down and started wiggling the rifle off Dylan's body where it was slung on its Blue Force Gear VCAS sling. As he was about to pull the rifle free, Dylan woke up. Dylan didn't wake up slowly; he regained consciousness suddenly, with the startled fear of waking from a bad dream. He opened his eyes and through the blood in them saw Hilton on top of him with Dylan's own rifle in his hands, trying to get it untangled.

Dylan panicked and lunged up, grabbing the rifle with his left hand and slamming Hilton in the face with it. Dylan clawed for his pistol and after a moment of struggling to shift Hilton's weight was able to draw it. In one motion Dylan rotated the Glock 17 up and started shooting. His first round struck the rifle, showering his face with fragments. Dylan kept pulling the trigger as he extended the pistol toward Hilton. The second, third and fourth rounds connected with Hilton's abdomen and chest, and his fifth round exploded from the Glock just as Dylan's Surefire X300U light touched Hilton's chin. The near-contact shot entered the roof of Hilton's mouth and burst out the top of his head. Hilton collapsed on Dylan, who struggled to get out from under the now dead man. Dylan felt like he was being suffocated. He was finally able to roll Hilton's lifeless body off of him and untangle his rifle. Dylan managed to get to his feet, but immediately got dizzy. He walked in a tight circle trying to clear his head and promptly slipped on a deep smear of blood, falling poorly and disorienting him even more.

The two thugs who had been following Dylan and his prisoner, intent on keeping them in sight, saw the entire deadly encounter. The fight and shooting had unfolded so quickly that by the time one of them got his phone out to take video, it was over. His phone didn't work anyway. When they saw Dylan stand up again, they ducked behind a busted-up car in the alley and continued watching, waiting for the sirens of more cops and the ambulance to tell them it was time to go. The sirens never came.

Chapter 5

City Police Range
Alliance, OH

"Are you sure this is really the apocalypse?" Kyle asked Mark with a grin. "It seems awful quiet. I mean, we aren't even raping and pillaging." "No, I'm pretty sure this is the apocalypse bro, but we are less than an hour into it. Be patient." Mark replied, then continued, "And no matter how bad it gets we won't be raping or pillaging." "Humph," Kyle huffed, "This apocalypse is dumb." Mark couldn't reply; he was laughing too hard.

They called off their quick and dirty inventory of the vault having decided the people were more important than the equipment. They called everyone at the range into the classroom. First, they started a fresh roster. Some of the civilian CQB students didn't understand why this was important enough to do first and started making soft complaining noises. All of the cops in the room understood knowing who was available, with what skills and equipment, was the first step to any plan. They also understood that things were about to get crazy; and keeping track of who was where, doing what, would prevent serious ass-ache in the future. They were delighted to discover that the classroom laptop and iPad, while not connecting to the Internet, both still worked. They were happy they didn't have to do all the organizing by hand.

As they were starting to build the roster in the laptop they heard a vehicle pull up and doors slam. Chris and Ed from the Brick Plant burst through the door, and Chris blurted out "We got EMP'd!" Everyone just looked at them. Mark said, "We know bro." Chris looked deflated. Mark continued, "I'm glad you guys made it. What vehicle did you find to run?" Ed replied, "My truck is a '71. Runs fine if you ignore the aftermarket gauges that don't work now." "Awesome." Mark said, "It's good to know some things you'd expect from an EMP are true. Have a seat guys." Ed laughed and while pushing Chris to the back of the room said, "Wait till I tell you guys about how Chris punched himself in the junk 10 minutes into the apocalypse." A low roar of chuckles erupted, and Kyle said, "Alright, let's get down to business. When we point to you, we need your full legal name. We will assign teams and roster numbers when we are done."

It took about 20 minutes to get through the process. They ended up with 31 people who could be assigned to an operational team, including instructors and range staff, and two support personnel. The support personnel were Burt and Lydia. Burt was the range maintenance man. A Vietnam vet, Burt hadn't been operational since then; but he was a dedicated member of the range staff and could build or fix pretty much anything. He was a Godly man and an accomplished hunter and woodsman. Burt was also blessed with the deep common sense and practical knowledge often found in older rednecks. Kyle was sure he would be a rock in the coming bad times. Lydia was a Deputy Sheriff who managed the work release program for the Stark County Jail. She spent most days shuttling around petty offenders to do one menial task or another. She happened to be at the range when the pulse hit, checking to see if Kyle needed any manual labor from her inmates over the next few weeks. Her van wouldn't start, but no one suspected she would stick around long. She seemed pretty dang soft.

Of the 31 "deployable" guys, 20 were Alliance SWAT officers, including Kyle and Mark. The other 11 consisted of the eight students in the CQB class, five of whom were cops in out of state jurisdictions, and three who were highly trained citizens, one was David, with Chris and Ed being the last two. Mark looked at the roster and let out a long breath. Whatever was coming at them 31 people wasn't a lot to meet it with. The good news was everyone in the room was a solid performer who Mark, David, and Kyle had trained or worked with before. Some of them were unproven under fire while others had been bloodied either as cops, while serving in the Military, or working for Private Military Companies. Either way, every one of them was trained to a high standard and was equipped with the right gear. Mark would go to war with any of them and it looked like he'd have that chance.

Mark, Kyle, and David pulled Chris and Ed aside and got a quick and dirty report of what they had seen. They reported the same phenomenon of the loss of power and cell phones, but found

40

that Ed's old truck still ran. They observed hundreds of stalled vehicles on the road and people milling around, and theirs was the only running vehicle. Chris said, "We saw an Alliance patrol car on Liberty Avenue but no one was in it, and we didn't see the officer between there and the station."

Mark came back and addressed the group, "Ok, here is the situation as we understand it. The power is off, most of our vehicles don't work and our electronics that weren't inside this metal building are dead. Our phones that do work don't have any cell signal at all. Electronics that were stored in our closed vehicles seem to have survived fine but anything wired into the car is dead." Mark took a second to think before continuing. "We haven't seen the skydiving plane overhead since this happened and they usually fly all afternoon. We haven't heard a train pass on the nearby tracks since the event; our handheld police radios that were in the vault and our cars work but we can't raise anyone on any of the frequencies, other than ourselves on the car-to-car channel. Chris and Ed are reporting the same general thing was happening through town on their way here and the same effect on their electronics stored in their vehicles."

Mark continued, "I propose we place Kyle in command. He is the highest-ranking police officer present, and should be the one to direct our operations, at least until we make contact with the Chief of Police." Kyle got serious for once and nodded his head. Mark drove on, "Those of you who are not sworn Alliance PD personnel, I'd like you to accept an emergency commission until we figure things out. As the Commander of the SWAT Team Kyle has the authority to deputize all of you." For some reason that was the moment it seemed to get real for some of the guys. "You mean you want us to become Alliance cops and respond to this in an official capacity?" Lee asked, with some incredulity in his voice. "I've never been to the police academy. I'm an electrical engineer working for a tech startup. I've only trained; I've never been shot at or pointed a loaded gun at anyone." Before Mark could reply David jumped in, "This situation is only a few minutes old but we don't know where it will go; how bad it will get. We need every trained gun we can get to help brother. If the time comes you will do fine, or you won't. We are in it now, and we are all we have." Kyle nodded and responded, "The good news is, we are all we need."

Another of the CQB students, Ernesto, a retired cop, spoke up, "Guys, if this is nationwide I need to get home to my family." "I understand completely brother," Mark said. "A temporary police commission is just that; temporary and a commission. Meaning you can resign and leave at any time. I'm not talking about conscripting anyone against their will." Silence reigned in the room. Mark continued, "OK, hear my logic guys. I know everyone with family somewhere else wants to ruck up, steal an old truck, and go all road warrior. The problem is, if this is a national emergency, by the time you get out of Ohio it will full blown Mad Max out there. Think through how you would travel, eat, fight, and where you would find fuel assuming you could acquire and keep a running vehicle. If you had to walk home to California Ernesto, it would take you 18 months in the best scenario."

Mark paused for a breath then continued, "Guys, in the end, this situation is what the Second Amendment is really all about. The right to bear arms we talk about all the time is only half the equation; the reason we have that right is because we need it to fulfill the obligation to be 'well regulated', which means well trained, and to serve in the militia in times of crisis, like now. The point is not hunting or target practice; it's about being ready when the day comes. Well, it's come. I know each of you guys, and I know you take that obligation seriously."

Mark noticed the nod of realization from several guys, including Ernesto, and kept going, "What I think we need to do is create a safe haven here in Alliance until we can get some idea as to the magnitude of this event, then make viable plans to get guys home who want to go. If it is a national level emergency, or even one covering several states, we will be far better off, both as individuals and as a team, if we gather resources and then act from a position of strength. Rushing off to face this alone, or even in groups of 2 or 3, will greatly reduce your likelihood of saving your families. If this turns out to be a fairly local thing we will probably know that within a few days; and if that's the case your families aren't in any danger."

Mark paused for a second and recalled a story he had seen on the National Geographic channel, and decided it may help. "Guys, what's the biggest, baddest predator in the ocean?" Ernesto said, "The great white shark. They're the apex predator." Ernesto grinned and continued, "I know that because all the white girls in college

42

called me the 'great Mexican shark'." Mark shook his head and drove on, "As individual animals, you are correct brother. But did you know white sharks are hunted too?" Ed piped up, "No way. Nothing could kill a great white other than a human with an M1 Garand and a scuba tank." Several guys chuckled at the Jaws movie reference. "Actually Ed, you are incorrect." Mark smugly said.

He continued, "Some Orca whale pods near Monterey have learned to hunt great white sharks using team tactics. They figured out that if they circle the shark as a pod they can distract the great white long enough for one of them to come at him from below and flip the shark on its back. A shark on its back is instantly put into a type of paralysis and when held there will suffocate. You see no matter how bad ass you are an individual will always lose to a determined and cunning team motivated by hunger." The reality of the challenge of moving a long distance in a non-permissive environment by themselves was dawning on some of the guys. "This isn't some end of the world fiction book guys. This is 'fo reelz' as they say 'in da streets'. If this is widespread, the entire country will be like Somalia within a week. Failure here means you die and never get to help your family." Mark concluded.

Kyle jumped in and said, "Why don't you guys think about it for a couple of minutes." He then turned to David and Mark and said, "Let's strategize for a second." The three of them walked outside to huddle. "Sorry to put you on the spot bro, but I think some semblance of legality is necessary until we know if things are completely off the rails or not." Mark told Kyle. "It makes sense. I need you guys to prioritize some tasks and let's start making a plan." Kyle said. Mark said, "I think we need to break the guys up into teams and assign some leadership, so we can share the work once we decide what to do." David nodded his head, and Kyle replied, "Sounds good. Mark, you are my #2." Mark ignored Kyle's grin of implication regarding the potty humor. Kyle looked disappointed to not get the satisfaction of a response to his hilarious poop joke, but continued, "I need you to get the teams organized, and by then David and I will have some tasks identified and prioritized." Mark said, "Ok, I'm on it," and went back into the classroom. Kyle and David went to the office and cleared off the whiteboards to start making lists.

When Mark re-entered the classroom, he saw that the five civilians were standing in the front of the room. Lee, apparently their elected spokesman, said, "We have discussed it and we are all in, at least until we have a clear picture of what's going on and can make a plan for these guys to get to their families." "Ok, thank you brothers." Mark said, then asked, "Why are you all up here in a line?" "To be sworn in as cops, dummy." Lee grinned. Mark sighed, and told them to raise their right hands.

Mark said, "I don't remember the entire oath but I'll cover the important stuff. I, state your name." They all did so. "Do solemnly swear to uphold the Constitution of the United States, the laws of the State of Ohio and the laws of the City of Alliance. To hold true faith and allegiance to the same, and to obey the orders of those appointed over me, so help me God?" All agreed and lowered their hands. Mark solemnly told them thank you and then led everyone in a prayer for their families, the country and for strength and wisdom in the days ahead.

*

In the range office, Kyle and David were furiously writing on the white boards that covered the walls. Kyle was listing every critical site and resource in town they should try to secure and assigning them a priority. His list included things like 'all pharmacies' with a sub list of all of them he could think of, 'city water wells' and their locations (Kyle had worked for the city water department for a year before becoming a police officer, and was generally aware of their resources), a list of Alliance's four grocery stores and one food supply warehouse, and all of the gas stations he could remember.

David was listing the team equipment available. Things like breaching tools, explosives and ammo were listed; and what needed to be checked to see if it would function, like vehicles, radios, optics, and spare night vision had its own list. Once he had an initial list done David started thinking about what they would need to turn the range into a functioning base of operations. The department had a robust 1033 DRMO program, and there were many items stored at the range for use in training events or during natural disasters. He listed the things he knew about like pop-up maintenance structures (basically a gigantic tent), large water purification units that could be towed behind trucks, and porta-potties. As he wrote this list a thought occurred to him.

"Hey Kyle," David asked, "If the power is out, the water treatment plant will shut down, right?" Kyle said without looking up from the list he was working on, "Yeah, with no power this place would be unlivable and…" Kyle stopped talking and looked up at David. "Shit, if the water isn't moving in the plant we can't stay here. It will be a cesspool in a matter of two days." "Can we run the essential parts of the plant and the water well here on a backup generator?" David asked. "Maybe," Kyle said. "I will put it on my list to go see the plant manager and find out what the bare minimum power required to at least keep the sewage moving. Let's put 'find alternate base' on our list of tasks."

"We need to get as much of this logistics stuff done as we can before things really fall apart," Kyle said. "I have a feeling once the public gets their minds around this it's going to be far worse than even we anticipate." David replied, "We're all we've got." Kyle responded with a sad sounding, "We're all we need."

*

With everyone on board, at least for now, Mark turned to assigning team leaders and teams while Kyle and David planned. "Alright Kyle is in overall command. He's assigned me as his Second. I don't think we have enough people to have a full-blown headquarters element, but I need to be free to be the assault commander or whatever else Kyle needs me to do. Dan, I need you to TL Alpha Team." Dan, like his brother Kyle, could be a goofball. But also like his brother was an experienced SWAT assaulter with exceptionally good tactical judgment. Dan, in addition to being the SWAT Team's reigning gay chicken champion, was a former Ranger (also like his big brother Kyle) with 4 combat deployments to Afghanistan with The Regiment before he got out and came to work at the PD. Dan just nodded his head and said, "Roger."

Mark continued, "Manny you have Bravo Team." Manny just nodded. Manny, while not a cop, was a West Point grad and former Ranger Platoon Leader, who, after getting out in 1992 had disappeared into the PMC world. He'd kept his tactical skills sharp over the years, and had worked with Mark on several projects. Manny and Mark had trained together a lot over the last 10 years; and he was as good a Leader of Men as Mark had ever worked with, and possessed a seasoned, proven judgment under fire.

Mark then pointed to Ben, one of his fellow TL's on the SWAT Team, "Ben, you have Charlie Team." Ben, a career cop with over 15 years on the SWAT Team, just nodded and said "Copy." Mark continued, selecting Troy, a Pennsylvania State Trooper assigned to their full time SWAT Team, to be the TL of Delta Team. Troy had already spoken quietly to Mark to tell him he wasn't going anywhere because he was single, had no family other than his brother, who was also a SWAT cop for the PA State Police, and couldn't think of anywhere he'd rather ride out the end of civilization. To lead Echo Team, Mark selected Trent, another of his fellow SWAT TL's on the Alliance Team.

"Ok," Mark said. "We have 5 teams. Team Leaders you need to get together and assign assaulters as you see fit. The only guidance I have is each team needs to have a qualified breacher and a medic. There are enough guys of each specialty in this room to do that." Mark paused to think, then continued, "Once you have your teams, write your rosters on a white board and separate your gear into team areas here in the classroom."

Dan asked, "What about David? Do you want him on a team?" Mark said, "No. David will lead our sniper element. Long guns are his calling and he has all of his gear with him." "Roger that." Dan answered, then turned to the group and said, "That leaves us 23 assaulters and 5 team leaders; so three six-man teams and two five-man teams." Mark then interjected, "As people trickle in, and I'm sure they will, we will plus up the 5 man teams before we form more teams." The TLs nodded, and went to work.

*

As Mark left the classroom to let the teams sort themselves out, he ran into Kyle. "How did it go?" Kyle asked. Mark replied, "Good. I swore in the civilians as temporary cops under your authority as SWAT Commander." Kyle said, "Ok. That was a smart call." "How is the planning going?" Mark asked. Kyle replied,

"Good as can be expected I guess. Too many tasks and not enough people." Mark nodded his head and said, "Well, we have 5 teams to work with. One of them will have to stay here on security, so 4 teams for missions." Kyle nodded and said, "We have work for them, that's for sure."

They stood quietly for a moment, each lost in their own thoughts, before Mark said, "I'm going to push one team out to set up security here." Kyle replied, "Yeah. It's just a matter of time before people start showing up." Mark nodded and went back in the classroom, while Kyle went into the office to start writing an operations order. He hadn't written one in longhand since Ranger School over 27 years before, but figured he could get through it. Kyle muttered under his breath, "First thing out of the gate I'm doing paperwork. This apocalypse is dumb."

Chapter 6

City Police Range
Alliance, OH

David held his breath as his hand hovered over the start switch of the BAE Systems Caiman Mine Resistant Ambush Protected (MRAP) armored vehicle. He said a prayer that God would grant them a miracle. David wasn't sure if the MRAP was designed to be EMP resistant; and was concerned that even if it was the shielding had somehow failed.

The MRAP was one of several vehicles the Alliance Police Department had acquired through the years from the US Military's law enforcement DRMO program. The other military vehicles in the Alliance fleet were two up-armored HMMWV's, two unarmored (or soft) HMMWV's, one M113 armored personnel carrier, and two M915 Military Semi Tractors with low boy trailers. Alliance had collected these vehicles over the years to serve as armored vehicles for SWAT missions, rescue vehicles in natural disasters, and as educational platforms for military and police units who used the range for training. If any of these vehicles still ran it would give them a considerable leg up in whatever was to come. If they didn't they were very expensive, poorly positioned pillboxes.

David let his breath out and turned the switch to the first position. The system powered up! He could have kissed a BAE engineer, if any were around. He gave the vehicle a few minutes to warm the glow plugs then turned the switch to 'start'. It fired right up! David could hear and feel the air system begin to feed the brakes.

As the MRAP warmed up several of the guys came out of the classroom and ran to the small military vehicle parking area. David couldn't hear the guys but he could see them cheering and jumping up and down. One of the guys ran up to his door and grabbed the key ring for the padlocks to the rest of the vehicles. The guys swarmed over the remaining vehicles, and soon they were all warming up. Even the two M915's started right up despite them being manufactured in the Carter administration. The Alliance SWAT guys were old hands at driving and maintaining these vehicles and soon each one was undergoing a thorough preventative maintenance check.

Mark came walking out to the vehicles and called the team leaders to him. He told the TLs to get the vehicles shut down after they were finished checking them then meet up in the team room (as he was already thinking of the classroom). Once they showed up Mark assigned people to build breaching charges, pull the belt fed machineguns from the vault and test fire them, and told everyone to make sure their guys had all their kit ready. He told them to make sure their guys checked their night vision to make sure it survived the pulse; and to ensure they had combat loads of ammo and water in their gear ready to deploy. Mark also ordered Echo Team to post security on the range. Everyone scattered.

Trent posted two of his assaulters at the range entrance gate with orders to build a fighting position and entry control point (ECP), and assigned his other two assaulters to start random patrols of the facility perimeter. All the guys quickly geared up, made their weapons ready with live ammo, and pushed out to their first mission of the apocalypse.

As soon as the guys manning the gate, Ernesto and Lee, got set up at their post they saw several of the water treatment city employees come out of the building directly in front of them. The water workers walked up to Ernesto and said, "Do you guys know what's going on? The power is out and nothing works." Ernesto turned to Lee and said, "Go get Trent," then addressed the workers, "We aren't sure yet. I think you guys should hang out in your office; we are coming up with a plan. I'm sure Kyle will come talk to your boss in a bit."

One of the workers said, "I'm the 'boss'," and put out his hand for a handshake, "Marty Jones, Water Treatment Manager." Ernesto shook his hand and said, "Good to meet you Sir. When my partner gets back he can take you to Kyle." "Sounds good," Marty said. Marty spoke to his people, "Go back in the building guys, I'll find out what's going on and come let you know." Lee returned with Trent in tow and Ernesto introduced Marty to them. Trent said to

Marty, "Common, I'll take you to Kyle." They walked away and Ernesto closed the gate.

Trent walked with Marty to the range office before he peeled off to go back to building firehose breaching charges for the teams to carry in case they needed them. Marty went into the office and got a warm greeting from Kyle. They quickly got down to business. Marty said, "What the hell happened Kyle?" Kyle explained what an EMP was and its effects, as well as what they had observed about metal buildings and vehicle interiors shielding from the pulse. Marty thought for a moment and said, "So, we are screwed. Without main power, we can't treat sewage or pump fresh water to customers."

Kyle asked, "Would it be possible with some limited power to pump sewage without treating it and keep the city well pumps working at least part of the time? If we can keep the city water towers full we could maintain some water pressure." "Maybe," Marty mused. "If we can find some working generators we could direct wire them into key systems and keep things moving I suppose. The environmental impact of pumping raw sewage out into the discharge canal could get us some big fines from the EPA; but if this is as big as you think it is I suppose the EPA don't exist anymore. The problem is working generators and fuel. If cars don't run we can't get fuel deliveries."

Kyle thought for a minute and then asked Marty, "We could check the city yard. The whole yard is a metal building. They have a couple of the big 150 kW portable generators they use for road construction, and one of the big semi-trailer sized 1500kW units the city got at an auction a few years back." "Those would definitely have the power, if they still run." Marty said. "How do we move them around with no trucks though?" Kyle smiled and said, "Our surplus military semi tractors still run. I'll have Mark send a team with you for security and you can go grab all three generators and bring them back here." Marty said, "Sounds good. I'll go get a crew together. We should be ready to go in about 10 minutes or so." Kyle replied, "Ok, we will need a little more time than that; we are still getting organized. How about 30 minutes at the range gate?" Marty looked at his watch, noticed it wasn't working, and said, "Sounds good."

Lee told Ernesto, "I hear a car coming." Both took cover behind the dumpster they had pushed next to the gate. They both saw a black Chevy SUV with a bunch of stuff strapped to the roof come tearing ass past the water plant buildings and turn the corner towards the range. The SUV swerved around the building in front of the gate and came to a screeching halt about 50 feet way. Ernesto looked at the front license plate and immediately recognized it as belonging to Kasey, Mark's wife. Ernesto knew Kasey almost as well as he knew Mark; he had been training with Mark for years and Kasey was often a student in those classes. Her personalized plate was hard to forget.

Ernesto broke cover and sauntered up to the SUV while Kasey got out of the vehicle. "You guys obviously know what's up if you are guarding the gate," Kasey said. "We do. It's good to see you sis. Mark is going to be very happy you're here." Ernesto said as they shared a quick hug. Ernesto noticed the two people in the SUV and nodded his head towards them, saying, "Who dat?" Kasey said, "JR and Sarah. They are friends of ours." Ernesto said, "Cool. Pull in and park, but leave room for the MRAP to move out the gate. David got it running." Kasey smiled and said, "OK, thank you!"

Kasey pulled through the gate and parked in front of the first building inside the gate, the bathroom. JR and Sarah got out, and Sarah ran into the bathroom in full pee-pee dance mode while JR started unloading boxes and stacking them by the vault door. Kasey made a bee-line for the office where she found Kyle writing on a white board. "Sis!" Kyle yelled and ran across the office to sweep her up in a bear hug, saying, "I'm so glad you made it!" Kasey replied, "Me too." After releasing her, Kyle said, "It's not crazy out there yet is it?" Kasey replied, "A little. I picked up JR and Sarah on the way and we had someone shoot at us. JR took care of him." "Wow," Kyle said. "Things went downhill fast." Kasey nodded her head and said, "Where's Mark?" Kyle said, "In the classroom I think," and turned to the coffee pot, "Want a cup of coffee?" Being greeted with silence, he turned to see Kasey had already left.

Kasey burst into the classroom and barreled head on into Mark, who was getting ready to walk out. "Hi Baby," Kasey said as

Mark snatched her up. Mark couldn't find his voice for a second, the shock of relief was so overwhelming. He finally whispered into her neck, "Thank you Lord for bringing Kasey safely to me." He kissed her tenderly and said, "Baby, I'm so happy you made it here." Kasey noticed Mark's eyes were welling up and said, "I'm here and I'm safe baby. That's all that matters."

Mark took a second to compose himself and said, "We are just getting organized. How did you get here so fast?" Kasey said, "I went to court and parked in the basement. I guess the pulse didn't reach my SUV." Mark wasn't surprised she had already figured out what had happened. Kasey continued, "I ran into JR on the way home and we went and got Sarah and loaded up some of their stuff. They came to the condo with me, we loaded what we could, and then drove here." Kasey omitted the shooting from her story for now. There would be plenty of time to talk about it later.

Kasey looked around the classroom turned team room and said, "What can I help with." Mark said, "We have assigned teams and are getting squared away to head out for a scouting mission and to make contact with city hall. David is the sniper team leader. You should go find him and check in." Kasey nodded, thankful to have a mission. They shared another quick kiss and Kasey jogged out to find David.

Mark went to the office and found Kyle. "I think we are ready to do the scouting mission bro." Mark said. "Ok," Kyle replied, "get everyone not working the gate in the classroom and we will brief. I'm only going to give the situation and mission. I need you to assign units and execution details. You and I need to be on this run; David will need to stay here and stand up a TOC. You'll be the ground force commander. I'm not sure what we are going to find at the PD and I may need to stay there for a while." Mark thought for a second and said, "Check. Everyone is in the team room... Oh, and FYI, I renamed the classroom the team room. Let's go get started." Kyle laughed and said, "You win. You've been trying to rename that damn building the 'team room' since we built it." Mark just grinned.

Mark stepped out the door and yelled in his best NCO voice, "Everyone not on watch meet in the team room." He saw David and Kasey round the corner of the team room from the shoothouse side and followed them into the building. When he stepped into the team room Mark saw JR and Sarah sitting down drinking some water. He went directly to JR and said, "Thank you Brother. I can't tell you how much I owe you for helping Kasey get here." JR stood up and replied with a smile, "Bro, Kasey got us here, not the other way around."

Mark hugged Sarah and said, "It's such a blessing to have you guys safely here." then smiled and said, "Sorry guys, but duty calls. JR, are you good to deploy?" JR said, "Yeah bro, I've got all my gear and everything still works." "Great!" Mark replied. "You're on Sniper team for now. David is your team leader. You know him, right?" JR nodded and said, "Yeah I took the SWAT Sniper Over-watch class from him last year." "Good, stand by for briefing then report to David afterwards." Mark said. JR just nodded and sat back down and pulled out his notebook to get ready for briefing.

Chapter 7

Alley West of Liberty Ave, Ward 2
Alliance, OH

Dylan knew he was in trouble. His head was pounding and he couldn't seem to focus his eyes. Why wasn't anyone coming to help him? He had called 'Officer needs assistance, shots fired' over the radio several times but got no response. Dylan realized he needed to calm down and think. He took several deep breaths and it came back to him. The reason he was in this alley in the first place was neither his radio, car, nor cell phone were working. He needed to communicate with Headquarters. He was injured and there was now a big messy crime scene to deal with. He knew that with his reputation in the press the city would explode when word got out he'd shot someone; especially a young black man.

He had to do something. Now that Dylan's vision was clearing he could see two of the teenagers who were watching him earlier hiding behind a busted-up car in the alley to the south of him. He wondered idly where the third one went when he ran off. His question was answered as he got to his feet. As he wobbled to a standing position, feeling the world spin for a second, he heard a lot of yelling to his north. As Dylan turned to look that way, he saw a group of about 15 people come around the corner into the alley from several blocks up, about 150 yards away. While Dylan couldn't make out what they were saying the group was pointing at him and spewing a cacophony of insults and slurs at him. He knew they were talking to him because of the repetitive use of his last name 'Nowak' in conjunction with some creative compound F words. He checked behind himself out of habit, in time to see the two thugs to the south of him emerge from behind the car they where they were hiding and advance on him.

Dylan knew he couldn't stay here, crime scene be dammed. He smartly didn't try to stand and fight or reason with this mob. Dylan hauled ass, a chorus of insults and several gunshots trailing in his wake. He ran west through the side yard of a house and burst out onto Seneca Avenue. Dylan kept running across the street and between the houses on the other side of Seneca, then turned north in the alley behind that block. He felt like vomiting, and blood kept running into his eyes. He kept moving. He heard a few more shots but nothing impacted or passed close to him.

After running for what seemed like 10 miles, but was actually closer to 200 yards, Dylan decided he needed to stop and make a new plan. Ahead of him he saw an abandoned house with a great big bush overgrowing the stone entryway to the basement. He looked around to try to ensure he wasn't seen ducking into his hiding spot then got under the bush and down the five steps to the basement door. He kicked on the door trying to breach it but it wouldn't budge. *It figures*, he thought to himself, *I pick the only abandoned house in Ward 2 with secure doors.* Giving up on the door, Dylan crouched at the bottom of the stairs under the bush and tried to control his breathing.

Unfortunately, Dylan didn't see the 320-pound woman with a baby on her hip on the back porch across the alley, looking right at him. The woman heard the riotous commotion behind Dylan, looked where he had disappeared under the bush, and looked back at the noise of the crowd who was obviously looking for him. It took a few seconds to penetrate her dim mind, then she started bellowing at the top of her considerable lungs, "That cracka Nowak right here! Nowak over here, Nowak over here!" She wished her phone worked; she'd be all up in Group Me tellin' eerrybody.

Dylan would recognize Adasha Rice's voice anywhere. He just couldn't catch a break. He was feeling dizzy again and was tired of running away. As he listened to the ghetto version of 'marco-polo' going on outside his bush, Dylan checked his rifle. He saw immediately the left side of the upper receiver had a hole in it. He vaguely remembered shooting the side of the rifle when Hilton was trying to take it. Dylan removed the magazine from the rifle then tried to cycle the action. The charging handle wouldn't move. *Come on God, I need some help here* Dylan thought. Dylan heard the crowd was in the alley now. He was out of time.

Thinking he would need to be running his ass off any second, Dylan took the useless rifle off his body and dropped it where he stood. He took a deep breath as he drew his Glock 17. Dylan didn't remember how many rounds he fired when he shot Hilton, so he did a quick tactical reload then and stepped out into the alley. As soon as Dylan broke cover Adasha started yelling, "There he is, there he is!" Dylan wanted to shoot her so bad. Discretion overcame his homicidal urge and he glanced to the south in time to see about 30 hood rats 25 yards or so away running towards him. Dylan didn't see who shot at him first, but the sonic cracks of the rounds passing by him were too much to ignore. He stopped, planted his feet and started shooting.

Dylan's first target was a guy in a black shirt with the Cleveland Cavaliers logo emblazoned on the front, standing on the far left, who was pointing something at him in his right hand. Dylan fired four rounds in quick succession and saw the target fall down. The rest of the crowd scattered. Seeing his chance Dylan turned and sprinted north down the alley. He cut west again between some houses, then turned north again when he hit Freedom Avenue. He sprinted about 100 yards when he saw an Alliance police car sitting in the middle of the road on Freedom Avenue. *Thank you, God,* Dylan thought.

He turned on his afterburner and sprinted to the patrol car. When Dylan rushed around the back of the car, he collided with a kneeling Officer John Card, knocking both of them ass over teakettle. After getting untangled and standing up, Dylan said, "Well, that was undignified." "That you they are shooting at Nowak?" Card asked. Dylan responded, "Yeah. Guess I pissed them off." Card looked closely at Dylan and asked, "You shot man? You're bleeding from the head." "No, a suspect kicked the shit out of me before I filled him in." Dylan said. Card shook his head. The power, phone and cars not working was bad enough; now Nowak had started a full-blown riot. Dylan continued, "I shot another one in the alley behind the 900 block of Seneca just now as well." Card raised his eyebrows and said, "Yeah, I heard a bunch of shooting." "Only four of the shots were mine bro." Dylan responded defensively. "If you say so Nowak." Card said.

Card changed the subject and asked, "Any idea what the hell is going on? None of my electronics or my patrol car work." Dylan said, "I'm not sure. Had to have been a nuke of some kind." Card said, "It could have been a sun storm too." Dylan ignored him, in his mind it didn't matter what caused the problem. Dylan noticed

Card wasn't carrying his rifle or wearing his hard armor and asked him, "Where's your rifle and plates bro?" Card looked at him derisively and scoffed, saying, "I'm here to protect these people Nowak, not attack them. I've been trying to calm people down and telling them to shelter in place." Dylan was not surprised. Card had always been a social worker cop who carried a gun because the department made him. Not exactly the kind of dude Dylan wanted with him right now.

The only thing Dylan could think to say was, "Can I have your rifle?" Card shrugged his shoulders, stood up and opened the trunk, and handed Dylan his patrol carbine. Dylan said, "Thanks. Do you have any mags?" The rifle didn't have a magazine in it. *Typical,* he thought. Card ignored him, looking intently to the south. "What is it?" Dylan asked. "A group is coming this way." Card said. Dylan was about to speak when rounds started impacting the patrol car and whizzing by in the air. Card didn't move and Dylan had to pull him behind the car. Dylan hurriedly loaded the rifle and snuck a peek downrange. They must have seen him because the incoming fire increased in intensity. Some of the incoming fire was much louder and the rounds snapping overhead began to crack painfully. The opposition had found their rifles. He and Card needed to move. Now.

Dylan began pushing Card backwards, trying to keep the rapidly shredding patrol car between them and the bad guys. Dylan grabbed Card by the shirt and shook him. When Card's eyes focused on him, Dylan said, "Sprint to the west side of the street, find cover and start shooting at these assholes. I'll cover you while you run. When you start shooting I'll sprint to you." Card nodded jerkily and got up and started running. "Thanks for the warning bro." Dylan said sarcastically to himself. He took a deep breath, switched which knee he had on the ground to reduce his exposure, shouldered the carbine, and rolled out to find some work.

As he extended past the car, Dylan saw a guy kneeling behind a car about 50 yards to his south-east. The guy had an AK in his hands and was firing at the patrol car. Dylan centered the EoTech reticle on the guy's head and fired once. Nothing changed. He centered the dot and fired again. He watched the round impact the guy in the hip and he fell over screaming. *What the hell?,* Dylan thought, *Where does Card have his rifle zero'd? That round impacted like 3 feet low.* Dylan transitioned targets to a dude who was standing in the middle of Freedom Avenue wearing a bright white parka, shooting at the patrol car with a pistol. Again, Dylan aimed at the guy's head and again the three rounds he fired hit the guy in his pelvis. The white jacket provided a great contrast to see his hits. *Kind of like a zeroing target* Dylan thought wryly.

Dylan realized Card wasn't shooting. He ducked back behind the patrol car and noticed the fire from the dirtbags was slacking off. Maybe shooting at the cops was less fun when some of them were getting burned down. He chanced a glance to his right and saw Card was down on the sidewalk on the west side of Freedom Avenue, writhing in pain and yelling incoherently. "Shit." Dylan said out loud. He moved the selector on the rifle to safe and sprinted at Card. As he reached him the fire from the hood rats picked up considerably. Gritting his teeth, Dylan stopped at Card and started to drag him west behind a house. When he got Card around the corner Dylan dropped him and collapsed in a heap himself. He was smoked.

Dylan had to keep going. He turned and started to evaluate Card's injury and asked him, "Where are you hit bro? We don't have a lot of time; you have to work with me here." Card gritted his teeth and groaned, "I'm not shot. I sprained my ankle." Dylan shook his head for a second. Keeping his thoughts to himself because they were counter-productive, Dylan just said, "Get. Up. Now. I need you to pull your weight and quit being a basic bitch, Card." Card just looked at him. Dylan tried again, "Card we have to move. These guys have rifles and are coming for us. We need to get in a spot we can hard point and fight from." Card finally nodded his head and dragged his sorry ass up to his feet. Dylan looked back around the corner at the dirtbags, and noticed they hadn't advanced on the patrol car yet, but they had stopped shooting. *They must be having the 'no, YOU expose yourself first' argument,* he thought.

Dylan ducked back behind the corner and told Card, "OK, let's get to the next alley west and look for a place to hard point. We can't keep up this running gunfight; there are too many of them. Eventually they will smarten up and get north of us to box us in." Card just nodded and hoped Dylan knew what he was doing. It was starting to dawn on Card just how off the rails things had become. His mind still reeled, trying to understand how in just an hour or so the day had devolved from a typical winter day shift into he and Dylan running for their lives, looking for a place to make a stand like they were some 19th century Indian fighters or something. Dylan could see the indecisiveness on Card's face and said, "Just follow me and do what I tell you to, Card. We will be fine." Card nodded and gathered himself to move.

Dylan and Card spent the next 30 minutes rushing from one piece of cover to the next. Alternating between running and hiding, they worked their way 8 blocks north. Their latest hiding spot was behind a bush on the east side of the St. Joseph's Church Rectory, just a few of blocks from the police station. Dylan knew they couldn't move much on such a sunny day without being seen but tried several times to stop and hard point a position, only to have someone see them and start yelling. They could hear the mob behind them; always stalking just out of sight like predators waiting for the prey to show a weakness.

As they hid they heard a commotion to their right and looked up just in time to see two young males banging on the front door of a house to the south of the Rectory. The two were let into the home and a moment later Card spotted a rifle barrel sticking out of one of the second-floor windows. The barrel was moving in a fairly tight cone in his and Dylan's immediate area as if searching for them. Card started to say something but was cut off by Dylan softly saying, "Contact left. Four armed subjects across the street to the north." Card said, "There is a rifle pointing at us from the second-floor window of the house to our south." Dylan said, "So shoot at them dude!" while his mind raced for a solution. He wasn't sure how the dirtbags accomplished it with no communications but they had the cops surrounded.

As Dylan tried to steel himself to assault through the four gunmen to the north, that being the only option he could see at this point, a window behind them in the Rectory opened. An elderly white man who Dylan recognized as the Pastor of this church stuck his head out and said, "What's going on officers? Everything OK?" Dylan said, "No sir things are not OK. Can we come in please?" As the man was formulating a response the rifle in the window to the south cracked and the man's head seemed to momentarily expand like a balloon. The 7.62X39 round caught the Pastor in the right temple and exploded out of his head just behind his left eye, painting the window sill and Dylan with the innocent man's gore.

Card recoiled in shock and froze. Dylan knew they were surrounded and exposed in broad daylight without the benefit of even the most basic of cover. He made a snap decision. As more rounds came into their position from the south Dylan grabbed the lifeless Pastor by the shoulders and shoved him back in the window. In the same motion, he threw himself up into the window, catching the bottom of the sill and pulling himself in as rounds impacted the wall around him. As soon as Dylan got inside he turned and began engaging the elevated shooter to the south with his rifle. He hoped to suppress the guy long enough to get Card into the window. It was not to be.

As Dylan ceased firing he heard several shots from the north and clearly heard the distinctive smacking sound of high velocity rifle rounds striking flesh. Card was hit in the head and torso by several rounds. He watched Card crumple to the ground and not move, a large pool of blood already pooling around his head. Dylan noticed Card's pistol was still in its holster. Card had never drawn his weapon during the entire ordeal, making Dylan wonder what made a guy refuse to defend himself.

Dylan ducked back into the room he now found himself in and tried to fight off the shock. This was all too much. One-minute life is normal and the next he's in a prolonged fight for his life. Dylan's psyche struggled to adapt to this virtually instant polar shift in his reality. He forced himself to move.

He realized there was no getting out of this building now that he was inside. The ghetto army had him pinned in. He decided to take as many of these assholes with him as he could. The Pastor and Card were both gentle souls, and had not deserved to die like that. He would make these people pay. Dylan took a moment to pray for his children, now resigned to the fact he would never see them again. All thought of escape or reuniting with his family were pushed from his mind. Dylan was all in. He would kill all of these hood rats, or die trying. Dylan started looking for targets.

Chapter 8

City Police Range
Alliance, OH

Kyle walked in the team room and spoke up, "Alright, listen up for briefing." Everyone settled down and pulled out their notebooks. Kyle began, "Everyone is familiar with the situation. It appears we have been EMP'd. We are lucky in that while it is bad, it could have been worse. Our first mission has three objectives. By priority, they are: One, make physical contact with the police department and city hall. Two, escort a team from the water department to the city yard to test three large generators and move them here if they work. Finally, objective three is to scout the city for problems and start recovering our families." Kyle paused and said, "While we are on this mission, David will be working on planning to secure critical resources and facilities, and will be the base commander. Expect follow-on missions as soon as you return or FRAGOS (Fragmentary Orders) while you are still out."

Kyle continued, "This is just the first of many missions. At least one team will be tasked with recovering their families every time we leave the base today, and everyone else should be looking for teammate's families during your missions. Team leaders, I need you to make a list of all of your team member's immediate family and their likely location. We will turn this into a comprehensive list and everyone will have a copy." Kyle paused to gather his thoughts then continued, "Barring some emergency we will spend tonight recovering whatever families are left out there that are within our reach." Everyone grabbed their notebooks and started writing family member names and likely locations before Kyle even finished speaking.

Kyle moved on, "Mark will be the ground force commander for this operation and will brief you on the execution, logistics and command and control." Kyle sat down.

Mark stood up and briefed the execution phase. He was taking Alpha, Bravo, Charlie, and Delta teams. Dan's Alpha team's objective would be to get Kyle to the police station and back to base. Kyle needed to brief the Chief and the Mayor on what he knew of the situation and give them his recommendation for a course of action, then return to base. He was pretty sure the Chief and Mayor would adopt his general plan, but didn't want to get caught up in a Chinese fire drill at city hall. Alpha's job would be to make sure Kyle got back safely to base and to recover whatever family members they could find between the two locations. Mark assigned Alpha the two up-armored HMMWVs for transport, and told them to mount one of the range's M249's in the lead vehicle's turret. The range maintained several M249 and M240 machineguns for military units to use in training so those units didn't have to travel with the guns. That piece of logistical convenience would pay off in spades in the days ahead.

Manny's Bravo Team would handle the escort to the city yard. They would take the two soft HMMWVs and one of the M915 semi tractors. These vehicles would allow them to transport all of the generators back to the water treatment plant in one movement. Mark didn't assign any of the machineguns to Bravo because their trip would not take them into the city proper; the city yard was only two miles from the range through an industrial area. The risk of unrest was very low in that area this early in the event. Mark told Manny they were not to brook any objection from the city yard, but to let Marty do the talking.

Ben's Charlie team was assigned to conduct a preliminary scouting mission of the city and to recover as many of their family members as possible. Charlie team ended up being made up of Alliance SWAT guys and Ed and Chris, so everyone knew the city intimately. If things were out of place any one of them would know it immediately; and most of them lived within the city limits, so gathering their families would be the simplest of the recovery missions. Mark told Ben to check State Street first, as that was where the majority of the large stores and other resource-heavy buildings were located. Charlie was told to scout and recover for no more than 2 hours then return to base. If they did not return by then a search team would have to be sent, so Mark stressed the importance of getting back on time. This was only an initial patrol, and Mark said, "Do not try to save the city on your own. Get your families and see what you can." Mark assigned Charlie the MRAP armed with an M240 machinegun.

Mark tasked Delta team to be the quick reaction force (QRF). He told them to stage at the Circle J convenience store on Union Ave and to be listening closely to the radio. The teams would be doing constant radio checks to test the range of the car-to-car channel, and would report the results to Lee when they returned. Lee had been drafted as the comms guy, at least until they could find someone else; and he would plot the radios' ranges on a map when the teams returned. Mark assigned Kasey's Equinox and Ed's pickup as Delta's transportation, and told them to take one of the range's M249 machineguns converted to a Mk46. Darren, an Alliance SWAT assaulters on Delta team who was qualified on the Mk46, volunteered to be the SAW gunner.

David asked, "Where do you want the snipers?" Mark replied, "Good question. I'd like to attach Kasey to Delta and JR to Charlie." David nodded his head and looked to make sure the two snipers understood. The last thing Mark wanted to do was send Kasey out into the apocalypse, but she was a warrior and it would be a waste of resources to not deploy her, in addition to pissing her off.

Finally, Mark tasked Echo team with maintaining base security.

In addition to the military vehicles, David had discovered the range's three quads and two dirt bikes still ran. Mark would use one of the quads (he never was a good dirt bike rider) and would float between the QRF and Alpha team during the mission. His plan was to be available to coordinate a response if one of the teams ran into trouble.

David briefed the medical plan. Each team had a medic and David would be at the base. Everyone hoped no medical services would be needed for this first mission; but David, a surgeon by trade, and Doc Zimmerman, an emergency room doctor and tactical medical director for the Alliance SWAT team, briefed the teams on medical procedures based on the austere conditions they suddenly found themselves in. Sarah volunteered to act as a medical assistant and would use the time to start converting the classroom pro-shop, with Burt's help, into a clinic.

The only wildcard was Lydia, the county work release deputy who was stuck at the range when the pulse hit. She just sat in the back of the room looking worried. Earlier Lydia told Burt she was a widow, and after thinking it about it had decided she had nowhere better to be. She wasn't sure this "EMP" was a real thing but Kyle and these SWAT guys seemed to be pretty sure, and she couldn't think of a safer place to be than right where she was. Lydia spoke up and said, "I'll help Sarah." Mark nodded his head and said, "Thank you."

Lee spoke up, "I wouldn't count on the radios to work very well right now. The ionosphere is probably so overwhelmed the range of any radio waves is going to be pretty short for the next couple of days or weeks. They should work OK for tactical comms within a mile or so, but not much farther than that." Everyone nodded and made murmurs of understanding.

Next, Mark issued radios and flashbangs to those without them (the non-SWAT people), and went over the individual assaulter load-out. Everyone leaving the base would be equipped with their ballistic helmet, active ear protection (most of the guys used MSA Sordins worn under their helmets), eye protection, plate carrier with level 4 plates front and back, two flashbangs, radio, six rifle magazines loaded to 28 rounds, a carbine or rifle with weapon mounted light (100% of the team was running Surefire) and multi-function aiming laser (all but two of the lasers in the room were the B.E. Meyers MAWL DA or C1+, which the Alliance SWAT team had only recently purchased for each assaulter, replacing the older Peq 15A models the team used for years. Most of the civilian students were running MAWLs as well because it was the "new hotness" and one hell of a good laser system), a tourniquet and IFAK medical kit, 10 chemlights on their belt or plate carrier, pistol and three loaded magazines, night vision goggles (several guys asked why they needed to carry their NVGs during the day, and the Rangers in the room all said, "REALLY?!"), three bottles of water, and a protein bar.

Mark thought about how lucky they were that everyone there was on the range in the first place prepared for day and night time live fire training, or had brought their own equipment with them when they bugged out to the range. The range had plenty of loaner gear and weapons, but everyone having their own gear saved them a monumental amount of time and effort.

Mark finished, "Last thing I have is IFF (Identification, Friend or Foe). We don't have a standard uniform for everyone, so grab four Black Knight patches on your way out and put them on whatever Velcro you have on each arm and the front and back of your plate carrier. It will have to do for now." The Black Knight patch started out as an inside joke many years previously. The range hosted so many units and students, who were always going into town to eat in their uniforms, with pistols showing, driving armored vehicles, that the public took notice. One day at the Mexican restaurant in town an elderly woman asked one of the Alliance instructors who all these men with guns were who were in town all the time. With a perfectly straight face he told her, "We're the Black Knight Squadron Ma'am. Please don't tell anyone."

It was a mildly funny incident until a week later, when the local newspaper reported the 'Black Knight Squadron' was in Alliance doing training. After that it was uproariously funny and quickly became legend. Kyle adopted the Black Knight Squadron as the range logo and mascot, a student had small patches made of a chess piece Knight, and the rest was history. Now a Black Knight patch was recognized the world over in the tactical community as a talisman of having trained at Alliance, and was something of an icon.

Lee stuck his head in the team room and said, "Water treatment guys are ready to go." Mark acknowledged him and said, "Bravo, get ready to push. Other TLs, let Bravo clear the range, then get your vehicles lined up." and the briefing broke up. As the teams began putting on their kit the team room door opened and Gary Willow walked in. Gary was another one of Kyle's volunteer range crew. A 20-something manager at the chemical warehouse next to the water treatment plant, Gary spent almost every free minute at the range. He was a graduate of almost every high-speed course the range hosted or offered.

Gary wanted to be a cop, and he had the skills and motivation to be a good one. The problem was Gary's job couldn't afford to let him take the time off necessary to go to the police academy. Still a single guy, he spent his time at the range helping Kyle however he could; doing everything from sweeping floors to acting as a role player in force on force training. Like Chris and Ed, Gary saved his money and only spent it on gear and training ammo, so he was fully equipped already. He was wearing all of that kit now, carrying his rifle and assault pack. He dropped the pack on the deck and said, "It figures I'm three miles away when the balloon goes up. That was a long ass walk!" Mark laughed and announced, "Ladies and Gentlemen, Mr. Gary Willow!" Everyone clapped, as was the tradition. Mark was busy but told Gary to stay kitted up and to go 'pre-flight' a quad. "You're riding with me for this mission. I need someone to watch my back and be a runner." Gary just said, "I'm on it." and disappeared out the door.

Two hours and forty-nine minutes after the world stopped, Bravo team was loaded, the vehicles were lined up at the gate, and the three water treatment employees were in the vehicles. They were told to stay in their seats and hold on; this was going to be a rocket of a thunder run. As they were about to pull out, Mark approached the lead vehicle and shouted, "We're all we've got!" Six voices responded, "We're all we need!"

Chapter 9

"Black Knight Six, Black Knight Five," Mark said over the radio, using Kyle's radio call-sign followed by his own. "Go for Knight Six," Kyle responded. Mark keyed up the PTT on his plate carrier, which connected his radio to his MSA ear protection, and said, "The Circle J is being overrun by looters. Recommend we bypass and just bring the QRF with us. We can have them stage somewhere closer to the PD." "Roger," Kyle responded, then without un-keying the mic said, "Delta One, Knight Six, did you copy?" Delta's team leader Troy replied, "Copy direct."

Mark stayed in his position for another minute or so, sitting astride the quad watching the looting through his Steiner 8X50 compass binos from behind the abandoned bank building catty-corner from the convenience store. Mark shook his head, wondering how things got so out of hand so fast. He had actually thought about this general scenario occasionally, and had always assumed it would take two or three days before things got out of control. Mark chastised himself for making assumptions; he knew better. When in doubt, count on mankind to be at their worst.

He looked behind him and asked Gary, "You ready to move?" Gary nodded and lowered his BCM carbine from where he was pulling security for Mark's six-o'clock then tightened his VCAS sling so the weapon sat tight against his plate carrier. Mark fired up his quad and got turned around then keyed the radio, "Knight Six, Five. We are ready to move. I'll lead back to Garfield and then south." "Roger, Move," Kyle replied.

Mark spent the next 20 minutes scouting and leading Alpha and Delta teams through a maze of neighborhoods. He was trying to find a route to city hall where the sidewalks and streets weren't full of people milling around. It was cold out and Mark thought these folks must be pretty unsettled to be out walking around in it. Mark could almost feel the anger radiating off the groups of people he saw.

Mark and Gary were finally able to lead the teams around the worst of the trouble, including the two different dollar discount stores that were being looted at Union Avenue and Main Street. As he and Gary came to a stop to scout the last intersection before they got to the police station they both clearly heard the sound of sustained gunfire to the south. It sounded like several weapons firing, and Gary said, "That sounds like quite a gunfight." Mark replied, "Yeah. We are going to have to check that out once we drop Alpha at the station."

Mark got on the radio, "Knight Six, Knight Five. This last intersection is clear. We are going to peel off and take the QRF with us. We are hearing a pretty heavy gunfight to the south." Kyle said, "Roger. Let me know if you need Alpha team." Troy cut in, "Delta copies direct. On you Knight Five." Mark waved Alpha team's two HMMWVs past him and said over the radio, "Delta One, Knight Five. Move to the corner of Union and Broadway and stage there. We will scout and give direction from there." Troy responded with a "Roger," and pushed out.

Mark and Gary rode down Union to Broadway and passed the QRF as they staged in an abandoned gas station parking lot. When they slowly turned the corner to go east on Broadway, the gunfire got loud. About 300 yards ahead of them Mark could see several people with rifles running back and forth in the street, firing to the south. As he watched he saw one of them fall down and stop moving. Whatever this was it was a real fight. Mark gestured for Gary to follow him and turned north into the driveway of a home across the street from the fire station. He shut down his quad and got off. Gary did the same and asked Mark, "So, how do we figure out who is shooting at who?" "It's 'Who is shooting at whom' Gary." Mark said with a grin, then continued, "We will move forward and bias to the north. We will see if we can figure out whom," Mark paused to grin, "they are fighting and if it's a good guy we will attack and destroy them." Gary said, "Ok. I'll follow your lead."

As they pushed off Mark hit Troy on the radio, "Delta One, Knight Five. We have eyes on subjects on the north side of Broadway, shooting into a house on the south side of the street about

68

300 yards east of our pos. We are moving northeast on foot trying to figure out who is fighting. Be ready to haul ass east on Broadway to support, but do not drive into the fight. The subjects are armed with rifles and your soft skin vehicles will just be in the way. If this is dirtbag versus dirtbag we will back off and let them sort each other out." Troy acknowledged.

Mark added, "Have your sniper deploy to the roof of the fire station just south of our quads and see if they can get eyes on." Mark tried to push the fact he was sending his wife up on a roof to act as overwatch out of his mind. She was a pro, and he had to treat her as such. "Roger. She's moving now." Troy replied.

Kasey bailed out of the Equinox where she had been riding. Getting her Sako M10 off the floorboard of the backseat was a chore; with the Surefire suppressor attached it was a long beast. Once she got the rifle free of the door she grabbed her assault pack and put it on, then picked up her tripod with the MOD 7 Hog Saddle on it and slung it on its two point VTAC sling behind her back and pulled it tight. She picked up her rifle, slung it, and stuck her head back in the door and asked Troy, "Should I bring someone for security?" Troy said, "Yeah, take Ken." Ken Branch was one of the Alliance SWAT assaulters assigned to Delta team. Branch bailed out, ran to Kasey's side of the SUV and said, "On you sis." They immediately started running east on Broadway on the south side of the street. Troy got on the radio and said, "Knight Five, Delta One. I'm sending a security guy with the sniper." When Mark replied it was obvious from the huffing that he was running, "Roger, thanks."

Kasey ran as fast as she could towards the fire station. Her heart already felt like it would burst out of her chest just sitting in the vehicle, so the running didn't effect her heart rate much. The sound of an actual gunfight, combined with knowing Mark was running toward it, scared the hell out of her. The running actually served to calm her down a little; having a mission helped focus her mind.

As Kasey and Branch ran towards the fire station, Mark and Gary were in the backyards of the houses on the north side of the street, jumping fences. Gary was wishing he'd spent more time in the gym and on the wall obstacle at the range; it sucked having to learn climbing fences with kit and a carbine on right now. They could hear the gunfire slacken considerably as they approached. By the time Mark snuck a peek around the corner of the house just west of the shooting, it had stopped completely. Mark stepped back from the corner and told Gary to pop the corner on a knee and keep an eye on the house everyone was shooting at on the south side of the street.

Mark started to go back the way they had come with the thought of flanking the shooters, but Gary stage whispered, "I see someone wearing an APD patch inside the one-side second floor second window." "Well, that answers that question." Mark said. He called Gary to him and then got on the radio. Speaking as quietly as he could he broadcast, "Knight Five to all units. The shooters on the street are firing at an APD officer barricaded in the rectory next to the church on Broadway at Linden Ave. We do not have eyes on the shooters, but are standing by to assault them from the west once we get overwatch from the fire station. Delta One, stand by to haul ass down here if we call for you." Troy immediately said, "Roger." Kyle came up on the radio and said, "Knight Five, Knight Six. I am at the station and in contact with leadership. Let me know if you want me to send Alpha to you." "Roger," Mark replied, then said, "Break. Delta Sniper, what's your ETA to overwatch?" Kasey replied, "One minute. We just got on the roof and I'm setting up now." Mark thought for a second before responding, then replied, "Copy. As soon as you are set I need to know what you can see." Kasey just said, "Ok."

In one minute and 35 seconds Kasey was set. It seemed like it took them forever to get a fireman to open the door (they were all in the basement hiding from the gunfire) and convince him they really were cops and needed on the roof. Luckily one of the fire Captains recognized Branch, and led them at a sprint up the roof access stairway and onto the roof. Kasey quickly found a firing point and set up her gear. She thanked God that she had found the motivation to practice getting set so many times. Within three minutes of setting foot on the roof she had her firing point set with her barrier bag resting on the roof's parapet and her Hog Saddle deployed to act as a stock rest. It took her about 20 more seconds to get a round in the chamber and her eye in the scope. She quickly found the shooters, all five of whom were armed were huddled in a line kneeling against the curb side of a tan Ford Astrovan on the north side of Broadway. She used the Horus H59 reticle in her Steiner 5-25 scope to range the target at 315 meters. She quickly dialed 1.2 mils of elevation and keyed her radio, "Sniper set."

70

Mark replied, "Report." Kasey looked around the target area again and composed her thoughts. She keyed the mic and said, "I see five subjects kneeling behind a tan Ford Astrovan on the north side of Broadway across from the rectory. I see one subject lying on his face in the grass behind them and another subject laying in a pool of blood in the westbound lane of Broadway to the southeast of the van. The subject in the street has an SKS rifle lying next to him." As she was letting off the PTT, she saw one of the men stand up and fire several rounds at the rectory then duck back down behind the van. She immediately got back on the radio and reported this.

Mark thought about the angle Kasey would be shooting from and decided he and Gary could safely assault through the position so long as Kasey lifted her fire once they got close. He made a decision and hit the PTT on his vest, "Knight Five to all units. On my mark, Sniper One, initiate the assault by engaging the subject farthest to the east that you can see, then work one more target west. We will assault through on foot. We are only about 30 yards west of them, so we will be on their position after that second shot. Cease firing after that second shot unless you see our assault fail." Kasey caught herself wincing at that last part, but refocused her mind on the task. Mark continued, "Delta team, we will call you up once we have this side of the street cleared." Everyone acknowledged over the radio.

Mark looked at Gary. "You ready to do this for real bro?" Gary took a deep breath and thought that this morning when he woke up, he wouldn't have bet a penny that before sundown that day he would be assaulting a group of five armed men, under the fire of a sniper. His brain was still trying to catch up. He'd shot guns at real people before, but always in training using SIMS guns. Truth be told he never thought he'd shoot at anyone in real life, ever. Gary finally nodded his head, put on a brave face and said, "Let's roll." Mark said, "Wait for Kasey's first shot to pass by, then give me a barrel release and we will take this last 'L'. As soon as you see a target with a gun, start shooting. I'd like to get all of these dudes at once so we aren't chasing squirters all day. Cool?" Gary nodded his head and Mark keyed his mic, "Sniper One, Initiate."

Kasey already had a beautiful sight picture on the furthest eastern subject's head. As soon as she heard the word, she pressed the trigger. This was the first time Kasey had actually shot live rounds at another human being. She felt a surge of something she could not describe as she came off recoil and saw her target on the ground. She quickly cycled the bolt and shifted to the next subject, who hadn't noticed the suppressed shot take his home boy down. She centered the reticle on his right ear, and worked the trigger. He went down as well.

As soon as Gary heard the crack of the round passing, he lifted his carbine barrel up then dropped it down. That was Mark's signal to launch. Mark pushed off and went wide around the corner of the house two addresses west of the dirtbag's position. As he moved quickly to the sidewalk he felt Kasey's second round crack painfully close over his right shoulder. Mark came to a stop, planted his feet and fired his first shots of the apocalypse. As Mark centered the dot of his Khales 1-6 variable powered optic on the right armpit of the guy closest to him, the dirtbag saw Mark in his peripheral vision and started to turn and lift his rifle. He was far too late. Four rounds from Mark's 14.5" BCM carbine slammed the dude to the ground before his body got all the way oriented to fight back.

As Mark was shooting, Gary was also busy doing work. He turned the 'L' as the inside guy and immediately saw he had a great angle on the douchebags farthest away from he and Mark. He didn't think. He saw the guy to the east had a rifle, centered his Aimpoint dot on the guy's head, and shot him twice. The dirtbag slumped over and stopped moving. Gary and Mark both transitioned to the last of this crew at the same time but that didn't prevent him from getting off one shot from his Hi Point 9mm carbine. His round went into the grass about 10 yards in front of Mark. Both Mark and Gary's fire pounded him into the sidewalk.

Mark immediately started looking for other targets but couldn't find any. He got on the radio and said, "All units, Knight Five. Splash five. Moving to assault through and establish contact with the rectory. Sniper stay on overwatch." Mark took cover behind a vehicle and yelled at the rectory, "Blue Blue Blue." A couple of seconds later a faint voice yelled from inside the rectory, "Blue Blue Blue. Thank God."

Mark called Troy on the radio, "Delta One, move up to the corner of Broadway and Arch. Dismount but leave the drivers for vehicle security. Come to me on the north side of Broadway." Troy responded, "Roger, on the way." Before Troy finished speaking, Mark could hear Delta's two vehicles roaring down Broadway.

Delta team parked quickly, and Troy and his last unassigned assaulter, the Mk46 gunner Darren, walked over to Mark. When they got there, Mark said, "Darren, take Gary and go to the one/two corner of the rectory and pull security. Darren nodded and took off, grabbing Gary on the way. "Troy, call the vehicles up. We need to grab the officer in there and haul ass." Mark said. Troy nodded and made the call.

When Darren and Gary were posted up on the northeast corner of the rectory and Delta team's vehicles arrived, Troy and Mark dead checked the seven down subjects and collected their weapons. Only one of them had an ID on his body, which they collected. Mark said, "We are going to have to leave them here until we can figure out how to get them collected up." The two of them then approached the rectory. As they reached the porch the front door opened and Dylan Nowak stepped out. "You look like shit bro," Mark said. "Where are you hit?" Dylan responded, "I'm not. I got my ass kicked and a couple of people bled all over me." Mark noticed Dylan's usual jovial attitude was gone. He looked broken. "Let's get you loaded up and out of here bro." Mark said.

"We need to get Card." Dylan said. Mark asked where he was and if he was injured and Dylan said, "He's dead Mark. Him and the Pastor here got shot. Card is under a window on the east side of the house. The Pastor is inside." Mark put his arm around Dylan's shoulder and quietly said, "OK brother. We will take care of them." Mark turned to Troy and said, "Get one of your vehicles to take Dylan to the police station. Have them brief Kyle then send one of Alpha's HMMWVs to transport the bodies." "Roger," Troy solemnly said, and he led Dylan to the Equinox.

Mark got on the radio, "Knight Six, Knight Five." Kyle responded, "Go ahead." Mark gathered his thoughts and said, "We recovered Nowak out of the rectory. He's injured but ambulatory and on his way to you in one of Delta's vehicles. We have one other officer down hard and a civilian as well. Nowak can brief on officer's ID when he gets there. We are standing by to recover them, then will be pulling off target and returning to you to…"

Mark was interrupted by the sound of several short bursts from the Mk46. He and Troy sprinted to the northeast corner of the rectory and did a high/low pop on the corner. Mark saw Darren running to the east then flop down in a prone position, obviously displacing after shooting. When Darren didn't shoot again Mark shouted, "SITREP?" Darren replied, "One armed subject came out of the house to the south and pointed a rifle at us. I dumped him." Mark said, "Roger. Go dead check him, get any ID he has, and collect his weapon." Darren and Gary nodded and pushed off.

Mark ducked back behind the rectory corner and got back on the radio, "Knight Five continuing. We just had an engagement to the south of our pos. We need to recover our bodies and get off this target." In a few seconds Kyle responded, "Copy Knight Five. Dan is bringing Alpha team to your pos now."

On the roof of the fire station Kasey was starting to shake. At first, she put it off to it being cold outside but after a minute or so she realized it was the adrenaline bleeding off from her system. She tried to focus and do her job watching Mark's back but a wave of nausea hit her suddenly. She came off the gun and vomited violently. Kasey was willing herself to stop, to get herself under control, but she couldn't stop the physical reaction.

Branch put his hand on her back and said, "It's OK sis. The same thing happened to me in Iraq the first time. You'll be ok in a minute." Kasey hated herself for showing weakness in front of a man other than Mark, but didn't realize at the time Branch thought no less of her. He knew the true test would be the second time she had to shoot; would she let this experience mess with her head and affect her performance next time? He didn't think so.

Kasey said a quick prayer turning the experience over to God and immediately felt better. She knew she would have to deal with it later but for now she could carry on. Kasey got back on the gun and said, "Thanks Branch." "Don't mention it sis." Branch said, and returned to watching to the west. She did a fresh scan of the area and saw two HMMWVs to her east coming at them. That would be Alpha team. She watched as the vehicles pulled up and everyone bailed out to pull security. They must have done some basic drills before leaving the range because they looked professional as hell with that dismount. Kasey saw Dan get out of the lead vehicle and go to Mark.

Mark was getting antsy. It was going to be dark in an hour or so. He could see groups of people moving between the houses to their southeast and knew if these people were already chasing cops around shooting at them in broad daylight, four hours into this

74

emergency, things would be completely off the hook soon. This part of town was going to be a war zone by tonight.

Dan came up to Mark and said, "Seems things have gotten sporting already." "Seems so brother," Mark replied, and then continued, "Can you peel off a couple guys to help us load Card and the other guy? I guess he was the Pastor of this church." Dan said, "Will do. I grabbed some body bags from the detective bureau when I heard the radio traffic. I'll go get them." Mark just nodded and went back to scanning for problems.

Dan and two other Alliance SWAT assaulters from his team collected the two bodies and gently placed them in the cargo bed of the lead HMMWV. When they were done Dan sent them and two other Alpha team assaulters to check the rectory. They cleared the building quickly and came back out with three bloody PMags, all marked with 'NOWAK' in yellow paint pen. All of them were empty. They turned them over to Dan with the comment, "There was brass everywhere in there. Nowak must have shown them what time it is." Dan just nodded. Before today he wouldn't have bet a single dollar Nowak had it in him. He was pleased he'd been wrong.

Chapter 10

Police Station
Alliance, OH

When Mark and Dan walked into the briefing room at the PD it was jammed full. Kyle and the Chief of Police, Harold Stone, were at the front of the room writing lists on the white board while others in the room were talking over one another. When the crowd saw Mark, they stopped talking. Kyle looked up and said, "Hey bros, glad you guys are OK." Mark replied, "Me too," then looked at Chief Stone and said, "Hi Sir." Stone walked over to Mark and Dan and gave them both a bro-hug. "You guys OK? Anyone else hurt?" Mark said, "No Chief." Mark really liked the Chief; he had always found him to be a calm, reasoned leader with good judgment, possessed of a finely tuned political subtlety that got shit done without unnecessary heartache, and a genuinely great dude. So, when the Chief's first question had been about the Men's welfare he wasn't surprised. No histrionics about the end of the world from Chief Stone; just solid leadership. He was thankful to be working for him.

"What have we done with Card's remains?" the Chief asked. Dan replied, "Sir, we placed him in the evidence room." Stone said, "Thank you. That will have to do for now. I know he was a single guy with no family, so we will have to decide soon how to deal with his remains." Dan said, "Yes Sir. I'll stay on it and handle whatever needs to be done." Stone replied with a simple, "Thank you Dan."

Mark looked around the room and took note of who was present. He saw and said hi to the Mayor, Ron Barnhart. He was happy Barnhart was Mayor at a time like this. Ron was a recently retired police officer and SWAT Team member, and he and Mark knew one another well. Mark trusted Ron's judgment and silently thanked God that Ron had taken office the month before.

There were four uniformed police officers, all of whom he recognized as Day Shift guys. That meant everyone else had made it back to the station. He also saw the Day Shift Sergeant and Lieutenant were present. That was less of a surprise, as both rarely left the station other than to grab lunch.

The last row back consisted of the Admin Sergeant Jim Wiggins, the City Attorney (also the city prosecutor) Kathy Jones, who also happened to be Kyle's fiancé, and the city's Maintenance Director Gabe Riley. Most importantly to Mark, besides Kyle's fiancé Kathy, was seeing Mitch "Bones" Clark in the back corner. Bones was a detective, and was the only SWAT team member who hadn't been present at the range when the pulse hit. Bones was a very experienced SWAT leader and assaulter, who worked full time as a Task Force Officer assigned to the Canton regional FBI Violent Crimes Task Force. His wealth of experience and unflappable attitude was a needed element of the team's dynamic, and Mark was very happy he was ok.

Mark had snatched up the Fire and EMS Chief Mark Dalano and brought him to the PD when they had recovered Kasey and Branch from the fire station. Dalano was just taking his seat.

Mark asked where the department's two Captains were. Kyle said, "They and two of the Lieutenants went to training in Columbus this morning." Mark said, "Damn. We need to make sure we grab their families if we can. Those guys won't be back for a while." He left off the 'or most likely ever' from the sentence. Everyone was already thinking it. Most of Columbus was a third world shit hole before the lights went out; now it would be the seventh ring of hell.

Kyle went back to leading the group through their thoughts on the priorities of work. Mark apologized and interrupted, "Things out there are off the rails already. I think our first priorities should be one; evacuating the police and fire stations and city hall and displacing to the range; and two; recover all of the family members and off duty officers and families we possibly can immediately."

Kyle nodded his head and said, "We were just talking that through." Mark said, "If that's our plan I'll head back to the range now and start coordinating. Bravo team should be back and available by now, and Charlie team's two hours expired 10 minutes ago. I'll send the MRAP here so you can start loading essential people and gear to get the move started. I'll wait to hear from you to start pushing out family recovery missions. It will probably take us some time to figure out where we need to go anyway."

Kyle nodded and looked at Chief Stone. Stone thought for a minute then spoke to Mayor Barnhart, "What do you think Ron? I think we should do it." Ron said, "Sorry, I thought it was a no-brainer. Yes, do it." Stone nodded and pointed at Mark and said, "Go." Mark and Dan both said, "Yes Sir." and left the room. Behind them everyone got up to start getting things ready to move.

When Dan and Mark exited the front door of the PD they joined a couple of Alpha team assaulters, one of whom was Jim Keel, one of the CQB students and a Las Vegas Metro SWAT cop who had come to Alliance to take the class and hang out with Mark and Kasey. Mark put his arm around Keel and said, "I'm praying for Becky (Keel's wife) brother." Keel said, "She's at her parent's ranch in Austin Nevada. She will be fine 'till I get there." "Thank God," Mark said. "In that case I bet you're glad you weren't in Vegas when the lights went out." Keel grinned and said, "Dude, you have no idea." From where they stood they could see two columns of black smoke coming from the area of Ward 2 where Card and Nowak's patrol cars had been left. Mark lit a Marlboro, slowly blew the smoke out of his nose, and said, "Well, this is going to suck."

*

City Police Range
Alliance, OH

Manny stuck his head in the office and told David, "The generators are placed. They put the big unit on the north side of the scum removal building. It looks like that one 1500 kW generator will power the entire water plant and the range as well." "That's great news. That will leave us the other two generators for other things," David said, thinking about the water towers in town. "How long until we have power back?" Manny said, "The electrician told me less than an hour, barring complications." David said, "Thanks. You guys ready for another mission?" Manny smiled and responded, "Oh hell yes. That escort was a milk run." Bravo team's mission to escort the water plant folks and pick up generators from the city yard had taken less than an hour, and the biggest challenge had been navigating around dead cars in the road.

"Alright, here's your next mission," David said as he handed Manny a hand-written op order. Manny read the order quickly and said, "Looks good. We will get the M113 warmed up and get ready to move. I'll check in before we go." David had ordered Bravo team to collect all of their own and several other guy's family members who lived within 5 miles of the city, four families in all, and to bring them back to the range. Manny said, "This will make some of the SWAT guys happy; they are worried about their families." David responded and said, "I figured. We have to take care of the guys so they can focus on the hard missions that are sure to come tonight." "Roger that," Manny said, and left the office to get things moving.

The last couple of hours had been a rough transition for David. The world changing so rapidly had shaken him up a little; after all, he wasn't 25 anymore. He was thankful, however, that he had his experience as a Special Forces NCO to carry him through. He was adjusting rapidly; but he would feel better when he went and got his family in a couple of hours.

David's planning and organizational skills, learned in the crucible of the extremely austere environment of the Central American drug wars of the 80's, were standing him and the entire team in good stead. While he would rather be out in the city gunfighting, he knew he had a critical mission to perform here; one he was uniquely qualified for. David liked practicing medicine, and he was gifted at it, but in his soul he was a gunfighter and leader of Men first. Knowing he had a lot of work to do, David stopped navel-gazing and got back to it.

Manny, on the other hand, was in his element. A near lifetime of leading teams in non-permissive third world hell holes, always fighting with limited resources and time, combined with his formal US Military Academy training and time in the Ranger Battalion, had prepared him for this challenge probably better than any of the other leaders in the group. It was almost as if God had lead him on a career then put him in this place, at this moment, to serve a specific purpose. The men he had selected for Bravo team, three SWAT guys and two out of state cops, were all US Army veterans with combat deployments. Two of them were fellow Ranger Qualified guys, though neither had served in the Regiment.

Manny was confident Bravo team could handle just about anything their leadership or the apocalypse could throw at them.

After leaving the office Manny gathered his guys together and briefed them on their next mission. He assigned tasks to the guys with the stated intention of launching in 20 minutes. The team bomb-burst and got to work. Manny grabbed Jerry, one of the SWAT guys, and went to the vault, where he signed out an M240 and 1000 rounds of linked ammo. He and Jerry took the weapon and ammo to the M113, where another team member already had the back ramp open and the engine warming up. After they mounted and loaded the 240, Manny directed the driver to close the ramp and drive over to the 300-yard range. As they moved Manny got on the radio and called David, telling him they were about to test-fire the 240. David cleared them to go hot.

By the time the M113 rolled back off the 300-yard range, the other three team members had pulled their assigned soft skinned HMMWVs into line near the gate and were standing by for a final check. With the M113 in place between the two HMMWVs, Manny lined everyone up and did his pre-combat inspection; making sure everyone had all their armor, mags, radios and so forth.

In their minds, it didn't matter that they had just done the same thing an hour ago before they left on the earlier escort mission; they all understood winning was in the details. After Manny checked everyone they lined up facing the range berm to the north and made their weapons ready. They loaded up with two assaulters in each vehicle and moved out. After exiting the water treatment facility onto Rockhill Avenue, the team turned left, taking the back way into town on county roads on their way to the first of the recovery objectives.

While the M113 had road treads on the tracks, it still moved at what seemed like a snail's pace, forcing the lead and trail HMMWVs to moderate their speed to match. The vehicles kept about 25 yards of separation, and all eyes were alert to the outside world. The guys alternated their scans between the far horizon, about 100 yards out, and 25 yards away; constantly shifting their focus in an effort to maintain awareness and hopefully see problems long before they got to them.

The first recovery involved picking up team member Phil's wife Linda, at Tractor Supply, where she worked. When the convoy pulled up in front, they found her waiting in her now useless car. After embracing Phil, she immediately started with the questions about what was going on. Phil told her that now wasn't the time, and she needed to just get in the M113.

As he was helping her load a few things from her car into the back of the lead HMWWV, Manny turned around from where he was pulling security and asked her, "Do you guys sell hand crank fuel pumps?" She looked confused and Manny repeated the question. She finally said, "Yeah I think I've seen them in the farm equipment section. Do you need one?" Manny replied, "No, I need all of them. We will need them to get fuel from gas station tanks." Phil's wife shrugged and said, "Well we can't take money, nothing works." "Is the manager still here?" Manny asked her. She pointed to a man standing with several employees near the front door staring at the heavily armed men and said, "That's him. Knock yourself out." She then turned and walked up the ramp into the M113.

Manny approached the manager and introduced himself. The manager said, "Oh thank God! See Mary," he turned to one of the women standing with him, "I told you the military would come to help us." Manny cleared his throat and said, "Sir, I'm sorry but we aren't the military, and we aren't in a position to help much right now. I actually have a request for you." The manager looked confused and said, "Well you have guns and a tank," the manager said, gesturing at the M113 armored personnel carrier, "So you're someone official. You're supposed to help us in a disaster. I demand you help us."

"Actually Sir," Manny said, getting annoyed, "I recommend you walk home and shelter in place for now. We have another mission we have been assigned." The manager got red faced now, "Oh, I see how it is! You have running trucks so you spend your resources going around collecting your families? Using public assets to take care of your own. I see what's going on here; I know Linda is married to that cop."

Manny was already tuning out the manager, but something he said gave him an idea. He said, "Sir, where do you and these ladies live?" The manager sensed he had gotten the upper hand and said, "I live over by the college (Mount Union, a private university in Alliance) and both of these ladies live right around the corner from here." Manny said, "Sir, I came over to talk to you to tell you I needed to buy some equipment from inside. If you can help me out I can bend the rules and take you guys home." The manager thought about it for a few seconds and said, "Deal!"

The manager let Manny into the store and helped him load several carts with hand crank fuel pumps and lots of hose and connectors. As they worked, Manny explained what had happened to the manager. Manny suggested they use some MDF board he saw in the store to cover the main doors and seal the back entrance from the inside. In less than 10 minutes they had the entrances boarded up and everyone loaded on the trucks. It was none too soon; the guys on security were getting nervous about the crowd that was gathering to look at them and ask questions. "Bravo One, Bravo Five," one of the guys said over the radio, "Some of these folks are getting pissed we aren't helping them. We need to go." Manny acknowledged him and told everyone to mount up. The convoy left immediately.

After dropping the two Tractor Supply gals at the apartment they shared nearby, the team drove to Mount Union College, by coincidence the location of the next family members they needed to recover. They were picking up Allison, the girlfriend of SWAT officer Dale Renton, and their child. Renton was driving the lead HMMWV, and as they approached the Athletic Department he saw Allison and their 4-year-old son waving at him. Dale's son had taken rides in both the HMMWVs and M113 during team family BBQs, and recognized them.

Dale pulled up and stopped next to them, then jumped out of the truck and swept them up in his arms. After sharing a quick embrace and kiss, he hustled them to the rear of the M113 where the ramp was just coming down. They loaded up and Dale quickly returned to his seat in Manny's vehicle. A couple of seconds later the radio cracked, "Vic Two is ready to move," meaning the ramp on the M113 was up and the driver was ready to pull out.

As they pulled out onto Union Ave from the college Manny commented, "This is going way too easy Dale." "I know," Dale replied, "But I'm grateful we were able to grab Allison and Dale Junior." Manny nodded and said, "Me too brother."

The Tractor Supply manager was riding with Dale and Manny, and gave them directions to his place, a dilapidated house on Milner Street, where they dropped him off with the suggestion to shelter in place. After the manager got out of the HMMWV he turned and started to say something to Manny, but the truck was already moving. Manny watched him turn and disappear into his house in the rearview mirror.

To get to the next address they had to go north on Freedom Ave, right through the middle of Ward 2. As they pushed the envelope of the M113's speed limitations, swerving around stalled traffic and marauding pedestrians, Manny saw a patrol car in front of them in the road. As they got closer he saw it had been shredded by gunfire. He reached for the PTT on his plate carrier but before he could broadcast he heard a series of shots and heard them striking the M113. Manny found the PTT and broadcast, "Push through, Push through!" Already traveling at maximum speed, the convoy just kept moving. Manny turned his body to allow himself to shoot out of the passenger side door opening (the soft HMMWVs didn't even have plastic roll down window covers), and heard the M240 on top of the M113 open up in a booming series of short bursts as Jerry gave someone the business. Manny couldn't find any targets.

The team drove out of the area, making several random turns. Eventually they were able to slow down a little and continue the mission. The next recovery location was a dry hole; the SWAT assaulter's wife wasn't at home and her car was gone. He had no idea where she could be, and looked devastated that she wasn't there. The team waited while he grabbed some belongings from the house and left a note for his wife. Manny promised him they would make sure all the teams had her description and would be looking for her. They reluctantly moved on to the next objective, where they recovered a member of Charlie team's wife from work, then the two kids from middle school.

As they moved west on Patterson Street returning to the range, Manny could hear heavy gunfire to the south. He thought back to the shot-up patrol car on Freedom Avenue, and hoped that if that gunfight involved Black Knight teams that they were stacking some bodies. *The more we handle early,* Manny thought, *the fewer we will have to deal with once they get organized.* Manny knew from hard won experience working in the middle of several miniature apocalypses, from Syria and Iraq to Sudan and Liberia, that as time went on the individual savages that survived would smarten up and form into organized groups of savages.

Manny shook off the big picture and refocused on the current mission, knowing the best thing he could do was knock the targets down one at a time, one mission at a time. Of all the people present on the range when the lights went out, Manny had the easiest transition from 'normal' to 'society is off the rails'. He understood from firsthand experience what it took to win in these types of situations; he just never seriously thought he'd be doing it in America. Still, he counted himself blessed, knowing how lucky he was to happen to be here, with these people and resources, when the pulse hit. For the first time in a long time he felt he had a genuine purpose in life. He realized he was all-in with the Black Knight Squadron.

*

When Bravo team pulled into the range Manny noticed that Burt and several of the Echo team guys had already erected one of the Army surplus vehicle maintenance structures on the grass on the breaching range, and were about halfway through putting the second one up next to it.

He also noticed smoke rising out of a chimney pipe sticking out of the first structure. Kyle must have gotten the duel fuel wood/coal heaters that were an option with the structures in the Army supply system. He shook his head in admiration at Kyle's prowess with the DRMO system. Manny went back to the M113 and told Dale to unload the families into the big tent, not the team room, because the maintenance structure was heated while the team room was probably already getting cold with the power to the heater out.

When Manny walked into the office, he surprised to see the lights were on. David looked up and smiled at him and said, "That electrician is a stud. I was just surprised the wiring was still intact after the pulse. None of the computers will work, but the heater, outlets and lights seem fine." All Manny could say was, "Holy crap Dave, that's amazing." "Nah, just hard work. The miracle will be finding enough diesel in a week to keep it running." Manny couldn't disagree and replied, "True 'dat.". Still, it really was a minor miracle that the electrician was able to get that big generator wired in that quickly. That dude deserved a medal.

David asked, "So how did the run go? Who were you able to recover?" Manny filled him in on the entire mission, including grabbing the hand crank fuel pumps. As he spoke David walked to one of the white boards and started marking off the families they had recovered, and made a note by the one that they didn't. When Manny was finished, David said, "Great work brother. Take a few minutes to refit, then relieve Echo team on base security. I'm sending Echo with Doc Zimmerman to the hospital to see what's up there." Manny said, "Roger that," and pushed out to his next mission, happier than he had been in a long time.

Chapter 11

City Police Range
Alliance, OH

It was fully dark when the first convoy from city hall passed through the gate checkpoint at the range. Kyle, sitting in the front passenger seat of the lead vehicle, immediately noticed the two maintenance structures Burt had erected on the breaching range; and more importantly the fact that there was light coming out of them. As soon as the HMWWV stopped moving Kyle was out of the truck and jogging to the office. When he opened the door, he saw the lights were on there too, and the heater was working! A big smile grew on his face as he said, "Damn David, I leave you alone for a few hours and you fix everything!" David smiled and said, "The water plant guys and city electrician really crushed it. They had that big generator wired in and running about an hour after Bravo team delivered it."

"Wow! That's awesome." Kyle said, then changed the subject, "City hall and the PD and Fire departments are moving out here. I have a bunch of them and their stuff with us. We still have Alpha team and four patrol cops at the PD we need to recover. Nowak is slightly injured and is being moved to the new clinic in the classroom building. Gean (the Alpha team medic) is with him." David said, "Roger, I will go examine him as soon as we are done, and we will put the city government types in the second tent." Kyle nodded, then brought David up to speed on the events in town, including the small battle on Broadway, and Officer Card's death. David digested the info for a second and said, "Holy shit things got bad quick." Kyle could only nod.

Kyle stuck his head out of the office and told Mark to put the city people in the far maintenance tent. Mark said, "Roger," then turned and started barking orders. Kyle returned to the office and said, "OK, where do we stand with the rest of the missions?" David spent the next 15 minutes briefing Kyle on Bravo's two missions,

Charlie's scouting mission return, and Echo's new mission to the hospital. "I haven't gotten Charlie team's report yet, they got back about 10 minutes ahead of you." Kyle replied, "OK. I'm going to go gather up the Chief, the Mayor, and Mark. If Ben comes to give Charlie's scouting report before then have him wait. We'll only be a minute." David replied, "Roger," and went back to work on his white boards as Kyle left the office.

Kyle spent the next five minutes gathering up Mark, the Mayor, and the Chief. They ran into Ben in the team room and all walked over to the office together. After everyone was inside and had found a chair, David gave a briefing on Bravo team's two completed missions, and Echo team's scouting mission to the hospital that had just launched. Ben then stood up and briefed the group on Charlie team's scouting mission while David prepared to write critical information on the board.

Ben gathered his thoughts, consulted his notebook, and began, "We started by heading towards Hwy 183 to come back into the city from the Atwater direction, but found a train stopped on the tracks blocking the road. We noticed the train had a bunch of CONEX boxes loaded, a mile's worth at least. We didn't stop to check the boxes, but some of them are sure to be filled with food for the ABC Food Superstores warehouse to the west of town; and at least some of the cars were hauling coal." David wrote 'check train for resources' on the missions list.

Ben continued, "We backtracked and made it into town on Rockhill. As soon as we got to the cemetery on Rockhill we noticed several groups of young males standing in the street mean mugging us. We kept going, but we did see them gather up and start walking south. When we made it to State Street we saw a lot of stalled vehicles, but not a lot of people, until we drove past the Texas Roadhouse. There were people stacked up outside the door and it looked like the building was full as well. It was probably people taking shelter from the cold. We drove all the way west to Walmart, and found a ton of people in the parking lot. They had the doors barricaded already, but I don't know how long they can hold out against a mob." David wrote 'Secure Walmart' and 'check on people at Texas Roadhouse' on the board.

"Then we went east on State Street," Ben said. "The Marathon gas station at Rockhill was being looted. We continued

87

east and turned south on Union, and saw the CVS Drug Store was being looted as well. Mount Union was a ghost town, I guess the students are on Christmas break." Ron, the Mayor, nodded his head and said, "They are." Ben gave him a thumbs up and continued, "The first people we recovered were Tom and Kim (Tom was a nationally known gunsmith and machinist, and close friend of everyone in the room; Kim was his longtime girlfriend). I figured his skills and tools would be critical." Everyone in the room made approving noises, and Kyle said, "Absolutely. Great call."

Ben nodded and drove on, "We weren't able to bring much of his stuff, but we locked the house up tight and figured we can go back soon and get it before the looting gets out of hand." David wrote 'get Tom's gear' on the board while Ben pressed on, "We were able to recover everyone on Charlie team's families except Ed's. His girlfriend wasn't at work and his kid wasn't at school. After that stop, we went to every school in town, and only found kids at the High School. The rest of them were empty and locked up. The admin must have sent the kids home somehow. The High School had about 30 kids left, and the Principal was making a plan to get the rest home." David wrote 'get high school kids home' under the 'Priority 1' heading on the board. Everyone knew that would be the next mission.

"After that we patrolled some of the residential areas," Ben said, "but there were so many people wondering around looking pissed we decided to go check on some other PD families we knew about, and off duty officers. We did hear a big ass gunfight somewhere in the Broadway area, but didn't investigate. I heard some of the radio traffic and thought you guys had it under control. We were able to recover two more officers and their families before the MRAP was assholes and elbows full. We got back late because we realized after we left, no one had a watch that worked, and none of our cell phones were displaying the time." Ben closed his notebook and sat down. Kyle said, "Great job brother."

The group in the office spent the next hour making plans and setting priorities. The first job was to get someone to the High School to check on those kids and to get them home. The Mayor also wanted the Principal brought to the range, to coordinate using the High School as an emergency shelter. Charlie team got the tasking and was pulling out of the gate within 10 minutes of Ben receiving the verbal OPORDER from David. They ran blacked out, the MRAP's infrared headlights and the MAWL on the M240 in the turret allowing the team to drive and pull security under night vision.

*

As Charlie team pushed, the command group decided to move the range office and team room / classroom to the newly erected maintenance tent closest to driveway, and to start calling it the TOC. The range office was equipped with a full kitchen and industrial ice machine, which now worked again thanks to the power from the generator; and they decided with so many people (over 30 women and children were already on site, and more were sure to be coming) living at the range, even temporarily, the space would be better utilized as a communal kitchen.

They spent some time moving people and gear around until they had the large classroom configured as a sleeping area for families (They had a limited number of cots, and put 'lots of mattresses' on the salvage list). Next, they set up the second maintenance tent as the temporary City Hall and City Emergency Operations Center. Burt spent several hours running extension cords and low wattage LED Christmas lights into the tents and building make-shift easels for all of the white boards they had taken down from the classroom and office.

David put on his doctor hat and went to examine Dylan Nowak. When he was done he reported to Kyle and Chief Stone that Nowak had a mild concussion and suffered from the psychological shock that could be expected of someone who had just experienced unexpected, sustained combat. He ordered Dylan to rest for 24 hours, and would check on him periodically. David told Chief Stone that Dylan would be fine in the short term, but was pretty sure he would have some long-term psychological effects from the fight.

Several SWAT wives volunteered to run the kitchen, and immediately started sorting through the LTS food Kasey had brought from the condo, and the few buckets of Wise LTS food Kyle kept on site. Mark and Kasey had decided to donate their LTS food to the group to make getting through the next couple of days easier for everyone. The three-month supply of food for four people wouldn't last long feeding the growing host of people living at the range, but it would give them time to gather more food and get a meal plan organized.

Using one of the M915 tractors and lowboy trailer, they moved the fire department mobile command trailer to the range from the city maintenance yard, and plugged it onto the makeshift power grid. By the time Delta team escorted Fire Chief Dalano back to the fire station all of the fire fighters were gone, despite his orders to stay there until he returned.

Bravo team caught the mission of going with Chris and Ed back to the brickyard to gather up the working frontend loader, backhoe, and bobcat. They returned shortly, having driven the large vehicles on the road back to the range. They swapped out the bucket on one the loader for large forks, and started moving most of the vehicles the pulse zapped off the range and up to the main entrance of the water treatment plant. They left Mark's Yukon and David's Ford Raptor to be used as storage.

Manny supervised the placement of the cars at the entrance to the water treatment plant to create a makeshift serpentine of broken down cars to force any traffic coming into the plant to slow down. He knew it wouldn't stop a real VBIED, but it gave them a framework to improve upon, and provided some small level of cover to the guys working what was now called the ECP. Mark ordered the access control team to move up to the treatment plant entrance and to expand the active patrolling area to cover the entire water facility.

Kyle discovered that Lydia, the Stark County work release deputy, had worked as an inventory control manager for a steel mill in Canton for several years, back when steel mills were still a thing in Ohio. He immediately christened her the supply guru, and she jumped at the job. Lydia had been worried she had nothing to contribute, and was scared she wasn't going to be able to pull her weight. She was very happy to have a purpose, and started working like a whirling dervish. Within two hours Lydia was reporting back to Kyle in the TOC with a list of supplies on hand, and an even longer list of things she thought they needed to go 'acquire'.

Once city hall was fully evacuated and all of the police personnel were at the range, Mark formed another Black Knight team, Foxtrot, from 14 of the non-SWAT police officers now present at the range. He assigned Sergeant Wiggins, the department admin sergeant, as their Team Leader, and tasked the team with providing security for the water treatment facility and the base 24/7 until further notice.

Chief Stone announced to the TOC that he was re-naming the police range 'Forward Operating Base Card'.

Of the department's sworn police officers, only six were unaccounted for at this point, with four of those being the supervisors who had been trapped in Columbus. After assigning 14 of the patrol officers to Foxtrot team, Mark had eight patrol officers and four detectives left over. He spread the eight remaining officers, all of whom were former SWAT officers or guys who spent a lot of time training at the range, out among the existing Black Knight operational teams.

Tasking the detectives was a little more delicate; they viewed themselves as special, and had to be handled by the Chief directly for now. Mark suggested to Kyle that the detectives be formed into the intelligence section because they knew everyone and had a great deal of experience gathering information and turning that information into useable intelligence.

Kyle discussed the idea with Chief Stone. Stone didn't expect his detectives to be investigating much crime anytime soon; besides, how would they prosecute or incarcerate anyone? He called the detectives to the TOC and told them they now worked for Kyle and Mark. He was greeted by blank stares, but the detectives didn't have much choice in the matter. All but one of them, Detective Becker, came around quickly and did seem to be happy to have a mission, especially one that so perfectly fit their skills. David, being a consummate pro, just ignored their attitudes and assigned them a place in the TOC. He then briefed them on what he had done so far with regards to planning and what kinds of intel he needed immediately, most of which was human terrain information.

Becker stood in the back of the group with his arms crossed over his Affliction sweatshirt, convinced all this 'end of the world' stuff was bullshit. He was sure this was a local event and the National Guard, Ohio State Police and FEMA would be rolling into town at any minute. He knew when they did there would be hell to pay. With the Chief letting these SWAT yahoos and civilians run amuck, he wanted as little to do with this fiasco as possible.

Becker had never been a SWAT guy, and frankly the thought of having a SWAT team in Alliance in the first place was stupid; he thought he could do any of the raids the SWAT team did with just a couple of other detectives and some patrol guys; and if they had a hostage situation or something they could call in the FBI. He'd tried out for the team when he was a young cop, and hadn't made it because the Chief at the time thought he 'lacked judgment'. *What a joke,* Becker thought.

Chief Stone knew his Men, and was well aware of what Becker was probably thinking. He decided to keep an eye on it, and step in to crush Becker's soul if he started acting up. He knew Becker could be an arrogant prick, but he was a good detective; and in the final analysis he knew Kyle and his guys would need every single gun they could get.

Stone was a man of exceptional intellectual and emotional intelligence; and he was smart enough to know this situation was beyond his experience. *Hell, this is beyond anyone's experience,* Stone thought. It was only a few hours after the event and this situation was already far beyond a 'police matter'. His heart told him they should all be out in town keeping the peace, but he understood Kyle's insistence that they had to get their own shit together before running out to save the world. Without safety and care for their families, and a plan, Stone knew his officers would disappear, valuing their families over their oath; and he wouldn't have blamed them for a second. Without the organization, planning, equipment, and operational ability Kyle and all of his people brought to the game, the department would cease to exist; and the 22,000 souls who called Alliance home would be left to the mercy of the tides of anarchy.

Stone trusted Kyle in an absolute way, and he trusted Mark and David's professional judgment and abilities to lead. He had already decided he would support Kyle and his team with all of the legal and moral authority he had. He hoped it would be enough.

*

Manny finished briefing Sgt. Wiggins on the ECP's operation and helped him establish a watch schedule. With 14 people on Foxtrot team, using 12 hour shifts, Wiggins would be able to keep four cops on the gate, two guys patrolling the facility's perimeter, and a team leader on duty all the time. Manny went to the TOC and found David, "Hey Dave, can I issue one of the quads to the base security team to patrol the perimeter with?" David checked his board and said, "Yeah, but only one bro; and I don't know how long we will have gas for it."

Manny got the quad and drove it up to the gate. When he got there, he gave some hip pocket training on patrolling, and told the guys to swap out riders often so everyone could learn the facility. A couple of the guys complained that one of the guys on patrol would have to ride 'bitch', since they only had one quad. Manny suppressed his urge to go all Major Payne on the cop, and settled for saying, "Sorry man, it's all we have."

With Foxtrot team settling into their new duties, Manny gathered up Bravo team and reported to the TOC. He told his guys to flake out or check on their families, then he went to David looking for a heads up on their next mission. Manny found David, Kyle, Mark, and Bones huddling in front of a white board with a map. "Hey Manny," Kyle said when he saw him, "Bravo ready for another mission?" Manny came to a position that looked an awful lot like attention and said, "Absolutely."

David turned and asked Manny, "Can you go find Dan and bring him here? We need to brief both of you guys." Manny said, "Sure thing," then took off to find Dan. After asking the Alpha guys in the team room side of the TOC if they knew where Dan was, without success, Manny went to the kitchen. The former range office was packed with women, but he found Dan there, joking around with Kasey, Sarah and some of the wives who were cooking. *Leave it to Danny to be where the women are,* Manny thought.

"Hey Dan," Manny said in his big voice, "On me. We are wanted in the TOC." Dan smiled at Kasey, then came to Manny and they walked outside. Manny, in a deadpan tone, said, "I see you found the women already." Dan chuckled and said, "I went in there to get some coffee for my guys and it felt like a funeral. Depressed soccer moms as far as the eye could see. So, I told some jokes, got them laughing. This sucks enough without the women-folk being down in the dumps." Manny got it, and felt bad for his initial reaction, thinking Dan had been shamming. "Good thinking bro," Manny said, "And a nice thing to do for them."

Dan shrugged and asked, "We have another mission?" Manny said, "I think so. Charlie and Echo teams are out right now, so I have no idea what's next." "Where is Charlie team?" Dan asked. Manny replied, "They are going back to the High School to try to set it up as a shelter I think." "OK," Dan said, "I'm worried about Echo team. The hospital is bound to be a mad-house." Manny replied, "No doubt man."

They walked into the TOC and found David, who saw them and said, "Stand by to copy an Operations Order." This apocalypse was getting busy.

Chapter 12

Alliance Hospital Emergency Room
Alliance, OH

Echo's team's TL, Trent, wasn't exactly sure what he was supposed to do with this shit-show. The team's mission had been to provide security for Doc Zimmerman so he could evaluate conditions at the hospital. While Doc didn't work at the Alliance ER, he did have privileges there. Doc was something of a mentor to ER doctors around Northeast Ohio, and he knew just about everyone in the EMS world in Stark and Summit Counties.

The backup generators must have been fried by the pulse, because there was no power whatsoever anywhere in the building. The ER ambulance bay, waiting area, triage room and treatment areas were all a mass of confused movement and yelling, made positively surreal by the rave-party like effect of the battery powered emergency lights high up on the interior walls, handheld flashlights, and red and clear head lamps the medical staff were using to try to treat patients.

Doc ran up to the first medical person he saw, an RN he knew, and asked her where the Chief of the Emergency Department was. The nurse didn't recognize Doc in his SWAT gear, and just ignored him. He repeated his question and added, "Cybil, it's me, Doctor Zimmerman." She looked up, shined her flashlight in his face, and said, "Oh, thank God you're here! Every Doctor and Nurse in the hospital is down here now, and we are still overwhelmed!" Doc paused for a second and said, "Cybil, I'm not here to treat patients, at least not yet. I need to speak to whoever is in charge and figure out what the city can do to help get this under control."

"I think Doctor Mills (the hospital's Medical Director) is in the pharmacy. Someone already came in and shot up the place and stole a bunch of meds." Cybil said, exasperation thick in her voice.

"Last I saw him he was trying to save a couple of gunshot victims there, and figure out what meds we have left."

Doc said, "Thanks Cybil," and started moving to the pharmacy. As he passed patients, some of them laying on the floor because there were no more beds, he saw several gunshot wounds, a bunch of burn cases, and more than a few obviously expired people. While he and Trent moved past the nursing station they heard, "Oh hell no! You taking care of my boy NOW! Screw all these other people!" coming from an exam room to their right.

They veered that direction and Doc entered the room. In the dim glare of the emergency backup light in the room, he saw a young female LPN being manhandled by a large guy dressed in sagging pants and a green puffy jacket, and an obviously expired guy with half his head missing laying on the exam bed. Doc yelled, "Stop!" trying to get the dirtbag to focus on him and let the nurse go. The dude looked up, saw Doc and Trent standing there in full tactical kit, roared, "YOU MOTHERF***ERS did dis!" and pushed the nurse aside while he reached for his waistband. Doc froze up for a split second. Luckily for Doc and the nurse, Trent did not.

In one motion Trent planted his feet, raised his 11.5" BCM carbine from the low carry, activated his weapon light, remembered to compensate for offset, and shot the guy three times in the chest as fast as he could get the Aimpoint's dot back on target. The gangster's FNS 9C pistol fell from his hand and he staggered back against the wall, his heart and lungs utterly pulverized by the 77-grain rounds from Trent's carbine. The LVN fell to the floor, holding her ears and crying, while the ventilated bad guy tried to make his lungs work, looking like a fish out of water.

In the moment it took for the light to leave the criminal's eyes, Doc got his shit together. He shook his head to clear the blast effect of the 11.5" rifle with a Surefire Warcomp on it going off in the small room, which rocked his world, despite the MSA hearing / comms set under his helmet. Doc went to the bad guy, his carbine light now pointed at the loser's head. He checked to ensure the guy was indeed dead, then turned his attention to the nurse, getting her gently to her feet and walking her out of the room.

Doc was just about bowled over by Ernesto and Lee barreling into the room, running to the sound of the guns. Doc said, "Slow down guys, it's over." Lee asked, "What the hell happened?" Doc ignored him and got the LPN to a chair at the nursing station. Trent answered Lee, "Homeboy here was beating that little nurse up, and when he saw us he drew his gun. I filled him in." Ernesto said, "Sounds legit to me." Lee just looked sick to his stomach. Trent told Lee to go pull security on Doc.

Ernesto picked up the little FN pistol the dude dropped, unloaded it and said, "Well, he had three rounds left. Not sure what he was planning on doing with that." Ernesto closed the pistol's slide after checking it to be empty and dropped it in his dump pouch. Trent searched both the guy he shot and the dead patent on the exam table. He didn't find any ID on either of them, so he wrote their physical descriptions in his notebook, making sure to note their tattoos.

Outside the room Doctor Mills and a security guard ran up to Doc Zimmerman and asked him who was shooting. Doc said, "We were. A guy was attacking a nurse and tried to shoot us." Doctor Mills looked at Zimmerman closely, looked down at the 'POLICE' patch on the front of his vest, and said, "Neal?" using Zimmerman's first name. "Yeah, it's me." Doc said. Doctor Mills exclaimed, "Oh thank God you're here! We are drowning in patients and are running out of meds and consumables. We lost the patients on life support already, and several who were on the bubble before the lights went out. I don't know what we are going to do about the rest of the admitted patients, and you can see this ER situation is untenable." Doctor Mills seemed to be having trouble keeping himself together, appearing to be on the verge of sobbing.

Doc said, "Mills, I am here to see what you guys need that the city can provide. It's obvious your first problem is security." Zimmerman paused for second to think then continued, "We don't have medical supplies in any quantity. I will ask if we can try to find you a generator. Where is your Engineering and Facilities Manager?" Mills said, "I don't know," and the security guard said, "He left as soon as the lights went out. I saw him walking away from the property." Doc looked at the guard's nametag and said, "Thanks Winterman," then paused to shake the man's hand. "Do you know if any of the facilities guys are still here?" Doc asked him. Winterman replied, "I don't think so Sir. I've been looking for them and haven't seen any."

Doc Zimmerman thought for a few seconds then called to Trent, who joined them at the nursing station. He asked Trent, "What do you think of the situation here? Is this place even tenable anymore?" Trent immediately said, "No Doc, it's not. It would take 50 well trained guys to secure the building at this point, and it sounds like they are running out of everything anyway, so I'm not sure what we would be protecting." Doc asked, "Do you know if Charlie team has linked up with the High School yet? If they are going to use the high school as a shelter anyway, it may make more sense to move what we can from here and set up in a wing of the school. That would mean we would only have to power and defend one location."

Trent though about it and said, "It would make sense. I guess we should check with Kyle and let him take a run at convincing the Mayor." "Alright, lets mount up," Doc said. He turned to Doctor Mills and said, "Have you implemented the JCSE Emergency Operations Plan?" Mills said, "Not yet. Things have been moving too quickly. Besides, I'm not sure we have a hard copy of it and none of the computers work." Winterman said, "I have one in the security office Sir." Doc suggested they get to work, and Trent got on the radio, "All Echo units, fall back to the vehicles."

Once they were mounted up and moving, Doc looked at Trent and said, "Thank you. I can't believe I froze up," referring to the shooting in the ER. Trent shrugged it off and said, "It's cool Doc. You lost your chance for an apocalypse kill, that's all," with a grin. Doc thought for a second, then said with a grin, "Something tells me I'll have plenty more chances. Besides, I'm a doctor… I've killed more people on accident than you've arrested on purpose." Trent laughed and spoke to Ernesto who was driving their vehicle, "Let's go west to Hwy 62 and hit the range from the Union Ave exit. I don't want to drive through the ghetto, and I'd like to get a look at Walmart on the way." "Roger," Ernesto said and focused on not slamming into stalled cars while driving with his NODs on.

*

Ben decided to avoid Union Ave and the ghetto entirely when selecting a route for Charlie team to take to get to the High School. David had changed out their vehicles, having them take the soft skinned HMWWVs instead of the MRAP, and Ben wanted to avoid a pitched gunbattle in the soft skinned vehicles if at all possible. As the team was traveling down Hwy 62, intending to come into town from the west, he noticed three sets of taillights traveling in the same direction about 500 yards in front of them. It took Ben a minute to realize this wasn't normal anymore. He didn't know how long he had seen them and just didn't register the problem.

All of the Black Night Squadron vehicles had orders to run blacked out with IR headlights and NODs, so these folks were someone else. Somebody had gotten some vehicles to run. Ben didn't know who they were, but if they were out in force and driving at night, it probably wasn't good news.

Ben elbowed JR, who was driving the lead HMWWV, and said, "You see those taillights?" JR jumped and said, "Holy shit, I saw them but it didn't register!" JR immediately slowed down while Ben got on the radio and told everyone there were vehicles ahead of them going the same direction. Vehicle two gave a 'roger', then Ben heard David's voice come over the air, "Charlie One, Knight TOC. We copy. Follow and KMA (keep me advised). Be advised we have no friendlies in that area." Ben said, "Roger," and squared himself in his seat. "Let's follow them and see what's up." Ben told JR, who nodded.

Ben hoped these people would continue out of Alliance on Hwy 62. *Maybe they are heading to Canton,* he thought. Two miles later Ben's hopes were dashed. They saw break lights ahead and watched the vehicles exit on State Street. When the vehicles turned east on State Street, Ben saw it was three full size pickups, two of which had people in the back. He was pretty sure he saw vertical gun barrels in the back of one of the trucks, and JR confirmed this by saying, "I see several armed men in the back of the two lead vehicles.

Ben got back on the radio, "Knight TOC, Charlie One. Be advised the vehicles have exited onto eastbound State Street. We observed armed subjects in the back of at least two of the three trucks." David immediately replied, "Roger. Keep eyes on please. We are spinning up some assets to head your way." Ben said, "Roger. We are exiting 62 now." JR waited for Ben to get off the radio then said, "I'll bet you these guys are raiding Walmart." Ben wouldn't take that bet.

*

David turned to Kyle, Mark, and Bones and said, "I think Walmart is getting raided by unknown forces." "Shit," Kyle said, "We have to defend Walmart. Losing those supplies would hurt." Chief Stone was standing there and interjected, "Kyle is right. Losing Walmart will be a disaster. Do what you have to do to defend it." Kyle nodded at the Chief and shouted, "All teams to the trucks! Stand by for orders." David asked the Chief if he could take over the radios. He would need to go if Walmart was being raided. Mark, Kyle, Bones, and David grabbed their kit. Mark had to search for his 11.5" BCM carbine and get the Surefire can attached, but he still beat Kyle to the trucks

The next five minutes was an exercise in organized chaos. Alpha and Bravo teams were already geared up and ready to push out on their next missions, so they just got in their trucks and the MRAP and waited while Delta team and Kyle, Mark, Bones, and David got their gear on and did pre-combat checks. Delta team jumped in the MRAP with Alpha team, while the command group found seats in the M113. As they got settled they heard Ben come on the radio, "Knight TOC, Charlie One. The three vehicles pulled into Walmart and are shooting at the front doors and into the crowd outside." They heard Chief Stone come on the air and say, "Knight TOC copies. Knight Six, launch." Kyle said, "Knight Six copies. All teams, let's roll."

The four armored tactical vehicles roared out of the gate, leaving a knot of wives and families standing outside the kitchen, wondering what was going on.

*

JR was working his way through the miniature jungle that bordered the northwest corner of the Walmart parking lot, his Tikka Tac A1 sniper system in his hands. The rifle was heavier than usual because of the TNVC / FLIR PVS 27 clip-on night vision device that now sat in front of his optic. Kyle had issued him the night vision

100

optic out of the vault saying, "No sense keeping this stuff locked up, and I don't think anyone is going to need it for training anytime soon."

JR was happy to have it now. Without it he would have been dependent on the ambient light of a 13% waning moon. With no man-made light anywhere in sight it was darker than the inside of a coal digger's ass; and without the night vision he wouldn't have been able to identify a target at 25 yards, much less across the massive parking lot of Walmart. JR reached a good spot on the reverse slope of a small drainage berm at the edge of the lot that was high enough to let him see over the sea of dead cars in the Walmart lot, and set his rifle down. He slowly took off his tripod and assault pack, laid them down next to his rifle, extended his bipod and got down in a prone position behind the gun.

He turned on the PVS 27 and gave his scope turret 0.2 mils of elevation to compensate for his known POI shift with the night vision optic. Getting behind the gun, he found the west entrance to Walmart in the optic, where he could see one of the raider's trucks parked, and started to observe. He broadcast on the radio, "Charlie Sniper set, northwest edge of the parking lot." After getting an acknowledgement from Ben, JR pulled his prized Swarovski rangefinding binos and ranged the building at 193 meters. After dialing another 0.6 mils of elevation to compensate for the range, JR started observing in earnest.

As he settled his optic's reticle on the west entrance, he saw a guy in a coyote brown tactical vest and armed with an AK walk out of the doors, go to the truck, grab what looked like a 12 pack of beer, and return inside. Scanning the parking lot, JR counted at least 30 bodies on the ground that were not moving, and about the same number of people, running to the east, almost out of sight beyond the buildings bordering the lot on that side. The unmoving bodies were obviously the result of all the gunfire they had heard as they pulled up on the side street to the west of the property.

JR forced his humanity down and focused on the mission. He turned his focus to the east entrance to Walmart and noted two pickups were parked all akimbo just outside the doors. One of them was running and the headlights were on. He couldn't tell if anyone was in the truck. He noticed all three of the trucks were newer, and wondered how they still ran. JR got on the radio and updated Ben

on the situation as he saw it. Ben replied, "Roger. We are standing
by for the other teams."

*

Trent began picking up the radio traffic about Walmart as
they crossed Sawburg Avenue on State Street. He listened to several
transmissions, and while he could only hear Charlie team's side of
the conversation, he got the gist of the situation. He got on the radio
and said, "Charlie One, Echo One. We are westbound on State
Street at Sawburg. Do you want us to come in and set up from the
east?" Trent heard Kyle break in and say, "Echo One, Knight Six.
That's affirmative. Set up in the Tractor Supply lot and keep out of
sight of Walmart. Let me know when you are set. We are about
three minutes out with three full teams." Trent said, "Roger," and
told Ernesto to haul ass.

Chapter 13

Walmart
Alliance, OH

Billy had never been so excited in his entire 28 years on earth. When the lights went out, he was at work at the Nifty-Lube in Louisville, a small town between Alliance and Canton. Being in the oil change pit, he obviously noticed the power going out, but didn't think much of it until he pulled out his smart phone to use the flashlight on it to get up the stairs. The damn thing was dead.

He made his way upstairs and looked outside, where he saw all of the cars on the road in front of the shop were sitting still. *This is it!* he thought. He knew what was going on and felt the almost sexual excitement growing inside him. He and his group of friends had talked for several years about the apocalypse or civil war or financial collapse they were sure was coming, and all of the fun they would have once it did.

But for once in their lives, Billy and his friends had actually done more than just talked. Billy and eight of his closest friends had grown up together, committed petty crimes together, fought together, beat up minorities together; and over the last seven years had graduated to making meth and selling it together. Billy was their leader.

Several years earlier, while in jail for one of his many drug arrests, Billy had read a post-apocalyptic book, and become fascinated by the thought of living in a time with no law, no rules, and no boundaries. The idea of being a warlord fascinated him. Soon he was reading everything he could find about the subject. He kept his passion to himself for a long time, since his friends 'didn't cotton to no book readin'; until one night when they were all at his single wide trailer, drinking beer and smoking weed, and a popular TV show about the zombie apocalypse came on TV.

They started talking about what they would do if the zombies came, and Billy was able to lead the conversation into what they would do if a big disaster happened. By the time they fell asleep, surrounded by the flotsam of a long night of drinking and smoking the hippy lettuce, Billy had convinced them they should all 'get ready'. The group spent the next several months attending gun shows. Three of them could still legally buy guns, and they spent a lot of Billy's meth dealing profits on SKS and AK pattern rifles, lots of magazines and ammo, pistols, and crossbows; and an assortment of Chinese knock-off tactical vests, survival knives, ninja stars, tomahawks, one blowgun and a ninja sword. They spent time in the woods near Billy's trailer shooting their new guns and drinking beer.

Billy's cousin Frank was a diesel mechanic, and helped Billy convert his truck and two of his friend's trucks to non-electric diesel. Frank had stolen several crate motors from work, and he sold Billy three of them for $1000 and 12 ounces of his best sports-drink-bottle made methamphetamine. They did the work over a long 72-hour straight speed bender that ended with Frank getting arrested for possession when he went to the store to grab beer and got pulled over for a minor traffic violation.

Some of the guys asked Billy if they should be stockpiling food and such, and Billy said, "Nah. If something happens we will just go take over the Walmart in Alliance. We can use it for food, and as a base to start rapin' and selling dope." The group got even more excited about that idea.

As soon as he realized what was going on, Billy jumped in his truck and hauled ass. As he was looking in his rearview mirror at his boss who was standing in the driveway looking at him drive away, he felt and heard the truck hit something. He looked forward in time to see a man going under the front of his truck. *Dumbass must have been standing in the middle of the road. Serves him right,* Billy thought. He realized he was only two minutes into the end of the world and he'd already gotten to kill someone. Billy smiled and hooted.

When he arrived home, he saw both Ronnie and Bobbie's trucks were in his yard. *Damn, they hauled ass to beat me here,* He thought. He jumped out of the truck and ran to the front door, flinging it open and shouting, "It's time to get our apocalypse on Bitches!" He was greeted with whoops and hollers from everyone in the living room. It turned out Ronnie and Bobbie had picked almost everyone up on the way to the trailer, along with several guys who weren't in the core group but hung out from time to time. Of the group, only Billy and Bobbie had jobs, so it had been simple to snatch everyone on their way. As Billy asked where the last guy was, he came up the driveway on a bicycle. "Hot damn everyone is here!" Billy yelled.

The group spent the next few hours drinking beer, loading magazines, smoking some weed, and plotting their first move. Billy decided they would wait until dark to hit the Walmart. He figured they had time; in all of the post-apocalypse books he read it always took a few days for things to get crazy. In their celebration of the end of the world, they lost track of time. By the time they got geared up and ready to go, they were about 2 hours behind Billy's schedule. The irony of them being late to the apocalypse was lost on them.

Before they left, Billy gave them his grand plan. "Alright, shut up and listen." Billy started. "Grab all your guns and put all the ammo and beer in the trucks. We won't be coming back here. We will convoy up to Alliance and stop at Walmart first. The security there is unarmed, and the cops in Alliance have probably already split to take care of their families. We will hunt them down later. The cops only have pistols and shotguns, so even if they are around we will f**k them up."

Billy paused to imbibe some Keystone Light then continued, "When we get to Walmart, we will shoot our way in or use Bobbie's truck to ram the doors. Once we get in, shoot all the men inside. Keep the bitches alive; we will have some fun tonight." All the guys yelled their approval. They mounted up with two guys in the cab of each truck and everyone else is riding in the pickup beds.

On their way to Walmart they had to take a detour around a bunch of semi's that were stalled out on Hwy 62, which forced them off the freeway and around the back way into Alliance. They never noticed the armored vehicles that ended up behind them.

When they tore into the Walmart parking lot, the truck headlights illuminated a big group of people hanging out near the doors. No one gave an order to start the massacre, but one of the guys in the back of the lead truck thought it would be fun to shoot into the crowd. *Screw it* he thought, *No rules.* He brought his prized AK to his shoulder and, bracing himself on the roof of the pickup, his magazine gouging huge rents in the paint as he rested it on the top of the truck, started firing randomly into the crowd as fast as he could pull the trigger. He was having a great time, and just wished he had spent the money on a bump stock. Others in the backs of the trucks joined in, figuring it was part of the plan.

Billy sped to the east doors of the store, slammed on the brakes and stopped. He left the truck running and jumped out, intent on getting into the store. The guys in the back of his truck were still shooting, so he ran around the front and rushed the big glass doors of the store. They were intact and when he tried pushing through them he bounced off of the locked doors. Looking down, he saw someone had wedged 2X4's between the walls and the back edges of the doors, preventing them from being opened.

Billy was stymied for a second until one of his guys ran up next to him and started shooting the glass out of the door. Billy joined in and one magazine each later they were in. Billy turned and yelled at the guys in the truck, still focused on mowing down the crowd now running away from them, to get in the store. They stopped shooting and bailed out, joining him inside.

A couple of hours earlier, the Walmart manager, already in a panic over the large crowd outside, had sent all of the employees and customers still in the store to lock themselves in the break-room in the back of the store. After arming himself with a Mossberg shotgun from the sporting good section, an action he was sure was going to get him fired, he had hunkered down on top of the women's fitting rooms located at about the center of the store, near the front. He was contemplating letting the crowd into the store to loot it, in an attempt to save his employees, when the gunfire started outside. He knew he was stuck.

The manager listened as Billy and his guys entered the east doors first, followed closely by the sound of them coming in the west side. He struggled to see anything in the cavernous, pitch-black store, and was able to track the intruders only by the sounds of their yelling to one another. The sound reminded him of the packs of jackals he had seen on the nature TV shows he watched with his kids.

Billy was kicking himself in the ass. *FLASHLIGHTS! I didn't plan on flashlights!* Ran through his head on a loop. Ronnie had a cheap light on his AK, but he was on the west side of the building. Billy could see Ronnie's light moving around, but it did him no good at all. He yelled at Ronnie to meet him in the middle, and jogged that way.

When they met up, Billy told him, "Get everyone over here. You will have to be the point man, none of us can see." Ronnie shinned his light around and spotted some cheap keychain lights in the shelves by the registers, walked over and grabbed a handful off the hook. He also saw some rolls of electrical tape, and remembering some pictures he saw of the Navy Seals, he said to Billy, "Hey, just have everyone tape these lights to their guns." Billy, initially pissed that Ronnie wasn't listening to him, stopped for a second and let Ronnie's idea pierce the weed-induced fog in his head. "Brilliant!" Billy exclaimed. They quickly distributed the lights and taped them to their guns. Now, they could go hunting.

The store manager watched all this from 30 feet away, and thought he was doomed. Figuring he was mere seconds from being discovered, he shifted his shotgun and pointed it at the group of men standing in front and slightly below him. Thinking only that he had to get as many of them as he could before they found his employees, he pulled the trigger once and promptly fell off the roof of the fitting rooms, and became entangled in a circular display of XXL flower print tank tops.

The shotgun blast caught the clumped group of would-be marauders completely unaware. One minute they were struggling to tape these little lights to their rifles and the next their world exploded. The store manager had loaded buckshot into the shotgun, and the 30 feet of separation had allowed for a pretty good spread. Pellets struck three of the men, one of them standing just to Billy's left. All of them panicked and started shooting.

Most of the raiders oriented in the general direction the blast had come from before they fired; but at least two of them, one of them the wounded guy to Billy's left, just started pulling the trigger of their rifles. By the time they stopped shooting, three more of them had been hit, this time by their own guys. Billy took 7.62X39 rounds to the left foot and left calf, and Bobbie had stopped a round the hard way behind his right ear, completely decapitating him.

Everything was silent for a couple of seconds, when the guy who had gone back out to get the beer from the truck came running up to the group, yelling his ass off. In the dim glow of the keychain lights he saw the carnage and promptly threw up, then dropped the beer and sprinted towards the west doors. The survivors of the dumbest gunfight of the apocalypse, so far anyway, took a minute to gather themselves, then began to re-group. Billy yelled, "Someone go get me some first aid stuff from the medicine isle!"

*

By the time the convoy from the FOB showed up, Ben had Charlie team set up in the ditch on the west side of the lot about 30 yards from the northwest corner of the building. When they arrived, Kyle had the vehicles drop Alpha team and the leadership group at Ben's vehicles on the side street to the west. He directed the drivers and gunners of every vehicle with a belt fed mounted on it to stay in place and stage near the two driveways into the lot. Walmart was on a slight hill above State Street, making it impossible for people at the building to see down onto the road, a terrain advantage Kyle planned to maximize.

Kyle directed the vehicles carrying Bravo and Delta teams to drop their assaulters on the east side of the lot, and for those teams to link up with Echo team. He ordered the MRAP to stage at the bottom of the west driveway into the lot, and the M113 to stage at the bottom of the east side driveway. The driveways were so steep that the trucks could sit out of sight from the store until they were needed.

"This is going to be shady as hell bro." Mark told Kyle, as they crouched in the reeds close to the northwest corner of the building. Kyle replied, "I know brother. There have got to be employees in there. This is going to suck." Bones and David soon joined them. Mark got on the radio, "Delta One, Knight Five. Place your sniper and a security guy in the woods on the two / three corner (the southeast). Once they are set we need them to provide intel and squirter control." Troy responded, "Roger, she's moving." Mark could visualize Kasey running in her gear, and again had to force down his emotions.

Mark thought for a second and keyed the mic again, "Charlie Sniper, you have sides one and four." JR immediately responded, "Sniper set." Mark replied, "Roger. Other elements hold what you got for a minute." Kyle said, "So we have about 10 dongs (Mark was constantly coming up with different nicknames for bad guys,

108

and 'Dongs' was his latest idea. Kyle liked it.) armed with long guns inside. They have already evinced their intent by shooting all these people in the parking lot. There are some number of unknowns, now hostages, inside the store and," Kyle was interrupted by a heavy volley of gunfire from inside the store. He continued, "Shit. Ok, we need to assault. Anyone disagree?" Everyone shook their heads no.

"Ok," Kyle continued, "Mark will lead Alpha and Charlie teams close to the west doors. Everyone stays dark (under night vision). Bravo, Delta and Echo will move to the rear of the store and figure out a good breach point close to the east end of the building." Kyle paused to think, then continued, "Once they are set to breach, they initiate and you guys hit it from multiple breach points. All teams will move clockwise. I will fall in but stay towards the rear of your element Mark, so I can coordinate. When we breach, the M113 and MRAP pop up and cover the front. They will need to be careful of their fire towards the building, but as long as they avoid targeting the doors we should be fine. That wall should stop 7.62. What am I missing?" Kyle finished.

David said, "Sounds good to me. Everyone here has trained in CQB under NODs with teams. It will suck but we should get it done." Everyone nodded and Bones said, "We're all we got." The other three replied, "We're all we need." No one else had anything to add, and Mark started giving the orders over the radio to send the Black Knight Squadron into the assault.

Chapter 14

It took about 10 minutes for everyone to get organized and move to their jump-off points. During that time, they heard nothing from inside the store. Mark appointed Manny to be the assault team leader for the second element, which would be breaching and entering the back of the store. Manny was currently standing just outside the assault line to the left of the door he had chosen for their breach point. Based on Trent's knowledge of the backend of the store, this eastern-most pedestrian door opened up into the far end of the main stockroom area on the edge of one of the two loading docks.

Manny watched as Delta team readied then set the firehose charge on the hinge side of the heavy steel pull door, carefully peeling the carpet tape covering off the back of the charge and sticking it into place. Next, Delta team placed a small 'C' shaped charge made of C2 explosive and a booster, just under where they could see the bolts holding the door's auto-return system in place. Once both charges were set, Trent capped in and unrolled the shock-tube to its full 25 feet of extension while moving to the right of the door, and took a knee. *This breach is going to suck,* Manny thought. *That's a lot of net explosive weight, and there is no cover for us to shield behind.*

Manny watched through his Sentinel NVGs as Trent connected the shock-tube to the Royal Arms firing device then pointed at Manny. Manny took a deep breath and keyed his radio. Speaking softly, he said, "Rear element set." For several seconds, no response came. Just as he was about to re-transmit, Mark came on the air, "Execute."

Manny lifted his barrel up and quickly dropped it back down, signaling Trent with the barrel release to blow the door, then averted his eyes. The sound was incredible, and combined with the pressure wave in the assaulters' chests, it rocked Manny's team. As a cloud filled with the scent of detonated high explosive billowed over the team, Manny looked to confirm the door was now open and hit his PTT, saying, "Positive breach." His four lead assaulters launched through the hole where the heavy door had once stood.

*

Holy crap that was a big charge, Mark thought when he heard the breaching charge detonate. He looked to Zach Shepard, an Alpha team assaulter and SWAT guy, and gave him a barrel release. Zach's position gave him the most advantage once they moved through the door, so Mark was giving him the initiative to lead the assault. Shepard activated the short-range mode on his MAWL laser and pushed through the busted-up glass doors. As he crossed the threshold he turned right as soon as he could to clear the hard corner, finding nothing but vending machines in the small alcove between the two sets of doors leading into the store. He took a couple of steps and collapsed his sector of fire while Dan, the second assaulter, had already cleared the left corner and was collapsing towards him.

The third and fourth Alpha team assaulters, Anson Cross and Jim Keel, entered on Dan's heels and set up to cover the center of the room; a space dominated by the second set of glass entry doors, which were open. Through their night vision, Keel and Anson had a clear view through the doors and all the way to the far back wall of the store, a little more than 100 yards distant. They activated their MAWL laser / illuminators and scanned for threats. Finding none, Keel began moving his laser vertically up and down on the doors in front of him, signaling to the others the next breach point. Communicating this way allowed the team to move and work without speaking, maximizing the stealth advantage the night vision technology gave them.

Keel moved forward and quickly ducked through the open doors, moving to the left once he cleared the threshold, with Anson on his ass, moving to the right. When Keel dug his corner, he found himself facing a complex set of problems, with angles of exposure all across his front and right flank. Directly ahead, only about 10 feet away, was the store's bank franchise, with its myriad of tables, counter, and other places a threat could be hiding. To the right of

111

that was the long open pathway behind the registers where shoppers transited to get out of the store. Next were the register stations themselves, with hundreds of places someone could be hiding and still see, and therefore shoot, him and his team mates.

Keel stopped scanning when he noticed a faint glow in his NVGs, on the other side of the registers, about halfway down the store. As he focused on the area, he heard a male voice in the same area say, "Damn that hurts!" followed by some scuffling and the sound of someone moaning. *Must be one of the victims,* Keel thought. A different voice said, "What the hell was that explosion?" The first voice replied, "I told you, it was probably a transformer blowing up. Now help me with this bandage."

Dan, who came in as the number three assaulter, falling in on Keel's side of the door, heard the same thing and immediately stepped up to cover Keel's right side. The problem was that while Dan was a normal sized guy, at 5'10" tall with his helmet on, Keel was one of the largest SWAT mammals on the planet. Standing a little over 6'9" tall in his helmet, and weighing over 300 pounds, Keel was a regular competitor in the World's Strongest Man series, and simply dwarfed everyone else in the Black Knight Squadron. Dan did his best to shield him, and kind of succeeded in covering part of Keel's chest.

While Keel and Dan were working on deciphering the muttered talking and noises coming from beyond the registers, Anson and Shepard were clearing the shopping cart holding area to the right. Mark entered the second doorway and looked around. He also heard the voice, and quickly called the remaining three assaulters from Alpha team to him with a hand signal. He pushed Anson and Shepard to Dan, then stepped out and marked where the light and noise was coming from with his laser. Concerned about crossfire, given where he knew Manny was leading the other team into the building, Mark pulled Keel and his team to the right, directing them to move down the wide isle on the store side of the registers. If they encountered threats, Mark wanted to be shooting directly east, not into the southeast corner or the south wall.

As soon as Keel and Dan quietly turned the L corner around the self-checkout area, into the store side register waiting area, they saw several people kneeling around a few other people who were lying on the ground about halfway down the wide isle. The entire group was lit up in the team's NVGs, cast in the glow of several small LED lights they could see were attached to rifles. *What the hell are these dongs doing?* Keel thought. Given their lack of reaction to the team's presence, the group of dongs obviously hadn't seen them.

The pitch-black store interior enveloped the Black Knights, allowing Dan, Keel, Anson, and Shepard to move up on line, with two other Alpha team members moving with them covering their flanks and clearing the dead spaces in the checkout lines as they glided past them. The team moved past the stand-alone displays designed to sell extra crap to people waiting in line at the cash registers, to within 30 feet of the cluster of people who they could see now were clearly dirtbags. The strong smell of burnt marijuana wafted into Keel's nostrils, confirming his visual assessment that these dudes sporting neck tattoos, ball caps and cheap-looking tactical vests, scrambling around and cursing, were indeed the dongs they were looking for. IR lasers from the four assaulters advancing on the group danced slightly as the team moved, confirming none of them were doubled up on targets.

As Keel noticed several of them had AK's in their hands, one of them stood up and looked directly at him, then turned his long gun towards Keel. He was trying to use the light on his rifle to see the vague specter he sensed in front of him. As the rifle lifted, Keel steadied his laser on the dong's nose and fired a controlled pair, sending two 62-grain Gold Dot 5.56mm rounds through the guy's brain and showering his buddies with the evacuated contents of his cranial cavity. The unsuppressed shot, with all the panic-inducing surprise that comes from a very loud gunshot at close range from a dark unseen foe, combined with the warm liquid splashing on them, caused all hell to break loose.

The next ten seconds were a bloody, chaotic, loud and confusing mess. The four Black Knight assaulters quickly delivered suppressed and unsuppressed hammered pairs to their selected targets, then searched for another target holding a weapon. The team worked hard to make sure everyone they shot had a weapon, but all of them were worried there might be hostages in the swirling mass of guns, moving bodies, and prone people they could see in the pile through their night vision. Several un-aimed panic shots came back at the team from the huddled group of dongs. Dan saw one of the shooters, a longhaired guy sitting on his ass, firing a pistol at the team, and drilled him with five rapid shots to the chest as soon as his laser stopped on the dude's armpit.

Dan's shots slammed the dong to the ground, but not before one of the guy's pistol rounds found the right-front quarter of Anson's helmet. Anson went down and Mark immediately moved to take his place on the line. By the time Mark got on-line, the shooting was over. He was able to clearly see the writhing mess of bodies in the white-phosphorous tubes of his Sentinel goggles, but didn't see anyone who posed a threat to the team. He quickly grabbed Anson by the shoulder strap of his Velocity Systems plate carrier, and drug him into the checkout line of the nearest register.

Unsure of the tactical situation and not wanting to project visible light, Mark turned on the Surefire IR light on his helmet and flipped the Phokus Research lens caps closed over the end of his NVGs, shifting the focus of his goggles from 'infinity' to close range. This allowed him to start a blood sweep on Anson, despite Anson's groggy bitching about how he was fine. Mark hissed at him to sit still.

While checking the back of his neck, Mark saw the butt end of a .45 ACP round sticking out of Anson's helmet. The Team Wendy ballistic helmet had stopped the round, but the blunt force must have rung Anson's bell. Not wanting to assume this was Anson's only injury, Mark checked him thoroughly; loosening his vest to sweep his torso, and doing a complete front and back sweep of his hips and legs. Finding no other injuries, Mark grabbed Shepard and told him to do another check on Anson and then keep an eye on him, then called Charlie team up. Mark told Ben to have his medic set up a CCP in the vending machine area inside the west doors, then use his team to clear the shops and restrooms on the north wall of the store.

Mark rejoined Keel, Dan, and the other Alpha assaulters, and oversaw the team as they secured the subjects they had just fought. Two Alpha guys watched the main store retail floor while Dan covered the subjects as Keel grabbed all of the weapons he could see and threw them up on register 15's conveyor belt. Keel then grabbed the dongs one at a time and dragged them off of one another, secured their hands with Cobra cuffs, searched and disarmed them, then laid them out in a line. All of them were wearing cheap tactical vests and were armed. *Thank God none of these guys were hostages,* Keel thought.

Of the eight subjects Keel found, only one was still alive. This dong was shot in the left buttcheek, and wouldn't stop running his mouth. Ronnie kept saying, "Please don't hurt me," over and over. Keel finally hissed at him, "Shut your suck, dumbass," in his mean voice. Ronnie promptly shut up. As his brain caught up with his eyes, seeing the giant of a man wearing night vision goggles, standing over him, Ronnie voided his bladder into his best pair of sagging track pants.

After quietly speaking with Keel, Mark got on the radio. He pushed the PTT and said, "Knight Six, Knight Five. Splash seven, one dong in custody. Anson is injured but mobile. I need you to push to me; we need you guys to help us continue clearing."

Within a minute David, Kyle, and Bones were at his side, surveying the carnage. Mark said, "We will take Dan and assault through. Watch your step, there's a ton of blood on the deck." Kyle looked up at the number above the cash register and grinned. Mark said, "Don't even say it dude." Kyle just kept grinning. As they started moving Kyle spoke softly to Bones, "Cleanup on isle 15."

*

Manny had Bravo team in front of him, clearing the stock-room and 'back of the house' areas from east to west, with Delta team trailing about 20 feet behind him, ready to pass through and continue the assault should Bravo encounter a problem. Echo team was staging at the exit from the stock-room into the main store, covering that door and the assault team's back.

After clearing the east side of the stock-room, Bravo team stacked on the double doors marked 'Employee Break Area'. After listening for a second, Jerry, who was set up as the lead assaulter on the door, looked back at Manny and touched his ear pro with his right index finger, indicating he heard people on the other side of the door. Manny gave him an exaggerated nod and waited. Jerry listened for what seemed like forever, but was probably only 20 seconds or so, then quietly verbalized, "I hear women and children talking." Manny nodded and swept his IR laser up and down on the door.

115

Dale, who was set up as the breacher on the door, tried the knob but found it locked. Not seeing any hinges on the outside of the door, he quickly looked up at Phil, who was stacked next to Jerry, and made the hand signal for 'breacher up'. Phil turned around and let Dale grab the collapsible JMSG Metalworks breaching hammer out of the carrier on his back, then got back in position. Dale quietly extended the tool and made ready to breach. When Jerry saw he was ready, he took a deep breath and gave the barrel release.

Dale swung the hammer as hard as he could, and scored a perfect hit on the door handle, sending it shooting into the room. As the momentum of the hit pushed the door ajar, Jerry pushed off, shouldering the door open and breaking left into the room. The room seemed abnormally bright, and it took Jerry a second to realize several Coleman LED lanterns were lighting up the room. Phil was right on his heels and went right. The rest of Bravo team flooded into the room behind them. The room erupted into chaos. The Bravo assaulters were yelling, "Get down. Get down on the ground," and all of the room's occupants, most of them wearing Walmart employee vests, were crying or yelling incoherent words.

On the right, Phil was confronted by a fat guy with a big white beard in a Walmart vest, wielding a baseball bat. He came charging at Phil yelling, "Get out of here!" Phil ducked inside the man's charge and avoided the bat's swing. Already having his 11.5" BCM carbine with a Surefire Mini suppressor at the high ready, Phil simply pushed off the guy, arrested his own rearward momentum, and struck the dude in the chin from below with the muzzle of his suppressor as hard as he could. The fat guy's head snapped back and he went down like he had been pole-axed. Phil jumped on the guy and quickly had him handcuffed.

Manny stepped into the room and flipped his NVGs up on his helmet. Taking in the situation within a couple of seconds, he did his best Sergeant Major voice and bellowed, "Police Department. Everyone calm down. Please get down on the ground people." He pushed the guys on the left to the far corner on their side, and started sorting people out. These folks all looked like normal, if terrified, people; and all but three of them were wearing Walmart employee vests. The three non-employees were an elderly couple and a girl who looked to Manny to be about four years old.

The team got the group calmed down and seated at the tables in the break-room as Phil, the team medic, began treating the man he'd muzzle thumped. Manny told the guys to pull security on the door, then looked at Phil and said, "Keep me updated on his condition," then added with a smirk, "I can't believe you cold-cocked Santa Claus bro. Probably won't be the last time you hear about that." The rest of the team laughed. Phil didn't think it was nearly as funny as the rest of them did, and he knew it would be a long time living that one down.

As Manny flipped down his NVGs and moved towards the door, they all heard the crashing of gunfire from the front of the store. Manny paused for a second, as the group of citizens in the room ducked down under their tables. Jerry said, "Sounds like the guys up front are doing work." Manny nodded and spoke to the room, "It's alright folks. We have another team in the building. That was probably them." Manny wanted to report his situation over the radio, but knew the other teams would be talking shortly.

Manny had to wait for about a minute before he heard Mark come on the radio and report on the gunfight. When that traffic was done he keyed his PTT and said, "Knight Six, Bravo One. Recovered 17 Hotel's (code for hostages) in the employee break room. One Hotel is slightly injured, medic is handling. Charlie Mike (Continuing Mission)." When Kyle responded it sounded like he was out of breath, "Roger Bravo One."

An older lady in the room, who Manny surmised from her Walmart nametag was named Rosa, asked him, "Can you see if you can find Harold, our manager? We haven't seen him in over two hours and I'm worried about him." Manny replied, "Absolutely ma'am," and asked her for Harold's physical and clothing description. Once he got that Manny got back on the radio, "Knight Six, Bravo One. A Hotel reports the store manager, Harold," Manny gave his description, "was foot-mobile in the store as of two hours ago." He heard David's voice respond, "Copy Bravo One. Thank you."

Manny made eye contact with his team and said, "I'm pushing. Stay Frosty." They all nodded, and Jerry said, "We're all we need Boss." Manny nodded, not trusting himself to speak. It was only a few hours into this thing and he was already proud of his team. He went back out the door, then pointed to Troy and quietly said, "Delta team. Assault through."

Chapter 15

Walmart
Alliance, OH

Despite all the cold weather gear she had on, Kasey was getting chilled. Lying in the icy grass at the edge of the southeast corner of the lot, forced by her mission to stay completely immobile, she could feel the heat being sapped from her body. Her Kestrel 5700 told her it was 24 degrees, but the temperature was dropping fast and it felt much colder. She struggled to maintain her focus, knowing the teams were relying on her for information, and cover if the fight came her way.

Kasey took her eye off the scope for a second to relax her neck and eyes, and when she got back on the gun something had changed. It took her a few seconds to figure it out. The Black Knight M113 had moved up to the north-east corner of the parking lot when Bravo team breached, and was covering the front of the building. The M240 on the armored vehicle was not equipped with a thermal sight, so the gunner was using his helmet mounted NVGs and the IR laser and illuminator on his MAWL to see and aim. As the IR beam moved around, it created some great contrast for Kasey as she looked through the PVS 22 clip-on night vision device on her Sako M10 rifle.

Kasey realized there was now a head in a ball cap and the upper shoulders of a man silhouetted in the IR illuminator from the M113. He was poking up from the top of a vehicle that was stalled in the driveway just to the east of the garden center. The man was on her side of the vehicle looking at the M113, and the M240 gunner had not seen him. Kasey activated the B.E. Meyers IZLID IR illuminator on her Sako and the man's image virtually jumped out at her. Now that he was illuminated from her position, she saw him clearly. He was a white guy wearing a tactical vest and a ball cap, and had an SKS rifle with a long magazine held low behind the vehicle. As she decided, given this guy's clothing and weapon, that he was indeed a dong, Kasey saw the M240 gunner in the M113 stop moving and focus his laser and illuminator on the subject. She got on the radio and said, "Delta Seven, Delta Sniper. That subject is a dong. I can see his entire body, and he is armed." The gunner replied, "Roger. On you."

Kasey centered the reticle on the dong's head, but as she prepped the trigger the guy broke cover and sprinted west towards the still running pickup in front of the east doors to the store. Kasey quickly led him and fired, but his full body flinch and continued running told her she had missed. The dong passed behind the northeast corner of the building before she could get another round off, and she got back on the radio, "Delta Sniper, negative hit." The M240 gunner replied, "OK. I've got him."

The Black Knight assaulter on the M240, Jared Venton, had retired from the Alliance SWAT Team 3 years ago, and now worked patrol on the midnight shift; but he had continued to help teach at the range when he had time. In addition to the years of experience Venton had with the M240 as an Ohio Air National Guard Security Policeman, he had been one of the original APD officers who helped spin the rest of the team up on the belt fed machineguns when Kyle had first acquired them. He didn't like to brag, but Venton was a surgeon with a 240. He saw the dong was sprinting for the running pickup, and decided to take that option away from him. Besides, it was easier to hit and disable a stationary pickup than a running dude from 150 yards away with a belt fed while shooting under NVGs.

Venton lit into the truck, sending short streams of 7.62 love into the Dodge pickup's engine compartment, driver side tires and wheels, and where he thought the gas tank should be. The truck was reduced to a burning heap by the time the dong could arrest his run and make a decision on where to go, now that his getaway ride was a useless hulk. Venton saw the dong make the turn towards the east doors into the store, but couldn't fire; his rounds would enter the store and probably hit one of his team mates. *That's fine,* Venton thought. *I'll just kill him with my radio.* "Knight Six, Delta Seven, one dong squirter coming to you through the east doors. I say again, a squirter is running INTO the store through the east doors."

When David and Kyle heard Kasey's initial radio traffic, they'd just finished clearing the shopping cart storage area inside the interior set of east doors. They stayed in place, not wanting to be in

120

the exposed east doorway if a Black Knight machinegunner needed to engage the dong outside. They didn't hear Kasey's suppressed shot, but they heard her next radio call and Venton's response. Unsure of Venton's angle of attack with the 240, they continued to hunker down in case he engaged into the north wall of the store.

When the hellish bursts of M240 fire stopped, and Venton radioed that the dong was headed back into the building, David and Kyle exchanged feral grins. They were perfectly positioned to ambush this dude as he ran into the door. They stood up, shoulder to shoulder, took perfect combat carbine stances, and waited. In less than five seconds the sound of falling glass and the running crunch of boots announced the guy was bumbling through the east doors. Then he was in their lasers, sprinting into the store but looking back at the parking lot. He never realized death was waiting with a smile in the other direction.

Both Kyle and David saw the SKS at the same time and started burning the dong to the ground with a broadside of 5.56 rounds, tracking and filling him in as his momentum carried him a couple feet past their position. "Knight Seven, splash one," David said over the radio. Kyle couldn't resist the chance to mess with Kasey. He pushed his PTT and said, "Delta Sniper, Knight Six. We wiped up your squirter. You're welcome." Kasey could hear David chuckling in the background on the radio, and couldn't help but laugh. Kyle was the king of lame tactical puns. After a quick fist bump David and Kyle tac loaded their carbines and went to find work.

*

It took over an hour for the assault elements to search the entire building. The multitude of small rooms, cubbies and nooks, and nightmarish angles of exposure on the retail floor forced the teams to spend a lot of time communicating to de-conflict their movements. These delays, while necessary, caused Mark some gray hairs in his beard. Momentum is life in CQB, and Mark and Manny were constantly forced to sacrifice momentum for angle coverage. With the hostages recovered, nothing else in the store was worth accidently shooting one another over, so they sucked it up and did what they had to do.

Delta team found one more dong while searching the infant supplies section in the southwest part of the store. He was found on his knees with his hands up, and a blowgun, an SKS rifle, and an XD .45 pistol lying on the deck, out of reach. After Delta team got him in Cobra Cuffs they removed his tactical vest, shoes, and hat. While searching him, they found three throwing stars in an ankle holster and a knife hanging down his back from some paracord around his neck. When they questioned him, Manny and Troy didn't even bother asking his name, they just called him 'Ninja'.

It seemed Ninja came to Walmart prepared to 'lay some hate', but had lost all his enthusiasm when he saw all his buddies get a mudhole stomped in their ass near the registers. He ran and hid in the infant care section and waited to surrender. Ninja denied even firing his weapon; and a quick check of the SKS told Manny he was probably telling the truth on that front. Manny had a Delta assaulter take Ninja to the employee break room, and their search continued.

Alpha team found the store manager, Harold, hiding inside one of the women's fitting rooms; and after a quick tactical questioning session to confirm his identity, they took him to the CCP to get checked out by the medic. Shepard knew Harold, and spent some time getting him calmed down. It turned out Harold was most worried about getting fired for shooting at the dongs. Shepard assured him that not only did he do the right thing, but that Walmart most likely no longer existed as an organization. Shepard knew Harold would be a critical resource as they tried to use the supplies in Walmart to keep the city from falling apart.

*

By the time the two elements linked up at the northwest and southeast corners of the store, everyone was smoked. Mark, Manny, Kyle, David, and Bones spent the next hour organizing their asses off. They set security, made sure the assaulters got some water and tac loaded their carbines, documented the scene (just in case the lights came back on), and got the Walmart employees sorted out.

Echo and Delta teams were tasked with searching the parking lot and sorting out the victims who had been gunned down there as the raiders had arrived. Troy and Trent reported back to Kyle that 34 adults and three children were down in the parking lot. Trent told

122

Kyle 29 of the adults and one of the children had perished, and that the survivors had been moved to the CCP at the west doors, where Doc Zimmerman was working on them.

Kyle asked Trent and Troy, "How are the guys handling the carnage out there?" The two team leaders shared a look. Trent responded, "They are mad bro. Several of those people could have been saved if we had gotten to them earlier." Kyle took the comment as a criticism and said, "What the f**k could we do? We had to handle the threat before we could help them." Troy quickly replied, "No one is questioning that brother. We are upset because we wish we had the emergency medical resources that could have been treating them while we were in here working." Kyle nodded and said, "Me too brothers. Me too."

At David's suggestion, they armed the Walmart employees from the stock of rifles in the sporting goods section, and set up a camp inside the store for them to live temporarily. David explained to them that the Squadron did not have the resources to get them all home right that minute, but they would work out a plan over the next several days to get them where they needed to be. The little girl was the child of one of the female employees, who had been in the store with her mom for some reason when the lights went out.

After speaking with the elderly couple, David tasked Charlie team with taking them home to gather up some belongings and their medications then return them to the store. The couple had decided that they wanted to help the community during the crisis, not hide at home; and thought they could contribute by staying at Walmart and helping however they could.

As the team was bringing some order from this chaos, Kyle was silently praying, asking for guidance on what to do with the two prisoners. It would be simplest to just execute them. That would be simple to justify, given the situation and what the dongs had done out in the parking lot. Mark walked up to Kyle and asked, "What are we going to do with these dirtbags we caught?" Kyle let out a long breath and said, "I'm not sure brother. I was just praying about that." Mark nodded and said, "Well, as far as I'm concerned the Constitution wasn't nullified by this EMP. How did they handle murderers before electricity?"

Kyle nodded his agreement and thought for a second. "We know where Judge Morris lives. We could go find him and make it his problem. We have a prosecutor, I suppose we could put them on trial." Kyle thought for a second before continuing, "I hate to waste what are sure to be limited resources feeding and guarding them, but doing anything else makes us tyrants." Mark replied, "I couldn't agree more brother. This event, whatever it is, only means the end of civilization if we let it."

They stood in silence together for a moment before Mark continued, "I am going to use Ninja as labor to get these bodies moved." Kyle nodded and said, "Task a team for security. We will turn both of them over to Foxtrot once we get back to the FOB. They can guard them." Mark squeezed Kyle's shoulder and walked away to organize things.

Mark assigned Bravo team to guard the prisoners and supervise the work that needed done. Manny immediately grabbed Ninja, gave him a casualty litter from the M113, and put him to work. Manny then got together with the store employees and organized a watch schedule for them. Mark had told Manny they weren't leaving any assaulters behind to guard the store for the night, so Manny spent a lot of time helping them get organized to defend themselves and the store's resources until tomorrow. It took until well after midnight, but Ninja eventually got all of the bodies moved to the west side of the parking lot. Tomorrow they would bring a backhoe from the FOB and bury everyone.

David approached Kyle and Mark as they stood in the CCP, and said, "Hey brothers. I need to go to the house and check on my family." David's home in Alliance was less than a mile from Walmart. He wasn't too worried about his family yet, but he needed to check in. "You should just stay the night there." Kyle replied, "No sense sleeping on the ground when you've got a perfectly good bed there. Take one of the unarmored HMWWVs." David said, "Thank you brothers. I'll be at the FOB before sunup." Mark said, "Please be careful brother. Why don't you take one of the single guys with you to watch your back while you travel?" David thought for a minute and said, "Sounds like a plan, I'll take Lee." He bro-hugged David and Mark, and took off to find Lee.

Mark found Bones and helped him organize getting the store's main doors, and the door Trent had blown up, boarded up for the night. By one a.m. they had everyone loaded up in the vehicles and heading back to the FOB. Everyone was exhausted and emotionally wrung out. There was so much that needed to be done in town, but they couldn't push the teams past the breaking point. This was only day one of what was almost sure to be a permanent situation.

By the time all the teams pulled back into the FOB, unloaded, got the casualties situated, and the prisoners turned over to Foxtrot team, the guys were asleep on their feet. Several of the wives got up from their make-shift sleeping areas in the classroom and made a hot meal for the guys. After resetting their gear and loading mags, everyone flaked out where they could and ate, then found a warm place to curl up and sleep. To a man, the guys with families that made it to the FOB said a quiet prayer of thanks for the safety of their loved ones.

The Black Knight Squadron command team, minus David, met up with Chief Stone in the TOC and gave him a full report. He agreed with the idea to find Judge Morris, and put it on his list for the next day. The group decided to get some sleep and meet up before the sun came up for a serious planning session. By the time Mark found Kasey sound asleep, wrapped up in the sleeping bag from her rucksack, he was as tired as he'd ever been. He noticed Kasey had already set up his blow-up ground mat and laid out his bag next to her, and said a prayer of thanks for his wonderful wife. Mark fell asleep thinking of how lucky he and Kasey were to be in this place, with these wonderful people, when the lights went out.

Chapter 16

Stark Towers Apartments
Canton, OH

Nicholas "Bookie" Lincoln wasn't your average drug lord. His 5'7", 140-pound stature, thick glasses, buck teeth, sunken chest, and slight limp, all conspired to create the impression of a thoroughly unimpressive and harmless handicapped man. Based on appearances, Bookie was absolutely the last guy you would peg as a dope kingpin. Bookie not only liked it that way, he worked hard to further that impression.

Bookie, now 29 years old, had grown up in these same projects were he now stood. The son of a crack addict mother, he had never learned his father's name; his mother couldn't remember it. He'd gotten his nickname young in life, the result of the boys who hung around this very project making fun of him for always having an arm-full of books in tow whenever he walked past them. They were learning to sell dope and pull robberies, while he spent all his time with his nose in a book. *Most of those losers work for me now,* Bookie thought. *At least the ones who aren't dead or in jail.*

Growing up in a truly desperate kind of poverty, driven by his mother's addiction, Bookie had never known when he was going to eat again. The only constant in his early life was books. Canton's public library system gave him an outlet to immerse himself in other worlds, helping him ignore his crappy life. Never a great student, mostly because he was bored, he stopped going to school when he was 12; choosing instead to educate himself. His mother never noticed he'd stopped going to school.

Bookie's studies were deep and wide-ranging. By the time he was 16, he understood his stature and physical abnormalities were the result of his mother's drug use while pregnant, and the severe malnourishment he'd endured as a small child. After deep thought and contemplation, he decided he would never be hungry again. As Bookie looked around his world for a way to make money to eat, he couldn't help but notice the only people who had lots of money were drug dealers and preachers. While he had read the Bible, being a preacher didn't appeal to him.

Having made his decision on a career, Bookie looked for a way in the door. One of his many interests was accounting, and by 16 he'd read and understood enough to be a good bookkeeper. His break came one night as he sat on the dirty floor of an apartment in the Stark Towers. His Mother's crack dealer, another young ghetto rat named Jigsaw, had engaged him in conversation. Bookie had impressed Jigsaw with his obvious intellectualism and knowledge of handling money.

Jigsaw recalled a conversation he'd overheard several weeks earlier with the kingpin of Canton's dope trade, Big Mook. Big Mook had been complaining to Jigsaw's boss, Ray-Ray, that he had been forced to 'fire' his accountant, because he thought the guy was stealing from him. After busting a cap in his account's ass, Big Mook was faced with a mounting pile of cash he didn't know how to get rid of.

The day after his conversation with Bookie, Jigsaw mentioned Bookie to Ray-Ray, suggesting Big Mook might be able to use the scrawny kid. The next time Ray-Ray went to drop off cash, he mentioned the kid to Big Mook, who said, "Bring that little nigga to me. Anything is better than trying to keep track of all this cash myself." The next day Jigsaw tracked Bookie down at the library and took him to see Big Mook.

It took Big Mook less than five minutes to realize Bookie was special. He had never met anyone as intelligent, well-spoken or street smart in his entire life. He hired Bookie on the spot, making him part of his posse. Bookie went to work immediately, and within a week had all of Big Mook's cash safely distributed, and much of it smartly invested. Within two months, Big Mook realized Bookie was not only making him rich, but his money was no longer visible to the cops. From then on Big Mook began asking the now 17-year-old advice on all sorts of subjects, and found Bookie's counsel invaluable. With Bookie's help, Big Mook expanded his operation into Akron. Things had never been better for Big Mook's organization. Over the next 10 years, Bookie and Big Mook built an illicit business empire, until one of the Mexican cartels decided Big Mook had shorted them on a payment.

The night Bookie got the text that Big Mook had been beheaded in the restroom of one of the Akron bars he owned, he'd been working at his desk in the modest three-bedroom home he'd purchased. He immediately called Jigsaw, who over the years had grown into Bookie's right-hand man. They spent the night visiting every dealer working for Big Mook's organization to tell them Bookie was now in charge.

Two of the dealers had resisted Bookie's calm and reasoned assumption of leadership, each claiming the throne for themselves. Bookie had merely nodded at Jigsaw, who promptly shot them in the face. Each of these executions had happened in front of the dealers' posse, and the message was received loud and clear: Bookie's hustle was not to be messed with.

This was the last time any of the dealers saw Bookie in person. Still a heavy reader, he'd spent several years studying how to insulate himself from the criminal activity he hoped to someday direct. Now that he was in charge, he put his plan into action. Word spread quickly that Bookie's name was not to be mentioned to the cops. Ever. He had managed to fly under the radar of police for years; and now that he was King, anyone who snitched on him in any way would find themselves on the wrong end of a drive-by, or a sharpened toothbrush while they showered, if they happened to be in jail.

When the lights went out, his cell-phone stopped working and no cars would run, Bookie knew what was happening immediately. He received further confirmation a few minutes later when he watched a Southwest Airlines 737 slam into the shopping mall a half-mile from his home. His voracious appetite for reading had led him to several books about CME's and EMP's over the years, and his mind quickly analyzed the implications. He grabbed his HK VP9 compact pistol and a wad of cash, then walked to Jigsaw's house, just three blocks away in their upscale Hampton Park Estates neighborhood.

Bookie found Jigsaw in the open 4-car garage of his house, looking under the hood of his 2017 Maserati Ghibli. Bookie said, "Hello." Jigsaw didn't look up and said, "What up Book! My new slide won't start." Bookie walked up next to Jigsaw and said, in his very precise form of speech, "And it never will again. Did you note your cell phone does not work?" "Yeah, the power is out too. You know what's up?" Jigsaw replied. Bookie said, "I do indeed. We have been struck with an electromagnetic pulse of some sort." Jigsaw stood up and looked at Bookie, "We was hit with a what?"

Bookie gave Jigsaw a smile, a facial expression Jigsaw knew Bookie only used when he was pleased that he knew more than you did. "An electromagnetic pulse, known more commonly as an EMP," Bookie began, "is a pulse of energy. A strong EMP can disrupt the power grid and destroy communications and transportation assets. They can be man-made, through a nuclear detonation, or a naturally occurring phenomenon as the result of coronal mass ejections from the sun." When he finished speaking, Bookie stared at Jigsaw waiting for a reaction. Jigsaw said, "Well ain't that some shit. So how long until they fix all this stuff?" Bookie shook his head and said, "They never will Jig. This is permanent. We are living in the pre-industrial age again."

Bookie raised his eyebrows and nodded his head at Jigsaw, then asked, "Do you still have that 1964 Chevrolet Impala you restored several years ago?" As usual, it took Jigsaw a second to noodle through Bookie's words. He pointed to a vehicle under a blue car cover and said, "Yeah Book, it's right there." Bookie asked, "Can you please uncover it and start it?" Jigsaw said, "But I think you just said no cars would work now." Bookie replied, "Just do as I ask please. It's more complicated than you understand." *No shit,* Jigsaw thought. He always felt like a retard around Bookie.

Jigsaw got the car uncovered and it started right up. Bookie had him lock up his house, and told him to make sure he had a rifle in the car. Jigsaw went to his Ghibli and grabbed a tricked out AR15 from the back seat then got back in the Impala. Bookie got in the passenger side and said, "We need to go see every one of our dealers. We have a lot to do in a very short time." Jigsaw shrugged and said, "You say so Book. We out." Jigsaw chirped the tires as he pulled out of the driveway. He loved this car.

The rest of Bookie and Jigsaw's day, and most of their evening, was taken up by driving around giving orders to their dealers. Jigsaw wasn't sure why Bookie was giving the orders he was, but he trusted Bookie completely. Besides, what he saw as they drove around town was the craziest shit he'd ever experienced. Their car was the only one he saw moving, and the streets were full of people wondering around. It was kind of scary.

None of the dealers Bookie gave instructions to really understood why they were doing what they were doing; but they all knew the consequences of defying or betraying him in any way would include Jigsaw or one of his crew shooting them in the face several times. Everyone knew the story of one of Bookie's dealers who refused to stop using the 'N-word'. It was a serious pet-peeve of Bookie's, a fact which was made clear to everyone several times. He thought using a word invented by the White Man to keep his people in their place was an act of self-degradation, and he hated it.

One day when Bookie was surfing his dealers' social media pages, something he did regularly to look for violations of his operational security, he watched a video on one guy's page where the dealer was dropping the 'N-bomb' repeatedly. Within 12 hours, two of Jigsaw's crew were dragging the offender out of his car while it sat in front of a liquor store. They made the dealer get on his knees, looked around to make sure everyone was watching, then blew his brains all over the side of his own car. Bookie never had to admonish his employees to refrain from using the N-word again.

Bookie understood tribal and dictatorial psychology better than most college psych professors, and utilized an almost perfect balance of carrot (money and power) and stick (bullets to the face) to keep his people loyal. Everyone understood there were no middling punishments with Bookie; either you were family, or Jigsaw was busting your dome with his favorite 'Glock Fo-ty'. His years of work building his organization in this way were about to pay off.

Before nightfall, Bookie was able to make contact with 23 of his 35 Canton based dealers. He told them what happened, and gave them all identical orders. First, he wanted them to gather as many thugs and street soldiers as they could. Second, they were to take over and secure all the grocery stores, gun shops and hardware stores in their area. He stressed that he wanted all of these captured intact. Third, they were to stop any looting or burning of buildings they saw. Bookie told them to shoot whoever they had to in order to stop looting. He wanted all of the city's resources intact.

Lastly, Bookie ordered all of his people to kill every police officer, sheriff's deputy, state trooper, firefighter, and government official they found, and to hang them by their necks from the nearest light pole or traffic signal. He wanted every single person of governmental authority dead and put on display. Bookie wanted it made perfectly clear he now ran the city.

*

It has to be past midnight by now, Bookie thought. It was cold standing outside the Stark Towers, but he was listening intently to the sound of gunfire echoing across the city as thousands of 'His people' vented years of pent-up wrath on their 'oppressors'. Youngsters on bikes came and went in a constant flow, delivering messages of progress to Jigsaw, who even now remained at Bookie's side. He could see the bodies of three Housing Authority policemen and one female city police officer swinging lightly from the traffic signal outside the Towers in the soft night breeze. The female was naked, and Bookie was sure her last moments were less than pleasant. *Serves that white devil right,* he thought cynically. *Soon I will be the King of Canton. I will keep the people focused on rooting out the white devils while I consolidate power.* Bookie turned to Jigsaw and said, "I'm going inside to rest. Please awaken me should anything untoward occur." Jigsaw nodded his head and replied, "We got dis."

*

Four Canton police officers crouched in the shadows of an old building, watching the Hwy 62 on-ramp from the south side of the bridge on Cleveland Avenue, on the northeast edge of the city. They had a good view of the half-assed roadblock six thugs had set up to restrict movement out of the city. A uniformed police officer's body hung from the freeway exit traffic signal, lit up in the garish lights of the headlights of the three dirtbikes parked at the roadblock. The sight made all four officers sick, but their experience in the last several hours taught them they needed to exercise calm, explosive, and planned violence to get past this latest hurdle to their escape from town.

Their trek began hours before when they realized they were being hunted. When the lights went out, all four of them had been in briefing with three other officers and a sergeant, preparing to begin their eight-hour shift. It took them less than 15 minutes to figure out what happened. Their Sergeant gathered up several other officers who were in the station, and ordered them all to gear up to deploy as a Mobile Field Force (MFF). It took very little effort to convince the Sergeant to allow the officers to bring their patrol rifles slung on their backs for the deployment, a decision that saved some of their lives.

Unable to find any working vehicles, and with the radio system not functioning, the MFF walked to the corner of Tuscarawas Street and Walnut Avenue in the downtown area, to stage. Less than 10 minutes after they arrived, the group of 13 officers came under sniper fire. As the fire intensified, the Sergeant stood up to direct some officers to begin a bounding-overwatch to retreat. He was promptly struck in the head and chest by rifle fire and went down hard. Five of the officers panicked and ran west. They didn't make it across the street before being gunned down.

The remaining officers decided it was time to get out of Dodge, and determined they would evade northeast. Miles Johnson, the senior officer present and still alive, decided he was going to head for the Alliance range. A former Marine and dedicated training junkie, he trained there all the time, and knew they had resources and people most departments didn't. If anyone could survive this event, he reasoned, it would be Kyle and the guys at the range.

Johnson led the surviving officers on a four-hour odyssey which saw the group fight its way on foot for over three miles to reach this position. At one point, they found themselves taking cover in a hardware store that sold Carhart clothing, and they all changed out of their uniforms into heavy work clothes, concealing their armor and other gear as best they could. They figured the clothing would keep them warmer, and serve to camouflage the fact they were cops. By the time they made it to the intersection of Hwy 62 and Cleveland Ave, only four of the original 13 officers who left the station to meet the crisis remained standing.

As the four surviving officers watched the roadblock, one of the criminals sitting atop a dirtbike pointed south on Cleveland Avenue yelled something at his homies. The officers had been observing this roadblock for about 10 minutes, and had seen several black families on foot pass though unmolested. As Miles looked to the south, he could see a white guy and young girl approaching the roadblock in the dim glow of the dirtbike headlights. Both were

132

wearing backpacks and the man was carrying a shotgun. Judging from the body language he was seeing from the thugs at the roadblock, this family would not pass by so easily.

Thinking quickly, he told the rest of his team, "Ok, here's our chance. When these dirtbags start talking to this guy, we attack. Jones and Miller," Johnson pointed to two of the cops with him, "you guys work around to our left and hit them from the flank. Wait to engage until I do. None of these assholes walk away from here, understand?" All of them glanced at the officer's body swinging on the traffic pole and nodded.

Jones and Miller took off at a quiet run, and disappeared around the back of the building where the team was positioned. As Johnson was waiting for them to get in position, he heard one of the scumbags at the roadblock yell out to the approaching man, "Well, what do we have here? Looks like a cracker brought us some honey." The guy stopped and squinted in an attempt to see past the headlights, then brought his shotgun to his shoulder as he stepped in front of the girl.

Having a bad feeling about what was about to happen to the man and little girl, Johnson brought his department issued Colt 6920 to his shoulder and lined up the Aimpoint's dot on the chest of the criminal farthest away from him, on the east side of the roadblock. He moved the selector to Fire and launched four rounds across the 50-yard gap separating him from his target. Johnson watched his target fall off the dirtbike and shifted to his left, looking for another target, as the officer next to him, Ermin Lisowski, started firing his Colt.

High velocity rifle rounds snapped in both directions as the degenerates at the roadblock zeroed in on Johnson's muzzle flashes. After Johnson and his partner put down three subjects, the gunfight turned into a pop-goes-the-weasel affair, when the remaining three scum took cover behind the vehicles used in the roadblock. Then the flanking officers got in the fight. Gunfire erupted from Johnson's left, and within 20 seconds all the return fire from the roadblock stopped.

Johnson heard Jones' voice, "Three suspects down behind the cars. I think it's clear." Johnson yelled in reply, "Stay there and let them bleed for a while." Looking to the south again, Johnson couldn't see the man and girl anymore. They must have smartened up and split when the shooting started. Johnson's watch didn't work, but when he thought about 10 minutes had gone by he yelled, "Jones, you guys move up and check them. We'll cover." Jones yelled back, "OK. Moving."

Jones and Miller found five dead bodies and one thug bleeding badly from his abdomen. The kid was writhing in pain and begged for help. Miller stood over him and looked down into a face contorted with pain and fear. Miller stared at him for a minute, then looked off into the dark night. Miller glanced up at the mutilated body of the police officer swinging from the traffic light, which he now recognized as Reggie Bershaw, a black kid who'd been a cop less than a year.

He remembered the party at the FOP lodge the day Reggie was sworn in. Reggie's dad, a long time Youngstown cop, had been so proud of his strong son, tearing up and joking about his 'allergies' when he stood to toast his son's new commitment to serving. Miller wanted to cry at the injustice of it all, but knew he had to harden up. The last several hours had changed Miller, probably permanently. He wiped some tears from his cheeks and told himself, *if they want it this way, so be it.*

Miller didn't say anything to the wounded piece of garbage; he just pulled his Glock from his duty holster and put a .40 caliber Gold Dot through the kid's nose. None of the other officers said a word. Miller holstered his pistol and put it out of his mind. This was no longer police work. This was war.

Johnson gathered his guys together at the roadblock and made them all reload their rifles. Miller and Lisowski were out of rifle ammo, and Johnson and Jones were down to their last full magazines. They searched the weapons and ammo left by the vermin they had just burned down, and found four Colt 6920's and seven full AR magazines. All of them were marked 'Canton Police Department'. They also recovered four Canton PD issued Glock 22's and 12 Glock magazines.

Johnson told the guys to mount up on the dirtbikes. Miller, being the smallest guy in the group, had to ride behind Jones on one of the bikes. Within minutes they were roaring east on Hwy 62, headed for Alliance, where they hoped to find some semblance of civilization remained so they could regroup. They were all determined to come back. There was a lot of killing they needed to do.

Chapter 17

FOB Card
Alliance, OH

What the hell is wrong with our mattress? I feel like I got hit by a truck, was Mark's first semi-conscious thought of the day. It took him a moment to remember where he was and why he hurt so badly. Cement floors make the worst box springs. When he opened his eyes, he slowly focused on a pair of Salomon boots in the dim light. A Glock coffee cup appeared in his vision, followed by a boot lightly kicking him in the thigh. Mark groaned, sat up and grabbed the coffee.

Kyle laughed softly and said, "I've been up for a while bro. I figured you should get your lazy ass out of bed before you slept the day away. It's got to be at least 0430." Mark groaned and said, "Wow, two hours of sleep, I must be on vacation." Kyle chuckled and said, "I'm getting the leadership up. Meet in the TOC in 10 minutes." Mark nodded and tried to get his legs to move.

Mark pulled his Surefire Minimus headlamp around his neck and turned it on, casting the room full of sleeping bodies in a red glow. He took the time to pray for wisdom and to thank God he and Kasey had a place to sleep this night, then found his travel bathroom kit in the top of his ruck. He stood up and weaved his way through the sleeping bodies to get out of the classroom. When Mark stepped outside he just about had a heart attack. It had to be close to zero degrees outside and he was in his wicking t-shirt and Arcteryx combat pants, not exactly great cold weather gear. He ran to the bathroom building and slipped into the heated men's restroom.

As Mark was brushing his teeth Bones and Chief Stone came into the bathroom. Bones was bitching up a storm about how early and cold it was, and the Chief was egging him on, saying things like, "I know right." and "Yeah, this is bullshit," with a sly grin. Mark smiled at the Chief, then finished brushing and said, "We need to find some shower trailers somewhere." Chief Stone replied, "I think there are some at the Walton Oil Company yard. They went bankrupt last year and all their field worker support gear is still there." Mark said, "Well, that goes to the top of the list." Chief Stone laughed and locked himself in a bathroom stall. Mark ran back to the classroom and grabbed his Arcteryx WX jacket then walked to the TOC. On the way there he noticed three random dirtbikes parked on the grass near one of the breaching walls used for training, and a few vehicles that weren't there the night before, in the parking lot. *Someone made it in last night. I hope they're assaulters,* Mark thought.

The TOC / team room tent heater was cranking. Mark immediately shed his jacket and said, "Holy crap it's hotter than Hades up in here." The detective who was working on the intel board and watching the radio overnight said, "Don't judge me Mark. I'm from Florida, I get cold." Mark laughed and grabbed a chair as the command staff started trickling in. Mark noticed the team room side of the tent was empty, and when Kyle sat down next to him asked, "Where are the single guys sleeping? I figured they would be in here." Kyle replied, "There was too much light from the TOC. They all moved over to the city tent." "Good call," Mark said. "It's going to get loud in here when we all start yelling at each other." Kyle laughed and replied, "If everyone would just do what I say, we could avoid all the leader on leader violence." Mark grinned.

They heard a HMWWV pull in the gate, and within one minute David walked into the TOC. "Morning Brothers!" David said, in way too chipper a tone. Bones grumbled, "Spoken like someone who slept in a real bed." David laughed and said, "Don't be hatin'. It was very nice. We had the gas fireplace cranked up and it was toasty warm. There was even hot water to take a shower." Everyone groaned and several people threw things at him. David laughed and found a cup of coffee and a chair. Mark got up and walked to the boards, and wrote 'gas service still on?' It was one more thing to check.

By the time the Mayor walked into the TOC, everyone else was in a seat and ready to work. Mark recognized most of the people present, but several were strangers. Chief Stone kicked the session off by having everyone stand up and introduce themselves, mainly for the benefit of letting the Black Knight leaders know who everyone was. The city was represented by Mayor Barnhart, who was obviously chairing the meeting, Chief Stone, the Alliance Fire Chief, the Director of Water and Power, the Manager of the water treatment facility, the Director of the public works department, and the Manager of the city maintenance yard, Jimmy. City Prosecutor Kathy Jones was also present, sitting next to her boyfriend Kyle, resting her head on his shoulder and nursing a cup of coffee.

The Fire Chief from Lexington Township, the small jurisdiction that butted up against Alliance, was also present. Two Alliance firefighters, a Battalion Chief and a Captain, had made it to the range at some point, and were sitting in the planning session.

Alliance EMS was represented by one of their Paramedic Supervisors, who so far was the only EMS asset any of them had seen since the pulse. She had come in on foot at some point last night. After discussing it with Kyle, Chief Stone had asked that Dylan Nowak be woken up to attend as well. Stone thought his deep knowledge of the city and its criminal element would help shape the group's planning, and Kyle told the Chief he would be appointing Nowak as the Squadron's Chief of Intelligence as soon as Dylan was cleared to work by Doc Zimmerman. The Black Knight Squadron command group, Kyle, Mark, David, and Bones, and the new supply manager Lydia, rounded out the meeting's 17 attendees.

The Mayor was normally a very outgoing and funny guy. Given the gravity of the situation the previous day, a lot of that had been missing from his interactions with everyone. It was back in full force this morning. "Alright folks, let's get started!" the Mayor said after the introductions were complete. "Thank you to everyone for getting up so early," he paused as everyone booed. "Seriously though, I cannot tell you how proud and thankful I am for each one of you. We are facing a crisis of unparalleled proportion in any of our lifetimes, and I intend to keep our little part of the world as safe and healthy as is humanly possible."

Everyone nodded as the Mayor continued, "We managed to get through day one of this event, but it was a rough, seat of the pants affair. We lost one police officer and only the Lord knows how many of the other 22,000 souls in our city. If we want to have any measure of success in keeping this place together we have to have a master plan; at least one laid out in general terms. The miracles Kyle and the guys pulled off yesterday are simply not sustainable, and that's just the security situation. We have many more areas to think about and plan for to avoid the host of other major problems that are coming our way; like water, food, shelter, heat, fuel, and on and on." The Mayor paused for a minute then continued, "Before we start planning in earnest, I think we need to call on the Lord's help and providence." The Mayor then led the group in a heartfelt prayer to God for wisdom, guidance, strength, and perseverance.

Mayor Barnhart then got down to business while David and Mark stood up to transcribe information on the whiteboards. Everyone in the room was also keeping paper notes, mostly to track the work they were assigned. They started out by listing all of the city departments and how many staff members they had on site.

The Police Department was obviously the largest so far, with almost 90 trained people on hand. Apparently cops from close-by jurisdictions had been trickling in all night, having been chased out of their own cities and townships; or simply deciding Alliance was the best-equipped place within traveling distance to weather the storm.

The Mayor said, "We've been discussing the issue of the police department, and this event is obviously well beyond what a traditional police organization can effectively respond to. We aren't really clear on my powers as Mayor in an emergency; the law puts most of the authority in the hands of the governor. But with no way to contact the State government, or even the county sheriff, the City Attorney," he gestured towards Kathy, "has told me I have the authority to do what I think is best, so long as it's constitutional."

The Mayor paused and looked at Chief Stone, then continued, "I've asked the Chief, given the severity of the security situation and unique nature of the emergency, to enlist the Unorganized Militia, as described in the Ohio Revised Code, and I've given him the authority to re-organize the police department in whatever way he thinks best, to manage the situation." The group responded with stone cold silence. Even Kyle was surprised.

Chief Stone stood up and said, "Given the war-like state that exists in the city, and presumably the entire State and Country, I am appointing the Black Knight Squadron, with Kyle as its commander, as the City's Militia for defensive and offensive operations, under my civil oversight." Several eyebrows lifted at that one, including

Mark and David's. Mark wasn't aware the Chief even knew what the Black Knight Squadron was; and this was a ballsy move by the Mayor and Chief. Mark agreed it was the right thing to do, but he presumed it would be several weeks before the city government realized it.

Chief Stone continued, "This is a time when we will need a functionally military organization. Police tactics and organization simply won't cut it. Kyle and his team are already doing the work, and have the expertise to do what needs done. State law is silent on the subject of who can activate the Unorganized Militia if the Governor is incommunicado, but Ron (the Mayor) has decided that, given the unique circumstance and our inability to contact the State government, he has the authority necessary. The City Attorney agrees." Kathy nodded her head.

Stone continued, "The Black Knight Squadron will take command of the Unorganized Militia, and it will report to the proper civilian authority. Me." Stone paused for a second then continued, "Until further notice, the police department will consist only of myself and detectives Becker and Wright. All other personnel and assets are assigned to the Squadron effective immediately." Even Kyle was stunned into silence, and just nodded his head in acknowledgement of the order.

Nowak, sitting the back of the room said, "Damn, Kyle!" in an impersonation of a popular Internet video meme. Several people just shook their heads, but smiled. "Nowak must be feeling better," Kyle quipped dryly. "Watch that white board or he'll have his signature drawn on it." Everyone laughed at that one; Nowak was known for drawing a male appendage on any whiteboard he chanced upon.

"Alright, any questions on that? If not let's move on," Ron said as the laughter died down. The Water and Power folks reported a lot of help available, with 23 people on hand, over 80% of their normal workforce. The rest of the departments reported between two and five personnel available. The Mayor's first directive was for each department head to work on finding their employees and convincing them to come to work. Having trained people, intimately familiar with the city's systems, would be crucial to keeping things going.

For the next hour, the group wrestled with big picture priorities, such as shelter and heat for the citizens of Alliance, water supply, gathering food and distributing it, transportation, fuel for vehicles and generators, communicating with the citizenry, and the security / civil unrest situation. Most of the issues required investigation by the departments before clear plans could be made, but the group was able to make some decisions. First, as many supplies as possible had to be gathered. With the area already in the troughs of what promised to be a cold winter, securing as much food, medicine and fuel as possible was deemed essential.

Mark spoke up for the first time, "I think we need a department responsible for identifying, gathering, and distributing supplies. There is simply too much out there that we need to secure quickly to do it by the seat of our pants. Something critical is going to get missed." Ron nodded and said, "That's a great point. Some of this stuff, like the trainload of containers we need to sort through, are going to need a lot of bodies, and a way to move and store it." Kyle interjected, "We have the military semi tractors, and I'm sure there are hundreds of CONEX semi-trailers at the train yard in town. We will need to find a way to unload CONEX boxes from the train-cars so we can get that train unloaded and the boxes moved someplace for sorting." Everyone was nodding. It would be a huge undertaking, but really was nothing more than an exercise in scale.

Kyle continued, "I think Chris Mason would be perfect for directing the on-the-ground salvage work. He has a ton of experience in heavy equipment and is a good leader. His partner Ed used to work in a container yard before he went into the Marine Coprs, so he knows how to move the CONEX's. We just need an organizer to coordinate all the moving parts and track the supplies." The room was silent for a moment, until Lydia spoke from the back of the group in a timid voice, "I can manage the supply situation until you can find someone qualified."

Kyle began to speak but paused, thinking about how little they knew about Lydia's abilities. She had done a good job so far in organizing the small amount of supplies at the range, but this was a monumental job for the steel mill supply clerk turned Deputy Sheriff. Failure in that position would endanger the entire community. The Mayor made the decision for him, "Thank you Lydia. You're hired. Coordinate with the Black Knight Squadron for security. Alright everyone, the sun will be up in a few minutes, let's get to work."

*

After everyone else left the tent the Black Knight leadership group, which now included Nowak, stood in the TOC to flesh out the day's missions. David said, "Well, that was interesting." Kyle shook his head and said, "I always wanted to be an officer... said no one ever." Mark grinned and said, "Well, I will be calling you 'Major Payne' constantly." Kyle replied, "Shut up Private." Everyone laughed at that.

Kyle got everyone back on track, "Alright, we had a bunch of hitters come in overnight. I spoke to Miles Johnson from Canton PD; he and Ermin Lisowski escaped from Canton with a couple of other officers." Everyone nodded; grateful Miles and Ermin had made it out. Both of them were good friends and proven assaulters. "It must be bad in Canton if they had to fight their way out," Mark said. Kyle replied, "From what Miles described to me it sounds like someone in the ghetto figured out what was going on pretty early. No one was rioting or looting. Instead everyone was hunting cops and firefighters and lynching them. Miles told me he counted over 30 dead cops and five dead firefighters; all of them were killed and left hanging from traffic signals. They also noticed hood rats were guarding all of the grocery stores and gas stations, like they were trying to protect the resources. That's too organized and consistent to be anything other than a centralized plan."

Nowak said, "Before the pulse I was working on developing information on a new criminal organization based in Canton. Information was pretty thin, which in itself is an indication of a high level of organization. Addicts like to talk, but someone was putting the fear of God into my snitches." Dylan paused to think then continued, "Based on some of the people involved, I'd say whoever is in charge took over Big Mook's organization after the Mexican's relieved him of his dome. Whoever is capable of that kind of organizational discipline could definitely put together and enforce the kind of plan you're talking about." Bones nodded; he'd been working a case on Big Mook when he was killed, but was having a

142

hard time tracking the money. Once Mook was dead, what little traces of his financial empire existed had vaporized.

"The only real info I've been able to get," Nowak continued, "is that the group is known as the 'Bookie Organization'. I've run the name though every database in the state, and I've only gotten one hit, but it can't be the right guy. It was listed as a nickname for some disabled kid in Canton." Kyle interjected, "Well, whoever is running it, they seem to be squared away. I think they will become a major threat pretty quickly." Mark agreed, "If they organized a genocide against public services that quick, it sounds like they are following the ISIL model; eliminate the local government and replace them with your own people. They are going to be a problem we need to deal with soon." Everyone agreed.

The group shifted focus to integrating the 50+ new cops and civilians who had shown up at the range overnight and wanted to join the Squadron. Some of them had brought their families, and Kyle was getting worried about their capacity to house so many people. In addition to all these folks, three National Guard Troopers had shown up last night as well. They reported that the Armory was locked up tight, and they knew their commanding officer was out of town on training. All three of them were 91S's, Striker Systems Maintainers, assigned to care for the National Guard Armored Calvary Company's tactical vehicles, which were stored at the Ravenna Reserve Base about 20 miles away. "Those guys will be helpful." David said. Mark replied, "Yes they will. I was thinking we needed to check out Ravenna anyway; there will be a lot of useful equipment there." It went on the list of scouting missions.

David said, "Ok. So how are we going to organize the Squadron? The teams as they sit now are staffed with folks who have basically the same level of training, or at least common SOP's everyone is trained on. Do we break the teams up and disperse the talent to fill leadership roles, or do we build more teams of like-qualified people?" Mark piped up, "I think splitting the current teams up would be a bad idea. We need combat effectiveness now; we don't have the time for our guys to train all these new people. We have to be running missions within an hour."

Kyle nodded his agreement and Bones said, "Can we just form more teams? Having six to eight guys on a team seemed to work. That would let us get more missions done at the same time."

Mark replied, "That's true, but we will run ourselves ragged keeping track of that many teams, and our transportation is pretty limited. What about this," Mark paused for a second then continued, "Since we are a 'squadron', in name anyway, let's stand up three "Troops", and assign each of the teams to a Troop. A Troop commander should be able to handle three or four teams of up to 10 guys each. That structure should be able to handle at least 160 assaulters. We have 90 or 91 guys now, if you include us."

Kyle said, "That would work. Keep in mind we will need support people as well; guards for the FOB and whatever off-site locations the city sets up, supply people, food service, equipment maintenance, etc. We should probably stand up four Troops, and make the fourth the Support Troop." David nodded and said, "We will also need some staff people. Intel," he pointed at Nowak, "planning and so forth."

Kyle was nodding and said, "Alright. David, you're my operations and planning officer, let's just call it S3 (military speak for OPS Officer) for my sanity. Nowak, you're the Intel guy, so you're the S2. Bones, you're my XO (Executive Officer); you will handle admin, keeping the roster up to date, personnel issues, that kind of stuff. You'll also be a task force commander when we need it. Mark, you will be the Deputy Squadron Commander, my number two," Kyle grinned again, while Mark just sighed and rolled his eyes, "and the other Task Force commander when we need it."

David said, "OK. Who do we want as our Troop Commanders? Obviously, Manny is a no brainer." Everyone nodded to that and David continued, "Mark, Dan has worked for you for a long time on the SWAT team, would he be a good Troop commander?" Mark replied, "Absolutely. He was the next name on my list. What are you guys thinking for the third, Ben or Troy? I think Troy has the slight edge in tactical ability, and Ben has it in team leadership experience and local knowledge." Kyle said, "Ben is our Master Breacher. Tying him up with that much responsibility might screw us at some point. I'd like to keep him in a TL slot." "Roger that, Troy it is." David said. Kyle nodded and said, "I'll explain it to Ben. He will understand."

Kyle left the TOC to go check in with Chief Stone while Mark went to go wake up Manny, Dan, and Troy. Bones, and David built new teams from the late arrivals and assigned them to the

144

Troops. Foxtrot team had done a good job of documenting who had arrived overnight, where they were from, and what their experience level was. This information was invaluable as a starting point for David and Bones in assigning guys, and a few women, to teams.

They assigned Manny to lead 1st Troop and gave him Alpha and Bravo teams, with a team of new arrivals they designated as the new Charlie team. Manny's callsign would be 'Knight One'. Next, they tasked Troy with leading 2nd Troop (callsign Knight Two) and assigned the old Charlie and Delta teams to him, renamed Alpha and Bravo, along with a team of seven SWAT cops from other jurisdictions who had straggled in overnight. Then they assigned Dan to command 3rd Troop, calling him 'Knight Three'; giving him the old Echo team, renamed Alpha, and two new teams of recently arrived guys. Without waiting to talk to Kyle, they assigned command of 4th Troop, the support group, to Sgt. Wiggins of Foxtrot Team, and called him 'Knight Four'. He had done an absolutely phenomenal job in organizing his guys and accomplishing his mission, and being the admin Sergeant for the PD, he knew everyone in the city. He was a good fit for that slot. They loosely organized the remaining available manpower into six-man teams and assigned them to 4th Troop, trusting Wiggins to sort them out.

By the time Mark returned with the newly minted Troop commanders, each of them appearing to be half asleep, Bones had a neatly handwritten roster for each of them. Mark got on the radio and put the arm out for Sgt. Wiggins, who appeared in the TOC momentarily. Mark briefed the Troop commanders on the new organization, all of whom took it in stride. When Mark finished, Manny said, "Well, I didn't have anything better on my agenda today anyway."

It was a little after 0630 when the Troop commanders left the TOC to find all of their guys and start getting things ready to receive missions. The sun was peeking over the horizon, casting a shadowed glow against the overcast sky. It looked like snow was coming, but nobody in the TOC could remember what the weather forecast had said about today before the lights went out. *I guess we will have to dress for the worst and hope for the best,* Mark thought. It was going to be a long and cold second day of the apocalypse.

145

Chapter 18

Walmart
Alliance, OH

When Troy's armored HMWWV made the turn off of State Street into the western entrance of the Walmart parking lot, he saw big clouds of smoke coming from the back of the store, and peed himself a little. He thought the building and supplies they had worked so hard to secure the night before were on fire. He yelled at the driver to haul ass behind the store. Troy's butthole unpuckered when they turned the corner and saw a long line of smokers, gas grill BBQs, and turkey deep fryers running full blast in the chill morning light.

As Troy's HMWWV came to a stop, he bailed out and walked directly to a guy in an employee vest holding an AR-15 rifle, obviously pulling security. "Good morning!" Troy said. The employee replied, "Thank God you guys are back. I was sure the smell of all this food cooking would draw the crowds." As Troy was formulating a response, Harold, the Walmart manager, walked up and said hello. Troy said, "Good morning Harold. What's up with all the cooking?"

Harold smiled and said, "Well, with the power out all the meats won't last long. I figured it was best to smoke or dehydrate everything we could, and cook the rest. We are starting with the fresh meat, and should have that all done by about lunchtime. Then we will start in on the frozen stuff that has already defrosted." Troy was impressed with the initiative and said so. Harold just blushed and said, "I couldn't let it go to waste. We have the means and fuel to cook it right now, so why not?" Troy said, "Hell yeah! Listen, we will be in the area all day, the Mayor wants to set you up as the center of a safe zone." Harold nodded and said, "That makes sense. With us, Lowes, the nursery and the big greenhouse produce farm behind us, it's a perfect spot." Troy asked, "Um, did you say there is

146

a greenhouse farm here?" Harold said, "Yeah, you didn't know? Come on, I'll show you."

Harold led Troy to the southwest edge of the lot and pointed south. Beyond the trees lining the Walmart property, Troy could see over 100 large transparent greenhouses. "Holy crap!" Troy whispered. Harold said, "Sorry, I thought you knew that was there. It's called Greenbrier Farms. We buy most of our out of season produce from them; it's local and much cheaper than importing from South America. I got a huge bonus last year for striking a deal with them. I know the manager, Anthony Barton, really well. I know the Mayor knows him too." "Holy crap." Was all Troy could say. This was an amazing resource. Troy snapped out of it and said, "Thank you Sir. We will secure the farm as well. I'll stay in touch today." The men shook hands and Troy walked back to his vehicle.

Troy had brought all of 2nd Troop to Walmart with orders to set up another FOB there. The store was situated perfectly to secure not only Walmart, but to use as a base of operations to secure the Lowes, Goodwill, Stapes store, Holiday Inn (the hotel where all of the visiting CQB students had rooms), and Organic Nursery on the other side of State Street; and the Tractor Supply, indoor shopping mall, and 200 room hotel just to the east on the Walmart side of the street. His briefing hadn't included the Greenbrier Farm property, but it was obviously now on his list. City leadership's plan was the entire area, once secured, would become the new 'center' of town. It was a lot of area to lock down and search with just the 26 assaulters of 2nd Troop, but Troy was confident they could have it done by nightfall. His orders were to have the area ready to begin distributing food and supplies to the city's citizens by daybreak the next day. He was told more manpower would be on the way to assist with the logistics tasks as soon as possible, but he was the main effort for the security situation.

Troy gathered his three team leaders and started giving orders. Alpha team was directed to search and secure the nursery and Goodwill stores, then set up a blocking position on State Street to the west. They brought the Brickyard's backhoe with them: after it was done burying the dead from last night, it would use its front end equipped with forks to begin moving stalled vehicles to set up an ECP on the west side. Bravo team was ordered to search and secure

Lowes, and to set a small security detachment on the roof of the building when done, then search and secure the office supply store and Starbucks coffee shop that shared a parking lot with the big box hardware store. Once those tasks were complete, they were to set up a blocking position to the east, to be built into an ECP once the west side was done.

Charlie team had the biggest task. Troy left the team's M113 on the east side of the Walmart lot with a driver, machinegunner and two assaulters, to act as QRF. The rest of the team was going to clear and secure the tractor supply, the mall and the hotel. It was a big job for six assaulters. He gave his team leaders a few minutes to get everyone set to move, then addressed the entire Troop. "Stay frosty 2nd Troop. We're all we got." They responded with a robust, "We're all we need!"

About 20 minutes later Troy was supervising as the backhoe was digging a trench for the mass grave of the marauders who died in the Walmart fight last night. He figured they would be fine laid to rest together. The real work would be digging the individual graves for their victims. Troy thought they deserved the respect of individual graves, despite the extra work. His train of thought was interrupted by the radio, "Knight Two, Knight Two-Alpha-One. We found the owner of the Organic Nursery sleeping inside the store. He is telling me he wants nothing to do with us." Troy sighed and replied, "Knight Two copies. I'm on my way."

Troy jogged north through the parking lot, down the berm, and across State Street. When he got to the front doors of the nursery, he found one of the Alpha team assaulters holding the door open, waiting for him. He said, "Thanks," and slowed to a walk. When he got inside, taking note of the 'Sanders 2016' sticker on the front door glass, Troy followed the sound of someone yelling until he found the Alpha team leader, Ben, being berated by an old skinny white guy wearing a green 'Earth Day 2001' t-shirt and sporting a slate-gray bonytail.

Ben was patiently listening to the guy vent about how he wasn't letting Trump's 'brownshirts' come seize his property just because the power was out. "The whole thing is a made-up emergency designed to let Trump complete his establishment of a dictatorship!" the man concluded. He folded his arms with a nod of his head and finally shut up. Ben said, "Are you done sir?" The guy looked like he was going to explode again when Troy stepped up to him and put out his hand and said, "Hello Sir. My name is Troy. What's your name?" Troy's conversational tone, the smile on his face and the firm handshake caught the man off-guard, and he gruffly replied, "Um, Bernard Getty." Troy quickly responded, "It's good to meet you Mr. Getty. I appreciate your patience with us." Getty was still trying to catch up with the verbal judo Troy was throwing down on him.

Troy spent the next few minutes explaining the situation to Getty, emphasizing the emergency nature of the event and its likely permanence. He told Mr. Getty about the raiders who'd killed about 30 people last night across the street from him, and how Troy and his team had helped stop them. Troy also told Bernard that he and his team were not from the federal government, but were representing the duly elected government of the City. Troy concluded with, "We are only here, Mr. Getty, to check on you and put you in touch with the Mayor; I think he wants to draw on your expertise to help everyone start gardens. This is going to be a long crisis and the people will need your help. You are also in the middle of an area we are setting up as a safe zone."

Troy had carefully chosen his words to ensure maximum effect, and the now beaming smile on Mr. Getty's face showed the wisdom of that tack. Troy knew the man's knowledge of small-scale farming were going to be invaluable to the community as the crisis continued. He could tell his appeal to Bernard's talent and ability to help others had struck him where it counted: Bernard's ego and his sense of duty to help others in need. Mr. Getty stood a little straighter, stuck out his hand for a shake, and said, "Troy, please thank the Mayor for me. I am more than happy to help however I can."

Troy smiled back and said, "Thank you Mr. Getty. I'm sure Mayor Barnhart will be by soon to get your input on planning. In the meantime, my men and I will be working in the area today. You may see us out on State Street; we are setting up a roadblock to keep men like those who attacked Walmart last night out of the area. If you need anything at all, please just contact one of them and we will get you squared away." Mr. Getty said, "Thank you son."

When they got outside Ben turned to Troy, grinned and said, "That was some ninja level verbal judo brother. Very nice." Troy laughed and said, "Easy day. He is someone we will need on our side when we run out of Vienna Sausages and Doritos." Ben's chuckle was interrupted by the sound of three slow gunshots to the east. Ben said, "One's a backfire, three's gunplay." Both started walking that way when they heard the belt fed on the M113 open up. "Venton must have seen something if he's shooting back," Ben said, as they both started running towards the gunfire.

They heard Venton get on the radio and say, "Two-Charlie-Two, some dong is shooting at the M113, from north of my pos. He's hiding inside the Starbucks." As they listened to Venton on the radio they could hear him continuing to work the M240, suppressing the shooter and pinning him in place. Troy keyed the radio as he and Ben changed direction to come up on the west side of the coffee shop, and said, "Knight Two copies. Fix him there while we get set. I'll call you to lift fire when we are ready." Venton replied, "Roger," in between bursts.

It took Troy and Ben less than a minute to run to the coffee shop, where they took cover behind a dead vehicle on the west side of the building. They gathered themselves, and took a second to catch their breath as Venton continued to send streams of 7.62 justice over the shop's patio and into the store. Venton saw Ben and Troy behind the Ford Taurus to the left of the shop, and keyed his PTT, "Knight Two I've got you. Let me know when you're ready to move." Troy looked at Ben, who gave him a muzzle release, then transmitted, "Shift fire. Assaulting through."

As Troy and Ben sprinted the 15 yards to the west door of the coffee shop, Venton shifted the M240 to the right on its mount and ceased firing. Making it to the already broken-out glass door first, Troy cleared the part of the store's interior he could see from the outside of the opening. As he finished that scan, Ben came to a stop on the right side of the door next to the handle. Ben gave another muzzle release and Troy yanked the door open. Ben launched through the opening, went left, and stumbled over someone crouched next to the wall by the door, sending him on a short but ungraceful flight to the ground. With his BCM 14.5" carbine in his hands, Ben didn't have time to let go of the gun, and broke his fall with his face.

The guy Ben tripped over was just as stunned. He had been crouched next to the exit door, waiting for the terrifying stream of machinegun fire to stop so he could make a run for it, and was taken completely by surprise when the dude in the Navy Seal getup had barreled him over. When Ben hit him, the guy dropped his Mosin-Nagant 7.62X54 bolt action rifle as he fell over on his butt. Panicked, the man kicked his legs and clawed for the Beretta 92 in an Uncle Mike's holster on his belt.

Ben recovered his senses quickly and looked over his left shoulder at the man. Seeing the guy was flopping around Ben launched himself at him, landing sideways on the man's chest and shoulders, with his head over the guy's right shoulder. He felt the air 'ooph' out of the man's chest, and pinned the guy's right arm against the ground. Ben grunted, "Stop resisting or I'll kill you." The man went limp. Ben found the guy's Beretta in the holster and took it out, skidding it out of reach, then untangled his own slung carbine and rolled the man over. Ben quickly grabbed his Peerless steel handcuffs out of the pouch on his plate carrier and handcuffed the guy. It wasn't pretty but it would do for now.

Once he was handcuffed, the man started writhing around on the ground, trying to get out from under Ben's weight. Troy stepped over to the two-man dogpile after clearing the rest of the room and put his Danner boot on the dude's head, pinning it to the deck. Troy said, "Stop moving." The man got still again. Ben finished searching the guy, finding a KA-BAR knife in a sheath on his belt and a Khar PM9 pistol in an ankle holster on his left ankle. Ben ditched the weapons out of reach then asked the man, "Why are you shooting at us?" The guy didn't say anything for a second and Ben asked him again, "Dude! Why did you shoot at us?"

The man replied, "I thought you was raiders. I walked up here before sunup. I was gonna get some supplies from Lowes, but that APC pulled up across the street," he gestured with his head to the south, "before I could get there. I saw ya'll weren't in a standard uniform and figured ya stole that M113 and was raidin'. Figured I'd whittle ya'll down some before I ran away." Ben turned the guy over, sat him up and asked him, "What's your name." The guy replied, "Hank Mentor."

Seeing Hank was a man in his mid-50's dressed in woodland pattern BDU's, wearing an old school surplus LBE and sporting a giant beard, Ben asked him, "You a prepper Hank?" Hank looked down and to the left and mumbled, "I ain't tellin' you that." Ben smiled and said, "You just did Hank. You've been reading too many books. We are the police department, well, we used to be anyway, and we are here to secure the area to distribute aid. You could've hurt someone with that Russian peasant rifle Hank. That was dumb." Ben stood Hank up and brushed him off.

Two Charlie team assaulters ran up to the door and called out, "Blue coming in!" Troy said, "Come in." When they stepped in Troy motioned for them to come with him, and they finished clearing the building. Ben pushed the PTT on his vest and said, "Two-Charlie-two, two-Alpha-one. We are secure. One subject in custody." Venton replied, "Roger." Ben turned back to Hank and asked him, "Where do you live Hank?" Hank replied, "Down the road a bit." Ben got annoyed, "Hank, we aren't going to come steal your stuff. I'm trying to figure out what to do with you." Hank cleared his throat and shifted his weight, then replied, "I have some property west of here on Reeder Avenue, off Highway 173."

Ben knew he'd seen the guy before, and now it clicked. Hank was indeed a prepper. About three years ago, Ben traffic stopped Hank for some minor equipment violation, and remembered it because he had seen a bunch of Wise food buckets in the bed of Hank's truck. He hadn't said anything about it at the time, but now it was useful information. Ben asked Hank, "What were you looking for at Lowes?" Hank replied honestly, figuring there was no use lying now, "I need a hydraulic log splitter. I ain't got nearly enough wood put up for winter, and I'm getting too old to split wood the hard way with this bum shoulder." Ben nodded his understanding.

Ben righted one of the chairs that had been perforated and knocked over by Venton's controlled fury of machinegun fire, and told Hank to take a load off. When Troy and the other two assaulters returned, Ben gathered up Hank's guns and knife and set them on the coffee shop counter, then motioned for Troy to join him. Troy walked up to him and said, "So, what do we do with ol' Hank?" Ben said, "I was thinking about that. He's not the sharpest tool in the shed, but I believe him. I'd say we let him go home and tell him to come back tomorrow with something to trade for the log splitter. It could be useful to have him splitting wood; someone around here will need it for heat. He could also serve as an outpost to the west."

"I agree," Troy said, "Just make sure he understands the consequences for shooting at us again." Ben nodded and walked over to Hank.

"Alright Hank," Ben said, "Here's the deal. This morning you are going to walk home. Return here tomorrow morning, and someone will be able to speak with you about trading for the log splitter. This area will be a safe zone for the near future, and I'm sure we will need split wood for heating." Ben paused and kneeled in front of Hank, looking him right in the eyes, "But I'll only say this once Hank. If you shoot at us again, we will kill you. Even if you get away, I know where you live. There will be no more chances; do you understand me?" Hank had lived a simple life, and was never really great at reading people, but he could tell by the look in Ben's eyes that he could take that warning to the bank. Hank nodded his head and said, "Thank you." Ben could sense the sincerity in Hank, and said, "Alright, let's get you out of here."

Ben took the handcuffs off Hank and led him to the counter where his guns were. Troy, who was now behind the counter said, "I have a Mosin-Nagant with a double shot of 9mm for Frank," obviously mimicking a barista mispronouncing someone's name. Hank didn't get the joke, but gingerly accepted his now unloaded guns and his KA-BAR knife. Troy told him, "These two nice assaulters will escort you to the overpass out of town. Remember Hank, no shooting at anyone wearing a Black Knight patch," while pointing at the patch on his chest. Hank nodded emphatically and replied, "Yes sir. I'll see you in the morning."

2nd Troop spent the rest of the day clearing buildings and setting up checkpoints. They didn't find any more people until they got to the hotel, where the team found 16 rooms were occupied. They made contact with everyone and explained the situation. Most of the hotel's guests were oil field workers with no place else to be, so Troy put them to work after feeding them from the food piling up from the grill-a-thon behind Walmart.

After thinking about what Troy had told him this morning about the City's plan for the area, Harold had commandeered the closed down chain restaurant building on the eastern edge of Walmart's lot. He and three of his employees set the place up as a dining hall, and by mid-day they were ready to start serving buffet style meals made up of the perishable food his crew had been cooking all day. Troy was able to rotate all his assaulters through the buffet, getting some of them their first real meal in over 24 hours.

By the time the logistic convoy arrived from FOB Card, with Mayor Barnhart in the lead vehicle, 2nd Troop and the oil workers had the area ringed with dead vehicles, and had two functional ECP's emplaced. The eastern ECP was already allowing citizens to enter the area, sending them under escort to the buffet for a meal. Everyone they allowed in volunteered to help in whatever work needed to be done; gaining a doctor (an Oncologist) and several master tradesmen in the process. The Mayor found Troy standing by the M113.

"You guys crushed it Troy! This is amazing!" Mayor Barnhart said by way of greeting. Troy smiled and said, "All we did was provide security Sir. Harold and his team, and some oil field workers we found in the hotel, really made the progress today." The Mayor nodded and said, "Well, great work. Any injuries?" Troy replied, "Nope. Venton about gave a guy a heart attack with the 240, but we are all good." Barnhart laughed and said, "Well, praise the Lord for small miracles."

Troy agreed and said, "Speaking of miracles, I found out this morning there is a giant greenhouse farm just south of Walmart. It wasn't on the orders, but we secured it and made contact with the manager." Mayor Barnhart slapped his forehead and said, "I can't believe we forgot the farm! That place grows massive amounts of fruits and vegetables year-round. Thank you for catching that." Troy said, "Don't thank me, Harold told me about it." The Mayor nodded and said, "I'll make sure I stop down there and say hi to the manager, I think it's Anthony, and coordinate with him." Troy nodded, then filled the Mayor in on the rest of the day's events, and told him about the issue with the owner of the nursery.

Barnhart said, "Sounds good. I'll go talk to Bernard as well. He campaigned against me, and I arrested him once for growing weed back in the day, but I'm sure we can come to an understanding. I need to catch up with Harold first." Troy nodded. He thought about assigning someone to guard the Mayor, but Barnhart was armed with his M&P 9mm and BCM M4. *Ron can take care of himself,* Troy thought, remembering the Mayor had been a SWAT guy before retiring. They shook hands and the Mayor jogged off to find Harold.

Chapter 19

Camp Ravenna
Ravenna, OH

Manny wasn't happy about his 1st Troop making the long
movement to the Camp Ravenna National Guard Base in soft
skinned HMWWVs, an M915 tractor and trailer, and Kasey's SUV.
The problem was he had 29 people to move, and there were only so
many armored vehicles. He dealt with the risk as best he could by
doing a detailed route briefing as part of his Op Order, and doing
several down vehicle drills in the water treatment plant parking lot
before they pushed out the gate. He also felt better that the
HMWWVs had belt feds mounted and manned.

While his primary mission was a reconnaissance in force to
Ravenna, he had several secondary goals. He was to check the truck
stop at the intersection of Hwy 14 and I-76, looking for semi-trailers
that may have supplies in them and marking them for pickup, and
doing the same on I-76 on their way to Ravenna. He was dubious of
the wisdom of stopping the convoy every 100 yards to check a
truck's load, but he understood the necessity of gathering every
single scrap of food and fuel now, before things got crazy. *Look on
the bright side,* he told himself, *at least the Troop will get lots of
'dismount and set security' drills done today.*

Manny positioned himself in the second vehicle, trusting a
police officer from Stow who had come in last night who was a
former Army Cav Scout, to run the scout vehicle mission in Kasey's
SUV. He had one assaulter on a dirtbike but decided to use her, a
female cop from Marlboro, for rear security. It felt shady as hell
deploying with a team he hadn't trained, much less who had never
trained before together at all. *We're all we got,* kept running through
his mind.

1st Troop spent the next three hours checking semi-trailers.
They found the truck stop at I-76 almost completely abandoned. The
only people there were three truckers who'd locked themselves

inside the convenience store of the truck stop and refused to come out. All their appointed spokesman would say to Manny was "We aren't coming out. We have this place by salvage rights, and we are staying here! Take our trailers if you want, we don't care."

Manny tried reasoning with them, pointing out they could only stay inside so long before the Twinkies and Diet Coke ran out, and offered to take them back to Alliance, but they wouldn't budge. He gave up after about 10 minutes. After opening every trailer in the lot, they found 16 that had dried or canned food inside and two fuel haulers loaded with diesel and gasoline. They re-secured them using heavy-duty pad locks, having cut off the shipping seals, and marked the trailers for recovery.

Moving on to I-76 itself, they checked over 60 trailers in the westbound lanes in the few miles between Hwy 14 and the Hwy 44 turnoff to Ravenna. They found, resealed, and marked 11 of them for recovery, including one fuel tanker. It surprised Manny that they hadn't found anyone on I-76. The roadway and all of the vehicles appeared completely abandoned. He had expected to find at least some people still in their cars less than 24 hours after the pulse.

When the scout vehicle exited I-76 onto Hwy 44 northbound, the vehicle commander got on the radio and said, "Knight One, Knight One-Alpha-Three. I found all the people." Manny replied, "Roger, One-Alpha-Three. How many and where are they." The scout responded, "There are several hundred people in the parking lots of the gas stations and fast food places at the bottom of the ramp at the Hwy 44 exit. I can see several of them looking at us through the scopes of hunting rifles, and some have already started walking towards us. We are backing out." The driver of Kasey's Equinox put it in reverse and backed up the ramp as fast as he could, then got turned around and headed east in the westbound lanes until they reached Manny's vehicle.

The scout got out, ran up to Manny's door, and found him already looking at the paper road map, looking for a way around the intersection. "OK," Manny said, talking to Keel, who was his driver, "We will turn around and go back to Hwy 14. If we go north on Hwy 14 it will dump us out near the Camp." Manny showed the scout the route on the map and held it while the scout pulled out his notebook and drew a strip map. He was pretty sure he knew where he was going, but getting lost wasn't an option. When he was done the scout mounted up and led the Troop east.

They made good time once they got back on Hwy 14, and within 20 minutes they were parked in a herringbone formation at a turnout near the southeast corner of the Camp Ravenna reservation. Manny called his team leaders to the center of the formation and gave his briefing. "Alright guys, we know the situation. Our mission today is to recon Camp Ravenna to determine if there are any resources available we can utilize. My intent is to observe the Camp and figure out who is in control, if anyone, before making any contact." Manny paused and made eye contact with his team leaders, then continued, "It is not my intent to attack the Camp. We are here to observe unless I decide otherwise. Everybody understand?" Three heads nodded.

Manny assigned Alpha team, now under Jim Keel's leadership since Dan was promoted to lead 3rd Troop, to recon the main gate, located on the northeast side of the Camp. Jerry's team, Bravo, was tasked with doing the recon of the southeast gate, a seldom-used entrance to the Camp. Charlie team, with Canton PD's Miles Johnson at the helm, was ordered to maintain security on the vehicles and operate the patrol base. Manny kept the three Ohio National Guard guys with him at the patrol base for now. He trusted them, but only so far.

Manny gave the TLs 10 minutes to get their guys organized; Keel's Alpha team was moving in seven. When he saw Alpha pushing out early, Jerry keyed his radio and said, "Overachiever." The only response he got was Keel's left middle finger up high pointing back at him. Alpha team slipped into the woods on the east side of the roadway, opposite the Camp, and disappeared towards the north.

Jerry's Bravo team, having a much shorter distance to travel, reached their objective first. When they got to the southeast gate, Jerry laid out his seven-man team on the east side of the road in a shallow arch, with the center closest to the gate, directly across the north-south highway running next to the camp. He kept his team about 20 yards inside the tree line, and placed them about 10 yards apart. When Jerry finally settled in, he reported to Manny over the radio and used his Steiner 8X50 binos to start his recon.

After about 10 minutes of detailed observation, it was obvious the gate hadn't been used in a long time. He could see the weathered chain and padlock keeping the gate secured hadn't been moved in quite a while, if the rust bridge connecting the chain to the steel vertical pole of the 10-foot-tall gate's center was any indication. A heavy layer of grass was sticking out of the unmarred layer of snow in the driveway. Jerry bet he could use the several layers of plastic garbage bags and fast food cups trapped against the mobile part of the fence to date the last time this gate was used, like an archeologist used layers of pottery fragments. The windows of the guardshack just inside the left side of the gate were yellowed and stained, and the step outside the shack's sliding door was overgrown with a small jungle of pine needles and moss.

Lee, the electrical engineer and tactics student turned Black Knight assaulter, was lying next to Jerry, watching the target through his Khales 1-6 optic. Lee leaned close to Jerry and whispered, "I'd bet every one of my Star Wars action figures this gate hasn't been used in five years." Jerry discovered new depths of self-discipline trying to keep himself from laughing. Instead, he keyed his radio mic and said, "Knight One, Knight One-Bravo-One. Negative activity at east gate. It appears to not have been used at all for over a year." Manny replied, "Roger One-Bravo-One. Hold your pos until I hear back from Alpha." Jerry clicked his radio mic twice to say 'roger' without having to talk, and turned his attention back to the objective.

Alpha team was discovering Jim Keel set a blistering pace. His legs almost being longer than some of his assaulters were tall didn't help, but his inhuman level of physical fitness had most of his eight assaulters breathing hard within the first 500 yards, just trying to keep up. Zach Shepard knew that if Keel kept this pace up Alpha would have guys fall out. Zach's limited patrolling experience as part of the Alliance SWAT team also told him that Keel, as the TL, shouldn't be the point man. Zach jogged up to Keel and stopped him. Keel took a knee, leaving him only slightly shorter than Zach when he was standing, and looked at him like 'what the hell dude, what is it?'. Zach put his mouth close to Keel's ear and said, "You need to slow down. Guys are already falling behind. Also, are you sure you should be the point man? You're the TL."

Keel's first reaction was anger. If an assaulter had questioned a TL in the middle of an Op on Keel's Vegas SWAT team, he would be punched in the face, followed by a rapid and unceremonious exit from the unit. *You're not in Vegas anymore Jim,* was his next thought, *and Zach has a point on both counts.* Keel nodded his head and whispered, "You're right bro. My bad. You take point, I'll follow." Zach breathed an inward sigh of relief that Keel hadn't been a dick about it, and pushed off at a more manageable pace.

Alpha team made the one and a half mile movement to the woods across from the main gate in just over 30 minutes. Keel thought that even the newest Army Ranger would have had a stroke had they seen (and heard) their fieldcraft during the walk, but he cut himself and his team some slack. They were a bunch of cops thrown into a situation calling for Ranger skills; but Keel knew the first thing he was asking Manny for when they got time to breath was dismounted patrolling training. He wished he'd taken some classes in it before the pulse. That, and his guys were going to PT until their arms and legs fell off.

The team set up in the woods across from the main gate and started watching. Keel immediately noticed a head in the guard shack positioned in the middle of the ECP. The cyclone fence gates leading into the base were closed on both the entry and exit sides, but the shack was definitely manned. A white ford pickup with the Camp's logo on the door sat with its hood up behind the shack. As he watched, a white kid in his early 20's, wearing a blue uniform coat and uniform pants stepped out of the shack and stretched.

He noticed the man's coat had a badge on the left breast and patches embroidered with 'HBD Security' on each shoulder, and he was wearing a gunbelt with a Glock pistol and two spare magazines, an empty radio pouch, and a Surefire light in an old Surefire light holder. The uniform matched the description of what to expect the guard to look like that Keel got from the National Guard troops riding with 1st Troop.

The team settled in to watch while Keel got on the radio. "Knight One, Knight One-Alpha-One. Eyes on. There is one uniformed guard, gates are closed. No other traffic." He heard

Manny say, "Roger. Charlie Mike." Keel settled in for a cold day sitting in the woods.

Across the road, the security guard was laughing to himself. Whoever that was in the woods across from him wasn't exactly Daniel Boone. Jeff Lewis was playing it cool; he heard the group moving through the woods opposite his gate several minutes before he saw them. He sat in his guardshack and watched them settle in about 70 yards to his east. Lewis was a former Marine who had taken this job because it paid well; and since it was on a government contract he got veteran's preference for hiring. Although young, Lewis had been out of the Marine Corps for five months. During his four-year enlistment, he had gone downrange to Afghanistan as a Marine Infantryman twice, and wasn't particularly worried about a bunch of yahoos who couldn't even sneak up on a $18 an hour security guard.

After coming outside to pretend to stretch in order to get a better look at the watchers, Lewis went back inside his shack. He slung his rifle on its single point sling, letting it hang in front of his body, and grabbed his small binoculars. Lewis spent the next 15 minutes finding and observing each of the four people he could see hiding. One of them was a great big dude with a large 'POLICE' patch on the front of his plate carrier. Being something of a gear queer, Lewis recognized that all four of the guys he could see were wearing high-end Velocity and Crye plate carriers, and Arcteryx or Crye uniforms and jackets. None of their gear was camouflage; in fact, it looked like the Ranger Green monster had puked all over them. Also, despite their obvious discomfort in the woods, they held themselves like professionals.

Ok, these are definitely SWAT guys, Lewis thought, *But what kind of cops can afford that gear?* When the big guy moved and he saw the knight chess piece patch, it dawned on him. These guys were Alliance SWAT. Jeff Lewis may have been a veteran Marine Corps gunfighter, but he was still a 23-year-old. Social media had been the center of his life, until yesterday at least. Being a gear queer and a gun guy in Northeast Ohio, he followed Alliance Police Training pretty closely on Facebook. He couldn't afford to train there yet, but it didn't cost anything to look at pictures and read after-action reports from classes. He'd recognize their Black Knight logo anywhere.

Lewis knew Alliance was close by; the SWAT team must be checking out Camp Ravenna for some reason. He weighed his options carefully. Lewis knew he was tired after sleeping in his car in short bursts last night. He knew he realistically couldn't hold his post until he starved to death. As much as the Marine Corps had ingrained General Order Number Five into him, 'To quit my post only when properly relieved', Lewis was honest enough with himself to admit if he'd had any family or a girlfriend, he would have started walking home by now. Based on his observations, Lewis knew they had been EMP'd, or hit by a sunburst or whatever that was called, and he knew no one was coming to help him.

He made up his mind quickly; he would make contact with these guys, and if they had any governmental affiliation he would join them. Lewis stepped out into the cold day and looked right at the group of guys in the trees across the road, pointed at them, then made the 'Rally On Me' hand signal. He repeated the gesture as he watched them squirm around, then he held his binoculars over his head and shouted, "I can see you guys. Just come over here."

Keel was taken completely by surprise by the guard's actions and words. He knew they weren't ninja's in the woods, but they must have sucked worse than he thought if the guy had seen them already. He keyed his radio and said, "Knight One, Knight One-Alpha-One. We've been made. The guard is calling us to him. I am making contact." Keel heard the tail end of a curse when Manny replied, "Roger, One-Alpha-One. I'm on my way. Delay if you can." Keel replied, "Roger," then said to Zach, "I'm going to go meet him, keep everyone here until I call you over." Zach merely nodded, a small smile on his face.

Keel stood up and walked across the road. When he got to the gate the first thing Lewis said to him was, "Damn you're huge. You play football?" Keel laughed and said, "What do you think bro?" and stuck his hand through the gap in the fence for a handshake. Lewis chuckled and said, "I bet you hear that all the time. Jeff Lewis. It's good to see you; I was starting to wonder if anyone was still alive out there."

Keel nodded his head and replied, "Very much so. We are from Alliance, scouting the area." Lewis smiled and said, "I know who you guys are, I saw the Black Knight patch. Is that what you call it, 'scouting'? You guys sounded like a bunch of drunk frat boys trying to use a brass band to disguise the noise of hiding a body in the woods over there." Keel grimaced and asked, "That bad huh?" Lewis replied, "Ha! That movement would embarrass a dumpster fire Jim." Keel sighed, "Well, we hadn't practiced yet." "I'm just glad it was me you were 'sneaking up on'," Lewis said, using his finger quotes, "and not a bad guy. I could have owned you guys." Keel nodded and sucked up the lesson.

Keel shook it off with an internal commitment to fix the problem, and had to laugh at himself. He said, "My commander is hauling ass up here as we speak, so expect to hear a HMWWV going mach 1.5 any second. What is your situation here?" Lewis replied, "As far as I can tell, I'm the only one left on post. I was following my Marine Corps General Orders and trying to figure out what to do when you guys showed up." Keel nodded then heard a HMWWV screaming north on the road. "That must be the Boss," Lewis said. Keel let out a breath and replied, "Yep." Lewis smiled and said, "Don't worry bro, I'll make you look good. No need for Officers to know NCO business." Keel just nodded and braced for the worst.

When the HMWWV pulled into the driveway leading up to the gate, it slowed to a crawl as Manny evaluated the situation. He saw Keel standing at the closed gate speaking with the gate guard. No one else was around. He had the driver pull close, then got out and walked towards Keel, keeping his carbine slung across his body, but keeping his firing hand on the grip. On the short drive from the patrol base he'd decided to play this straight, and see where it went.

As they watched Manny approach, Lewis took one look at him and said, under his breath, "Holy crap that dude's all Officer." Keel replied out of the corner of his mouth, "Ranger Officer. Awesome guy." Lewis nodded slightly and stood up straighter.

When Manny got within 10 feet of them he said, "Good Morning." Both Keel and Lewis replied, "Good morning." Keel felt a little silly, as he'd just seen Manny less than an hour ago, but there was something about Manny that made you want to treat him like a General. Keel shook it off and said, "Manny, meet Jeff Lewis. Jeff Lewis, Manny." The two shook hands through the fence while Manny said, "Nice to meet you Lewis. We are from the City of Alliance and wanted to come check-in with the Camp. Is the Post Commander on site?" Lewis said, "No Sir. According to my access roster, I'm the only one left on post. The Commander never came to work yesterday; I think he was on leave. The three employees who were working on the Camp left on foot yesterday evening. I haven't left my post to check, but I'm pretty sure I'm it."

Manny nodded his understanding and said, "Does the Camp have a plan for this sort of emergency?" Lewis replied, "Not that I know of, but I'm just the gate guard. I know the base doesn't have a lot of missions these days. So far as I know all they do here is National Guard training and equipment storage." Manny replied, "Ok. What do you plan to do? You can't stay here forever." Lewis said, "I was just thinking about that. My initial reaction was to remain at my post until relieved, but your HMWWV is the first vehicle I've seen that runs, and I have no comms. As far as I know I'll never get relieved."

Manny raised his eyebrows and nodded then said, "Well, you've gone above and beyond, staying on your post this long." Lewis straightened up a little and said, "I'm a Marine Sir. They made me memorize the General Orders for a reason." Manny said, "Yes they did. Well done. When did you eat last?" Lewis replied, "I haven't eaten since lunch yesterday. The lights went out after lunchtime, and I had eaten everything I brought."

Manny nodded and turned without another word and walked back to the HMWWV. He returned with an MRE and a bottle of water and handed them to Lewis, who thanked him profusely. Manny asked, "Can I consolidate my guys here at the gate?" Lewis replied, "Absolutely." Keel got on the radio and called his team over to the gate and set them up to pull security. While waiting on the rest of the teams to move up, Manny explained the situation as he understood it, and briefed Lewis on the Alliance city government's response, and the Black Knight Squadron.

Lewis took it all in and said, "Sir, as far as I can tell you guys are the only legitimate government entity around. I am willing to take my orders from you." Manny nodded and said, "Alright. That's how I see it as well. I know it's not a textbook solution, but I think keeping the equipment stored here out of the wrong hands, and putting it to work for the right purposes, is the smart call." "I agree 110 percent," Lewis replied, then continued, "I have no idea if it's legal, but I know it's right."

Manny nodded and said, "I have some National Guard troops with me. We will search the post and take as much equipment back

164

to Alliance as we can, then lock up the Camp as well as possible. I'm hoping it takes the bad elements of society a while to figure out what's here, and by then we will have most of it moved." Lewis agreed and said, "I have the keys to get into the storage control office. We should be able to access whatever we want." Manny replied, "Good. That will let us save our breaching equipment for other needs. Now, eat and relax for a few minutes. We are about to be busy." Jeff Lewis didn't need to be told twice it was time to eat.

The next few hours were a whirlwind of activity. 1st Troop was able to get 11 Strykers running, all of them M1126 ICV's. They were taking all of them. The three National Guardsmen spent an hour teaching everyone how to drive the armored vehicles, and Manny was confident they could get them back to the FOB intact. A lot more training would be needed before they fully deployed the vehicles, but everyone was happy they found them. The Guardsmen loaded all of the spare parts they could find, filling the troop compartments of four of the Strykers.

The rest of the vehicles were loaded with the contents of the Arms Rooms of the four resident National Guard units, including 18 M2 .50 caliber machineguns, 31 M240 machineguns, nine M249's, and over 130 M4 rifles. They also located four M203 grenade launchers, but couldn't find any ammo for them. They loaded as much 9mm, 5.56, linked 5.56, linked 7.62, and linked .50 cal ammo as they could fit. Some of the Strykers were overloaded, but Manny figured they would just drive slowly and hope for the best.

Radios were high on Manny's wish list, and they grabbed every piece of portable radio equipment possible. As far as he knew, no one in the Squadron knew how to use the complicated radios, crypto fill devices, and antennas, but he decided that was a problem for another day. Having the equipment was as good as he could do for now. He would have to trust God to send them someone who knew how to program everything.

In addition to the Strykers and other gear, the Troop took five soft-skinned HMWWVs from the motor pool of vehicles awaiting the DRMO process. The grass DRMO lot had at least 80 HMWWVs parked in it, but Manny was out of drivers. The rest of the Troop's time was spent location and marking other vehicles and equipment they wanted to recover later.

It was late in the day by the time Manny decided they had done all they could for now, and they locked everything up as best they could. He gave a full convoy briefing and mounted up. The 20-vehicle convoy kept a sedate 25 MPH pace all the way back to FOB Card, while Manny tried to figure out where he was going to park everything. *If the lights come back on,* Manny thought ruefully, *I'm going to have some 'splainin to do to the Ohio Army National Guard.*

Chapter 20

Ward 2
Alliance, OH

A cold artic wind blew in from the north, making the job of holding their rifles still enough to see clearly through their magnified optics much harder than normal. Mark, Kasey, and Gary had parked their quads on the north side of the railroad tracks where Bond Road crossed over into downtown, and were hunkered down observing what was left of the City municipal center, about 100 yards to their south. From their vantage point, Mark used the Schmidt & Bender 1-8 Short Dot scope on his 'heavy' rifle, a Knights Armament SR-25 EC 7.62mm Carbine, to see Freedom Square, a small park on the north side of the courthouse. It was relatively intact, but the Municipal Courthouse and Police Department buildings behind it were burned out hulks. The 2nd story corridor that connected the two buildings had collapsed, and it looked like the weight of that structure was pulling down the east wall of the courthouse.

Kasey quietly said, "For a fire to get hot enough to make that sky-bridge collapse they must have used a ton of accelerants." Mark shook his head and said, "Leave it to the dongs to waste fuel, now that no one is making any." Gary, who was behind them watching their six-o'clock, said, "If they were smart they wouldn't be dongs." "True dat' my friend." Mark replied, then said, "Let's move east to Seneca then south. Judging from all the smoke in the air, I'm guessing the PD and Courthouse aren't the only buildings that were burned down last night."

Mark's small team's mission was to probe the Ward 2 area of Alliance from the north, and gather information. The Mayor wanted to help all of the City's citizens, but not at the expense of running gunbattles like had happened yesterday afternoon in this very neighborhood. Mark, Kasey, and Gary's job was to assess the damage these people did to their own neighborhood, and determine what, if anything, could be done to help them. Bravo team from 3rd

Troop, under Trent's leadership, was assessing the damage on the south side of Ward 2, on and around State Street. If the teams could get an idea of the 'blast radius' from last night's fighting and looting, David could develop a plan to contain the problem. That was the idea anyway.

Mark's team got back on their quads and slow rolled east, then turned south and cut over the tracks through a vacant lot, and out onto Seneca Avenue. As soon as they got on Seneca, they had a fairly straight line of sight south for about a mile, and what they saw shocked them. Most of the homes they could see lining Seneca, and all of the buildings they could see to the west on Main Street, were smoldering ruins. "Holy crap." Mark heard Gary mutter from behind him. Mark quietly replied, "Holy crap indeed." Kasey said, "Why would they burn down their only shelter? Don't they know it's winter? I could see the logic, from their point of view, of burning down the police station, but burning their own homes? This is crazy." Mark replied, "I bet most of this destruction is accidental. The wind was from the north last night. When they set the courthouse and PD on fire, it probably got out of control and was driven south by the wind."

As they were about to push south, Kasey shifted on her seat to get a more comfortable position. As she leaned forward, a shot snapped through the air. She could tell it was close because the shockwave of the round passing her head felt like someone slapped her. Mark happened to be looking to the southwest, at about his 2 o'clock, and saw the muzzle flash come from the corner of a burnt-out home, about 80 yards away. He immediately brought his rifle up, put the Short Dot's red dot on the corner of the burned wall where he saw the flash, and fired five 7.62X51 rounds through the structure, hoping to hit the shooter on the other side of that corner. When no more fire came at them, he chanced a glance to his left to see if Kasey was alright, but she was already gunning her engine, leaned forward as close to the quad as she could get, as she charged right at the house where the muzzle flash came from. Mark immediately cinched up the rifle on its Blue Force Gear VCAS sling and launched to follow her, with Gary right on his tail.

No more shots came from the spot, and when they arrived about 10 seconds later, the shooter was gone. As Kasey jumped off her quad Mark screeched to a halt and said, "Stop. Do not chase him." Kasey stopped but didn't look happy about it. Mark got off his quad and said, "That probably wasn't random. He might be leading us into an ambush." Kasey nodded her understanding, but still looked pissed. Mark tac reloaded a fresh Magpul 20 round 7.62 Pmag into his heavy carbine. While he was putting the partial mag away, he said, "The ground is wet, we can track him. Relax and get your mind right," and stared right into her eyes. Kasey visibly relaxed and got herself together, then nodded.

As they disabled their quads and Mark checked in on the radio, to let Trent's Bravo team know what they were doing, it began to dawn on Kasey how close she had come to eating that bullet. She had felt the air on her face move when it snapped past her, it had been that close. She thanked God for saving her, then tried to put it out of her mind. She had been through several tracking courses with Mark, and instead focused on what would be expected of her while he tracked the spoor. She focused hard on that. Within a minute of arriving at the burned-out house, they were moving out on the track.

Within 50 feet Mark found a fresh blood smear at about shoulder height on the north-facing wall of a small shed. The smear looked like it was made by a hand. *Something tells me I won't need to be a Navajo Scout to follow this track,* Mark thought. He warned Kasey and Gary to be hyper-vigilant; their prey was wounded and was probably looking for a place to hide. About 30 feet west of the shed Mark started spotting very fresh blood drops on the ground. He stopped and called his small team together. "This guy is seriously hit. He's going to be close." Mark said. Gary and Kasey both nodded and got ready to move out again.

Another 100 feet to the west Kasey called a halt. She saw a bloody white basketball sneaker sticking out of a bush at her 11 o'clock, about 20 yards west of them. The team spread out, on guard for a trap. Mark looked at Gary and said, "Overwatch," while pointing to a stalled vehicle in the alley. Gary ran to the car and set up to lay some hate if it was indeed a trap. The weight of the Magpul D60 in his BCM carbine gave him some confidence, in case the hood rats decided to dance.

Mark and Kasey moved wide to their left, and were finally able to get eyes on the down subject's body through the bush. Kasey was pretty sure he was still alive, given the fact he was blinking, but his breathing was shallow and he was lying in a pool of what looked to her like 50 gallons of blood. As she watched, Kasey saw him trying to speak then it appeared he fell asleep. She noticed his labored breathing had stopped, so that was probably it. Mark quietly told her, "Move to this car with me and pull security to the south. We will give this guy some time to expire." Mark ran to a parked car, one of the seemingly endless numbers of Kia sedans in Ward 2, and took a knee, pulling security to the west.

Mark kept an eye on his wristwatch, thanking God for manually wound timepieces, and after 10 minutes he figured the guy was a goner. He said a quiet, "On me." To Kasey's back, then got up and cautiously approached the hopefully dead guy tangled up in the bush. When they got to him Kasey held cover while Mark grabbed his left foot and dragged the dude out from underneath the untrimmed Spicebush trees. Once they had his body exposed, Kasey saw a wooden rifle stock lying in the pool of blood next to the dead guy. She walked over and drug it out of the blood, and saw it was an M1 Garand.

"Holy crap!" she exclaimed, and told Mark what it was. He said, "Well, grab it up while I search and try to ID this guy." Kasey replied, "It's literally covered in blood." Mark looked up at her and calmly said, "Then wipe it off Baby. The faster you wipe it down, the easier it will be to clean up. We can't leave it here." Kasey looked around and finally saw a towel on the rear window deck of the Kia they had used for cover. She used the little window break tool she kept on a loop of paracord on her First Spear plate carrier to break the rear passenger window, and grabbed the towel. After seeing Mark glove up, she stopped and put on a pair of latex gloves out of her left cargo pocket. No sense getting the dead guy's cooties on her.

By the time Mark was done searching the dead guy, finding a Hi Point .45 ACP pistol with a half-loaded mag in it, two Garand clips and an expired Ohio ID card with the dude's name on it, Kasey was finished wiping the rifle off, as best she could anyway. As she cleaned, she kept stealing glances at the dead man, wondering how Mark could deal with the bloody body so clinically. Kasey felt sick to her stomach and decided to just ignore the guy.

When they were both done, Mark stood up and took the dead dude's jacket off of him, then wrapped it around the guy's face. Mark grabbed the dead man by the foot again and dragged him out of the alley and next to a burnt-out house. "He'll have to keep for now," Mark said, "We need to get moving." He updated Trent over the radio, and the three-person team formed up in a wedge, then moved east, back to their quads. *I hope this isn't what the rest of our lives will be like,* Kasey thought, knowing full well things were probably going to get far worse before they got better.

*

Trent acknowledged Mark's transmission and turned to Ernesto, who was driving the MRAP, and said, "You copy that? We can resume our mission. Knight Five is fine." Ernesto hadn't heard the transmission; his radio was turned down too low. He nodded and slowed down. He made a series of left turns and managed to get back on State Street without doing a Big Foot monster truck impression on one of the stalled cars on the road. When they were again heading west on State Street, Ernesto asked, "Do you still want to stay in the area? Charlie team has Kyle with them and they are almost to the Judge's house. We are close enough to help them if they run into trouble." Trent thought about it for a second and replied, "No, let's hit Giant Eagle and see how they fared last night. We still have to check the hospital before we head back to the range. I mean FOB." Ernesto said, "Roger that."

When 3rd Troop's Bravo team pulled into view of the Giant Eagle grocery store, they were surprised to see an orderly line of about 100 people formed at the main entrance. "What the what?" Trent asked. Andy Card, a Sebring cop and former Army Infantryman who had walked the 20 miles from Sebring to the range last night, who was manning the M249 in the turret of the MRAP, yelled down, "Hey, do you guys see this?" Trent yelled up, "Yeah."

Ernesto brought the huge combat vehicle to a halt in the far northeast corner of the Giant Eagle parking lot. Trent grabbed his binos from his assault pack and started glassing the store. All of the folks he could see standing in line looked cold, but they seemed to be bearing the wait well enough. A lot of them were holding or sitting on bicycles. Trent told Ernesto to pull up to about 50 yards from the doors, next to the building, and to park facing north so Andy could pull overwatch. After Ernesto got the MRAP positioned

171

and shut down, Trent told Andy, "We are going to go see what's up. I'm leaving you and Ernesto here." Andy said, "Roger," and Trent told the four assaulters in the back, "Let's go." They exited the MRAP, formed up into a loose diamond, and walked up to the main doors, all eyes in the line watching them closely.

When they got to the door they were met by a very thin guy with a big mane of white hair, wearing a Giant Eagle polo shirt, who was holding a Mossberg hunting shotgun with a Realtree camo stock in the crook of his arm like a bird hunter. As he approached the man, Trent could see his nametag said 'Bill, Store Manager'. "Good Morning Bill." Trent said in greeting. Bill looked Trent and the Bravo team assaulters up and down, taking in the full view of the men carrying rifles and wearing plate carriers with 'POLICE' on the front, and ballistic helmets. After a moment Bill said, "Hello. I assume you guys are from the government, and you're here to help?"

Trent laughed and said, "No sir. We are just out checking on folks and saw the line. What's the plan here?" Bill chuckled and replied, "You can call me Bill. Well, after the lights went out we were able to seal up the store. Most of us slept here last night. This morning, I figured we have food people need, so when folks started coming around, we decided to open up for the day." Trent said, "That's awesome Bill. Are you charging people for the food?" Bill shook his head, "No, hardly anyone has cash, and I'm not sure paper money is worth anything right now anyway. Besides, none of the credit card machines work; so we are limiting people to four perishable items, thawed meat or a cooked chicken, veggies and bread mostly. After they make their selections we do a simple IOU and have them sign it."

"That's a great idea Bill," Trent said, "Thank you for distributing the food. It's a good idea to get rid of the perishable stuff. Why let it rot if people can eat it now." Bill said, "Exactly. Most folks can cook on their gas grills, and some houses still have gas service, so they have a way to cook it. We are not letting anyone take anything canned or shelf stable for now. I figure the fresh food will be mostly gone today. We still have gas service so the ovens in the bakery and the rotisserie chicken cooker still work, so we are cooking our asses off, baking bread and cooking our stock of chickens."

Bill stopped talking as three people came out of the store, each with two plastic grocery bags. Trent noticed they each had a whole chicken in one bag and a bag salad and loaf of bread in the other. Two of them got on bicycles they had left outside. Bill passed three more customers into the store after they parked their bikes. When he was done, he turned back to speak to Trent, "I only have three employees to escort people, so we are doing three customers at a time. Anyway, I figure by the time we are out of fresh food the frozen stuff will have thawed, and we can start distributing that. I'm saving the shelf stable foods for last."

Trent nodded, impressed with Bill's leadership and organizational skill. He said, "Well, this crowd looks calm, but sooner or later you are going to have issues with people trying to force their way in or robbing these folks after they leave. Also, people are already looting and burning buildings over in Second Ward, and I'd imagine that crap will make its way here later today. I can't leave anyone here now, but I am going to put in a request to assign a team here for security as soon as possible. You're doing God's work here Bill, we need to do what we can to keep you going until the store is out of food." Bill nodded and said, "Thank you. I've only got six people here, including me, and this one shotgun one of my stock clerks had in her truck." Bill then lowered his voice and said, "She only had three rounds of birdshot for it, so it's mostly for show."

Trent raised his eyebrows and said, "Well, that's something I can help with. Do you know how to use an AK?" Bill nodded and said, "Yeah, I got some trigger time on one when I was in the Marines, in a foreign weapons FAM course." Trent got on the radio and said, "Knight Three-Bravo-Two, Knight Three-Bravo-One." Ernesto said, "Go ahead." Trent replied, "I'm sending someone back to the truck to grab one of the spare rifles and some ammo. One of the AK's we captured last night. Have one ready for them please." "Roger that." Ernesto responded. Trent pointed at one of his assaulters, who turned around a hauled ass back to the MRAP.

When he returned with the AK, three magazines, and one of the cheap vests they'd captured last night, Trent had him hold the rifle so he could transcribe the serial number into his notebook. No one had said anything about it, but he figured David or Bones would want accountability for all the captured weapons at some point.

173

When he was done, he handed the rifle, vest and magazines to Bill and said, "This should work a little better than that duck gun. I have no idea if it's zero'd. If the blood stains on the vest bother you just shoot some spray paint over them." Bill chuckled and said, "Thank you! I was pretty worried about having to shoot someone with this mallard slayer. I'll use the stains to remind me this is a new world." Trent nodded and asked, "Do you need to use the bathroom or anything while we are here?" Bill said, "Oh my goodness yes! Thank you. I'll be right back." And was gone like a shot.

While his guys watched the door, Trent took a minute to walk up and down the line of people waiting to get in. He answered their questions about what had happened ("We think it was an EMP") and what was going to happen now ("We all pull together and do what we can to help each other recover"). People started getting out of line to listen to his answers, so he waited until everyone gathered around and raised his voice so he could be heard, "Folks, my name is Trent, and I'm a Police Officer here in Alliance. We don't know exactly what happened, but we think we were hit with an electromagnetic pulse, which fried the power grid, most vehicles and our long-range communications networks. We are pretty sure this is a nation-wide event. The city is getting organized to help, but we need everyone to try the best they can to help themselves and their neighbors. It's only been about 20 hours since the event, so we are still scrambling, but we are moving as fast as we can. We need your help. We are Americans, and we help one another in times like these."

Trent could see a lot of people nodding their heads and murmuring agreement, and continued his impromptu speech, "Right now we are trying to secure the area around Walmart to be our base of operations for the recovery, and the plan is for it to be open for business tomorrow morning. If you can help in some way, please come there and check in. In the meantime, take care of your families and your neighbors. 911 is obviously not working, so please use your best judgment and handle your own security for now." He paused and tried to think of anything else he could say, then Trent remembered the water treatment plant. He continued, "The Water Department has been working hard, and managed to stabilize the water supply and sewage treatment. Your tap water at home is safe to drink and your toilets will still work, and as long as we can find

174

fuel it will stay that way. Please conserve bottled water in case something else goes wrong." The crowd made understanding noises.

Someone in the crowd asked, "Any idea where we can get medications? I'm not out yet but I will be in about a week." Trent said, "I'm not sure. I know we are working on plans for medication, but I don't have an answer for that." He heard an "OK, thanks." from the crowd, and decided it was time to wrap this up before he said something stupid. Trent said, "Folks, I hate to cut it short but we have to get moving. Thank you for your calm and understanding. We have to help one another through this, and you folks taking responsibility for yourselves goes a long way. Thank you." Several people said, "Thank you," and "Thanks for your service," as the crowd broke up and got back in line.

When Trent got back to the main doors he saw an older man in a Vietnam Veteran hat standing with Bill and chatting with the team. Bill said, "Trent, this is Harry. He and I see each other at the VFW a lot. He wants to help me run the door, and I could use a hand. Any chance you have another one of these commie rifles for him?" Trent smiled and said, "Absolutely Bill," and shook Harry's hand. When Trent turned to ask an assaulter to go grab Harry a gun, he saw one was already jogging to the MRAP.

Once he came back with another AK and some mags, and Trent wrote down the serial number, he said, "We have to take off Bill. You and Harry should make a plan to get the employees out of here if things get out of hand. The food here is important in the short term, but your lives are worth more long term. Be smart please. We will check on you as much as we can." Bill gave a curt nod and said, "Understood. You guys be safe out there. I think this thing is going to get bad soon."

Once the team was mounted up Ernesto pulled out of the parking lot to head to the hospital, while Trent wrote some notes about the situation at Giant Eagle. When he was done he looked up at Ernesto and asked, "You ready to do the hospital thing again?" Ernesto grimaced and said, "No, but it needs doing. I feel like we abandoned them last night, but I don't know what else we could have done." Trent replied, "I know what you mean. We showed up, shot some dude, and left. I hope they've gotten things under control." Ernesto said, "That's the key in my mind bro. We can't do everything, even for the hospital. These people have to help themselves." Trent shrugged and replied, "Everyone is going to have to harden up. Personal responsibility is back in style." Ernesto nodded and said, "We're all we got Bro."

Chapter 21

Eastern Avenue SW, Ward 4
Alliance, OH

"I should have sold my Bitcoin! I'm out like $57,000. This apocalypse is ruining my hustle!" Anson Cross complained bitterly to Kyle as he drove the lead vehicle in the two-vehicle up armored HMWWV convoy towards Judge Morris' house in south Alliance. Kyle sat in the passenger seat of the HMWWV trying to tune Anson out. Taking a bullet to the helmet the night before in the Walmart fight had gotten Anson put on light duty for the day, making him miss 1st Troop's mission to Camp Ravenna. But after examining him, David declared him 'fit for driver duty'. Kyle quoted David to Anson earlier at the FOB when he'd told Anson he was driving for 3rd Troop's Alpha team on the Judge recovery mission. "How is 'fit for driver duty' even a thing? I think he made that up," Anson said. Kyle's reply was simple, "Ya' think? Get your gear and get in the Humvee."

As they turned the corner onto Eastern Avenue from Stark Drive Kyle knew something was wrong. As soon as they crossed the apex of the right-hand turn, Kyle could see three bicycles laying akimbo in the street in front of Judge Morris' house, on his right only 30 yards or so away. As the HMWWV completed the turn, and the Judge's front yard and home were exposed to his vision, he saw two hood rats standing on Judge Morris' lawn. Both were over six feet tall, and both were armed. The guy closest to Kyle's direction was wearing a red beanie on his head, a gold colored jacket and black pants that sagged below his butt, and was holding a black long gun Kyle didn't recognize. The second dong was wearing a black puffy jacket and similarly sagging pants, and was armed with an AK. Neither one of them were pointing their rifles, but that didn't matter. They didn't belong there, and whatever their purpose was, it was bad.

By the time Kyle processed what he was seeing Anson had brought the HMWWV to a screeching halt. The assaulter on the belt fed above Kyle's head was yelling at the two dongs on the Judge's lawn in his cop voice, "Drop your weapons and get down on the ground!" Kyle would have just burned them down, but the cop on the machinegun was a young Akron SWAT cop who was still making the mental transition from cop to assaulter that Kyle had made about an hour into the crisis.

Before Kyle could tell the Akron kid to mow the two of them down, a 5'1", 90-pound ball of fury, who Kyle recognized as Ward 2 City Councilwoman Shimla Musk, came running out from the side of Judge Morris' house, waving her arms and yelling something no one in the HMWWV could understand. Luckily for Councilwoman Musk, the kid on the belt fed hesitated again. Kyle grabbed the kid's leg and said loudly, "Hold fire unless one of those dongs gets sideways." The kid replied, "Roger."

The vehicle commander in the second HMWWV, 3rd Troop's Alpha team leader, Ken Branch, saw the armed men and directed his driver to pull up on the left side of the lead vehicle, giving them two machineguns on the scene without making the Judge's home the backstop for their rounds. Kyle managed to get the up-armored HMWWV door open, reminding him he needed to start lifting weights again, and calmly spoke to the irate Councilwoman, "Shimla, what the hell are you doing at the Judge's house, and why do you have these guys with you?"

"Screw you Kyle Wilson!" Musk began. "You racist cops are killin' my people in Ward 2, takin' advantage of this disaster to kill as many black folks as you can before the Army gets here! I come over here to get Judge Morris to make ya'll stop, but that cracker ass cracker too scared to come on up out his house! I brought these young black men to protect me from yo' genocide!" Kyle remembered all the times Shimla Musk had insulted the police in general, and the Alliance Police Department in particular; the 'no' votes on contracts and equipment requests, the resolutions in support of cop killers, the constant drumbeat of 'community activism' targeting specific officers who were just trying to do their jobs.

Kyle seriously considered just shooting her. Shimla Musk was very close to being 'caught in the crossfire' as his team engaged

178

the two armed men they came upon in Judge Morris' yard. *No,* Kyle stopped himself, *I'm not a savage.* Instead, Kyle just said, "Shimla, you must have gotten some bad information. Our guys have only fought back when attacked. You need to leave and go home. Ward 2 needs you to lead them through this crisis. I am here to take the Judge to see the Mayor. I am sure the Mayor will let you know when he can gather a quorum of the City Council. That is the proper forum for your concerns, not in Judge Morris' front yard."

Councilwoman Musk screamed in response, "No! I demand you take me to the Mayor right now and stop all police work until the City Council meets and issues you orders!" As she spoke, her two goons moved up to stand on each side of her, keeping their guns pointed at the ground, but making it obvious they were ready to shoot it out. Kyle looked up at the sky and closed his eyes, letting out a long breath before responding, "Councilwoman Musk, that is not going to happen. I suggest, for the last time, that you take your 'guards', get on your little bicycles, and pedal on back to Ward 2."

As Musk was formulating a response, Judge Morris quietly stepped out onto his front porch, which was located on the left side of his house and out of the line of fire from the HMWWVs. He was dressed in Carhart pants and a heavy tan hunting jacket, wearing a large backpack, and carrying an M1A. Kyle knew the Judge could shoot, they practiced High Power rifle together in the summers. Judge Morris spoke, using his 'judge voice', "Shimla, take your thugs and get the hell off my lawn." Musk startled when she heard the Judge's voice, and spun around to yell at him. The Judge also startled Shimla's hood rat on her right, and he spun around and brought his rifle to his shoulder. That was all Darren, the assaulter manning the machinegun in the second HMWWV, needed. Already sighted on the thug on the left, Darren simply pressed the trigger of his Mk46 for two short bursts, sending nine rounds of high cyclic rate 5.56mm fire into the dirtbag. He went down like a puppet whose strings were cut.

Before Musk could react to her nephew's death from a terminal case of stupid, Judge Morris raised his M1A and shot her other nephew in the head. After the heavy 7.62X51 round plowed through the center of the dong's head, it struck the second HMWWV in the armored right-front quarter panel and careened off into space. Councilwoman Musk stood frozen in horror, covered in her two

179

nephews' blood, and unable to form a coherent thought. Judge Morris stepped off his porch and walked to her. He stopped about 12 inches from her and said, "Shimla, go home. You are out of your depth. The City is in a state of emergency, and your position on the council means very little right now. The Mayor is in charge. If you foment unrest in Ward 2 I will have you arrested." Musk continued to stand perfectly still and did not respond.

The Judge shrugged his shoulders at her lack of response and walked to Kyle. They shook hands and Morris said, "Thank you for coming to get me Kyle." Kyle replied, "My pleasure Sir. Where is your wife Sir?" The Judge looked down and said, "I don't know Kyle. She was on a plane headed across the Atlantic Ocean when it hit. I fear the worst." Kyle put his arm on the Judge's shoulder and quietly said, "I'm sorry Sir." "It's God's will Kyle, I just have to deal with it." Judge Morris said sadly, then continued, "On the bright side, I can cancel the three felony domestic violence warrants I issued for Shimla's nephew, Tareek Musk, last week," motioning with his head to the thug whose brains the Judge had just used to fertilize his lawn. Kyle sighed and said, "Well, there is that Sir." as he opened the back-passenger door for the Judge and motioned him into the vehicle.

Once the Judge was safely inside the vehicle's armor, Kyle picked up the two long guns from the front yard that were no longer needed by their owners. He saw the one he couldn't immediately identify was a Kel Tec .223 carbine. He was tempted to just leave it there. The guns had such a poor track record he hated to keep it, but maybe one of the hundreds of static security people they were going to need could use it. Kyle unloaded it and the AK, tossed them in the back, then got in his seat. He took a deep breath and told Anson, "Let's move." As the team pushed out Councilwoman Musk was still standing motionless in the Judge's front yard.

*

"This doesn't look good at all," Trent told Ernesto as they pulled into the Emergency Room parking lot at the hospital. Ernesto tried to formulate a response but couldn't. The ambulance bay and ER entrance looked like a bomb went off. The entire north side of the three-story hospital was charred black from fire. Bloody,

180

blackened and frost covered bodies were strewn all over the ambulance bay. Ernesto had been a Marine and cop in a large city, and thought he'd seen the worst humanity had to offer. Every other horror he had experienced paled in comparison.

After the team was parked and dismounted, leaving their machinegunner in place in the turret of the MRAP, Doc Zimmerman led them through the carnage. It was sickening beyond description. All of them knew they would quietly struggle for the rest of their lives with the scenes of dead nurses and doctors, their bodies draped over prostrate corpses of women, children, and the elderly, having obviously been executed from close range trying to protect their patients. In the garden just outside the ER waiting area, they found a pile of bodies burned beyond recognition after being stacked and set on fire. The smell of burned meat and lingering odor of gasoline would haunt their dreams.

Trent stopped the team and asked Doc Zimmerman, "Do we need to go inside?" Doc stopped and slowly began to break down. Once he got control of himself, he choked, "We have to make sure no one needs our help." They took a moment to collect themselves for the task ahead. Trent finally said, "Alright guys, we have to focus. Harden up." He was forced to go to each man and touch them lightly, trying to lead them to suppressing their horror and grief long enough to get the job done. He finally said, "First, finish the fight. Come on guys, there might be someone we can help inside." This truth finally spurred them into action. The team formed up on the ambulance doors and started executing their CQB procedures like the professionals they were.

It took more than three hours to clear the building. During the search, they noticed several bodies of men who had obviously stood and fought; CCW holders mostly, who died in piles of brass trying to slow the horde who attacked. It was to no avail. Those people in the hospital who did not die by gunfire or the flames perished from smoke inhalation. The team did find 11 bodies of what were obviously ghetto rats, all of them armed, who had died from the smoke. It looked like they had gotten lost in the building and died when their 'compatriots' set the structure on fire. "Too bad we can't kill them twice," Doc Zimmerman commented. Everyone agreed.

By the time the team was done, without having located a single surviving victim, they were numbed. They regrouped at the MRAP, but no one wanted to stay there for a break. Trent had Ernesto drive to a small park on the east end of town on State Street. Once there the team cleaned up as best they could. Trent ordered everyone to eat something, but no one bothered.

It was Doc Zimmerman who broke the silence, "If we had stayed at the hospital there is no way we could have held off a force big enough to do that kind of damage." No one responded, but they all knew he was right. Given its position at the edge of Ward 2, the indefensibly large size of the property, and the fact that every dirtbag within walking distance knew the building was full of narcotics, the hospital was a lost cause the moment the lights went out. One hundred assaulters would have had a hard time holding that hospital against what was probably as close as you can get to a real-life zombie horde.

Finally, after realizing even he was basically useless after experiencing trauma on that scale, Trent ordered the team back in the truck. When they were ready to go, he told Ernesto to take them home. They rode in silence, their bodies rocking gently with the rhythm of the truck's suspension. If trauma was the father of vengeance, then Bravo team, 3rd Troop, Black Knight Squadron determined they would be its children.

As they drove north on Arch Avenue, Ernesto was spacing out. He knew they shouldn't be returning to the FOB by driving through Ward 2, but part of him was hoping they would get attacked. After the hospital, he felt the old hate building in him. While it was a comforting feeling, he knew it would ultimately destroy him. He needed a violent outlet.

As they travelled, Trent noticed several groups of hood rats, all armed, on the side streets, and commented to Ernesto, "It's awfully early for the dongs to be awake. It can't be earlier than 1100. Must be a special occasion." Ernesto replied, "They don't want to miss out on the looting. The early dong gets the looted sneakers." Trent laughed and said, "You hate to see a dong lose a sneaker."

Trent was still chuckling when he saw, out of the corner of his eye, an obviously unconscious woman being drug by the hair up

182

the porch steps of a house just east of Liberty Avenue on Auld Street, by a male in an all red sweat suit with an AR15 hanging from his shoulder by a sling. By the time he could open his mouth and yell, "Stop the truck!" Ernesto had passed by the cross-street. It took Ernesto an entire block to get the 30,000-pound combat vehicle stopped. Trent raised his voice so the guys in the back could hear him, "Emergency hostage rescue. Two blocks back on Auld Street, to the east of us. Second house on the north, White with brown trim. One unconscious female being dragged inside by the hair by an armed male. Ernesto, circle to the east and come up Auld Street from that direction." Everyone nodded and started checking their gear as Ernesto got the vehicle moving again. They all happily focused on the new mission, putting the hospital behind them for now.

Trent got on the radio and called it in, hoping someone with a radio was close enough to hear him, "Knight TOC, Knight Three-Bravo-One. We are conducting an in-extremis hostage rescue on Auld Street, two houses east of Liberty on the north side of the street. White house with brown trim. Any units in the area please radio relay to the TOC. If responding, approach from the east. I say again, approach from the east."

*

The ionosphere must have been clearing up, because every police and fire radio in the city that hadn't been fried by the pulse, including the one in the TOC, heard Trent's transmission. From his chair in the TOC, Bones immediately replied, "Knight TOC copies direct." Bones jumped up and stuck his head out of the tent, and yelled, "I need David in the TOC!" His effort turned out to be unnecessary; David had been monitoring the radio while having a late lunch with his wife and kids in the range office / kitchen building. He was sprinting to the TOC before Bones finished his bellowed sentence.

Trent's voice jumped into Mark, Kasey, and Gary's MSA headsets at the same time. Mark had just decided to lead his team back to the FOB and regroup. He had given up on scouting Ward 2. The entire area was a cesspool in the best of times; now it resembled a civil war battlefield. Blocks of burnt out homes, random clumps of

183

dong militia roaming around, and dozens of bodies lying in the street told him everything he needed to know. Since being shot at earlier in the morning, they hadn't had any more violent encounters, but that was more a function of the speed and maneuverability of their quads than any skill on their part.

Mark didn't have to give any orders. They were already pointed in the right direction, and were less than a mile from the target. All they had to do was turn left on Auld and they would be positioned perfectly to help. They all sped up while Mark got on the radio, "Knight Three-Bravo-One, Knight Five. Less than two minutes out with three assaulters. Where do you want us?" Trent replied immediately, "Knight Five, we are about 30 seconds out from the target. We had to get turned around. I'll advise when we get there." Mark clicked his radio PTT twice and focused on pushing the quad as hard as he could without smearing himself on one of the stalled vehicles on the road.

Kyle and 3rd Troop's Alpha team, with Judge Morris in hand, were moving north on Sawburg Avenue when they heard the call on the radio. Not wanting to tie up the radio, he tugged on the machinegunner's leg and yelled up, "Tell the other vehicle to go to that call." The gunner nodded and turned the turret to point backwards. He made eye contact with Ken Branch in the rear vehicle and pointed to his own MSA headset, then pointed at Branch, then made a 'go away' motion. Branch nodded and the second HMWWV slowed and made a u-turn, then sped away on the quickest route to the hostage job.

Kyle told Anson, "Speed up. I want to get the Judge to the FOB and head back out." Anson replied, "So you're telling me to drive fast?" with a grin on his face.

While Judge Morris couldn't hear the radio traffic, because everyone was routing their radios through their headsets, he could tell something was wrong. He leaned forward and asked Kyle, "What's up?" Kyle turned around and told the Judge, "Another team is dealing with a hostage situation over in Ward 2. I sent the other half of our team to help, and we will go after we drop you off." Judge Morris replied, "You don't need to drop me off, I can take care of myself." Kyle shook his head and said, "Sorry Sir, but no way. Ward 2 is a war zone; Chief Stone would kill me if I took you

184

in there." The Judge sighed and nodded his understanding. He sat back and tried to relax. He had known Kyle since before Kyle went in the Army, and the Judge was a college student at Mount Union. He trusted Kyle, and if he said it was a bad idea, it probably was.

In less than five minutes Anson was guiding the HMWWV to a stop in the FOB parking lot, just inside the gate. Kyle jumped out of the HMWWV and helped the judge get his door open. He quickly escorted the Judge to what he thought of as the 'city tent' and found Chief Stone. He told the Chief, "I have to go Chief. We good?" Chief Stone said, "I heard the call. Go." Kyle nodded then jogged back to the HMWWV and jumped in. Anson had already turned the vehicle around, and as he was getting the door closed Kyle said, "Push out." Anson grinned and said, "Let's go kick some dong!" Kyle sighed and said, "Seriously bro, how long have you been saving that one? You're better than that." Anson laughed.

Chapter 22

710 Auld Street, Ward 2
Alliance, OH

Pain and nausea filled Carol's mind as she regained consciousness. The pain seemed to be constant, radiating from her back, hips and abdomen; while the nausea came in short but intense waves. As she struggled to remember why she hurt, she opened her eyes. Everything was blurry, and it took Carol a moment to realize she was looking at the faded pink baseboard and stained white paint of a wall, from about five inches away. *Where am I and why do I hurt so bad?* Carol thought. She was very cold, and realized whatever she was lying on was damp. *It smells like mold in here,* she thought.

Carol closed her eyes and focused on her breathing. She had to move, but fear of more pain made her hesitate. Finally, she opened her eyes again and sat up. The pain was worse than she feared, and she had to put her left hand on the damp carpet to keep from falling back onto her side. The cold wet feeling on her hand helped her focus, and she was able to finish sitting up. Carol kept her eyes closed as she let the waves of nausea wash over her. Once her world stopped spinning, she opened her eyes and tried to figure out where she was. When she looked behind her, moving slowly because of the pain, she saw two women huddled together in the corner. They looked like they were asleep, sharing a dirty zip-up Cleveland Browns hoody as a blanket. *Where the hell am I?* Carol demanded her brain to work.

Then it all came rushing back. Jeff, the sales manager at the Brickyard, had convinced her to let him walk her home after the lights went out. When they got to her house Jeff had refused to leave, telling her it was too dangerous to be alone. Carol asked Jeff to walk with her to her daughter's babysitter's house to pick her up, but he had been insistent that they stay in her house because it was too dangerous. Hearing gunshots outside had convinced her Jeff was probably right. A longtime victim of abuse as a child and teenager at the hands of her father, Carol seemed incapable of resisting even the mildest forms of manipulation by men. Her subconscious mind would find reasons to agree with whatever man she happened to be with at the moment.

Once it got dark, Jeff told her it was best to leave her daughter at the sitters for the night. They would walk over and pick her up in the morning after things calmed down. She wished now she had just gone on her own. During the night, Jeff had joined her in her bed, and she had done what he wanted, more out of a habit of submission than any desire to be with him.

When they woke up in the morning, it took several hours of crying and begging to get Jeff to walk with her to get her daughter. About half a mile into the three-mile trek, they were attacked by a group of young men. One of the men had shoved Jeff down on the ground, then shot him with a handgun a bunch of times. Carol had tried to run away, but was quickly caught and beaten until she lost consciousness. It was the last thing she could remember before waking up on this cold, damp floor.

Carol dragged herself to the other women and collapsed against one of them. She curled up as close as she could and began to cry. When she heard several very loud bangs from inside the house she made herself even smaller and prayed they weren't gunshots. The thought of escaping through the window right in front of her never entered her mind.

In the living room a couple of hood rats in their early 20's, known on the street as P-Hound and Jelly, were chilling on the couch sharing a blunt, when they heard a loud diesel engine rolling up the street. "That got to be them cops I saw creepin'." Jelly said. They both jumped up and grabbed their guns, and Jelly said, "I ain't takin' this no mo'. Can't be that many of 'em." P-Hound replied, "I'll go keep 'dem bitches quiet. Keep da cops out da house. As soon as the hood hears us shootin' they will all come rollin'." Jelly said, "Ah-right. I can't wait to use my laser site on 'dem po-po," and readied his rifle, an older Bushmaster AR15 with a cheap red laser clamped to the barrel, and no sights. He took the gun in a residential burglary several years before, but the laser sight was his customized touch.

As P-Hound bounded upstairs to guard their new 'ladies', Jelly cautiously peeked out the living room window through the curtains, and saw a big tan armored truck with a cop sticking out the top pull to a stop about two houses east of his house. *Maybe them dumb asses are going to the wrong house,* Jelly thought. He brought the rifle to his shoulder and started shooting at the truck

*

Trent crawled back into the troop compartment and briefed the team. "Some of you new guys don't have radios, so in case you missed it, we are doing a hostage rescue in about one minute." Trent said loudly, speaking over the roar of the engine. "It is a white house with brown trim, and will be on our passenger side front, about two houses in front of us. When we exit the back of the truck, go to the driver's side. We will form up there, and I will lead us up to the target." Trent paused as Ernesto wrestled the vehicle around a sharp right turn, jostling everyone around. He continued, "Remember the priority of life puts the hostages above us. The hostage I saw was a white female adult, and the suspect was a black male adult in a red jumpsuit."

One of the new guys, a SWAT assaulter from Akron PD, asked, "So we are containing and making contact?" Trent looked exasperated and said, "No! Brother, the old way of police work died yesterday. You were at the hospital with us, you know things have changed bro. We will immediately assault the house and rescue that hostage." The Akron guy nodded his head, and said, "I gotcha, still trying to flip that switch." Trent nodded his understanding and said, "Me too. I still have to remind myself bro. We are only 20 hours into this thing."

Trent felt the truck brake hard and heard Ernesto say, "Last Turn!" Trent looked each Bravo team member in the eyes then said, "We're all we got." The team responded, "We're all we need!" Trent nodded and said, "Good. When we go out the back, go right and form up. Go right and form up." Trent swiveled on the hard steel deck to face the door, thankful for his Crye pants' integrated kneepads, put his hand on the doorlatch, and waited for Ernesto to stop the vehicle. He knew that unless Ernesto said something else,

188

his 'last turn' call told the team that when the truck stopped again they would be in front of the target.

The truck began to brake and Trent looked out the thick ballistic windows on the back doors. He saw Mark, Kasey, and Gary coming up fast on their quads behind the MRAP, and smiled. He pushed his PTT and said, "Knight Five, Three-Bravo-One. I see you." He heard Mark respond, "Roger. On you." The truck stopped and Trent broke the seal on the left rear 160-pound door, then pushed and held it open as he exited. He waited at the top of the MRAP's back stairs until the next assaulter was able to hold the door. He carefully climbed down the stairs, not wanting to fall the three feet to the pavement in 50 pounds of kit. Not only would it suck to fall, he'd never hear the end of it.

Trent made his way to the driver's side of the MRAP and met Ernesto there, out of sight from the target house behind the truck. As he came up on line with Ernesto, getting two guns on the threat area, a fast string of rifle fire came at them from the target house, about 40 yards away. Muzzle blast carried the stained curtains through the now broken windows, giving the Black Knight assaulters a great target indicator, as rounds snapped overhead and struck the front of the MRAP with loud clanging smacks that rang like a bell. Ernesto immediately took a knee and sucked up to the MRAP near the front, at an angle where he could shoot at the window while exposing as little of himself as possible. Trent sucked up close and put his carbine over Ernesto's head, with the muzzle past his body, but neither of them returned fire.

Both of the assaulters had been conditioned by years of training to not fire into a building where hostages could be present. Luckily Andy, the Sebring cop and machinegunner on top of the MRAP, had no such conditioning. In fact, his training in the infantry had been the direct opposite; if some shoots at you, kill them. Andy immediately began putting bursts into the window where he saw the rifle firing, pushing the billowing curtains back into the house. The fire from the target house stopped, however Andy kept working over the window with bursts of fire. Trent yelled, "Cease fire! Assaulting through!" It took two times yelling and finally banging on the vehicle with his ASP baton before the 7.62mm belt-fed went quiet. Trent yelled, "Cover the neighborhood. We are assaulting." Andy replied, "Roger."

Trent looked behind him and saw his seven assaulters and Mark, Kasey, and Gary behind him, ready to go. He stepped to his left and pulled Ernesto up by the shoulder strap of his plate carrier, while saying, "Stand." As soon as Ernesto was on his feet he barrel released Trent, and the entire group moved up to the target house. As they moved Mark pulled a small 'C' shaped explosive charge from the breacher's pouch hanging from the left side of his plate carrier, and a pre-made section of shock tube with a loop of detcord and a blasting cap at the end of it, called a red devil, from his right cargo pocket. As they jogged to the breach point he clipped the red devil to the charge and said, "I've got breach." Gary and Kasey adjusted their path to work the breach with him. Mark was peeling the carpet tape off the door side of the charge as they ran up the steps of the porch, and quickly checked the door handle. It was locked.

The knob was on the side of the door opposite the living room, so three assaulters, one of them Doc Zimmerman, turned their back to the door to cover the big window through the broken glass and shredded curtains. As Mark was placing the charge around the door handle, Doc called out, "I see one armed dong down in the far-left corner of the living room." Trent said," Roger." As Mark was unspooling his shock tube from the small PVC piece he used to contain the loose end, he said, "Doc, anchor shot that dude if he's armed." Doc shrugged, aimed at the dongs head, compensated for offset, and shot him once in the head.

Mark finished unspooling the shock tube, taking the time to make sure it wasn't wrapped around anyone's legs (especially his), and handed it to Kasey, who held the Royal Arms ignition device she pulled from her breaching pouch. She quickly made sure there was a cap in the device, then loaded the end of the shock tube into the receptacle on the top of the initiator, tightened the locking lug, and pulled the safety pin. Mark brought his 7.62X51 carbine up to cover her as she nodded to Trent. Trent checked to make sure his assaulters were placed safely, and quickly gave Kasey a barrel release.

Less than four minutes from Trent seeing the unconscious woman being drug by the hair into the house, the 50 grain detcord C shaped breaching charge cut the entire handle and deadbolt mechanism out of the door. The team surged through the breach point, with Bravo team focusing on the first floor and basement, while Mark took Kasey, Gary, and Doc Zimmerman to the immediate right of the breach point, where they found the narrow stairs leading to the second floor.

Mark and Gary led up the stairs, with Kasey and Doc staying one landing behind them in case the point element needed room to back up. There wasn't room for both Mark and Gary in the space, so Mark was slightly ahead of Gary on the outside of the first angle, where the stairs turned left. As Mark got a couple of steps from the first landing, and the 90-degree angle of exposure of the left turn, he heard shots from upstairs. Whoever it was, they weren't shooting at them, which concerned him. In a hostage rescue you want the bad guys shooting at you, not the hostages. Mark sprinted up the stairs, Gary right on his heels and Kasey and Doc at a full run, taking two steps at a time, to catch up with them.

Mark could see the muzzle flash and hear the reports of what sounded like a pistol coming from the right side of the second floor, so when his feet hit the second floor landing he pivoted right and drove hard in that direction. His Knights heavy carbine was in the high ready position, with its stock down near his holster and the tip of his muzzle even with where he was looking. Mark liked this position a lot, and preferred it to low ready, when it was safe to use. He was happy he was using it today, because as soon as Mark drove to the right he came face to face with a dong holding a pistol aimed at the floor and a dumb look on his face.

P-Hound didn't have time to react, as Mark's momentum covered the 3 feet separating them faster than his mind could process the giant man in SWAT gear pointing a giant rifle in his face. Before Mr. Hound could process what was happening, Mark had rammed him in the face with the conveniently located muzzle of his 11-pound rifle. Mark's Surefire flash hider somehow found its way past P-Hound's lips, through his teeth and against the roof of his mouth. Mark continued driving to the far corner, now with P-Hound swinging from the end of his gun.

Aside from some missing teeth, this wouldn't have been too terrible for P-hound; except that when his back found the hallway wall, his sudden stop was met by the mass-times-velocity of 220 pounds of assaulter and 60 pounds of gear, focused on the very small surface area where the top half of the tip of Mark's flash hider was touching the roof of P-Hound's mouth. The result was messy.

Mark's continued forward momentum not only turned his flash hider into a bayonet, but it imbedded P-Hound in the drywall.

Mark held the dong against the wall and let go of his rifle with his left hand. He took the Taurus Millennium 9mm pistol out of the guy's hand as he continued to convulse and leak blood, and grey gelatinous matter, out of his mouth, all over Mark's rifle and boots. Looking around and seeing that Gary and Kasey had flowed past him, he waited for Doc to come into his peripheral vision before he let the pressure off the guy. When Mark stepped back and ripped his muzzle out of the dude's face with one hard tug, the dong remained trapped in the drywall. Doc grimaced and said, "Not much I can do for that wound. Holy shit."

Mark reached up, grabbed the still convulsing body, and succeeded in getting it out of the drywall. He let the dude flop to the ground, then kicked the guy over onto his face, Cobra cuffed him and searched him for weapons. Finding nothing other than some bunk weed rolled inside blunts, Mark and Doc looked for more work to do. Doc said, "Everything behind us is clear." Mark nodded and led Doc into the closest room. The door was marked with a chemlight, so Mark knew Gary and Kasey had already been here.

As they did a quick secondary search of the room, they heard Kasey broadcast on the radio, "Three-Bravo-One, Knight Five-Alpha. Three Hotels' recovered on level two. We are going to need a few minutes to get them ready to move and…" Kasey was interrupted when Gary, who was looking out one of the bedroom windows to the southwest, brought his rifle optic up to his eye, dialed more magnification on his Khales 1-6, and fired 10 rounds quickly. The three hostages screamed and tried leaving the room, probably because the BCM 5.56mm 14.5 inch carbine with the Warcomp on the end felt like a flashbang was going off in the room every time Gary fired.

Kasey managed to get the women under control as Mark and Doc moved inside the room. Doc helped Kasey with the girls while Mark went to the window to see what Gary was shooting at. When Mark looked out the window he said, "Shit." then pushed his PTT, "Three-Bravo-One, Knight Five. Two large groups of armed dongs are approaching from the west and the southwest. Both are less than 100 yards away. You need to get out of here now. We will try to fix them in place from up here, Kasey and Doc are moving the Hotels to you. Get them to the truck and haul ass. Don't wait for us." Gary resumed firing as soon as Mark stopped talking, and Kasey and Doc pushed the hostages out of the room and down the stairs.

Mark motioned for Gary to take a knee, then stood behind him in the high/low position, and both of them began shooting. Mark could hear the M240 working on top of the MRAP, and saw dongs falling down in the group to the southwest, as that group scattered under the intense machinegun fire. He focused on the group of about 10 dongs filtering through the houses to the south, an area that wasn't visible from the MRAP. Mark picked out a white kid in a Nike hoodie carrying a lever action rifle, and tried to steady the red dot of his Short Dot optic as much as possible, given the target was jogging and he was shooting from an unsupported standing position, and fired two rounds at him.

With so many bad guys, Mark didn't want to become too focused on any one threat. He moved onto the next target, then the next, delivering controlled pairs to everyone down there as fast as he could transition targets. The dongs finally wised up and scattered, taking cover behind the houses in the area. Even with the active hearing protection provided by their MSA headsets, the concussion of the unsuppressed rifles in the 10X8 foot room was deafening. The only way Mark knew the MRAP was moving off target was Trent came on the radio and said, "Three-Bravo-One off target. Knight Five, move."

Gary and Mark didn't need to be told twice. They reloaded their rifles, then sprinted out of the room, past the Cobra-cuffed dong on the floor, and down the stairs. They paused long enough at the front door to regroup, then Mark gave Gary a barrel release and they pushed outside. Sporadic gunfire snapped around them, but none of it seemed to be impacting close to them. Mark took a knee on the front lawn, facing the south, and said, "Set." Gary sprinted about 25 yards east, turned around and took a knee and yelled, "Set." Mark got up and ran about 50 yards east to their quads, turned around and took a knee and yelled, "Set." Gary got up and sprinted the last 25 yards to the quads, got on his quad and started it. Once it was running, he brought his carbine to the high ready, prepared to cover Mark.

Mark got on his quad and started it, then hesitated. He hated to leave Kasey's quad here; he didn't want to give the dongs any transportation. As he thought about how to destroy it, the answer came in the form of a ranger green HMWWV screeching around the nearest corner to their east and skidding to a halt. Ken Branch got out of the passenger seat and said, "Where do you want us?" Mark replied, "Get on this quad and let's get out of here." Branch didn't hesitate; he ran to the quad, got on, and started it. Mark turned his quad around to face east and said, "Moving." He gunned the engine and took off to the east, with the other two quads and the HMWWV on his tail.

After they turned north off Auld Street onto Mahoning, Mark pushed his PTT and said, "Knight Five off target. Last man. Units rally back at the FOB."

In the MRAP, Kasey breathed a prayer of thanks to the Lord. When Mark ordered her and Doc to get the hostages to the MRAP and leave, she hadn't hesitated. But as soon as the MRAP pulled away from the target she realized Mark and Gary were still stuck in that house, and were being surrounded by dirtbags with guns. She should have stayed behind once the hostages were secure in the armored vehicle. In the two minutes or so between them pulling away and Mark calling off target, she had convinced herself he had sacrificed himself for her, and he wasn't going to make it out. She said her prayer of thanks and tried to let it go.

As she watched the chaotic scene in front of her inside the cramped MRAP troop compartment, she found something new to focus on: Doc Zimmerman was having a rough time checking one of the hostages, a young black girl who looked about 12 years old. The girl kept batting his hands away and yelling, "Get off me!" Kasey fought the motion of the truck and the confined space until she was next to the girl and said, "He's a doctor, let him check you." The girl stopped resisting and let Doc check her for gunshot wounds. Finding nothing, Doc checked the last hostage, then started making the rounds of the team, making sure no one was wounded or hurt and unaware because of the adrenalin dump of the hit.

Kasey wanted to say something to the girl to comfort her, but the noise of the truck and the general pandemonium in the troop compartment prevented anything but the most basic communication. It didn't help Ernesto was obviously trying to qualify for the pole position in a NASCAR race, the way he was driving. Carol, her already nauseous stomach pushed over the edge by the violent and

194

unpredictable movement in the virtually windowless troop compartment, croaked, "I'm going to be sick," and promptly projectile vomited all over Trent, who was sitting across from her. Trent, a blank look on his face, stared straight ahead into space.

After a few seconds, he yelled up at Ernesto, "Slow down bro, it's like a roller coaster back here." The roller coaster reference, along with the smell of fresh vomit, was apparently enough to make the girl next to Kasey violently toss her cookies, followed closely by a chain-reaction of assaulters spewing the contents of their stomachs all over one another. Kasey looked at Trent and said, "Have fun cleaning this up. Not it!" Looking pretty green himself by now, Trent could only flip her off before he too lost his dignity.

Chapter 23

Norfolk Southern Railroad Right-of-way
One mile north of Alliance, OH

Earlier that morning, as day two of the apocalypse dawned, Chris was walking to the FOB bathrooms and looking at the cold grey sky, after waking up from whopping 3 hours of sleep. As he strolled along minding his own business, Kyle stopped him and said, "Good Morning Chris! Congratulations, you've been volun-told! You're now in charge of 'Salvage and Resource Recovery' for the City." Chris could only stare at him blankly for a minute, not really understanding what Kyle was telling him. When he didn't speak Kyle said, "It'll be fun buddy!" with a grin. Chris replied, "What will be fun? I don't know what the hell you're talking about."

Kyle grinned and said, "You've been reassigned to be in charge of all the salvage work the city needs to survive; gathering all the food, fuel, stuff like that. We were just discussing who would be best to do that job, and I dropped your name. Aren't you excited!" Chris began to understand what Kyle was telling him and said, "You're an asshole Kyle." Kyle laughed then got serious for a second, "Seriously bro, You're perfect for the job. We really do need you in that slot." Chris sighed and replied, "Buddy is only half the name. Holy crap that's a huge undertaking." He paused to think, then said, "Can I have Ed to help?" Kyle said, "You know I'm the King of the Blue Falcons buddy. Yes, you can have Ed; and the Mayor is instituting a plan to gather as much manpower as we can get. You'll have priority for all of the appropriately skilled labor."

Chris made one last-ditch attempt, "I'm not sure I'm the best person for the job bro, and my team needs me." Kyle shook his head, "You are the best person for the job; and I have trigger pullers coming out of my ears. What I don't have is anyone else that can plan, think logically, organize, and execute big jobs with no supervision, who also has your depth of experience moving and keeping track of lots of big things, and leading the huge amounts of manpower needed to get it done." Chris sighed and said, "Well, alright I guess." Kyle smiled and said, "That's the spirit of half-hearted indifference we've come to expect from you! You're welcome," then walked away laughing.

Chris spent the first 5 minutes of his new job trying to find Ed. He finally tracked him down in the FOB kitchen, eating a peanut butter sandwich and sipping a Diet Pepsi. Chris stood over him and stared. Ed ignored him. Chris sat down across the narrow plastic classroom table and continued to stare. Finally, Ed said, "Do you have to register with the cops for that thing?" "What 'thing'?" Chris replied. Ed said, "That weirdo perv thing you're doing, watching me eat like you're putting cash in your spank bank. I doubt I'm your first victim." Ed looked at Ken Branch's wife, who was in the kitchen having an early morning cup of coffee, and continued, "I mean, seriously Karen, you seeing this sicko assaulting me with his eyes? Hashtag 'me too', right sister!"

Karen spit coffee out her nose laughing. Chris couldn't help himself, and busted up. When the laughter died down Ed said, "What's up brother Chris?" It was Chris' turn to smile, "We got a special mission buddy, just me and you." Ed was a former Marine, and noticed the 'buddy' Chris just dropped on him. Anytime someone called you buddy, you were about to get the big green one in the exit only chute. He groaned and said, "Uh oh." Chris smiled even bigger and said, "That's right buddy, you and me. I just got assigned as the City Salvage and Resource Recovery Director, and guess who is now my right-hand man? That's right buddy; you! Aren't you excited!"

Ed groaned louder and exclaimed, "Oh no you didn't! No way bro, I'm a shooter, not a supply clerk. I'm on a squared away team; we are deploying in like 20 minutes. For the first time since I got out of the Marines, I feel useful bro. No way; not happening! Find someone else." he crossed his arms and gave Chris his best mad-dog Marine scowl. Chris just grinned and said, "Squadron Commander Kyle Wilson himself assigned you to me buddy. If I gotta come off a team and do this job 'for the greater good', you do too buddy. Look on the bright side." Ed waited for Chris to tell him what the bright side was, and when he didn't Ed said, "What bright side?" Chris grinned and said, "Oh, there isn't one. I was just trying to sound positive." Karen found that one much more amusing than

Ed did. Ed finally sighed and said, "Alright. We're burning daylight. Where do we start?"

Chris and Ed spent the next hour in the TOC with David, Bones, Chief Stone, Lydia (the Squadron's Supply Clerk), and Sgt. Wiggins, the 4th Troop commander, planning their first moves. The first priority was the gun store just east of town on State road, because it was the only other place near town to buy guns, besides Walmart. The Chief wanted control of those weapons as soon as possible. Chris flexed his new power by asking Wiggins to send a 10-man team to secure the gunstore and hold it, until Chris could get transportation over there to move the weapons and ammo. Wiggins left the meeting to organize that mission.

Next, they made a list of resources they needed to secure, move, inventory and store. Using the list of critical resources David started on the white board early in the crisis, they decided to focus their energy today on the loaded train sitting on the tracks north of town along Hwy 183, and the large grocery store distribution center a few miles southwest of town, off Hwy 62. These two targets seemed to represent not only the largest payoff in terms of supplies, but also the least risk of problems to secure them. Both the train and the food warehouse were in rural areas, and were not known by the general public.

"The Mayor's intent," Chief Stone concluded, "is to secure as much food and fuel as possible, so we can make it through the winter and summer, before bulk crop harvesting, with as much of our population intact as possible. David's job is to use intel from the Troops and Teams to locate as much of these resources as possible; while Chris, it's your job to get them secured, transported to a central area if possible, and inventoried. Once you have done this, whoever the Mayor appoints as the supply manager later today will be responsible for allocation and distribution."

Chris said, "OK Chief. What is my direction if we find supplies that someone else is already claiming?" The Chief replied, "Well, that depends. If it is the property of a locally owned company, leave them be. We won't be seizing private property when the owner is present; and if someone else has taken it, we will use force to return it to its rightful owner."

The Chief paused to think, then continued, "If it is owned by a corporation whose headquarters are not in our city, we will be

198

seizing it under the Mayor's Emergency Declaration. If it's someone's personal property, and is not obviously abandoned, leave it alone. If it was bought by taxpayers on any level, federal, state, or local, seize it. If someone else has already taken something that falls into a category marked for seizure, take it back. If you can't do it with your own resources, call the TOC, and the Squadron will give the mission to one of the Troops Commanders."

Chris looked up from his notepad, where he had been furiously scribbling, and asked, "Would it be possible to get those rules in writing Sir? I don't doubt for a second you would back me up if there was a problem, but I am going to need a ton of manpower as this ramps up; and I'd like to have a clear, written order for my people to follow." Chief Stone nodded and said, "Absolutely Chris. That's a wise request, on many levels. I'll have it drafted and get the Mayor to sign it as soon as we are done here." Chris replied, "Thank you Sir."

The rest of the meeting was spent allocating resources. David assigned Dan's 3rd Troop to send a team to secure the ABC Food Superstore distribution center. Chris decided he would go to the train himself and evaluate what they needed to do to get it unloaded. David tasked 4th Troop to provide a five-man security element to watch Chris' back while he worked. Chris tasked Ed with finding a working mobile crane. They would need it if they hoped to unload the train before hell froze over, and he was sure it would have many other uses down the road.

Within half an hour everyone was moving. Chris sat in while David briefed Dan and 3rd Troop's Charlie Team leader, Phil, on their mission to the food distribution center. Dan was leading the mission, and would seize and hold the facility until 4th Troop could organize a guard force to come relieve them. Once 3rd Troop pushed out of the gate, Chris helped Ed get two of the dirtbikes ready to go; one for Ed and one for the 4th Troop guy Wiggins had assigned to go with him.

Ed didn't know the new guy being sent with him, a Sebring cop named Ray who had come in last night; but he claimed to be both an excellent dirtbike rider and a former diesel mechanic before he became a cop. Chris had to get into the vault to get Ray a long gun; apparently, Ray had walked to Alliance in his patrol uniform and didn't have any gear other than whatever was on his patrol belt.

It turned out Ray had never fired an M4, but was comfortable with a shotgun, so Chris grabbed him an 870P with a sling and Surefire fore end light, and 50 rounds of Federal Flight Control 00 Buck. It wasn't a perfect setup for someone who was going to be out running around in the apocalypse, but it would have to do.

After Ed and Ray pushed out, Chris gathered up his little 4th Troop security element and showed them how to run a pre-combat equipment check. Once he got through that little piece of hip pocket training heaven, made better by having to give one of the guys some extra training on not pointing his pistol at his friends while using his fat little fingers to attempt a press-check, Chris gathered the team around and briefed them on the mission. He ended the briefing with a hearty, "We're all we got!" The team just stared at him.

Chris sighed and explained, "Guys, here at the Black Knight Squadron we do a little thing to remind ourselves of who we are. When someone says 'we're all we got' you reply, all together, with 'we're all we need'. Got it?" A couple of the guys nodded their understanding, but Fat Fingers objected, "What kind of high school football hoo-rah BS is that? That's dumb." Chris stared at him for a moment then said, "We do it to remind ourselves that in this shitty apocalypse, all we have is each other, and that's enough for us. While you're a member of this Squadron you will do it. If not, I'm sure Lydia could use help counting ammo or something."

Fat Fingers looked offended. *Who does this kid think he is,* Fat Fingers thought, *I'm a cop, and twice his age. Screw this guy.* As he was about to open his mouth, one of the guys he worked with at Louisville PD told him, "Shut up Bill. This kind of stuff is important, trust me. Be part of the team or go away." Fat Fingers reluctantly followed the advice, and when Chris hit them again with a, "We're all we got." he even participated in the, "We're all we need," that followed. With that behind them, they loaded up in Ed's old Chevy pickup and headed for the train.

After passing out of the ECP, they turned right and sped up Rockhill to Hwy 183, the guys in the bed of the truck freezing their asses off the whole way. It took about five minutes for the team to make it to the first locomotive engine of the southbound train. Chris pulled the truck up onto the right-of-way and parked, then got the team deployed. Wiggins hadn't appointed one of them as team leader, so Chris was having to do that job too.

Once he was fairly certain the team could protect themselves and the truck, he walked to the lead engine. As he got close, a short middle aged white guy in a Norfolk Southern uniform opened the crew door on the engine and stepped outside. Chris was surprised; it never occurred to him that the train would have a crew he would have to deal with. *That was dumb,* Chris thought, *Of course the crew isn't going to just say 'well, I guess our train don't work, lets walk away'.*

Chris decided he'd have to play it by ear, and said, "Hello sir. I'm Chris Mason, and I'm from the City of Alliance. I'm here to check on you guys." The crewman looked relieved and said, "Thank God." He climbed down off the engine and walked to Chris, sticking his hand out and saying, "Hello sir, I'm Roman Stewart. I'm the Conductor for this beast." Chris nodded and said, "Nice to meet you Mr. Stewart. How many of you are there in the crew? Is everyone alright?"

"I'm fine, thank you. Just a little hungry," Stewart replied. Chris nodded as Stewart continued, "The Engineer took off last night. Said he was walking into Atwater to steal a bike and ride home. He and I were the only crew. I manage the train with remote sensors and a drone these days, so we only need two crewmen for a train this size." Chris let his carbine hang on its sling and pulled a protein bar and water bottle out of his right cargo pocket, handing both to Stewart and saying, "Take my lunch. It will hold you over until I can get someone to bring us some food." Steward thanked him and invited Chris into the engine cab to get out of the wind to talk.

Once inside the cramped cab, Chris asked Stewart, "So, do you know what you're going to do? I assume the train engines are fried, right?" Stewart nodded and finished chewing a bite, then said, "Yeah. Whatever happened it killed all our electronics, even my cell phone and our radios. I read a lot of end of the world type books, and figure this was an EMP. If it had been a CME, it probably would have caught the engines on fire, and I didn't see any northern lights last night. So, I figure the North Koreans finally got one off on us. When you showed up I was trying to figure out what to do. I live in Iowa, so walking home in the winter is a non-starter."

Chris nodded his understanding and said, "Well, you are welcome to stay here in Alliance. The reason I'm here is I was just appointed to head up the City's salvage operations. I could use your help; and it seems like you're now unemployed, at least temporarily." Stewart looked at Chris and said, "I don't suppose it pays much, but money probably won't matter much after today or tomorrow. I reckon it's the best offer I've had all day." Stewart stuck out his hand and they shook on it.

Stewart spent the next 45 minutes answering Chris' questions about the train and cargo. Chris learned the 214-car train was a mixed cargo of double stacked Conex shipping containers, 15 full cars of processed coal, and 14 full DOT-111 34,000 gallon diesel tanker cars. With the cargo management computers not working, Stewart couldn't see the manifests that would tell them what was in the individual Conex containers. They would have to unload and search every one of the 370 individual Conex boxes to discover what was in them.

"Well, Stewart," Chris said, "This is going to suck. Where do we even start?" Stewart blew out a long breath and said, "Yeah it is. Unloading a train by hand is crazy." He paused to think for a second, and Chris said, "I have a guy out looking for a mobile crane that will run. He knows of several that are stored inside large metal buildings that may still work." Stewart looked confused and asked, "Metal buildings?" Chris said, "Yeah, we've found that things that were inside a properly grounded metal building at the time of the pulse still work.

Stewart nodded and continued, "OK. First, we need to figure out how to get the Conex's off the cars. If we can find a crane it'll be pretty straight forward. If not, it will be a cast iron bitch. I have no idea how to do that." Chris said, "I guess we should go look at the cars and see what we can come up with."

When they jumped down Chris called to his security team, "I need two of you to stay with the truck, and the other three come with me." It took a moment for the guys to get their stuff together and three of them to walk to Chris. "What's up?" one of them asked. Chris said, "We are going to go look at some of the train cars and try to figure out a way to move Conex's off of them by hand." All three of them looked surprised, and one of them said, "You mean, like, take the Conex's off the train by hand, without a crane?" Chris nodded and said, "If we have to, yes." One of the guys in a Sheriff's uniform shrugged and said, "I suppose if the Egyptians could move big ass rocks up, we could move big ass boxes down. Lead the way Chris."

When they turned to walk north, along the length of the train, Chris was immediately struck by its enormity. Sitting in his car waiting for trains to go by, while parked at a railroad crossing, was a part of daily life in Alliance. But only ever seeing trains from that perspective hadn't prepared him for just how big everything was when you were standing next to it. He mentioned this to Stewart, who said, "It still boggles my mind every day."

It took them several minutes to walk past the three locomotive engines that had pulled the train until yesterday. Once they reached the first Conex car, stacked two-high with grey 40' long Conex boxes, Stewart gave them a quick safety briefing on where to climb, what to hold, and where not to step. They carefully climbed up on the cars and Stewart showed them how the boxes locked into the car, and one another.

As they walked to the back of the car, Chris noticed that the bottom Conex sat in a tub in the train car, and asked, "I don't suppose there is room to just open the doors on the bottom Conex and unload them?" Stewart grunted and said, "Unfortunately no. The bottom box sits in a tight space, and there isn't room to even get to the door mechanisms, much less open the doors." One of the 4th Troop guys with Chris asked, "But we could open the doors on the top box?" Stewart started to reply then stopped himself.

By now they were at the back end of the train car and were looking at the doors from up close. Stewart looked around, then said, "We could use a ladder anchored there," pointing at a flat spot on the edge of the car, "But once you got the doors open, how would you sort through what's in the box to see if it's even worth taking? Most of these boxes will be loaded with palletized goods, stacked to the ceiling, all the way to the doors. Even if we could get them sorted, the pallets would have to be broken down inside the box and moved out by hand."

Chris grimaced and said, "Well that shoots down my first idea. I was thinking we could just cut the hinges off the Conex doors and move them out of the way with block and tackle, but that won't work if we still can't sort them." Stewart nodded and said, "I don't think we are going to be able to get away with not unloading the Conex's, Chris. I hope your man can find a crane that works." "Me too," Chris replied. The next couple of minutes were spent with Chris and Stewart looking the cars and boxes over, trying to figure out a way to do it by hand.

While Chris, Stewart, and the three security guys were walking the train, Fat Fingers was trying to convince the guy who stayed with him to guard the truck, one of his Louisville PD co-workers, to leave with him. "Come on Rich," Fat Fingers was saying, "the keys are in the truck. This whole 'Black Knight' thing is bullshit. We could take the truck and head to my dad's place over in Columbiana County. He has a small farm. Besides, we are armed. I'm sure we could 'acquire'," Fat Fingers used his fat little finger quotes, "some supplies in between here and there, one way or another."

Rich Masters was shaking his head, and replied, "No way dude. I know Kyle, and this group here in Alliance is far and away our best chance of surviving. You have no idea how lucky we are they let us stay. Things haven't really even gotten bad yet, but when they do I want to be part of the biggest, baddest dog on the block. I'll stick with them, man."

Both men were standing at the tailgate of the pickup, about three feet from one another. Fat Fingers weighed his options and made a decision. He nodded his head and raised his eyebrows as if to agree with Rich, and making an exaggerated move back from the truck and stretching, he pointed over Rich's shoulder and said, "What the hell are those guys doing?" When Rich turned to look, Fat Fingers made his play.

Fat Fingers was able to draw his Glock 22 .40 caliber pistol and fire four rounds into Rich's body from less than two feet away before Rich knew what hit him. Three of the 180 grain Gold Dots' found their way into the open space of Rich's soft body armor under his left armpit, and one of them blew the center out of Rich's aorta. Rich let out a terrified scream and fell down. He was dead within 30 seconds. By then Fat Fingers was in the truck roaring back onto Hwy 183 heading north.

Chris and the rest of the team heard the gunshots, followed closely by the sound of the Chevy truck starting up and peeling out in the gravel. Chris jumped off the train car and grabbed his carbine off his back, where he had cinched it down with his Blue Force Gear VCAS sling. Looking to the south, he saw Ed's truck pull out onto Hwy 183 and turn towards him. He ran to the edge of the elevated railroad bed and stopped. Chris saw the truck was only about 75 yards away, and was closing the distance fast. He brought the T1 optic up to his eye, stabilized his stance, and started shooting at the driver.

He got six 5.56 mm rounds launched from the BCM carbine before the truck passed him, no more than 50 feet away. Chris pivoted with the truck's motion, continuing to pour fire into the driver, who he could now clearly see was Fat Fingers, his face contorted with rage and fear. When the truck was beyond him but still at a shallow angle, Chris saw one of his rounds connect with Fat finger's head through the rear truck window.

He watched as blood and grey matter misted out of the driver's window like cigarette smoke, and the truck immediately went out of control. Chris watched as the truck slammed into a tree on the east side of the road, about 60 yards beyond where he was standing, driver's door first. He watched the truck break in half from the force of the impact, debris flying in all directions.

Chris reloaded his carbine and turned to give orders to the rest of the team. Everyone had looks of shock on their faces and seemed frozen in place. "Hey!" Chris shouted at them, "Someone go check on the other security guy at the truck, and someone come with me. One of you stay here with Stewart."

No one moved, and one of them said, "What just happened?" Chris gave the guy a withering glare and said, "This is the apocalypse bro. Try to keep up. Now move!" The guy nodded jerkily and turned and ran to where the truck had been parked. One of the other guys came to Chris and they jogged down the right-of-way embankment to the road, then up to the wreckage of the truck. Before he got there Chris remembered he had a radio.

"Knight TOC, Knight Eight. Shots fired. Splash one, and unknown friendly injuries. I need some help here at the south end of

205

the train." He didn't hear anything and re-broadcast the same message. When they got close to the wreckage, he noticed his ears were ringing and thought, *That's weird. My ear pro should have blocked the gunfire noise... Crap!* Looking down Chris saw his MSA ear pro / comm set swinging by the carabiner attached to his plate carrier, where he had stashed it after taking off his helmet and headset to climb on the train. *That would explain why I can't hear anyone answering me on the radio,* he thought, and quickly donned his headset.

When it got close to his ears he could already hear the TOC replying to his message. He keyed up again and said, "Knight TOC, Knight Eight. Sorry about that, was busy. Say again?" He heard Bones' voice say, "I said Roger, Knight Eight. A team has already pushed out to you with backup and a medic. Are you still engaged?" Chris replied, "Negative TOC. Threat is down." Bones replied, "Roger."

Chris and his partner found the bottom half of Fat Fingers lying on the passenger side of what was left of the truck's bench seat, with a trail of intestines still connecting it to the upper half of his body, which was pinned between the truck's A pillar and the tree. Chris' partner backed up and turned away, his years of police work being the only thing saving him from yacking all over the scene. Chris just stared at what was left of Fat Fingers and ran the event over in his mind again, trying to make sure his instinctual judgement had been the right one.

Then he remembered the other guy he'd left with Fat Fingers at the truck, and the sounds of shots. He started running south on Hwy 183, hoping he would find the other guy alive. When he got to within 50 yards of where he'd left the truck, he knew it wasn't to be. He saw the guy he'd sent to check on Fat Fingers' partner standing over a body with his head down. Chris slowed to a walk and arrived at the same time as David, who had ridden a dirtbike to the scene from the FOB. David dumped the bike on its side and ran to the down assaulter, dropping his med bag next to him as he slid to a knee and started checking him.

In less than a minute David stood up and looked at Chris, shaking his head. "I'm sorry Chris," David said quietly, "He's gone." Chris could only nod. *Less than 24 hours in and I've lost four people under my leadership,* Chris thought, remembering his three employees who died in the opening minutes of the event, *and I don't even remember this guy's name. I watched him kiss his wife goodbye at the FOB before we left.* Chris looked down at the body and saw a nametag, 'Masters'. He prayed for Masters' and his family, and dreaded returning to the FOB.

David, seeing Chris' mind at work, tried to get him to focus, "What happened, Chris?" Chris snapped out of it and gathered his thoughts. The assaulter Chris sent to check on Masters spoke up, "When we showed up we parked here. Chris took us to check on the train, and we left Masters and Panovich," *That must be Fat finger's name* Chris thought, "here to guard the truck. We heard several shots and saw the truck come speeding out onto 183. Chris ran down and shot at the truck and it wrecked. From what I can see here," he pointed to some shell casings about 5 yards to the southeast of Masters' body, "Panovich must have murdered Masters and stolen the truck."

David looked at Chris, who said, "That's about it. When I heard the shots, and saw the truck hauling ass, I figured someone was stealing the truck. I engaged him on the road, and he crashed about 300 yards north of here. Panovich is dead as well." David nodded and said, "Ok. Let's get this cleaned up and get back to the FOB."

It took about 15 minutes to collect Masters' body and get it loaded on the M915 semi-tractor that came to the scene after David called for it. With all the Troops out on missions, it was the only working vehicle left at the FOB. Chris helped Stewart load his overnight bag into the cab of the semi, then they all jumped on the back of the truck around the 5th wheel plate and held on for dear life.

Shortly after returning to the FOB, Chris participated in his first ever death notification. It was even worse than he could have imagined. Lost in the moment, he didn't notice the rush of activity around the FOB caused by the hostage rescue going down over on Auld Street, until Ed opened the door into the kitchen and said, "Need to see you bro," then closed the door.

Chris let out a long breath and hugged Masters' wife, then stood up. Chris' wife, Amanda, came to the range when the PD was evacuated last night, and he went to her before he left the kitchen. They shared a quick hug and kiss, and Amanda quietly told him,

"Stay strong Chris. Rely on the Lord and these people. We will get through this." Chris nodded, gave Amanda another kiss and said, "I love you." She smiled and said, "I know. Now get back to work." Chris gave her a weak smile, and she knew she would have to spend a lot of time helping Chris heal after things calmed down. Until then, she needed to help him stay focused.

Chris walked out of the kitchen, finding Ed just outside speaking to David. Chris looked at Ed and said, "Sorry about your truck brother. I should have kept the keys." Ed shrugged and said, "Meh. As much as I'd love to blame you, it wasn't your fault; that asshole was willing to kill for it. Don't worry about it bro. I'll come up with a way for you to pay me back." Chris groaned. He knew 25 years from now Ed would still be bringing it up. David said, "Alright, next problem. The 4th Troop guys you sent to check the gun store found it looted and two employees tortured to death. They said the place was literally stripped bare, and all the safes were empty. They must have sweated the combos out of the clerks. We did recover their FFL book, so we know what got loose, but consider that one a loss."

Chris said, "Roger, does the Chief know?" and David replied, "Yes, the TL briefed him." Chris nodded and David continued, "Next, Bravo team of 3rd Troop just pulled off a hostage rescue and are on their way back. We need to get ready to receive them. Can you two organize the wives in there," David pointed at the kitchen door, "to get ready to deal with three female hostages?" Chris and Ed nodded and turned back into the kitchen to get things organized. Chris decided grief would have to wait for its season.

Chapter 24

Stark County Main Library
Canton, OH

Bookie always felt most comfortable in the library. Growing up, it was the only place he felt at ease; not feeling like he had to be hyper-vigilant watching for someone trying to hurt him. Knowing Bookie better than anyone else alive, it was no surprise to Jigsaw when Bookie told him this morning they would be setting up their headquarters at the Stark County main library.

Bookie now traveled in a three-car convoy, with 12 OG gangsters as bodyguards. As they sped through town, Bookie admired the handiwork of his designs. Dead cops, firefighters, bus drivers, and plain old white folks hung from traffic lights almost every block. Every gas station and grocery store they passed had armed black men standing guard outside.

Most of them looked asleep, but Bookie could tolerate that. It was, after all, only day two of this new world, and they had enjoyed a long night of rape and pillage. He made a mental note to have Jigsaw slowly implement his plan for discipline. Better to boil the frogs slowly, and before they knew it these hood rats would be transformed into a real army.

Jigsaw was surprised when they got to the library and found it intact, with not even a single window broken. *Makes sense,* Jigsaw thought, *none of these Canton crackheads ever read one page of no book, so they don't know it's here.* Bookie asked his guards to find a way into the locked-up building, and one of them raised his AK to shoot out the glass of the main doors. Jigsaw had to say, "Stop. This is our new crib; don't break nothin' gettin' in. One of you OG's gotta know how to jimmy a door."

It turned out several of them did. Within three minutes one of Bookie's bodyguards was opening the main doors from the inside of the building. Bookie set up what he called his 'command center' in the second floor reading area, and ordered Jigsaw to have all the runners, kids between eight and 12 years old on bicycles, report to the first floor prepared to work. Jigsaw left the command center to pass the word, and to make sure security was tight on the building.

Bookie's first order of business was to get in touch with the leader of the Canton chapter of ANTIFA, a crazy school teacher lady named 'Dragonlord'. Bookie didn't know her real name, and didn't care. She'd first come to Bookie two years ago, seeking financial assistance and 'muscle', as she called it, to back her plans for some Black Lives Matter protests.

They had developed a good working relationship, and Bookie had continued supporting her when she'd decided BLM was too tame for her. In late 2016, she founded her own ANTIFA group, telling Bookie, "We got to get revolution up in here if we want things to change. Anarchy followed by communism is the only answer." Bookie didn't necessarily agree with her grammar or her views about communism, but anything that spread chaos was a win for him. The weaker the bonds that held society together were, the better Bookie could exploit the resulting misery for a good profit.

Bookie decided now was the time to let Dragonlord go hog wild. He sought maximum chaos right now, in order to allow him to seize all the resources within his reach. Once he felt he was in full control, he could dispose of Dragonlord and her band of useful idiots, and implement his end game: an African Kingdom in the heart of Ohio, with him as King. Only then would he allow enough stability to let free markets develop, under his strict control of course, and usher in a golden age of African dominance of middle America.

Jigsaw entered the command center and paused. He could see Bookie was deep in thought, and hesitated to interrupt. While Jigsaw wasn't especially gifted intellectually, he was an emotional intelligence powerhouse. Jigsaw had a natural ability to read people's moods and expressions with uncanny accuracy, and this allowed him to always know how to best deal with someone, especially Bookie. He and Bookie had been close since they were kids, when Jigsaw took the handicapped kid under his wing. As they grew up together, raised each other really, Jigsaw had learned to see through Bookie's undiagnosed PTSD and sociopathy, and communicate with him to maximum effect.

Jigsaw waited patiently until he saw Bookie's expression change, then softly said, "Hey Book. We're set up downstairs. I sent some peeps to snatch up Dragonlord, but there is a dude one of the runners just brought in, who is saying he has information for you. He used to work for us as a dealer until he got popped, now he's on parole and was laying low." Bookie asked, "Why does he insist on speaking to me?" Jigsaw said, "He thinks the info is valuable, and wants you to know it's from him."

Bookie said, "OK. Bring him to me, please." Jigsaw said, "Ah-right." and walked downstairs. Bookie sat down and composed himself. He hated face to face dealings with thugs, but maybe this guy had something useful. Jigsaw escorted the young black man wearing a white coat and red pants into the command center and introduced him, "This is Jordan Williams. He has information." Bookie nodded and raised his eyebrows, waiting for the guy to speak. Jordan was obviously intimidated, and stammered his sales pitch, "Yo, so... so I work at this ABC grocery warehouse for my parole job. It's a big ass place, with tons and tons of food. The place is bigger than a prison, and it's full of food. They send food to all the grocery stores. I figure the info on the place worth a lot." Bookie stared intently at Jordan, making him even more uncomfortable.

Finally, Bookie said, "Thank you Jordan. Please wait downstairs for Jigsaw; He and I will discuss your information." Jordan replied, "How much chedda I get?" Bookie ignored the question and instead said, "Jordan, how long did you work for me?" "Bout fo' years." Jordan replied. Bookie nodded and said, "In that time were you ever treated unfairly?" Jordan said, "No, you was always straight up wit me Bookie." Bookie nodded again and said, "So what makes you think you can walk in here and insult me by assuming I would not pay you a fair price for your information?" Jordan got very still, and looked to Jigsaw like he was pooping his pants. He finally said, "Mr. Bookie, I'm sorry. I never meant no disrespect." Bookie said, "If that is the case, please do what I told you to do." Jordan turned and fast walked out of the room, happy to be leaving with his skin.

Jigsaw chuckled and shook his head, then asked Bookie, "What do you think?" Bookie said, "I think that is indeed valuable information. I didn't think to find food distribution centers. We need to send people to take that warehouse; that much food will make our long-term prospects much stronger." Jigsaw nodded. Bookie continued, "Pay him in cash, it won't be worth much after today anyway. He only gets half the money now, the other half when we control that food. Choose a trustworthy group to go; that much food could make a man wealthy next week when people get really hungry. Send Jordan with them as a guide." Jigsaw said, "Will do Book. I got just the right crew in mind." Bookie nodded and said, "Thank you. Now, I need to think about clean water supplies before that crazy ANTIFA woman gets here." Jigsaw left to go organize a raid on the warehouse.

*

ABC Food Superstores Distribution Center
Near Intersection of Hwy 62 and Hwy 44

Dan was glad he had the Steiner Miniscope 8X22 monocular in his SWAT kit when the lights went out. He bought the little monocular last year after a SWAT call where he wished he'd had some sort of magnified optic. After that mishap, he considered throwing a small pair of hunting binos in his assault bag, but he'd seen the little Steiner monocular on sale online for less than $100, and figured it was small and light enough to just put in the GP pouch on his plate carrier.

He was using the little optic now to glass the north and west sides of the ABC Food Superstores regional distribution center. Dan was perched on a tree-covered hill about 150 yards from the northwest edge of the facility's sprawling apron of concrete, used to park and move the hundreds of trailers constantly cycling through the property. All four sides of the enormous rectangular structure were lined with loading docks, most of which were occupied with semi-trailers, with the exception of what looked like an office and entry area on the southwest corner of the building.

All of the loading dock doors Dan could see on the north and west sides of the warehouse were closed. He didn't see any people around, but there were about 60 cars and trucks in the parking lot. There had to be some employees still on site; it had only been about 24 hours since the lights went out, and at least some of the people

212

working here had to understand the value of the massive amounts of food in the distribution center.

Dan lowered the monocular and turned to Phil, the 3rd Troop Charlie team leader, who was lying next to him on the cold ground. He noticed Phil was shivering, and asked, "You cold?" Phil said, "It's colder than my ex-wife's heart bro." Dan chuckled and said, "Remember when I told you to get some good cold weather gear, and you were all like 'it's too expensive', and I was all like 'but you'll be comfortable', and you were all like 'I'm saving for a cruise'. How's that cruise treating you now big guy?" Phil just shook his head.

"I'm not seeing any movement down there," Dan said. He thought for a few seconds and continued, "We have nine assaulters including us, plus JR with his long gun. I think we will set JR on overwatch here, then put you and three assaulters on the southeast corner in case things go sideways. I'll take the M113 and four assaulters with me to go make contact." Phil replied, "I don't know if it's a good idea for us to split up brother. You, me, and JR are the only guys who have worked together before. My team are SWAT guys from two different teams and one squared away civilian, but I've had them for like three hours." Dan nodded and said, "I know brother, but this is all we got, and we have to secure this warehouse. We need the food in there to keep the city going through the winter and summer, until we can get some crops harvested. We are just going to have to wing it." Phil let out a long breath and said, "Alright. I'll go get JR."

Phil crawled backwards off the crest of the hill and jogged the 75 yards down the hill to where the M113 was parked. When he got to the armored vehicle, he saw JR was in the turret manning the machinegun, and the rest of the team was congregated around the back ramp, doing what SWAT guys seemed to enjoy most: standing around talking. No one but JR was pulling security, and the driver had turned the vehicle off. At least the driver had stayed in his seat. When one of the SWAT guys saw Phil, he said something and the group turned to look at him.

Phil's Charlie team consisted of seven assaulters; four from Canton PD SWAT, two from Akron SWAT, and an armed citizen, Martin, who had been one of Mark and David's students for several years. When the lights went out Martin, a paramedic and single guy in his 20's, had walked home from where his ambulance stalled out from the pulse, piled his gear in a game cart he kept in the garage, and walked the 13 miles to the Alliance range. When he got there he was immediately assigned as 3rd Troop's Charlie team medic.

It took a lot of self-discipline for Phil to not go off on the guys standing around. Instead he said, "Guys, we don't know who's out here with us. We need to maintain security." One of the Canton SWAT guys replied, "JR is in the turret, he's got us." Phil asked, "Can JR see 360 degrees?" No one had anything to say to that. Phil let it go for now, but he knew he would address the issue later. Although he was a fully qualified SWAT assaulter, his team knew Phil was a Firefighter and SWAT medic; and he was sure they didn't take him as seriously as they probably should. The only Firefighter / SWAT medic in the state with a shooting under his belt, his assaulters took him lightly at their own peril.

"JR, I need you to grab your sniper kit and get up on that hill with Dan." Phil said. "You'll be on overwatch while we make contact." "Roger," JR replied, and disappeared from the turret. Phil turned back to the group around the back of the M113, "We will be splitting into two teams. Three of you will be coming with me. We will move on foot to the southeast corner of the target and stand by. Our mission will be to support the other team if they get into trouble. The other team will go with Dan in the M113 to make contact with the people in the warehouse." Phil paused before continuing, "We have no idea who is inside, so we need to be ready for anything. We also don't know yet if anyone else is watching the warehouse, so everyone but Dan's team needs to stay covert."

Everyone nodded their understanding as JR came out of the back M113 hatch and slung first his sniper pack, then his Hog Saddle tripod and finally his rifle. He nodded to Phil and took off at a jog up the hill. Phil pointed to three guys and continued, "You guys will be on my team. We will be Three-Charlie-One on the radio. Take a few minutes and check your gear for noise. Jump up and down, check each other out, and secure any gear that's making noise." Phil then pointed at the other three assaulters and said, "You guys and the driver will be Dan's team. You guys will be Knight Three on the radio. Make sure you have your kit checked and are ready to go. As soon as Dan gets here we will push off. Any questions?" No one had any, and they got to work.

When JR got close to Dan's position, he got down on his belly and crawled the last 25 feet or so, until he was next to Dan, looking down on the warehouse. His first whispered words were, "Damn, that's a huge building." Dan chuckled and replied, "That's what she said." JR looked at Dan and said, "Common bro, you're better than that," with a smile. Dan smiled back and said, "No I'm not. Ask anybody." JR chuckled softly and started getting his gear set up.

While he worked, Dan briefed him quietly, "No activity so far. I can hear an engine down there somewhere, but I can't pinpoint it. It almost sounds like a generator. I'm wondering if their backup power system was shielded." JR said, "It would make sense to spend the money when a good chunk of your inventory is probably frozen food, and would be ruined if the power went out and the generators didn't work. Seems like a no-brainer for a business man." Dan nodded and handed over a hand-drawn range card from his Rite in the Rain notebook. Dan said, "I didn't get too detailed; figured you would want to do that. I also don't have any way to range, so that'll need to be done." JR took the card and said, "Thanks. What's the plan?"

Dan said, "I am taking a team to the Southwest corner of the building," Dan pointed to the spot, where JR could see the facility's office was located, "in the M113, approaching from the southwest driveway. Phil is taking a team to the southeast corner of the property and will set up in the trees there. They will be available for support from there. You have both the west and east driveways, and the north and west sides of the buildings." JR replied, "Roger. Which side do you want to be side one?" Dan said, "Let's call the north side the one side, east is side two, south is side three and west is side four." JR nodded and said, "Please tell Phil. There are so many doors down there I'll have to use the building numbering system to communicate almost anything." Dan agreed.

Dan stayed in place until JR finished setting up his position and spent some time with his laser rangefinding binos, finishing his range card. When JR was ready, he said, "Sniper set." Dan nodded and said, "Thanks Bro," and backed off the hill to join his team.

215

It took over an hour for Phil's team to walk to their position. Dan was getting impatient when he finally heard Phil get on the radio, "Knight Three, Three-Charlie-One. We are set at our standby pos. We ended up on the two / three corner, inside the trees about 100 yards from the building. We are at ground level, and do not have a clear view of the full length of either side of the building, but all the doors we can see are closed, and there is no activity." Dan replied, "Knight Three copies. Hold there. Break. Sniper One, Knight Three. Any changes? We are about to move." He heard JR say, "Knight Three, Sniper One. Negative. Move."

Dan got his team loaded up and stuck his head in the driver's copula, where Martin was strapped in, and said, "Let's roll." Martin started the M113 and let it warm up for a moment, before putting it in gear and pulling out. Kyle taught Martin to drive the lumbering tracked vehicle several years ago on a lark, during downtime at a CQB class he was taking from Mark and David. Learning to operate the vehicle had been fun; he'd never imagined he would be driving it in a situation like this.

Martin managed to get the armored vehicle into the distribution center's parking lot and backed up near the office doors with the ramp facing the building without damaging anything. *Not too bad for only 30 minutes of training several years ago,* Martin thought. Dan told him to leave the vehicle running, make sure the driver's hatch was locked from the inside, and join him in the troop compartment. Before he dropped the ramp, Dan briefed the guys one last time, "OK, we are taking everyone except the machinegunner," he pointed at one of the Canton SWAT guys who was qualified on the M240 from his time in the Marine Corps.

"We will lock you in," Dan continued, "and the rest of us will go see what's up." He made eye contact with everyone and said, "We're all we got," and was happy with the, "We're all we need" he got in return. He dropped the ramp and the team got out and set up security. Once the ramp was closed again, the team moved to the main entrance doors. The glass entrance doors were locked, and heavily tinted, forcing Dan to use the 1500 lumen Surefire M600DF Scout light on his carbine to see inside. All he could see was an empty lobby and a closed door on the wall across from the entrance.

Dan looked at his team, and seeing they were more or less set up on the door properly, he banged on the glass with his gloved fist, rattling the doors in their metal frame. When he got no response after several attempts, Dan decided they would need to find a way in. He was hesitant to break the glass doors, wanting to keep the building as intact and weather-proof as possible. Dan looked at one of the Akron guys and said, "Take someone and go find another door. I don't want to breach this glass if we don't have to." The assaulter nodded, grabbed an assaulter from Canton, and moved towards the southwest corner, looking for pedestrian doors.

Dan was about to give up on the main doors when he saw the interior door into the lobby open, and an older black man in blue suit pants and a button up white shirt walk into the lobby. He saw Dan and looked startled. Dan yelled through the glass door, "Police department. Can you let us in?" The man turned around and went back to the interior door and stood there. Dan yelled, "Sir! We are here to help you. Please open the door so I don't have to break it." The man replied, but Dan couldn't hear him. Dan said, "Sir, I can't hear you."

The man looked frustrated and yelled, "Go away. We don't need any help." Dan shook his head and replied, "Sir, I can't do that. I've been ordered to secure this facility. We aren't here to hurt anyone, but I am going to come in." The man shook his head and said, "Stay out! We just want to be left alone." *I bet you do,* Dan thought. He tried a different track, "Sir, I'm Dan Wilson, and I'm a SWAT officer." Dan took his badge off his battle belt and held it up to the window and pointed to the large police patch on the chest of his plate carrier, "What's your name?" The man said, "You any relation to Bill Wilson over in Alliance?"

Dan chuckled and said, "I'm Bill's son." The man softened a little, and yelled to be heard, "I used to shoot trap with your Dad. He still like to fish?" Dan laughed and replied, "Nope. He's always hated fishing." The man visible relaxed and walked to the glass doors. He unlocked the right-side door and opened it, sticking out his hand, "How are you son, I'm Richard Helms. Your pops and I were close when you and your older brother Kyle were young. We travelled the trap circuit together quite a bit." Dan said, "Yes sir, Dad talks about you from time to time."

217

Richard chuckled and said, "I bet he does son. So, you are a policeman now?" Dan replied, "Yes sir. Can we come in?" Richard said, "Of course, come in." Dan turned and spoke to his guys, "On me." The two assaulters who went looking for a door came back and all four of them filed inside. As soon as he stepped into the building, Dan could feel the heat inside the lobby and saw the lights were on. He was surprised the backup power systems were running the building's creature comforts in addition to the food storage systems. Richard locked the door behind them and gestured to the M113 sitting near the door, "I can't believe you guys are still using those old 113's. I rode one of those things all over Vietnam." Dan replied, "I can't believe you still have power here."

Dan left two guys in the lobby, and told the other two to find the access to the roof. Richard gave them directions to the access ladder and the combination to the lock on the hatch. Richard said, "I sent everyone else home last night, so you shouldn't run into anybody." Dan nodded and told the assaulters, "Go ahead and get on the roof. One of you has a radio right?" Both nodded. "Alright," Dan said, "Off you go."

Dan followed Richard into his office. Richard sat down behind his desk and asked, "So Dan, do you know what happened? I guess the power went out, but we have redundant power generation for that, and we didn't even know there was a problem until our second shift folks didn't show up. When I couldn't get the phones to work, even our cell phones, I sent everyone home. Then nobody's cars would start. I can't figure what the hell is going on." Dan said, "As best as we can figure the country was hit with an electromagnetic pulse." Richard had no idea what that was, and Dan took a few minutes to explain.

Richard was quiet for a while, then asked, "So this is a long-term thing; a new reality so to speak?" Dan said, "Yeah, I think so Richard." "So that explains why you and your guys are here in combat gear," Richard said grimly, putting all the pieces together, "The city wants to secure this food because no more is coming." Dan raised his eyebrows and said, "Yep." Richard let out a long breath and started speaking, but Dan didn't hear him over JR's voice in his headset, "Knight Three, Sniper One. A large group of vehicles just turned onto Hwy 44 from 62."

Dan jumped to his feet and replied, "Roger, do we have assaulters on the roof yet?" When he let off his PTT he told Richard, "A large group is headed this way. This can't be good." In his headset Dan heard, "Three-Charlie-Six is on the roof and has eyes on. Looks a large group of thugs coming our way fast. Estimate at least 30 subjects." JR stepped on him, saying, "Sniper One, I see AKs sticking out of windows. Permission to engage?" Dan thought through the information he had, balanced it against the situation, and made a decision.

Dan yelled for Martin, who was in the lobby, to get back in the M113 and be ready to move, and for the other assaulter to come with him, then keyed his radio, "Sniper One, engage." Dan turned to Richard and said, "Take us to the roof."

Chapter 25

ABC Food Superstores Distribution Center
Near Intersection of Hwy 62 and Hwy 44

JR fired his first shot as soon as his left hand got back on the bag he was using to stabilize his stock in the prone position. He fired before Dan's permission came. The situation was obvious, and he wanted to stop these dongs as far away from the facility as he could to minimize the effect of the enemy's superior numbers. His first target was the driver of the lead vehicle, about 300 yards from him, and only about 175 yards from the west driveway entrance. He lost the target in recoil, but knew he'd connected when he came back on target and saw the lead vehicle, a beautifully restored 1950's era four door Chevy Bel Air, swerve to his right, jump the curb and plow into a telephone pole. It looked like the dong sitting in the passenger seat ate his AK in the collision.

JR got on the second vehicle, a 1970's Ford van, which was braking hard after seeing the first vehicle careen off the road. It just made his shot easier. JR used the Horus reticle to hold one mil high and launched the next 168 grain Amax into the face of the Ford Van's driver. That vehicle was almost at a complete stop, so there was no spectacular crash, but as JR cycled his bolt and checked his work, he could see a hole in the windshield, and it looked like someone had thrown a 5-gallon bucket of red paint on the windshield from the inside.

By this time the five remaining vehicles had stopped in the middle of the road. JR could sense their indecision, and took maximum advantage of it. Another suppressed 168 grain round screamed through his Surefire suppressor, and another dong's head exploded, this time the front seat passenger in the third vehicle. The gore expelled by the supersonic round turning their homeboy's head into a canoe was enough to get the three dongs in the back seat, and the driver of the 1970's Lincoln Towncar, to jump out of the car and run into the woods on the east side of the road, putting them directly south of the facility JR was protecting.

The rest of the dongs in the convoy must have thought this looked like a good idea, because they all quickly followed suit. JR was able to shoot two more of them before they reached the woods, one of whom was only wounded, and was crying out for his friends to come get him. They must not have been good friends, because no one came. JR swept the vehicles in the road through his optic again, and found one guy had cracked the side door of the Ford van, and was trying to search for where the shots were coming from. JR watched him for a moment, and when the dong slowly slid the door open a little further, he saw this dong was apparently a 'sniper dong'.

This guy had a black Remington 700P, complete with the Leupold scope and Harris bipod, and 'CPD' stenciled on the stock. JR would recognize a Canton PD sniper rifle anywhere; he had been shooting and training with their Snipers for over 10 years, and had always given them crap about the off-the-shelf guns with the goofy stenciling.

JR had heard the stories about the dirtbags in Canton killing and lynching cops, so there was little doubt in his mind about where this dumbass in the Gucci hat and red jacket had gotten the rifle. JR placed the two mil elevation dot of his Horus reticle on Sniper Dong's nose and stroked the trigger. The Amax bullet did its work, and Sniper Dong fell into the crack of the van door, what was left of his head sticking out of the gap.

JR smiled, then returned his attention to the wounded guy in the road. It was obvious no one was going to help him, so JR finished him off with a shot to the head. He hoped his buddies were looking at him when the round bounced his head off the pavement. *You guys think you're bad asses? That's cute,* JR thought. If things were reverting to the law of the jungle, these dongs were nothing but jackals; and like jackals, they would regret stealing meat from the lions.

JR saw movement in his peripheral vision and returned his focus to the van. The side door was slowly sliding open, and he figured there had to be more of these dumbasses in there. JR decided see if he could provoke a reaction. He centered his two mil Horus dot on the center of the van's side door and put a round through the cargo compartment. About a second later the back doors of the van flew open and three dumbasses burst out onto the pavement, firing wildly in all directions with their motley assortment of long guns as they ran to the east woodline. JR expended the last three rounds of his Tikka's magazine, scoring only one hit, before they were out of sight.

JR quickly swapped out mags in the rifle and chambered a round. As he was getting back on the glass to try to find these guys in the woods, Dan called him on the radio, "Sniper One, Knight Three. We are up on the roof now." JR saw Kyle waving at him. "Sitrep? We could hear your rounds going supersonic past us, but hadn't heard any return fire until that last volley."

JR keyed his PTT and said, "Roger Knight Three. I'm good; they were doing the Iraqi wedding dance, nothing serious. Splash seven so far, the dongs bailed out of their vehicles about 125 yards south of the facility, and are now in the woodline to your south. I need to finish cleaning up the vehicles, then I'll start working the woods. Break. Three-Charlie-One, Sniper One. Be advised you have dongs to your southwest in the woods."

Phil pushed his PTT and said, "Roger. Break. Knight Three, do you want us to skirmish north to south and push them west back onto the road?" "Negative Three-Charlie-One." Dan replied, annoyance creeping into his voice. "You only have four guys. Hold your pos until I can get set up here." Phil responded with a curt, "Roger." Dan set himself up on the south parapet of the roof and grabbed his monocular, cursing himself for not carrying full size binoculars. He resolved to change that when they got out of here; he'd deal with the weight.

Dan scanned the woods to the south but didn't see anything moving. *Those dongs are probably cleaning out their undies and gathering themselves,* Dan thought, *I need to get ahead of their thinking,* as he racked his brain for a way to keep these guys off balance. He wanted to keep these guys as far away from the facility as he could, but he also didn't want any of them to get away; He didn't want any of them going to get more friends. Dan turned to Richard and said, "You know what I need, Richard?" Richard chuckled and replied, "A 90mm recoilless rifle?" Dan said, "I was thinking a 60mm mortar, but I'd take it. It would be nice to smoke check all those guys with some indirect fire while they are clumped up, before they get their shit together."

As Dan thought it through, he knew they were in trouble, despite how well JR had worked the dongs over. The enemy had between 20 and 25 guys left, while Dan's team consisted of 10 shooters; 11 if he could find a rifle for Richard. The enemy had freedom of movement, while Dan had a very large building to protect. Defending a building this size with 11 guys and a sniper was a losing proposition in the long run, no matter how much the opposition sucked. His radio wouldn't reach into Alliance, so he had no way to get help, short of sending someone back to town, which would reduce his effective force by 10%. Dan slowed his thinking and focused. *What are my options?* He asked himself.

First, he could evacuate everyone in the M113, allowing the dongs to take the warehouse without a fight. This would guarantee his force, and Richard, would make it out intact, but would mean failure of the mission; and virtually guaranteed casualties when the Squadron had to raid the facility to take it back. Not to mention the damage the dongs were sure to do to the building, and the food inside, while he gathered a force to come take it back.

His second option was to defend the warehouse, and hold out until David figured out something is wrong when they didn't report in at about 1600 hours as planned, and sent a relief force.

Dan's last option was to take the 240 and all its ammo off the M113, and bring the gun up to the roof; then send Martin back in the buttoned up armored vehicle to within radio range, to call for help. This would allow them to defend the warehouse almost as well as option two, and hopefully get a relief force back to him before the dongs got smart and came at them from multiple directions.

He made a decision. Dan got on the radio and, not knowing Martin's call sign, said, "Martin from Knight Three." No answer. "Anyone in the 113, Knight Three." Still nothing. Dan turned to one of the Charlie team assaulters on the roof with him and said, "Do either of the guys in the 113 have a radio?" The assaulter, who was resting his carbine on the parapet, exposing way too much of his body, shrugged and said, "I don't know." Dan sighed and said, "Give me your radio. I'll be right back. Let me know if the dongs move." The assaulter who was on the parapet nodded handed over his Alliance radio, and said, "Will do."

Dan climbed down the west roof access ladder, unlocked the main doors and ran out to the 113. He opened the rear door from the outside, and jumped in. "Gunner, take the 240 down and take it in the building, then come back and load all the ammo for it," Dan pointed to three wooden crates, each holding four 200-round cans of 7.62 ammo for the gun, "and get it inside." The assaulter manning the gun said, "I don't know how to get the gun down." Dan sighed and said, "Get out of the way, start carrying ammo into the building. Hurry up."

Dan got the gun off the mount and into the building, then ran back and closed the gunner's hatch. He stuck his head into the driver's compartment and spoke to Martin, "Hey bro. This is important," Dan handed Martin the radio he'd taken from the assaulter on the roof, "I need you to drive back to Alliance. Shit, I need to write a message, hang on." Dan ducked back into the troop compartment and pulled out his Rite in the Rain notebook and pen. He wrote a situation report and request for assistance, ripped it out of his notebook, and climbed back into space next to the driver's compartment.

Dan handed Martin the note and told him to read it. Once he was done, Martin looked up from the paper and said, "Ok. Who do I give this to?" Dan thought about that, then said, "When you get in radio range, call the TOC and tell them you need to get this to David. If he's not available, Mark, Kyle, or Bones will know what to do, but I'd prefer David." Martin said, "Roger." Dan continued, "Keep the vehicle buttoned up; use the viewports to drive. We can't risk losing you, the vehicle, or that message, understand?" Martin said, "I do," then repeated the instructions back to his Troop Leader.

Dan said, "Alright, you're good to go. When you pull out, make lots of noise. I want them to think we left. We're going to surprise those dongs." Martin replied, with a grin, "Surprise dongs was the name of my rave techno music DJ act in college." Dan laughed and said, "Get out of here, stud," then got off the vehicle, closed the door and went in the building, locking the door behind him. He heard the M113 rev up and pull away, and said a quick prayer for Martin's mission.

Dan's next problem was how to lead a bunch of cops in an infantry fight. He suspected he would have to use every ounce of skill developed during his years in Ranger Battalion. He knew these dongs had to smarten up at some point, he just prayed it wouldn't be today.

*

In the woods, south of the food warehouse, Theo Jackson was trying to get things organized. Theo worked as an enforcer for the Bookie Organization, and had since Big Mook's days. Today, when Jigsaw asked him to go along on this job to take and hold the big food warehouse outside the city, Theo was less than thrilled. He hadn't been to sleep in the last 36 hours, having spent the entire first night after the pulse driving around town keeping young gangsters in check, working to enforce Bookie's rules for this new world. He understood why Bookie was so adamant about the 'no looting' rule, but it made for a lot of work for Theo and the 13 guys who made up his crew. They'd had to show several young thugs what time it was; and while Theo had zero qualms about killing when it was necessary, he didn't enjoy it; especially when he was killing young black men whose only crime was refusing to respect Bookie's rules.

Like everyone at the higher levels of the Bookie Organization, he'd been selected for his intelligence, emotional stability, loyalty, and ability. Unlike anyone else in Bookie's employ, Theo was a Military Veteran with combat service. There were other Vets in the Bookie Organization, but most of them had been thrown out of the service, and none had any combat time. His four years in the 502nd Infantry Regiment during the GWOT shaped him in ways he barely understood.

A 68W Combat Medic, Theo had deployed to Iraq twice as part of the 101st Airborne Division's 2nd Brigade Combat Team. When he got out of the Army, Theo returned to his native Canton, intent on going to college. He quickly found college wasn't for him, and dropped out after less than one semester. Unable to find any work, Theo quickly fell in with the crew he grew up with in the projects. Not content to sling dope until he ended up dead or in jail, he leveraged his military experience, quickly proving himself to Jigsaw as a valuable member of his enforcement crew. Before Bookie had finished his sentence about taking over the food warehouse, Jigsaw decided to have Theo lead the crew.

The sniper attack on his convoy as they approached the warehouse hadn't been much of a surprise to Theo. He could see the gigantic building, sticking up out of the hills like a giant white blister, from Hwy 62 when they made the turn onto Hwy 44. A facility that big had to employ hundreds of people, and the amount of food stored there had to have made it the first target on any organized group's radar as soon as the lights went out.

So, Theo wasn't surprised when they'd come under fire as they approached; what surprised him was the effectiveness of the sniper. In less than a minute the sniper had whacked seven of his guys, destroyed several vehicles, and forced his platoon-sized element of fighters into the cold woods, still over 100 yards away from their objective. That wasn't some cracker hick with a hunting rifle; that dude was shooting a suppressed rifle from a good distance, he didn't hesitate to shoot, and his target selection and accuracy was too good to be luck. Theo was sure they were facing a professional Sniper. The important question to him now was whether the guy was alone, or was he part of a group or unit?

While Theo had never been a combat leader, he had served with some of the best small unit leaders in the world: Airborne NCOs. The US Army, despite all of its faults in Theo's mind, raised exceptional platoon level NCO's; and during his 26 months in combat, Theo had the opportunity to watch dozens of them in action. He began to do what he thought they would do in this situation. First, he rallied the people he had left and got them to chill out, trying to instill calm with his quiet confidence. When that didn't work, Theo gave up and told them the next one to speak was getting shot. Their excited babbling and yelling was going to get everyone killed. It finally got quiet. Next, he did a head count. He had 24 warriors left. Theo broke the group up into three teams of eight, and had them spread out in a roughly equal sided triangle with 25 yard sides. This would be his patrol base.

His second in command didn't make it out of the kill zone when the sniper lit into them, so Theo appointed a new one from his personal crew. He left his new 2IC in command at the patrol base and went to do a leader's recon. When he was about 50 yards away from his patrol base, walking northwest, Theo heard the sound of a poorly muffled diesel engine rev up and begin to move away. Not being close enough to see the distribution center through the trees, he missed seeing the M113 pulling out of the warehouse lot and turn north on Hwy 44.

Theo quietly worked his way north through the woods until he could see the distribution center through the trees. The view wasn't great, there were too many semi-trailers parked around the edge of the lot for him to see much of the building itself, but it was a start. Over the next hour he quietly worked his way around the giant building. During that time, he saw no evidence of anyone being there, other than all the dead cars in the parking lot. He decided the vehicle he'd heard must have been the sniper getting away, afraid of being encircled. Theo finished his wide circle of the property and crossed the road back into the woods near where they had abandoned their vehicles. It was time to get his guys organized, and go claim that warehouse.

*

Up on the roof of the warehouse, Dan tracked Theo's progress via radio. JR spotted him as he approached the distribution center from the woods to the south, his ACU camo uniform sticking out like a sore thumb in the leafless trees. The way he held his carbine, an M4 of some sort with a Trijicon ACOG and older Surefire light, combined with his head to toe ACU getup, complete with Gortex jacket and well-worn circa 2005 load bearing vest, screamed 'Army Vet' to JR. Between he and Phil, they were able to keep eyes on the guy during his entire circuit of the facility. Dan kept his and the roof team's heads down, hoping to entice the guy into attacking.

"Someone needs to tell this guy ACUs only work when you're lying on a gravel parking lot." JR commented over the radio. Phil replied, "No kidding. You can probably see this dude from space." JR watched as he crossed the road to the south of the earlier kill zone around the vehicles, and saw him disappear back into the woods. He got back on the radio, "Knight Three, Sniper One. The dong scout is back in their nest." Dan said, "Roger. Given what you and Phil observed about this guy, we have to assume he's had some infantry training. We can probably expect an attack straight out of FM 7-8." referring to the Army's Field Manual on small unit tactics.

JR replied, "Agreed. He will probably set up his base of fire on the south side of the property, and send his maneuver element to loop around wide and attack east to west. That's the avenue of approach with the most cover and he won't have to cross the main road." "Great minds think alike Sniper One." Dan replied, then continued, "Break. Three-Charlie-One, move to the northeast corner of the building, in the woods to the north, oriented south. If they attack like I think they will, you should be able to counterattack the right flank of their maneuver force."

Dan paused, thinking about Phil's frame of reference. Phil was a great Fireman, and an exceptional SWAT assaulter, but he'd never been in the infantry. He felt the need to clarify, "Three-Charlie-One, for clarity, it is my intent that you counterattack their flank with gunfire, not physically. Wait for me to initiate over the radio. Do not advance on the dongs unless I tell you to, and don't start shooting until I give the word." Phil replied, "Roger that. Moving." Dan looked again at the situation on the roof. It was an enormous expanse up there, at least 2000 feet on each side, littered with assorted HVAC systems and crisscrossed by air and electrical ducts. The four-foot-high parapet was solid concrete, obviously part of the monolithic pour when they erected the warehouse's walls. If he had about 50 more assaulters, it would be a dream defensive position.

Dan started placing his three assaulters in position, being careful to keep them away from the edge of the roof and hunched over. While he couldn't see the tops of trees next to the property from the center of the roof, if they got within about five feet of the edge they could be seen from the woods.

Dan placed his machinegun on the east side of the building, with a gunner and assistant gunner. He broke open all of the 240 ammo crates, and started ferrying 200 round cans to the east side of the roof, leaving 400 rounds on the south wall near the west corner, in case the enemy's anticipated support by fire position turned out to be their maneuver side. He also had the guys break the cans open and remove all of the 100 round linked belts from their individual cardboard boxes. He didn't want unfamiliar fingers fumbling with the boxes, like a teenage boy trying to unhook a bra clasp, when the shit hit the fan.

Dan took the machinegunner's carbine, after some quiet protest, and gave it to Richard, along with 4 of the gunner's M4 magazines. He placed Richard and his last assaulter on the south wall, about 25 yards from the southwest corner, with orders to stay out of sight unless he said otherwise. Both of them had small drain ports to look through where the parapet met the roof, but Dan gave them specific orders to not stick their carbines out of them, and once set to not move around. "If I tell you to engage," Dan concluded, "You'll be shooting to the south. Make sure you don't shoot over the parapet; use the drain openings from the prone position." While the assaulter, a guy from Canton SWAT, looked anxious, Richard actually looked excited. Dan could tell it had been a long time since Richard had a mission that meant something, and was probably happy to have the clarity a life and death situation provided. Dan could relate.

As he waited with the machinegun team on the east wall, one of the guys said, "I always wondered what people did with downtime before smart phones." Dan laughed and replied, "I guess now you know. No YouTube for you G.I." The gunner chuckled and said, "But a selfie with this gun just before I get a CONUS kill would totally get me, like, a million re-Tweets. With no internet, how am I going to watch my '600 pound hoarder storage auction addicted goldmining life' show on TLC?" All three of them laughed quietly, and the A-gunner got the last word, "If an apocalypse comes and no one Snapchats it, did it really happen?"

*

Theo managed to get back into the perimeter of his patrol base without getting shot by one of his own guys. He'd forgotten to tell them about challenge and response, but he was finally able to get his 2IC's attention without attracting the fire of his own guys. Once he was inside the triangle, he saw he needn't have worried; most of his guys were huddled in small clumps trying to keep warm, not paying the least attention to the world outside their little make-shift safe zone. He had a lot of work to do to get this rabble trained if the Organization hoped to accomplish anything other than ambush some cops and generally terrorize the population. As he saw earlier, any encounter with a trained group of people would result in someone cleaning his guys' clocks.

Theo sat down for a minute and took a pull of water out of his Camelback bladder, then called his core group of guys to him. Using a stick, he drew a quick diagram of the target and laid out

229

what he wanted them to do. Unknown to Theo, his plan was basically the one the Black Knight Squadron assaulters, who he didn't even know existed, had anticipated.

His '1st Squad', with eight guys, would move to the southern edge of the huge concrete apron around the building, and set up in a line. Their job would be to shoot anyone they saw, but they were not to advance. "If we are getting shot at," Theo told them, "it's your job to suppress them…shoot at them to keep their heads down. If we aren't taking fire, do not shoot. Does everyone understand?" Eight heads nodded.

Theo's '2nd Squad', with 16 guys plus him, would walk east, then north, then west, to approach the warehouse from the east. He would lead this element himself, and their orders were to work in eight man teams to rush the building. He kept the plan loose and vague, mostly because none of these guys had the training to understand what he was talking about. He would have to lead them from the front, and be ready to direct them on the fly.

"Alright, I think the power is on in there. I heard a generator. Do this right and we will be livin' large tonight." Before Theo could stop them, the entire group starting cheering, yelling 'whoop whoop', and generally acting like savages. It took Theo several seconds to get them to shut the hell up.

Chapter 26

Rural Stark County
Near Hartville, OH

Martin was lost, and it was taking every ounce of mental energy he possessed to push down the panic he felt. When he left the food warehouse, heading to the FOB, he was absolutely sure he knew how to get there. Martin had been a paramedic in Stark County for over 10 years, and was as sure as a man could be that he knew every inch of the county. After over two hours of driving the M113 through the idyllic countryside, he came to realize just how dependent on GPS navigation he'd become. He kicked himself for not spending more time navigating with a map book, to keep his skills up to date; but the thought that one day he might not have access to GPS never entered his mind. Until the GPS was gone.

The narrow field of view through the armored viewports Martin was using to see the outside world weren't helping. Dan had been insistent he remain locked in the armored vehicle, but Martin couldn't see jack shit through the viewport; it was all he could do to keep the 14-ton vehicle on the road, and avoid hitting the stalled cars blocking every roadway. "Screw this," Martin said out loud, and reached up and opened the driver's hatch, then leveraged himself up to drive with his head sticking out of the vehicle. The frigid air blowing on his face was a relief, and helped him clear his head.

Martin looked around, trying to get his bearings. The sun was almost down, and he was driving directly into it, so he knew he was heading generally west. He hadn't crossed a freeway in his travels, so he knew he was going the wrong direction. He was on a rural two-lane road, surrounded by fallow farm fields as far as he could see. He needed to get turned around, then start looking for street signs. It had proven impossible to read street signs through the viewport, and Martin decided he should have cracked the driver's hatch an hour ago.

He tried the radio again, "Any Black Knight units, Knight Three-Charlie-Two." and got nothing in return except the radio's chirp telling him the battery was almost dead. *I can't believe I'm failing my first mission of the apocalypse,* Martin raged at himself, *I had one job!* He saw a side road on his right, and was able to get the big armored vehicle slowed in time to use the space to turn around. He knew it was possible to turn the vehicle around in a small space just using the tracks, but he wasn't confident enough in his driving abilities to try. Instead, Martin executed the ugliest five-point turn in history, and headed back to the east.

Within three miles he knew where he was. Filled with renewed confidence, Martin navigated the county backroads until he made it to Hwy 173, then turned east. This highway would take him right to State Street, where he could check in with the Black Knight Troop at Walmart, and get a relief mission started to go help Dan and his Charlie teammates. Felling his oats, and wanting to hurry, Martin gave the 113 some gas. He was only a few minutes away from help now.

Martin didn't see the ice underneath the snow on the unplowed road as he approached the downhill S curve in the two-lane road. When the road tracks of the 113 hit the almost inch of solid ice, Martin felt the vehicle lose traction, and his lack of experience driving the APC sprung up to screw him. His first reaction was to steer into the spin, as he would do in an ambulance. The problem was he wasn't driving an ambulance. Martin didn't fully understand the differences in steering dynamics involved in driving a vehicle that was steered by applying power to tracks, instead of turning the front wheels. What he thought were gentle steering inputs caused a bad overcorrection, turning the vehicle's slide into an out of control spin.

Really God? Really! was Martin's last thought before the M113 plowed into the solid row of trees lining the edge of the golf course. The force of the APC demolishing the first tree slammed his face, just under his helmet, into the rim of the driver's hatch. His loss of consciousness saved him from the horror he would have felt when he was thrown from the driver's compartment as the armored vehicle smashed through the trees like a bomb going off.

*

232

ABC Food Superstores Distribution Center
Near Intersection of Hwy 62 and Hwy 44

"Sounds like the dongs are getting themselves motivated," the east wall machinegunner commented as he listened to Theo's guys whooping and hollering to the south. Dan grinned and replied, "Motivated Dongs was my punk-jazz fusion band in college. We played a lot of frat parties." Both assaulters laughed loudly, and Dan had to shush them. The guys calmed down and Dan said, "I'm going to go check in with the south wall. That yelling was probably them psyching themselves up, so expect to see them soon." The assaulters nodded and Dan moved off the wall.

When he got to the southwest corner of the roof, he saw Richard and the Charlie team assaulter had set up pretty nice firing positions. Both of them were in the prone position about three feet back from the wall, looking through the drain openings at the bottom of the parapet. As he approached them he saw they were moving from side to side, trying to get as wide a view as possible through the 12 inch wide by 8 inch tall openings. He dropped to the prone next to the assaulter, and saw a Velcro name strip on the back of his Multicam plate carrier that said 'Anderson', and said, "Hey Anderson. Cold enough for ya?"

Anderson came off the ACOG optic on his 16" BCM carbine and chuckled, "It's so damn cold bro. I'm kicking myself for making fun of guys for buying all that Arcteryx gear." He paused to shake his head at his own stupidity and continued, "Only activity was a bunch of ghetto squealing a few minutes ago. I haven't seen anything move yet." Dan said, "Yeah we heard it too. Sounded like someone was pumping them up to attack." Anderson nodded and said, "They need to get on with it. I'm freezing my wedding tackle off."

Dan crawled over to Richard and asked him, "You doing alright sir?" Richard replied, "Never been better son. I have a gun and there are gooks in the woods. What more could a guy ask for?" Dan smiled and said, "I saw a coffee pot in your office. Do you have a thermos anywhere? I'd like to get these guys something hot to drink before this kicks off." Richard said, "I do. It's in the credenza below the coffee pot. Good job watching out for your guys." Dan nodded and crawled away until he was far enough from the wall to stand up without being seen.

He quickly went down the roof ladder and into Richard's office. The coffee pot was hot and full, and Dan quickly found the thermos and filled it up. The coffee smelled a little stale, but no one would care. Dan grabbed a few disposable cups, screwed the thermos lid on tight, and headed back up to the roof. He went back to Richard and Anderson's position, and poured each of them a small cup of coffee. Anderson asked, "Can I pour it down my pants?" Dan replied, "In this cold it's not like there's anything outside your body to burn." Anderson laughed and said, "That's no joke." Dan poured Richard a cup, then moved back to the machinegun position on the east wall.

The guys were happy to have the coffee, and after they had a cup Dan pushed them through more dry drills with the M240 machinegun. Dan worked with them on loading, reloading, malfunction clearance, and fire control. He knew he wasn't going to turn them into Ranger Regiment machinegunners in 10 minutes of dry-fire, but he wanted to get them as ready as he could in the time he had available. Dan knew he should be on the gun for this attack, but he was responsible for the entire fight, and wanted to keep himself free as long as possible.

JR got on the radio, "Knight Three, Sniper One. Movement to the south. Can't tell numbers yet, but there is a group of black males in street clothes filtering through the woods, moving from south to north, about 100 yards out. They are on a line to come out about 50 yards east of the west end of the building on the south side, if that makes sense." Dan replied, "Roger, that makes sense." JR continued as soon as Dan let off his PTT, "Do you want me to pin them down now?"

Dan thought about it, and replied, "Not yet. I'd like to see if they have a second group before we let them know we are here. I also want them to commit to moving out into the open. We don't have enough ammo for a drawn out 'pop goes the weasel' fight." JR replied, "Roger. I'll keep you updated. Be advised once the group to the south gets to the edge of the pavement, I won't be able to engage them; at my elevation, my view is blocked by the building." Dan said, "Roger."

Phil broke in over the radio, "Knight Three, Three-Charlie-One. We have dongs crossing the east driveway heading north, about 75 yards from the building. Counted four so far, all armed with long guns. One of them was the scout dong." Dan acknowledged Phil and tried to visualize the battlefield. He struggled with the decision of when to initiate the defense of the building. If he waited until the enemy committed to a course of action he had a chance to mow them down in the open. The problem was, in order for his guys on the roof to engage, they would have to expose themselves. His fighting positions up here sucked. Phil's team was in a good spot to flank the enemy's east element, but Dan wasn't sure if that would be the dong's maneuver element of not. If they hunkered down behind cover on that side Phil would have to advance and assault through their position. He trusted Phil would advance on a fighting enemy, but he had no idea if the guys with him had the stones to attack with the aggressiveness required to pull that off.

If he initiated now, they could pin the enemy down farther away from the building, and disrupt whatever plan they had in motion. He really didn't want to get into a long drawn out fight with these assholes, but he was confident the dongs they were facing would fall apart under fire. If they started now, he had the chance of breaking the fight down into a bunch of little gunfights, allowing him to focus his combat power on one small group of dongs at a time. His only hesitation was the amount of ammo the team had for their carbines. Everyone had between six and ten mags, and that may be cutting it close if this thing went on for a while.

Dan thought about the advantages his team had over the dongs, and realized the decisive factor was training. His guys had an advantage in marksmanship. Stopping this attack further away from the building would maximize that advantage. He made his decision, "All Knight units, Knight Three. We are going to attack now. Pin and hold these dongs by the throat where they are, and we will pick them off one at a time. Conserve ammo and make your shots count. Remember, we're all we got. Sniper One, initiating on you."

JR smiled as he heard the command. He was already tracking a dong in a bright red puffy jacket about 150 yards to the south. The dong was armed with a Kel Tec PLR 16 .223 caliber pistol, with a drum magazine of some sort in the magwell, and was

235

confidently walking down an open row between trees, straight at JR's position. He centered the one mil dot of the Horus retile on the dong's upper chest, let out his breath, and allowed the Tikka rifle to fire when he reached the natural respiratory pause at the bottom of his exhale. The suppressed round removed the dong's heart from his body, and after cycling the rifle JR watched as the guy slowly crumpled to the ground.

While no one but JR heard the gun go off, everyone in the little valley heard the suppressed shot break the sound barrier, and the 'a hand just slapped a chunk of meat' sound of that round smacking flesh; but the suppressor masked the shooting's origin so effectively the dongs couldn't figure out where it came from. In the woods on the east side of the building, Theo's head came up, recognizing the sound for what it was. "Find cover and get down." Theo said in a stage whisper. *So, the sniper didn't leave after all,* he thought.

On the roof, Dan was down in the prone behind one of the drain openings on the east wall, about 40 feet to the left of the machinegun team, looking for targets. He saw some hurried movement in the woods about 50 yards out, but nothing defined enough to shoot at. He heard JR fire another suppressed shot, then heard several unsuppressed shots come from the woods to the south. He looked to his rear, but couldn't see his guys on the southwest corner. He was considering going to check up on them, mainly because there were obviously good targets over there, when he heard JR fire again, followed by both Anderson and Richard's unsuppressed carbines laying down some fire.

Richard and Anderson did indeed have some good targets. JR's third shot had flushed out some of the dongs to their front, about 75 yards out. Richard fired first, putting a few rounds on a guy in a green parka and white hat, who was standing next to a tree getting ready to shoot in their general direction. He watched as his first two rounds went wide, and was pleased to see his third and fourth rounds connect with the dirtbag's abdomen. This was Richard's first time shooting with a red dot sight on a rifle, but he kind of liked it. He moved on to find another target, leaving the guy he'd shot to writhe around on the ground in pain.

Anderson was having less luck. He'd fired five rounds so far, at two different folks, and as far as he could see all of them were clean misses. He found the spot where the last guy went to ground, and waited. Within 10 seconds, the dong stuck his head up to see what was going on. Anderson controlled his breathing and trigger, and was rewarded when his sixth round fired in this apocalypse smacked the dong in the forehead, snapping his head back.

The dongs started firing back in earnest, and Richard and Anderson were forced to move after a few rounds made it through the drain openings in the parapet, passing too close for comfort. Both of them crawled to different drain holes and set up again as JR poured precision rifle fire into the line of dongs trying to take cover just inside the wood line on the south side of the facility. In less than a minute JR was able to use five rounds to put three of the dongs down hard, and was now firing slowly into probable hiding places, trying to keep the bad guys' heads down until the two assaulters he could see on the southwest corner of the roof could displace to new firing positions. He fired the last round of his 10-round magazine before the assaulters were ready to work again, so he dropped the stock of his Tikka precision gun and scooted to his right, picking up his Hodge Defense AU-Mod 2 carbine, equipped with an Aimpoint T1 and 3X magnifier. He snapped the magnifier into place and got a quick sight picture.

Several dongs were up and shooting again, and JR settled his dot on the center of the Cleveland Browns logo on the chest of a dong who was shooting at the building with his SKS rifle. JR sent three Federal Gold Medal Match 69 grain 5.56mm rounds screaming through his Surefire suppressor, and the worthless football fan with the cheap commie rifle was disappointed in his winless Browns for the last time. JR looked for more targets. He knew trying to gain fire superiority with a semiautomatic rifle was doomed to fail against any professional enemy, but he hoped it was possible against these dumbasses.

In the woods to the east, Theo was trying to get in a position to see the target building. Only 12 of his guys had made it across the east driveway before the shooting started; and not knowing where the sniper was, Theo used simple hand signals to tell the guys who hadn't crossed the open area yet to just stay there. He moved west to a tree where he could see the warehouse, and brought his Smith & Wesson M&P 15 carbine up to his shoulder. Looking through his 4X ACOG TA1, he started scanning the building's roof looking for the sniper. Not seeing anything on the east end of the warehouse, he started scanning down the south side of the huge structure towards where he could hear his base of fire team shooting.

When Theo got towards the far west end of the south side of the building, about 600 yards away from him, he stopped. He had a hard time holding the rifle still enough to focus on something at that distance, but he was pretty sure he was seeing smoke and snow being blown out one of the rain spout drain things. He thought he'd found the sniper.

Theo quickly retreated the 30 yards to where he had his guys gather up, and told them, "Alright, time to get ours. There is a sniper on the far south roof," he paused to show them which direction was south, "We can move up on this side without him seeing us. Who has a gauge?" meaning a shotgun. Two of his guys nodded, and one of them said, "Yeah, that's what's up!" as he showed off his Kel Tec KSG 12-gauge shotgun with the laser sight. He wasn't really sure how to use the complicated shotgun, but he wasn't going to tell these guys that.

Theo nodded once and said, "Alright, you're with me. When we get to the building we are going to use your shotgun to breach one of those doors on the east side." Theo got his guys split into two teams, and explained that only one of the teams would be moving at a time, while the other team was ready to fight. The gunfire on the south side of the building had died down a little, and Theo wanted to get the movement done while that sniper was engaged, so he pushed his guys to the edge of the woods, placed the team on the left to cover the first movement, and ordered the team on the right to move out into the open, stopping at the line of semi-trailers parked around the facility's perimeter.

Phil and his guys had used the time after getting in position on the northeast side of the warehouse wisely, and were in fairly good fighting positions looking for targets when the first dongs stepped out of the east woods. He keyed his PTT and said, "Knight Three, Three-Charlie-One. Dongs are coming out of the woods to the east." Dan replied, "Roger, I got 'em. We will initiate on you." Phil responded with two mic clicks and carefully turned to the assaulter next to him, whispering, "When I fire, light them up. Pass it on." The assaulter nodded and passed it on.

When Phil figured the word had reached the end of his small line, he put his Aimpoint's dot on the dong farthest from him. As he prepped the shot, the dong stopped and got down on a knee next to the front stands of a semi-trailer about 50 yards from the building, and about 75 yards from where he sat. The trailer's stand partially blocked Phil's view of the dong, but he had enough meat in the guy's side available to make a good shot. Phil let out a breath, then fired two rounds at the guy. Both 55 grain 5.56mm rounds struck the dong under his right armpit and he fell down.

By the time Phil's second shot was leaving the barrel, the three carbines next to him unleashed a wall of rapid, aimed fire at the six other dongs in the group near the trailer. Phil could feel the noise and concussion of four rifles firing simultaneously in such close quarters in his chest, and he struggled to find another target. Seeing one of the dongs running east, away from the fight, Phil centered his red dot between the guy's shoulder blades and pressed off several rounds. He must have missed, because the dong kept running, escaping into the woods and out of Phil's sight.

On the roof, Dan waited patiently for Phil to fire while he watched a second group of dongs break cover and advance while the first group waited near the trailer. *These guys are doing a bounding overwatch,* Dan realized. Deciding he didn't like the idea of hood rats using real tactics, he determined none of these dudes were going to make it out alive. *We have to kill the good ones early,* Dan thought, as he heard Phil initiate the ambush. From his rollover prone position, Dan centered his Aimpoint dot on the chest of a dong in a Cleveland Indians sweatshirt and an orange beanie in the second group.

As Dan pressed the shot, the guy ducked down and turned to his right in response to the sound of gunfire in that direction, and Dan's round hit him on the left side of his nose. The 5.56mm FMJ pierced the dong's septum and blew off the tip of his nose, and the guy dropped his AK and grabbed his face with both hands. As Dan was moving on to another target he saw his machinegun team on his right pick the 240 up and set it on the parapet. Within seconds his assaulters had the gun running, shooting short bursts into the exposed group of dongs below as they ran back towards the woods.

Theo was wondering what kind of buzzsaw his guys walked into on the right when he saw a big dude in full kit with POLICE patches on it stand up on the eastern edge of the warehouse roof, and haul a freaking belt fed machinegun into view. He was momentarily transfixed by the horrible elegance of the ambush he'd walked into. As he watched, the machinegun opened up on his second team, who were caught in the open while bounding forward. Snapping out of his frozen stupor, Theo brought his M&P 15 to his shoulder and found the machinegunner on the roof in his ACOG. Seeing the guy was a cop, from the POLICE patch on his plate carrier, Theo centered the crosshair on the pig's face and started pulling the trigger.

Dan saw muzzle flashes from the woods to his right, and heard the unmistakable sound of rounds hitting a human head close by. As he quickly focused on tree where the shots came from, he saw the 240 falling off the roof and stop in midair somehow, in his peripheral vision. He shook off the sight and let loose at least half a 28-round magazine at the spot the shots had come from. He saw a rifle fall, followed quickly by a dong in ACU's. The army dong was still alive, at least for now, based on the way he was rolling around on the ground in agony. He watched as the Theo pulled a tourniquet out of his left BDU pocket and began applying it to his right leg. Dan knew how much leg wounds and the application of tourniquets hurt from first-hand experience, and hoped it was extra painful for that soldier turned murderer.

Dan let him finish getting the tourniquet on and synched down nice and tight, before he shot the asshole in the head. He was happy to send that dude to hell with pain having been his last conscious thought.

Only then did Dan look to his right and survey the damage. His machinegunner was down hard, his face distorted from the overpressure created by the passage of a high velocity rifle round through his cranium. A large pool of blood was already seeping around his head, while the assistant gunner struggled to haul the M240 back up on the roof by pulling on the belt of ammo he had been feeding into the gun when it fell off the roof.

Dan ran and helped the assaulter muscle the machinegun the last few feet over the ledge of the parapet as rounds started snapping overhead. He heard Phil on the radio, "Knight Three, there are new muzzle flashes coming from the woods to the southeast. It must be the guys they didn't get across the road before we initiated." Dan and the assaulter he had left got low, and dragged the 240 toward the south end of their side of the building.

Up on the hill, JR was continuing to work over the treeline on the southwest side of the building, and while the fire was slacking off, it hadn't stopped. He took a second to check on the guys on the roof, and immediately saw something was wrong. On the southwest corner of the warehouse, only one of the assaulters was moving and shooting, and he thought he could see blood pooling underneath the other one in the waning daylight. "Knight Three, Sniper One. It looks like one of our guys on the southwest corner is down. I'll keep the dongs off the building as long as I can but I'm Winchester on .308, and I'm down to my last two mags of 5.56."

Dan heard the transmission and stopped crawling for a second to think. *Where the hell is the rest of the Squadron!* his mind raged. He took a deep breath and calmed down, then said as calmly as he could, "Roger, Sniper One. I have one assaulter down hard on my side as well. Keep them back and let me deal with this group on the southeast side. They are doing a good job of suppressing us."

Phil knew he needed to move south to take the pressure off Dan and JR, but he also knew several of the dongs from the second group in the failed attack on the east side made it back into the woods. It would suck fighting through them, but it needed to be done. Phil pushed his PTT and said, "Knight Three, Three-Charlie-One. We are going to push south and try to assault through the dongs on the southeast corner." Dan didn't reply, so Phil took that as permission, and got his guys moving.

They ran east through the woods until Phil thought they were well into the east treeline, then turned south. He got his guys on a skirmish line and they advanced at a fast walk. Within 50 feet they encountered their first dong, an unarmed wounded dude lying in his own blood, who appeared to be hit in the stomach. The dong begged for help, but the team ignored him. One of the assaulters stopped long enough to handcuff and search him, then laid him on his face. Phil pushed the team on, until they got shot at from their front. All four assaulters fired at the shape partially obscured by a tree, and the shooting stopped. When they got to the spot, they found a dong lying on his back, eyes open and buck teeth bared in death. They found a Kel Tec shotgun next to his body, and one of the assaulters picked it up, not wanting to leave it for another dong to pick up.

On the roof, Dan got the 240 ready to rock by unloading it, doing a quick function check, and reloading it. He looked at the assaulter he had left on the roof with him, and saw the man was grimly determined. The assaulter, whose name Dan didn't remember at the moment, said, "I'm ready to lay waste to these assholes. We're all we got bro."

Dan tried to think of something funny to say, to lighten the mood before they stood up into the river of gunfire passing nearby, but all he could feel was the fire of an all-consuming anger. He hadn't felt the warm blanket of hate in his soul since his last trip to Iraq; and he embraced the darkness, knowing unleashing the hate in his heart on their enemies was his team's best chance of mission accomplishment. Dan gathered his legs under him, and steeled himself to pop over the top of the parapet to start the killing. He settled for a simple, "We're all we need brother," and stood up.

To be continued in Book 2 of the Black Knight Squadron Saga

Glossary

ACU: Army Combat Uniform. A recent U.S. Army uniform with a camouflage pattern not known for its effectiveness.

APD: Alliance Police Department

AR: ArmaLite Rifle. Pertaining to any AR-15/M-16/M4 type rifle.

Assaulter: The core designated skillset for tactical operators, common to all team members. Additional skillsets include Breacher, Medic, and Sniper.

Breaching: Skills for gaining entry into denied areas. Includes mechanical, ballistic, thermal, and explosive methods to forcibly defeat barriers.

CCP: Casualty Collection Point

CME: Coronal Mass Ejection

Comms or Commo: Communication

CONEX: Container Express box system. A generic name for any large metal shipping container.

CQB: Close Quarters Battle. A type of combat focusing on the tactics, techniques, and procedures for fighting at short distances and within and around enclosed spaces like structures.

Det Cord: Detonation Cord. Plastic flexible tubing filled with explosive that can be used to detonate larger explosive charges or used by itself in different configurations to produce explosive and cutting effects.

DHS: Department of Homeland Security.

DRMO or 1033 Program: Defense Reutilization and Marketing Service. A Defense Logistics Agency program that lets the Department of Defense transfer excess military equipment to U.S. law enforcement agencies.

ECP: Entry Control Point

EMP: Electro Magnetic Pulse

EMS: Emergency Medical Services

EOC: Emergency Operations Center

FEMA: Federal Emergency Management Agency

FOB: Forward Operating Base

FOP: Fraternal Order of Police

Fragmentary Order or FRAGO: An abbreviated operation order used by subordinate units frequently used for follow-on missions or changes to the OPORD, focusing on the first three paragraphs of the OPORD.

HMMWV: High Mobility Multipurpose Wheeled Vehicle. Pronounced "Humvee". A military light truck that can be a light utility vehicle or armored.

Hotel: Hostage

IFAK: Individual First Aid Kit

M2 Browning. A heavy machine gun in .50 caliber.

M113: A tracked armored personnel carrier.

M4 or M4 Carbine: An updated and lighter version of the M16 style rifle that has become predominate in military and law enforcement use.

Mk46: A lighter weight, Special Operations capable variant of the M249 light machine gun.

M240: A general purpose machine gun in 7.62 caliber. Weighing over 30 pounds loaded it is frequently mounted on vehicles.

M249: A light machine gun in 5.56 caliber. Weighing less than 20 pounds it is used as a squad automatic weapon in infantry units.

MAWL: Multifunction Aiming Weapon Light. A weapon mounted device that utilizes a choice of visible or invisible infrared lasers to aim at or mark a target for identification.

MRAP: Mine-Resistant Ambush Protected vehicle. A heavily armored vehicle designed to resist improvised explosive devices common in overseas operations that is frequently used as a rescue vehicle by SWAT Teams.

NCO: Non-Commissioned Officer

NODs: Night Observation Devices, i.e., night vision goggles

NVGs: Night Vision Goggles

Operation Order or OPORD: A five paragraph format for organizing and disseminating information for the conduct of infantry type operations. The five major paragraph headings are Situation, Mission, Execution, Sustainment, and Command and Control.

Overwatch: To support another tactical element by observation and fire.

PMag: A plastic magazine for the M4 family of weapons.

PMC: Private Military Corporation

POI: Point of Impact
POS: Position
PTT: Push To Talk switch
QRF: Quick Reaction Force
RMR: Ruggedized Miniature Reflex Sight. A type of miniature electro optic red dot sight frequently used on pistols.
SIMS: Simulated Munitions for training.
Squirter: Bad guys who are trying to get away.
Stryker: Wheeled armored personnel carrier, infantry fighting vehicle.
SWAT: Special Weapons and Tactics. A law enforcement unit with special training and responsibilities for conducting tactical missions to resolve critical incidents including High Risk Warrants, Hostage Rescue, Barricade Suspect, and Active Shooter.
TL: Team Leader
TOC: Tactical Operations Center
VBIED: Vehicle Borne Improvised Explosive Device

About the Author

Born and raised in the tony suburbs of Sacramento, California, John Chapman (known to his friends as Chappy) joined the Navy at 18. After his enlistment, Chappy returned home to Northern California and embarked on a law enforcement career while attending college.

Over 20 years later, Chappy has served in Patrol, SWAT, Investigations, Training and Admin assignments. Chappy became a firearms and tactics instructor in 1994, and has traveled the US and the world teaching armed citizens, SWAT teams and military units combat marksmanship and tactics. Best known in the tactical community as a SWAT and Night Vision instructor, Chappy continues to teach, now exclusively for Forge Tactical, a training firm serving law enforcement and armed citizens.

He maintains his police commission, and serves as a Police Officer with the Alliance, Ohio Police Department, where he serves as a SWAT Team Leader. Chappy also volunteers his time to serve as the Director of Training for the Ohio Tactical Officers Association, the largest tactical officers association in the country.

Chappy lives in northeast Ohio with his wonderful wife Kris and their cat Duce. When he's not chained to his desk writing, he can be found at the Alliance Police Range shooting, developing curriculum, testing gear, or teaching.

To learn more about opportunities to train with Chappy and his partner John Spears, visit forgetactical.com. To learn more about the Alliance Police Training Center (yes, it really exists) visit alliancepolicetraining.com.

Stout Hearts

Coming in Spring 2018

Black Knight Squadron

Book 2

Consolidation

Made in the USA
Las Vegas, NV
20 June 2023

73676288R00146